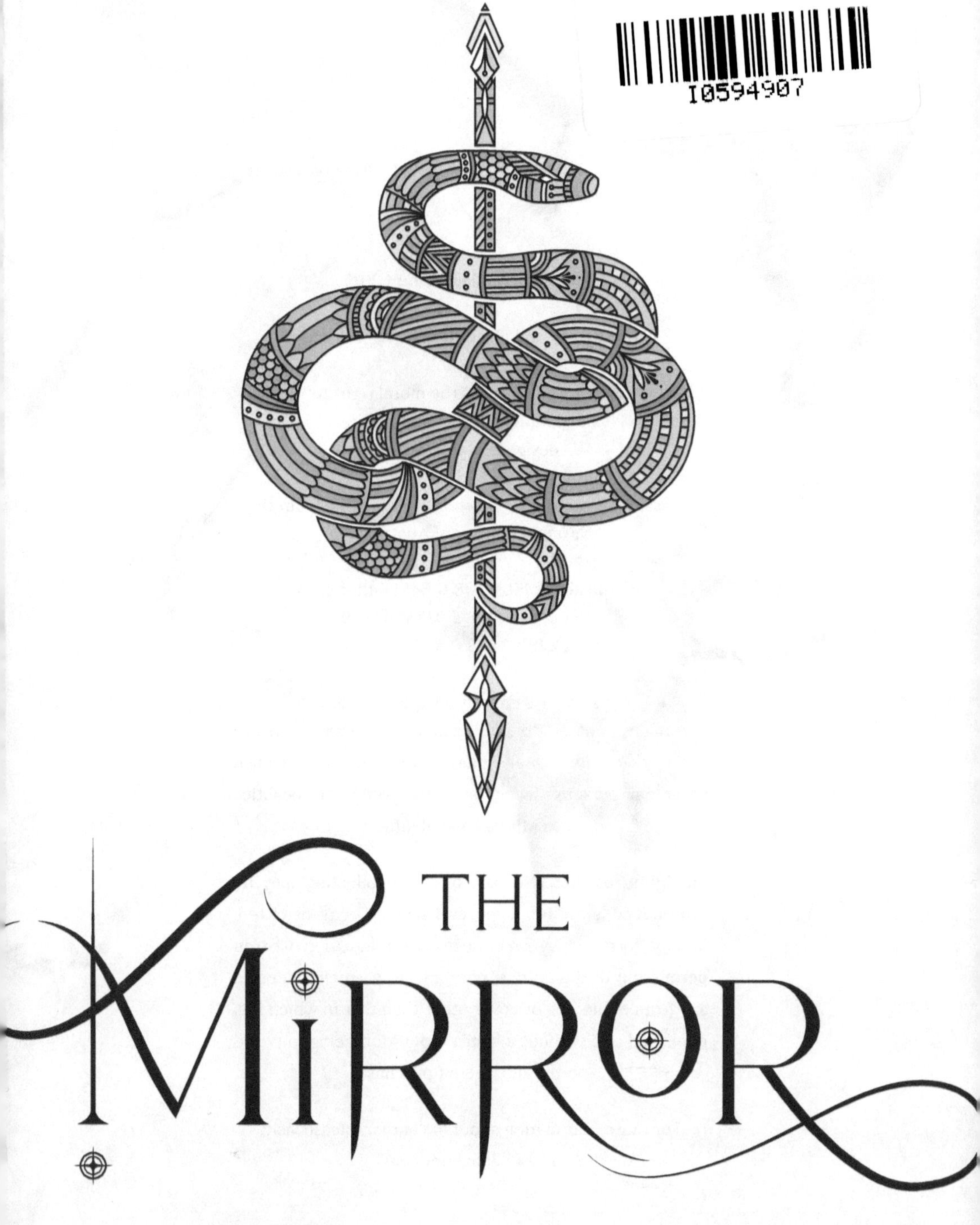

THE MIRROR

ELLEN A. HUNT

First Published in 2019 by Ellen A. Hunt

1

Copyright © Ellen A. Hunt 2019

Cover design and illustration by Ellen A. Hunt

Ellen A. Hunt asserts the moral right to
be identified as the author and
designer of this work.

A catalogue record for this book is available from the
National Library of Australia.

Hardback ISBN 978 0 6486943 2 8
Trade Paperback ISBN 978 0 6486943 1 1
eBook ISBN 978 0 6486943 0 4

For more information about *the author*, please visit:
www.ellenahunt.com

THROUGH NEGATIVE THOUGHTS WE WALK,
INTO FIELDS OF SHINING STARLIGHT.

For those who think they aren't enough.

You can do wonders.

Just let yourself believe.

THE MIRROR

ELLEN A. HUNT

The Fall

Ten Years Ago

A THUNDERING ROAR ERUPTED in the blinding-black silence. The roar of a nightmare bellowing its' rage. The roar of the wind, wrenching and wrestling with the limbs of a plummeting form.

A woman.

Lost to the weight of gravity, which dragged her.

Down.

Her burnt-orange dress snapped like a feral beast, the wind seizing its' edges, catching and tugging at the light, cotton scarf wound tightly around her head.

Her ears were ringing.

Her temples were throbbing.

Her lungs were aflame and threatening to convulse.

Breathe.

The woman's golden eyes flew open, ringed in white and wide with terror. Her nostrils flared, panicked, useless. Her breath was lost among the thundering wind, ripped from her lips by the sullen, relentless force.

BREATHE.

The air yielded.

The woman gasped, hauling in great gulping breaths. Mouth gaping.

Muscles straining.

Air filled her lungs.

Light filled her eyes.

And her crippling fear shattered. Replaced by a sudden, serene balance.

The sky spread above her, pale and cerulean, painted across the heavens and softly smeared with clouds. The deafening wind began to fade, stifled as it rushed over her flushed, creamy skin, filling and abandoning the mass of fluttering fabric clinging to her form. She watched, mesmerised, as the burnt-orange dress skittered, twisting and flicking in a frantic dance across the smooth surface of her thighs, beating with the unending throb which pounded in her temples.

The woman closed her eyes for the space of a pain-filled breath. Then, slowly, she turned her head, struggling to understand where she was.

Her disoriented gaze brushed the faint wisps of clouds, the smooth, day-lit sky, the curve of the imminent horizon—

The woman's heart faltered.

The horizon.

Her stomach contorted, fear becoming acid in her throat.

She was falling.

Her hands began to tremble.

Her lungs began to heave.

Terror lunged at her as she dropped, barreling towards the waiting ground, like Icarus with his burned and smoking wings.

She clawed at her chest, at her stomach, desperately searching for something, anything, to stop her unfettered descent.

She squeezed her eyes shut and found only oblivion, memories choked by darkness and an oily, smothering veil. She did not remember who she was. She did not remember why she was falling.

The heat of the earth kissed the ridges of her spine.

The woman gritted her teeth.

Swallowed her scream.

Her shoulder-blades hit the ground first.

Death is darkness.

Not the comforting darkness of night, nor a tombs' suffocating black, buried beneath the earth, crushed beneath the soil.

Death is the darkness of nothing.

Disappearing.

Into

Oblivion.

Part One

A Message in Murder

PROLOGUE

THE OPAQUE SHADOWS OF dissipating clouds crept across the soundless, moonlit streets. The occasional pool of warm light pulsed over the ice-laced cobblestones as lamps struggled to keep the cold at bay, their flickering beams illuminating the streaming fog which wafted through the frozen night.

A frosted breeze stung the flushed skin of a woman's cheeks, her pouting lips pale beneath a layer of rose-tinged gloss. An involuntary shudder trembled through her bones despite the thick coat nipping at her heels, the soothing layers of cashmere and cotton gingerly brushing the curve of her waist.

Deserted buildings rose above her, disappearing into the star-smeared night. The apartments had been abandoned for as long as she could remember, the gleaming cobblestones below all but forgotten as they extended through the gently curving street. Withered moss and vines wormed up the stone façades, twisting around the shadowed balconies and iron railings like the corpses of reaching snakes.

The woman stopped, a single boot hovering over the cobblestones, as she caught a glimpse of an ink black shadow shooting through her peripheral vision. Her chest rose with a deep breath, the cold air penetrating her lungs, her vast caramel eyes combing the depths of the dark for movement.

She stood, as still as a statue, waiting for what seemed an eternity. Nothing.

Her shoulders shuddered as she released a steaming breath of relief. She lifted a hand, sweeping gloved fingers through her river of honey-blonde hair. Her hovering boot connected with the ground and she continued walking, ignoring the flicker of fear which lingered in her stomach. Her paranoia was unnecessary. Flinching at every shadow was irrational.

Particularly after the night that she had had.

An appreciative sigh trickled from her lips as the echoed whisper of a man kissed the backs of her eyes.

Irises of muddied brown flecked with the spattered green of moss. A strong jaw. A seductive smile.

The woman's blood heated in her veins, her stomach tightened and a flush bloomed across her cheeks as she remembered the way he had gazed at her, his eyes full of want, his smile full of promise. It almost made her forget about the sculpture at the exhibition. Her favourite. A beautiful dancer carved of marble. The woman smiled, a quiet tilt of her lips, losing herself in thought as she continued walking down the cobblestone street.

Behind her a figure emerged from the depths of a shadowed door.

A street lamp sputtered violently.

Then died.

The woman turned.

And a black form streaked through the night air, a breath from her face.

The woman shrieked and leaped back. Her hands flew to her chest as the form landed on the ledge of a shattered window, quietly rustling its' feathers and watching her with wide eyes of moonbeam silver.

An owl.

The woman let out a short, sharp laugh. Her paranoia had been triggered by an *owl*. She shook her head, her honeyed hair shining in the dull street light as the edges of her mouth lifted in amusement. She glanced at the dead lamp, barely giving it a thought, then turned back and continued on her way.

She was almost home.

Almost to her apartment.

She slipped a gloved hand into her pocket to retrieve her ring of keys. They glinted, striking one another, and their song was a sharp chime as she held them aloft to admire the attached pendant. The palm-sized mirror had been a gift from the exhibition, an obsidian snake coiled possessively around a shining, silver frame. The creature's body seemed to slither as the mirror rotated in her fingers, reflecting the night-veiled street at her back.

Reflecting a figure, shifting in the dark.

The woman froze.

The silhouette's onyx cloak flowed like a torrent of spilled ink amid the fog.

The woman took a step forward.

And the figure followed, lean legs stalking through a gleaming pool of streetlight.

The woman tightened her grip on her keys, skin barking painfully as the metal bit into her palm. She did not hesitate. She sprinted towards the end of the street. Heart pounding against her sternum. Breaths coming in short, nervous gasps. Her apartment would be safe. She would slip inside and the silhouette could not follow.

The woman glanced over her shoulder, searching for the figure and finding the pool of streetlight empty.

She bit down on her panic.

She could avoid the figure. If only she knew where it *was*. The shadows between the lamps were too deep. The clouds had almost entirely engulfed the moon. The black cloak would be too difficult to find.

The woman launched herself along the street. She could almost feel the door of her apartment. Urging. Beckoning. If she could just make it inside...

Her heart crashed like a caged bird as she rounded the corner, panting through her teeth, breaths heaving, lungs burning. Her form shot through the halo of a street lamp.

And a hand emerged from the darkness.

The woman loosed a strangled cry as gloved fingers closed around her shoulder, hauling her back.

Her stomach dropped. She struggled to turn, attempting to see the figure as she fought an onslaught of dread.

She found herself pinned.

Trapped.

Captured by the stranger's unnatural strength.

The woman choked as the figure moved forward, heated breath caressing her ear, taut, muscled body pressing against her spine. "...Wh-who are you?" She gasped a frigid breath and forced herself to calm. To think clearly. She needed to find a weapon, a method of surprise. "Wh-what do you want?" She fumbled with the keys in her hand, the sharp metal of their teeth glinting in the street light.

The stranger lifted a shoulder in an apathetic shrug and shifted the grip on her shoulder.

The woman's heart stuttered.

She grabbed one of her keys, stabbed its' tip into the figure's hand and *twisted* as she struggled to haul herself away.

The figure hummed a laugh, brutal fingers digging deeper into the woman's flesh.

She opened her mouth to scream.

And was slammed back against a solidly muscled chest, the blow forcing the air from her lungs.

The woman lost her scream beneath a barrage of gasping coughs. Her keys dropped from her fingers, the metal colliding with the ground, the mirrored pendant shattering at her feet.

"I'm afraid a key isn't going to be of much help." The hand on the woman's shoulder moved, snapping to her mouth, pressing her head into a collar of stone. "Neither is your voice, for that matter."

The woman howled into the figure's glove, her jaw aching beneath the force of the grip, fighting with everything she had.

Calmly, the stranger removed the glove from its' free hand, catching the fabric between a gleaming set of teeth before dragging it off and tucking it into a pocket. The figure stood a moment, feeling the woman struggle, watching her eyes widen as its' ungloved index finger began to lengthen, the tip stretching, curving, shifting into a glinting, obsidian talon.

The woman hesitated, caught in a stunned paralysis, then she began to thrash hysterically, tears spilling from her white-ringed eyes, sobs wracking her straining throat. She clawed at the hand still gripping her mouth, only to find it steady. Immovable.

The figure breathed the woman's fear.

The talon lifted to her neck.

Pressed into her skin.

It began as nothing more than a bead of warmth, trickling down the woman's neck. Then the blood began to spread, following the path of the talon as it leisurely dragged across her throat, the honed tip neatly slicing flesh, coaxing the life from her with the artful grace of a chord from a violin.

The pain took a breath to unfold.

But when it did, it *exploded.* Rupturing the woman's anaesthetic shock.

Excruciating.

Effortless.

Blood spewed from her severed arteries, pouring in morbid streams onto her clothes and over the ground. A choking gurgle escaped as her hands flew to her throat.

She felt the warmth of her own blood pouring through her fingers, draining from her face.

Her skin turned cold and damp and tingling.

The woman collapsed beside the shattered glass of her pendant, blood bubbling in her mouth.

Her gaping eyes lifted to the cloaked figure as the talon retracted, shifting back to a blood-stained finger, smooth and slow as the moons descent.

The woman's strength trickled through the gaps in the cobblestones, leaking towards the jaws of an ever-waiting grate. It was then that she realised no one would come. No one would see her last moments as she slipped into the eternal dark.

A tear dribbled from the corner of the woman's eye.

Her hand slid from her neck.

The street began to blur.

And the life spilled from her like rain from the sky.

CHAPTER ONE

A SINGLE DROP OF WATER FELL from the leaden sky, splattering across Adalinda's cheek as she emerged from the mouth of a desolate alley. She glanced at the swollen clouds, her golden eyes flashing, and wiped the liquid from her skin in a smooth, sweeping movement. The frozen pavement made no sound beneath the silent soles of her boots, and she walked towards the Mirror Gallery with an unnatural quiet, even the rustling of her clothes seeming hushed by her presence.

The gallery sat across the street like a cut diamond amongst sand, its' glass façade supporting four stories of towering stone split by gleaming windows and balustrades of twisted iron. The neighbouring buildings stood sentinel, near perfect duplicates, save the caution tape obstructing the gallery's entrance. Stark and vivid. Separating the murmuring crowd from the curtained windows which shielded the chaos inside.

Adalinda lifted a hand to her scarf, smoothing the ruffles of fabric which coiled tightly around her head, as a series of restless shivers prickled over her scalp. The sensation crept down her spine, raising her skin in delicate mounds beneath the woollen fabric of her clothes. She sucked in a breath, the winter air clouding in her lungs, and curled her fingers into softly clenched fists as she willed the prickling to stop.

It refused.

The ghost of a frown curved Adalinda's lips. She paused a moment, her eyes flicking over the gathered crowd, before straightening her shoulders, lifting her chin, and weaving through them as gracefully as the wind through whispering leaves. She slipped beneath the caution tape, choosing a section which remained unmanned, and pinned her gaze on the officer standing guard.

The officer met her stare, pale scars and tribal tattoos shimmering on a face as dark as midnight. The woman waited until Adalinda slowed to a halt before opening her stern lips to speak. "Miss Adalinda Veil?"

Adalinda nodded, examining the swirling patterns of the officer's tattoos before peering at the gallery's entrance. "Why was I called?"

"To provide input." The officer narrowed her unusual eyes, her right gilded amethyst, her left a depthless coffee. She assessed the woollen cloak flowing over Adalinda's shoulders, allowed her gaze to linger on the scarf binding Adalinda's head. "My name is Tzali'ka, I was asked to escort you inside."

Adalinda frowned, aching to placate her prickling scalp as it sent another shiver down her neck. She began to reach for the base of her scarf. Stopped.

"Come, they will have questions." Tzali'ka shoved the door open, holding it just long enough for Adalinda to step inside.

It took a few breaths for Adalinda's eyes to adjust to the subdued light. The gallery echoed with countless footsteps, with the hushed murmurs of officers and forensics and the quiet sniffs which follow tears.

"Wait here."

Adalinda glanced at Tzali'ka as the officer turned her back, striding across the gallery floor to a man partially hidden behind a cluster of forensics.

"A bit intense, isn't she?"

Adalinda blinked, then turned, responding involuntarily to the familiar, lilting voice of the gallery owner. "Iveta."

The copper-eyed woman stepped up beside Adalinda, fiery, ginger hair flowing over one shoulder, tall, with the limbs of a willow. "That woman is like a raincloud on a summer day. Honestly, I don't think she has a bone in her body that isn't made of granite."

"You know her?"

Iveta shook her head, shifting her weight to the side. "I only spoke to her for a minute or so, but I figured that was enough. Especially after—" The words caught in the woman's throat and she bit her lip as it began to tremble. "... After what I found this morning..." Iveta looked over her shoulder, her eyes landing on Adalinda's marble sculpture, placed near the back of the room. The sculpted dancer seemed about to swoon, her arms elegantly extended, her unseeing eyes gazing eternally up.

Up towards the roof, painted a pale, bleaching white.

Up towards the woman.

Hanging silent.

Lifeless.

Murdered.

She dangled from the ceiling, suspended by smoothest silk. Her figure unnervingly bent, her back forlornly arched, as if wilting with the transient grace of a pale and fading bloom.

The silk coiled around her waist like a mourning lover's arm, the supple fabric circling the curve of her thighs, and reaching beneath her back, to stream through her dangling hands in a wistful, pearlescent cascade. A matching circlet of ribbon surrounded her slim neck, the perfection of her skin almost appearing porcelain beneath the fabric.

And her figure had been adorned with the spilling cloth of a beautiful, burnt-orange dress. The edges ragged yet stainless. One shoulder torn and hanging uselessly over her collar.

Adalinda stilled as a memory struck, cold and cruel as steel.

A thundering roar erupted in the blinding-black silence. The roar of a nightmare bellowing its' rage. The roar of the wind, wrenching and wrestling with the limbs of a plummeting form.

Adalinda clenched her teeth, her fingers curling in trembling fists, barely able to hear the incorporeal fog of Iveta's voice as the woman began to explain.

"I came to the gallery early this morning and she was just—" Iveta swallowed thickly, lifting a shaking hand to her neck, silver lining her bright, copper eyes. The woman shook her head, unable to hide the quivering of her chin. "She was just *hanging* there."

Adalinda forced herself to turn away from the suspended corpse, focusing her attention on the officer who had escorted her inside. Tzali'ka stood before an imposing man clad in a black, leather jacket, a frown tugging at her lips. She gestured to Adalinda and the man dragged a broad palm across his shaven jaw, his ebony features shifting as his eyes flicked in Adalinda's direction.

"... Do you recognise her?"

Adalinda dragged her attention back to Iveta, blinking at the woman as she spoke. She was combing her fingers through her flaming hair, still staring at the lifeless woman hanging from the ceiling.

"I don't recognise her. I've spent so much time in this gallery, preparing for the event last night, and now there's a *murdered woman—*" A sob clawed up Iveta's throat.

Adalinda placed a comforting hand on the woman's shoulder, unable to stop her gaze from returning to the burnt-orange dress. She swallowed the tension beginning to constrict her throat as she noticed the steady beat of approaching footsteps.

"Miss Veil?"

Adalinda gently pulled her hand from Iveta's shoulder and turned to find the man in the leather jacket standing at her side.

"I'm Detective Christensen." The man extended an introductory hand, his ebony skin dark against the pale gallery walls, his emerald eyes assessing. "I have a few questions for you."

Adalinda lowered her chin in a nod and took his offered hand. She suppressed a chill as her eyes slid back to her sculpture, catching on a broken pendant discarded at its' base. An obsidian snake, its' body curled protectively around the silver frame of what should have been a mirror.

Christensen released Adalinda's hand, his lips pulling in a deep frown. "That's your sculpture, isn't it?"

"It is." The pulse skipped in Adalinda's veins as the detective's gaze shifted over her head, focusing on a dark form which had begun to cross the room.

"Do you recognise the deceased?"

Adalinda shook her head, inwardly fighting the urge to sooth the aggravated prickle of her scalp as Christensen returned his attention to her. "No, I don't."

"Where were you last night?"

Adalinda tensed as the dark form stopped behind her, speaking with a voice as rich as molten honey, his presence a heavy rift in the cool gallery air.

She had not heard him arrive.

But she had *felt* him.

Slowly, Adalinda turned, her boots silent as midnight on the cold marble floor.

Quivers danced beneath her skin.

Her pulse stuttered.

Stopped.

A man stood with his hands clasped behind his back, his broad shoulders supporting the flowing length of a dark, storm-cloud coat.

Confident and powerful and elegant.

Adalinda's eyes wandered the exquisite planes of the man's chest, his steady breaths sighing against the fabric of his shirt, his scent of woodsmoke and rain folding over her, drifting through her.

Adalinda swallowed as pain lanced through her palms and she realised her nails had bitten into her skin.

Focus.

She forced herself to look up.

And her simmering gaze collided with that of gleaming steel.

The breath rushed from her lungs, leaving her empty, leaving her aching.

The man peered down at her with eyes of bluest ocean, their depths brewing with amusement, smothering an almost imperceptible flash of hunger as he noticed her white-knuckled fists. The corner of his stern lips softened, curving in a devastating smile.

Adalinda set her jaw, sensing a faint, impossible familiarity.

"Forgive me for the abrupt interruption. I'm Detective Donovan, I work with Detective Christensen."

Donovan extended a hand and Adalinda accepted it, all too aware of the shiver which charged up her spine. His warm, roughened skin grazed her palm, his touch consuming her, carving away her senses until there was only his staggering gaze. Wildfire coursed through her limbs, her nerves igniting in response to the contact as something inside her unraveled.

Phantom hands brushed her hips, causing heat to bloom in her core.

His grip was *wasted* on a handshake.

Adalinda forced her lips to part, to drag a word from the void consuming her thoughts. "I—"

Her scalp began to prickle.

The world slammed into her, a surge of colour and noise with the stinging lash of a whip, as she remembered herself. Remembered where she was.

Adalinda shook Donovan's hand. Once. With inadvertently unnatural strength. "To answer your question, I was working on a sculpture in my studio and returned to my apartment around midnight."

Donovan arched a brow, eyeing Adalinda's hands as they curled into fists and disappeared beneath the folds of her ivory cloak.

Christensen crossed his arms. "Did anyone see you return home?"

"Yes... My landlady, Diana, she has a habit of staying up." Adalinda paused, loosing her fingers and pressing a palm against her trouser pocket, feeling the shape of the keys to her apartment. "... She made me tea before I went to bed."

Another frown curled the edges of Christensen's mouth. "We'll need to confirm that with her."

Adalinda dipped her chin in a confirming nod. "I'll forward you her details."

"Can you think of anyone who would want to threaten you?"

Adalinda's eyes shifted to Donovan as he turned, slowly beginning to walk towards the murdered woman and her sculpture.

A shiver crawled across Adalinda's scalp and she lifted her fingers to the base of her scarf, moving to follow the detective. "... No."

"And you, Iveta?"

"No!" Iveta shook her head emphatically, her long hair whispering around her fair features, her boots echoing as she followed them across the floor. "I don't understand why anyone would..." The woman swallowed again, averting her eyes as Adalinda stopped before the sculpture to stare up at the suspended corpse.

The dead woman's honey-blonde hair shifted in a soft breeze as Tzali'ka swept out the door.

"Whoever did this clearly had a lot of time to prepare. I imagine suspending a person from a ceiling would be difficult." Adalinda gestured to the hook which held the silk, its' dark metal faintly glinting beneath the fabric. "They would've had to attach that hook to the ceiling, tie the silk and haul her body into position."

Donovan looked at Adalinda, the gallery light burnishing the thick waves of his chocolate hair, his ocean eyes dark and intense.

Adalinda kept her focus on the lifeless woman, attempting to ignore the weight of the detective's stare. "The murder was committed elsewhere." She nodded to the pristine, stone floor. "The gallery is too clean. There's no blood, no glass—"

"No glass." Christensen let his arms fall to his sides, glancing at Donovan and beginning to circle the sculpture.

"That is one of the gallery's promotional keychains." Adalinda pointed to the broken pendant discarded at the base of the sculpture. "It's mirror has been shattered but there's no glass here."

Christensen narrowed his eyes, peering at Adalinda around the curve of the sculptures back. "I take it crime solving is a hobby."

Adalinda hesitated, the corner of her lips twitching, as a medical examiner stepped around Donovan and reached for the murdered woman's dangling wrists. "You have a sense of humour, Detective."

"I think you know more than you're letting on." Christensen came to a stop by Adalinda's side, his brows knitting together in a deep-set frown. "What are you hiding, Adalinda?"

Adalinda met Christensen's stare, set her jaw against the inflamed prickling beneath her scarf. "I'm not hiding anything. I'm simply observant. I'm an artist, it comes with the territory." She shifted, catching sight of one of the many cameras scattered throughout the gallery. "... I take it the cameras didn't catch anything helpful since this looks as if the murder was clearly thought through. Did you speak to the security guard?"

Donovan nodded, crossing his arms over his chest and assessing the layout of the room. "We've already requested the security footage from last night. The guard was convinced that all possible entrances on the premises were locked and the alarms were activated. At no point during the night did he let anyone in, nor did any of the alarms trigger."

"The only people with keys are the security guard and myself." Iveta dragged her eyes away from the medical examiner still examining the murdered woman's wrist. The examiner's brow furrowed as something on the skin began to shimmer, catching the gallery light. She angled her head, the piercings lining the curve of her ear subtly winking.

"So how did the body get here?" The corner of Christensen's lips twitched as he looked to Iveta.

Adalinda lifted her gaze to the ceiling. "Perhaps the balconies above the gallery?"

"My apartments?" The blood drained from Iveta's face. "No. I reinforced all of the windows and doors with the same security as is in the gallery." She pursed her lips as Adalinda turned to her with a question brimming in her eyes. "What? I collect art. You really think I'm going to leave my own collection unguarded while I'm out?"

Christensen rubbed his palm across his forehead and over the cushioned surface of his tightly coiled hair. "What other entrance methods are there?"

"There's only the one." Iveta swept a hand towards the glass door of the gallery. "That's it."

Adalinda pressed her lips in a line. She twisted, momentarily studying the entrance before returning her attention to the murdered woman and the examiner standing beneath her.

The examiner released a low hum, muttering to herself before glancing at Donovan and then Christensen, her eyes of jade and topaz bright, the short side of her platinum hair rustling ever so softly as she moved.

"What is it, Clarke?" Christensen stepped around Adalinda, closing the distance between himself and the bright-eyed woman.

Clarke rotated the murdered woman's wrist and the silk draping from her waxen hands slipped...

To reveal a tattoo.

Adalinda froze, every muscle in her body becoming stone, her blood turning to ice in her veins.

Inked in shimmering ivory, in the centre of the lifeless woman's right wrist, was a curling snake, its' body looped and knotted, elegant in its' symmetry, simple in its' design and impossibly, sickeningly familiar.

"My guess is that this was tattooed post mortem. There's no aggravation on the skin even though the ink itself has not completely dried." Clarke released the wrist, lowering herself so her feet were flat on the floor.

"The murderer tattooed the victim?" Adalinda forced herself to relax, to erase the panic she could feel leaking into her eyes. Beneath her cloak, she discretely adjusted the right sleeve of her jacket, feigning calm as she ensured the cuff still concealed her wrist.

Clarke nodded, the piercing in her lip glinting as her gloved hands dropped to her sides. "And the ribbon around her neck is concealing a sliced throat. Professionally stitched." She turned to Donovan, revealing the long side of her platinum hair, the length rolled into a tight bun, the underside gleaming a deep shade of lavender.

Donovan narrowed his eyes, calculating the difference between her height and the suspended woman's neck. "... Do I want to know how you reached that?"

Clarke chewed her lip, gaze flicking to a chair behind the white desk on the far side of the room. "I used the chair."

A growl rumbled in Donovan's throat. "Clarke..."

Clarke's elven features contorted in a grimace as the detectives glared at her. "In my defence, I put it back *exactly* where I found it."

Donovan released a sigh, his expression shifting, becoming evaluative, as he noticed the fingers Adalinda had wrapped around her wrist. "I suspect the murderer wanted to convey a message."

Adalinda forced her eyes from the dead woman's tattoo, deliberately meeting Donovan's gaze and releasing her wrist. She could feel the spark of the detective's suspicion, seeping through his features as he locked his stare with her own.

As he took a step forward and she felt the air thicken in her throat.

"I don't suppose you have any idea what that message might be?"

Chapter Two

ADALINDA HELD DONOVAN'S STARE, feeling the anxious tension of her nerves, skin prickling, heart stuttering, as Iveta began to speak. "Snakes are often associated with fertility and immortality since they appear to be reincarnated when they slough their skins." The woman paused, looked between the detectives. "They're also regularly regarded as guardians of the underworld and, therefore, are connected with negativity and evil."

Christensen shuddered, crossing his arms over his chest, his words barely audible as he muttered under his breath. "I *hate* snakes."

Adalinda felt a contraction in her chest as a crease formed in Donovan's brow. "That doesn't explain why the murderer would tattoo it on a corpse."

"Perhaps the murderer sees death as a form of art and simply created a signature to ensure recognition."

Donovan's eyes flicked to Adalinda, his expression darkening in response to her suggestion. "... Hence the art gallery."

Adalinda nodded, inhaling deeply as she looked up at the murdered woman and fought to control her fragile state of calm.

"But why here?" Christensen frowned, sharing a look with Donovan before turning to Adalinda. "Why *this* gallery? Why *your* sculpture?"

A subtle ringing built in Adalinda's ears, leaking over Christensen's voice, swelling and surging as her calm began to fray, as her instincts began to scream at her to *run*.

The killer had chosen this gallery, had chosen her sculpture, because the *murder* was for *her*. She understood the macabre gift for what it truly was.

A warning.

A message.

Someone knew who she was.

Someone knew *what* she was.

Adalinda pressed her fingers into the flesh of her palms, struggling not to reach up and calm the crawling sensation beneath her scarf. The prickling had become constant, an incessant, unending reminder.

She was a *monster*.

And she could not run.

She would not run.

But if she remained looking at that burnt-orange dress, at that dead woman hanging from the ceiling, she would find herself defenceless. She would be unable to protect herself from the prowling memories she was constantly keeping at bay.

The blood heated in Adalinda's veins as she forcibly released her fists, dragging her eyes from the suspended corpse long enough to answer Christensen's questions. "If I knew why the body had been left here I would not hesitate to tell you, Detective, but I don't. I don't know why it's here. I don't know why it's above my sculpture." Adalinda inhaled an unsteady breath, re-establishing a few threads of her unravelling calm. "I apologise but I don't think I can help you any further. If you'll excuse me, I have some personal matters to attend to." She extended her hand to Donovan, deliberately ensuring her wrist remained hidden.

The detective hesitated, assessing her, before finally lifting his hand to take her own in a firm, unyielding grasp.

Adalinda exhaled a shallow breath, some of the tension bleeding from her bones as Donovan released his grip and lowered his arm to his side.

"How do we contact you? We'll have further questions."

Adalinda looked to the gallery owner. "Iveta has my details." Her gaze shifted to Christensen and she lowered her chin in an acknowledging nod before turning and striding for the doors, breaths unevenly shuddering, ignoring Donovan's piercing stare as it burned the planes of her back.

She dared not look back as she passed the officer still guarding the door, Tzali'ka's attention possessed by another woman slipping through the caution tape. Another woman who watched Adalinda, her eyes flashing silver, her auburn tresses strangled in a knot atop her head. She swept past in a river of confidence, head held high, the corner of her lips quirking.

Adalinda suppressed a shiver and lifted her fingers to brush the base of her scarf as she ducked beneath the barrier, narrowly avoiding a man clothed entirely in black. He watched Adalinda as she pushed through the crowd, his mud-brown eyes decorated with glittering moss, his muscular shoulders forcibly relaxed.

For a moment, the cuff of Adalinda's right sleeve fell, revealing smooth skin and a shimmering tattoo. An ivory snake. Looping and elongated. Elegant in its' symmetry. Simple in its' design.

Identical to that which was inked on the murdered woman's wrist.

The man's stare locked on Adalinda's tattoo as she tugged at her sleeve, once more concealing the pearlescent design.

His handsome features set in grim determination.

He shoved his hands into his pockets. Ducked his head.

And disappeared into the crowd.

Chapter Three

The enormous steel door stood before Adalinda like a demon in the recesses of her studio, appearing entirely effortless despite its' dominating, leaden features.

The door was old.

Enormously old.

With its' scratched and dented surface, rusted and eternally taunting.

Adalinda's tattoo glinted as she reached out with both hands, grabbing two of the six massive spokes protruding from the vault's radial handle. She flicked her wrists and the handle span, its' inner mechanism groaning loudly.

It spat a metallic *clunk* as it popped open.

The vault was not locked.

The vault was never locked.

And Adalinda felt the cool darkness inside it calling to her.

Tendrils of shadow sucked back as Adalinda pulled the door open further, the studios' light intruding on the airless, blackened void.

She heaved a long breath, dropping her hands from the door and rubbing a soothing thumb over the lines of her tattoo. She stayed there only a moment, then moved forward, slipping into the all consuming dark without a second thought.

A step to the left found her the light switch, clinging to the wall like a mulish parasite. Adalinda glared at it, her brow deeply furrowed, her golden irises glowing like embers in a dying fire. She flipped the switch. The electric current hissed.

And a single, naked bulb flickered to life, hanging precariously from the roof as if at any moment it might choose to fall.

Gradually, its' light expanded, banishing the darkness of the vault and replacing it with a warm, buttery glow.

Adalinda pivoted on her heel to face the room. Her bare feet absorbed the cold of the metal floor, the chill causing her skin to sing and her bones to gently ache. She followed the vault's great, steel walls with her eyes, then let her gaze sweep over the interior.

The vault was filled with figures of partially carved stone, all of them illuminated by the light of the fragile bulb. Their surfaces were smothered with crosshatching indents, chiselled and unfinished, dead and unseeing, misshapen and ruined and wrathfully banished to the darkness of the ageing vault.

A shudder spread beneath Adalinda's skin as she navigated through the statues, shifting and rotating with the dexterity of a dancer, her gaze locked on the wall at the end of the vault. A low hiss drove through her clenched teeth as she arrived at the wall, glowering at the small safe welded securely into its' surface. The safe was scratched and dented, its' door hanging from a single hinge.

This safe had been locked. Left without a key.

Though, that had not stopped her.

She had seized the door and wrenched it open with Pandora's ignorant curiosity, not fearing what was inside, nor what it would do to her if she found out.

Adalinda slipped hesitant fingers around the safe door.

A shudder crept beneath her scarf as she gently pulled it open.

The doors' hinge screamed in violent protest, the dull light from the single bulb creeping into its' mouth, crawling possessively over the item inside.

Adalinda pursed her lips and snatched the object up, her skin absorbing the rough feeling of ancient, worn leather. The abnormally light cover stared at her expectantly, the foiling on its' surface gleaming a bright and brilliant silver.

Adalinda's chest expanded as she inhaled a cavernous breath.

Her fingers curled around the cover.

She opened the book.

The inside of the spine was stripped, lined with the torn edges of the paper that had once filled it.

Adalinda's heart contracted as she stared at the splintered sentences scrawled across the inside of the back cover. A swirling script edged with panic. Sharp yet flowing like the sting of airborne sand.

Sentences which had remained vague and useless for nearing a decade.

Sentences written in her own hand, in a book she did not recognise.

Don't let − find you. She's −

Run.

Hide from the owls.

Find − The man who holds the ocean in his eyes.

I hope that will be enough for you to remember.

Some words had been removed, scraped and torn from the cover and smothered with bleeding black ink. Adalinda had searched for indentations, had tried to take rubbings with charcoal and tried to remove the ink.

Nothing worked.

She couldn't understand why she would have written so obscure a message. She couldn't understand how the book had appeared in the safe, waiting as if placed like a torturous, infuriating clue.

Adalinda had found the man with the ocean in his eyes, she'd found him, and *still* she did not remember.

Her mind was empty.

Wiped.

Save the decade in which she had been a sculptor.

The man peered down at her with eyes of bluest ocean, their depths brewing with amusement, smothering an almost imperceptible flash of hunger as he noticed her white-knuckled fists.

Fire surged in Adalinda's core at the memory of the detective. She snapped the book shut. Threw it into the safe. Slammed the *damned* door.

Metal shrieked as the remaining hinge ripped, peeling like the missing pages of her book.

The door of the safe crashed to the floor.

A growl lathered in Adalinda's throat as she glared at the book laying face up in the safe.

Smugly.

Taunting.

Adalinda stepped back, hands collapsing to her sides, and stood, barely moving for long, arduous moments. Her stare seared into the covers' shining indentation, twin, in every aspect, to the ivory tattoo inked onto the murdered woman's wrist, onto *her own* wrist.

Monster.

Fury bloomed inside her, throbbing and growing until it became overwhelming. Her fingers curled in straining fists. She spat a curse and bared her teeth, driving her knuckles into the wall beside the safe, her anger flooding into the steel, where it steamed, where it cooled.

Adalinda's nostrils flared, she pealed her fist away from the crippled metal, revealing a perfect imprint, as if she had struck nothing more than a pile of moistened clay, adding another impression of her knuckles to those already spread across the surface of the wall.

Marks of her frustration.

Her inability to understand.

She knew *what* she was. She simply couldn't remember *why*.

Adalinda twisted, storming back through the mangled sculptures, angered and frightened and alone. She stalked out of the vault and slammed the door, banishing the page-less book to the dark and leaving the naked bulb swinging, ever so slightly, from the force of her frustrated rage.

Chapter Four

FRIGID RAIN POURED IN SHEETS from the darkened sky, seeping into the heavy fabric of Donovan's coat, spilling down the ridges of his angular features and plastering thick waves of hair to his head.

He stood like a shadow amidst the glittering street, ocean stare locked on the warm glow leaking from the windows of the building before him. A hotel which had been converted into a luxurious orphanage.

"*Bloody hell*, it's cold!" The car door slammed viciously as Christensen stepped out, shoulders hunched against the downpour. "This weather makes my refrigerator look like the tropics." He muttered a string of curses, snapping the collar of his jacket up over his neck and stomping through the icy puddles to the building across the street. "... Let's just get this over with."

Donovan flexed his fingers, watching the freezing water collect in his palm, watching as the droplets trickled from the edge of his dark lashes and down the bridge of his nose.

Pattering.

Whispering.

Clinging to his skin as if it did not wish to leave.

The hypothermic cold didn't bother him. He felt the chill of it, the bite of the winter wind as it pinched his cheeks, the sting of iced rain as it nipped at his skin. Though it was more of an afterthought. An inconvenience.

He'd been through worse.

"Donovan." Donovan's attention snapped back to the building. Christensen huddled beneath the overhanging balcony, his gloved fingers curling irritably. "It's cold as hell. Stop standing in the rain, you're making me feel worse."

The corner of Donovan's mouth twitched in amusement and his eyes glinted as he strode forward. "It isn't that bad."

Christensen narrowed his eyes in response, shoving his finger into the bell and listening to the sharp melody of the chime as it echoed through the door.

Donovan and Christensen had found a suspect late that afternoon, a man clothed entirely in black, smooth as night as he crossed the security footage from the gallery exhibition the evening of the murder. The man had raked his fingers through his combed, chestnut hair, grinning and flirting with the victim while she admired Adalinda's sculpture.

They had yet to uncover a name.

Though they had obtained hers.

Leena Rosenberg had been studying sculpture, attending one of the top art universities in the city, and had attended an exhibition at the Mirror Gallery on the night of her murder. Her parents had identified the body, crumpling by her side and sobbing as they explained that she volunteered at the orphanage, that she was kind and caring, that she did not deserve to die.

Donovan slowed to a halt just shy of the sheltering balcony, considering the water pouring from its' edge, his boots half-submerged in a puddle.

Icy liquid nudged against his bloodless lips, urging him to open his mouth, pleading with him to suck in breath.

Donovan stepped under the balcony, raking gloved fingers through his soaking hair. He waited until the memory sank, drowning with the nights' shadow as the orphanage door swung inwards and warm light flooded the pavement.

A young woman peered at them through the opening, her dark hair kissing the curve of her jaw, wire-rimmed glasses perched on the bridge of her precipitous nose. "Can I help you?"

Christensen parted his lips in a charming smile, ivory teeth gleaming against ebony skin. "We were hoping to speak with whoever's in charge."

The woman's amber eyes widened as she raised her thick brows. "And you just assumed that wasn't me?"

Donovan watched Christensen's smile falter almost imperceptibly and then leaned forward, catching the woman's attention. "I'm Detective Donovan, this is my partner, Detective Christensen. We wanted to ask a few questions about Leena Rosenberg."

The woman frowned, her thin lips curving awkwardly as she pulled the door slightly further open. "... What about her?"

"She was found dead this morning."

The woman's jaw slackened, her eyes gaping as Christensen shot Donovan a chastising hiss.

"Her parents mentioned that she volunteered here. Did you notice anything strange in her behaviour over the past week?"

"I—" The woman raised a trembling hand to her cheek, her gaze sliding to the pavement. She shook her head. "No... No. She's like me. She comes to the orphanage once or twice a week... I barely know her..." She blinked, focusing on the crease between Donovan's brows. "How... How did she die?"

Donovan opened his mouth to reply.

The words caught in his throat as Christensen shoved an elbow into his ribs. "No. You don't get to break any more news, Mister *Sensitive*."

Donovan closed his mouth and moved aside to avoid another impromptu strike.

Christensen blew out a steaming breath, rubbing a palm across the back of his neck. "You don't want the details, Miss...?"

"Anna Winter." The woman straightened her shoulders, pulling her clothes tighter around her waist as she shivered. "And yes, I want the details. How did she die?"

A shadow dragged Donovan's attention away from Christensen's explanation. His eyes grazed the interior of the lobby, falling on a pale, dark-haired girl standing on a set of oak stairs, clinging to the bannister and staring at him with a hollow intensity. He watched as she gingerly climbed the steps, her movements stiff and awkward, her wrists a sickening shade of purple. Bruises flourished in sporadic patterns across her face, her neck, her ankles.

The murdered woman from the gallery whispered behind Donovan's eyes.

Rage flared through him and he clenched his jaw, teeth quietly grinding. "What happened to that child?"

Christensen stopped speaking, his eyes flicking past Anna Winter to the girl on the stairs.

Anna wiped shivering fingers across the tears which had begun to spill down her cheeks as she turned and saw the child. "River? What are you doing up, sweetheart?"

The girl pursed her lips, shaking her head as she continued up the stairs, her eyes deliberately averting from the painting of a man hanging on the wall.

Donovan stepped forward, gently nudging Anna aside and striding across the lobby.

"Donovan, we can't just..." Christensen trailed off as he scanned the child, the discoloured marks on her face and wrists. "Are those *bruises?*"

Anna scrambled away from the door, following the detectives as they crossed the floor. "River fell down the stairs the other day, I was told that she and some of the other children were playing chase and she slipped. It's lucky she didn't *break* anything."

"Who told you this?" Donovan stopped at the base of the stairs, watching the girl shrink into herself, her shoulders curved and shuddering as she stared vacantly across the lobby.

"Leena did. She said that she'd been in the kitchen with the cooks when it happened. She found River later trying to hide the bruises with a hat and scarf because she was embarrassed about falling down the stairs." Anna frowned as Donovan ascended the first step, holding his hands out in supplication.

River didn't move as he drew closer, she simply lifted her chin defiantly, revealing a set of large, deep bruises stretching across her neck.

The remnants of a choking hold.

Donovan kept his voice low, his murmur barely audible as he crouched before the child. "Who did this to you?"

River shook her head again, dark hair swishing in a tangled mess down her back, blinking rapidly to clear her wide, dark eyes. "I fell."

"No." Donovan struggled to keep his face calm, to keep his brows from furrowing as anger began to spread through him. "I don't think you did."

"Donovan..." Christensen started up the stairs, his boots reverberating through the wood.

River flinched, her hollow eyes flicking over the painting which hung on the wall. Fear momentarily shadowed her features before she pivoted. Fled.

Donovan straightened from his crouch, disgust and anger leaking onto his face as he glared at the oversized painting, an exquisite oil rendering of a tall, steel eyed man, his ink-black hair slicked smoothly back. The man glared out of the canvas, a crooked smile slicing his face.

A steel plaque sat below the rendition, a name etched onto it in bold, capital letters.

Wyatt Shade.

The politician who had converted the hotel to increase his popularity after having been accused of associating with black market trading.

Though no evidence had ever been uncovered.

Donovan passed Christensen, slowly descending until he stood before Anna, his fingers flexing and curling into dangerous fists. His skin began to tingle, a current of warm energy causing the air to thicken around him as it might before a storm. "Was Leena acting strangely when she told you River fell down the stairs?"

Anna shook her head, glancing at Donovan's fists and taking a cautious step back. "No, she seemed fine. I only saw her that one time but she didn't mention anything strange... I can't believe she was murdered... I can't think of anyone who would want to hurt her."

A growl bled from the sky outside, the thunder causing the building to shudder, the floor to vibrate.

Christensen muttered a curse under his breath as he headed for the still-open door. "Just my luck. The storm's getting worse."

"Let us know if you remember anything you might have forgotten about Leena. My number is on the card." Donovan paused at the entrance, placing a calling card on the table beside the door and looking over his shoulder at Anna. The woman stood in the middle of the lobby, arms wrapped firmly around her waist, eyes glittering with silver tears. "And see if you can persuade River to tell the truth. She didn't fall down those stairs and as much as I'd like to find the man I assume is responsible, I can't touch him without any proof."

Anna lowered her chin in a nod, staring vacantly as Donovan slipped from the building after Christensen and closed the door. He shoved a hand into his soaking pockets, fishing for the key to unlock his car as he crossed the road.

"What do you think happened to the girl?" Christensen hauled the car door open and slumped into the passenger seat, slamming it to shield himself against the still-pouring rain.

A frustrated sigh tumbled like smoke from Donovan's lips as he slid into the waiting car. "I have a feeling we're going to find out soon enough." He slid his key into the ignition and the engine rumbled to life, warm air bursting from the heaters. "Men like Shade can't hide behind their wealth forever."

Christensen frowned, turning to stare out the window as Donovan drove his boot into the accelerator and pulled the car into the street.

Streams of icy water leaked from his clothing, spilling over the seat and onto the floor.

His anger remained a heated tingle in his veins long after they had left the orphanage behind.

DONOVAN LOWERED HIMSELF onto his woven, charcoal couch, listening to the rain pounding against the window. He had dropped Christensen at his apartment on the way home, the other man muttering and discussing possibilities about what leads to follow next. Donovan had been only partially listening, his focus still glued on that bruised and beaten child.

The fire flickered before him, gilding his frowning features as he lifted a glass of whisky, condensation trickling down its' surface in a pathetic imitation of the pelting rain outside. An image of Adalinda invaded his thoughts as the cool liquid spilled through his lips.

She shook his hand. Once. With inadvertently unnatural strength.

Adalinda had been a pleasant surprise, a compelling puzzle waiting to be solved.

Donovan placed his glass on the wooden coffee-table, his frown softening slightly.

Her alibi had been checked and confirmed. And her observations of the murder had been enlightening, intriguing. He would not be surprised if, in future, she proved to be an asset.

Delicate fingers combed through his hair, velvet lips pressing against his neck.

Donovan stared into the blazing fire as he banished the thought from his mind. He could not allow anything to cloud his judgment.

Especially a potential target.

Adalinda had to be involved, despite her alibi. There were too many connections for it to be a coincidence. Donovan had seen her reaction to the murdered woman's tattoo, the quivering fingers which had adjusted the cuff of her sleeve beneath her cloak.

She knew more than she was letting on.

Donovan plucked his glass from the table and took another swallow.

The forensics had found no evidence at the gallery, not that he had expected them to considering the precision of the murder. Clarke had taken the body back to the morgue, promising to call when she found anything. So he sat, contemplating, thoughts shifting from the orphanage to the murder, simply waiting with an eternal patience while the fire burned the wood to embers, then to ashes, and died.

CHAPTER FIVE

SLASHES OF STREETLIGHT BLED through the blinds of Adalinda's studio, illuminating motes of dust, aimlessly drifting. She worked in a room softly lit by flickering candles, their viscid wax trickling down the fading walls and creeping down the legs of tables to spread over the ageing, wooden floor.

Adalinda stood, silent, staring at the marble slab in the centre of the room. Her delicate fingers clutched a chisel and hammer, her golden gaze hollow as she considered the progress of her work, partially lost to the events of the day.

She pursed her lips, determined not to glance at her wrist, at the tattoo which seemed to call to her in a faint, phantom throb.

Her figure had been adorned with the spilling cloth of a beautiful, burnt-orange dress. The edges ragged yet stainless. One shoulder torn and hanging uselessly over her collar.

Adalinda tensed, feeling the handles of her tools begin to groan beneath her grip. A prickle crept across her scalp. She shook her head and set the tools on the table at her side, attempting to remove the memory. The lurching nausea. The familiarity.

The woman's death was not her fault.

Monster.

Adalinda glanced at the fluttering candles, their collective glow toying with the darkness in the room. It licked over sculpted faces, over bodies posed elegantly on pedestals, the carvings scattered like trees in a forest.

She returned her attention to the slab before her, the partially carved chest and curve of the shoulder beginning to emerge from the marble. Uncut stone appeared to pull away from the carved features as if it were a body simply submerged in water, waiting to rise from its' tomb.

Adalinda turned as a memory clawed through her, fear and disgust seizing in her chest. She swept towards a window, parting the blinds with her fingers and peering down at the abandoned street.

Glittering rain plunged from the dark above in a seemingly unending torrent. Light burst from the few faltering street-lamps, their shine spreading unevenly over the drenched and drowning cobblestones.

A reflection of Adalinda's eyes stared back at her from the glass, her golden irises seeming to glow like an explosion of sunlight and fire.

The blinds snapped up as Adalinda released them and returned to her work, her loose, white pants flowing around her slim legs, her bare feet soundless on the floor. She lifted her hands and tightened the scarf around her head, the folds of fabric almost appearing to writhe in the shadows cast by the dancing candlelight.

Adalinda wiped her hands on her shirt. She reached out to retrieve the delicate, silver clock which sat next to her sculpting utensils.

An hour past midnight.

She returned the clock to its' place and plucked the hammer and chisel from the table, gently pressing them into the stone.

Phantom hands stroked her hips, grazing up her sides, ocean eyes flashing in the velvet light of a smiling moon.

Adalinda's lips pursed in response to the unwelcome thought and her hammer slammed into the chisel.

Too hard.

A fragment of marble fell, colliding with her naked foot, the mild ache in her toes barely registering as the shard of stone rolled onto the wooden floor.

Adalinda inhaled a calming breath.

The ink on her wrist flashed as she resumed her work, obstinately forcing the body to materialise from the stone as the rain began to taper and the sky began to brighten.

She never paused.

Never rested.

Refusing to avert her focus as the bust began to take shape, the damp buildings outside reflecting the hues of the rising sun, bright orange and burning crimson, as if the morning were painting the stone in an image of fire and blood.

As if the heavens were providing Adalinda with a warning of what was to come.

Chapter Six

Early morning light kissed the soaking cobblestones, warming the frozen buildings and caressing the velvet skin of Adalinda's cold-flushed cheeks.

She strode along the abandoned street, her aching stomach threatening to growl, her boots silent as the dying breeze. She relished the quiet, the calming trail of the winding road, never wondering at its' desolation, never questioning its' solitude.

She brushed a fleck of powdered marble from the shoulder of her cloak, the dust the only symptom of her entirely sleepless night. No shadows bruised the delicate skin beneath her lids. No veins of scarlet burned her eyes. The night appeared to simply give and never take away.

Adalinda raised her fingers, brushing the base of her scarf as she peered up at the wilted vines which clung to the looming walls. Their dried stems twisted, the leaves trapped beneath a cage of wickedly glinting claws. The owl was almost hidden, perched like an apparition on the ledge of a broken window, watching with eyes of fractured moonbeams as Adalinda faltered in her stride. Her mouth twitched, the corners lowering in a frown as her scalp began to prickle.

Hide from the owls.

Adalinda rolled her shoulders, consciously dismissing her unease as she glimpsed something glittering among the cobbles, remnant stormwater still leaking between the stones and into the mouth of a waiting grate.

She peered at the glittering particles, wariness flitting across her delicate features.

Shattered glass.

Something pulled at Adalinda's subconscious like a thread beginning to unwind. Something important, though forgotten, somehow distanced by the night.

Adalinda's frown slipped as she stepped around the corner and her momentary unease vanished. She could see the window of her apartment behind a rail of curling balustrades, the buildings stone façade washed clean by the rain, the carved, wooden door patiently observing the street.

She plucked her keys from the depths of her pocket, drifting around the body of an ink-black car parked in front of the building opposite her own. The morning air chilled her lungs as she stepped onto the road, crossed to her building and placed a key in the elegantly engraved doorknob. The door swung open smoothly, sunlight pouring through for nary a moment before she closed it and began ascending the oak stairs which lead to her apartment. She could almost see the book waiting on the table beside her bed, almost feel the invigorating warmth of an essential shower.

Adalinda reached her door, gently inserted another key and stepped into the waiting room. Beams of sunlight streamed through her windows, warming the fabric of a single, smoke-grey couch. Light flooded the floorboards, reaching towards the kitchen folded into the farthest reaches of her apartment.

A contented smile curled Adalinda's lips as she moved inside, the weight of the past day rising from her chest as if it were nothing more than evaporating frost. She grazed her eyes over the wooden coffee-table pressed against the back of the couch, its' surface lined with books, their peculiar gravity tempting as the door swung softly closed.

A whispering prickle swept beneath Adalinda's scarf.

She grazed her fingers across the fabric, chest becoming tight, smile leaking from her face as she noticed the open door leading to her bedroom.

The door she had left closed the day before.

Adalinda's stomach twisted.

A pale wound sliced the door's polished frame, the mark akin to the scratch of a claw, the scrape of a talon leisurely dragged across its' surface.

Adalinda crept past the kitchen, her stare pinned on the mark as she moved into her bedroom.

The trail lazily continued around the frame and along the plaster of her walls, carved paint dusting the floor in a fine layer which lead to her ensuite bathroom.

Adalinda barely registered the sun-warmed sheets draped across her bed, the book of mythos laying open, forgotten, on her dresser.

The pulse stuttered in her veins.

Panic pounded in her temples.

Hesitantly, she touched her fingers to the carved marks defiling her bathroom door. And pushed.

The door swung open.

She crept into the bathroom.

Froze.

Adalinda's golden eyes gaped, her shocked expression reflected in the ruined surface of her bathroom mirror.

The entire mirror had been artistically etched, leisurely scratched like the walls of her room. The design a perfect rendering of her ivory tattoo.

A shattered breath spilled from Adalinda's lips.

Fractures spread across the glass like the woven strands of an intricate web, splitting her face in a mosaic of dread. A sheet of paper had been impaled on a shard marking the epicentre of the splintering glass, one edge torn, aged and worn and smothered in rows of bleeding black ink.

Ink which erased sweeping lines of swirling script.

Ink which erased sweeping lines of *her* swirling script.

Identical to the sole remaining writing in the journal still hiding in her studio's vault.

And peaking through the striking black, at various positions on the page, were the disconnected words of a taunting sentence.

... don't... You... remember...?

Adalinda lowered herself to the edge of the bath, the cool of the porcelain seeping through her clothes and into her trembling palms, as the blood drained from her face.

Don't you remember?

A broken whimper tore up her throat, those haunting words smouldering like flames behind her eyes as she dragged her horrified gaze from the mirror and dropped her head into her hands.

LOST

TEN YEARS AGO

HER EYES SHOT OPEN, *gold and wild with panic.*

She hauled herself upright, gasping through a fit of coughs. The air rushed her lungs in a thick, fevered mass as a burnt-orange scarf fell from her fist, rustling a sigh and crumpling in her lap.

It took a few moments for her to calm. A few steadying breaths. A few flexed limbs. She remembered the terror of falling. The pain of hitting the ground. Though from what she could tell, her body was undamaged.

She let out a long, shuddering breath and instinctively lifted the scarf from her lap, deftly tying it around her head despite her shaking fingers. Her feet dragged through rasping sand as she drew her legs to meet her chest, coiled her arms around her thighs, dropped her forehead against her knees.

Gradually, her body's trembling began to calm and her heart began to cease its' struggle, content to remain in place behind the bones of her sternum. She didn't know how long it took, possibly minutes, perhaps hours. The curve of her chest rose with a final, cavernous breath. She released her rigid grip on her legs. Lifted her head. Returning to herself as her vacant eyes squinted in the impossibly white light. Brightness which devoured all save the deepest shadow.

Her hands dropped to the ground and she stared, with parched and gaping lips, as her pupils began to adjust. She lifted a handful of sun-scorched sand and began sifting the granules through her fingers, watching in stunned silence as it drifted in an unbroken stream, collecting in an insubstantial mound by her side.

The sun hung, suspended, just above the horizon, beams of glowing amber illuminating mountainous desert dunes, their peaks reaching greedily for the sky. In her shock, she had been oblivious to the blistering heat, the dense air which rippled around her in waves atop the sand. Air that might be plucked from the sky as if it were a piece of shimmering fabric, suffocating her figure in its' tremendous, hostile beauty.

Her features contorted in the faintest cringe, air sucking viciously through her clenching teeth.

Her limbs sang the tormented melody of skin burned scarlet, screaming for shelter from the suns' wounding rays. She tried to moisten her cracking lips with a light flick of her tongue, only to find its' surface dry as dust, rough as stone.

She could see no water.

If the cold of the night neglected to kill her, surely dehydration would. She could not remember the last time she'd had a drink. She could not remember herself, her face, her name.

Only a fall...

An impossible fall.

A whisper interrupted her rising fear as the last of the sand sifted through the gaps between her fingers. Her hand remained in its' position, hovering amid the suffocating heat, as her gaze slowly lowered to the whisper's source.

Sunlight glinted off a twisted, streamline form, its' scales a sighing kiss against the surface of the dune. The cobra hissed, stretching its' hood as it raised its' rounded head from the sand and spat an aggressive warning from the tip of its' flicking tongue.

Her right hand instinctively reached towards the snake, an unfamiliar, pale tattoo gleaming inside her wrist. "It's alright." Her voice came like the sand, rasping and slow, her golden eyes locking with the cobra's slitted pupils.

It snapped forward, a trail of shadowed sand abandoned in its' wake.

"Calm yourself." She leaned forward, mimicking the movements of the snake as her scalp began to prickle. "I'll not hurt you."

The cobra hesitated, forked tongue scenting the air, slitted pupils refusing to leave her own.

She fought the urge to stroke her scarf as she listened to the symphony of her breaths, the beating of her pulse. Her heart expressed an anxious flutter.

Almost imperceptibly, the cobra narrowed its' eyes. Its' hood deflated, head lowering in submission.

It curled on itself, pivoted and slipped down the side of the dune.

Her hand collapsed to her side, her palm facing a sky of shifting colours. The pearlescent tattoo on her wrist flashed as she stared after the cobra, leaving her to the rapidly cooling desert.

She pushed herself up and brushed a cloud of sand from her skirt with quivering hands. "I just told a cobra to calm itself." Her parched throat bobbed as she straightened, flustered tremors shuddering down her vertebrae. "I just told a cobra to calm itself." A disconcerted laugh trickled from her chapped lips, bleached and tight with hysteria. It withered as she turned in a slow circle.

Mountainous dunes reflected the warm colours of the sunset, peach sand shadowed a deep lavender, momentarily transforming the harsh landscape into a thing of rare beauty.

Her dark lashes shifted as she blinked, the hurriedly cooling breeze grazing her flushed face. She took a few steps forward, climbing the crest of a dune, and buried her toes in the heated sand as she admired the distant horizon.

The dunes rose and fell before her like seemingly infinite waves. Bare and never ending.

An overwhelming sense of dread rose in her hollow stomach, heavy and swollen with confusion and fear. She raised a forcibly steady hand, the crimson skin of her shoulder screaming as she smoothed the folds of her scarf.

A prickle swept across her scalp and she shivered, then whispered a cursing breath.

"Where the hell am I?"

CHAPTER SEVEN

DONOVAN FROWNED AS HE reached for the door of his ink-black car. He and Christensen had just emerged from Leena Rosenberg's apartment, their thorough search of her rooms providing only one link.

Adalinda.

The murdered woman's apartment had been overflowing with university projects. Sculptures and sketches lined the walls, books explaining techniques and referencing artists were crammed into rows of shelves. Leena had documented Adalinda's work for the past half decade, gluing photographs of her sculptures into books crowded with sketches and notes, developing an apparent obsession with Adalinda's sculpting.

The calendar hanging on her bedroom wall had the date of the Mirror Gallery's exhibition circled in vibrant crimson, the event dramatically underlined and followed by a string of exclamation points.

"Donovan?"

A hum rumbled in Donovan's throat as he paused, glancing at Christensen over the roof of the car, his hand resting on the handle of the door.

"I swear..." Christensen leaned forward, narrowing his eyes at a window in the building across the street. "I *swear* I just saw Adalinda."

Donovan's dark brows narrowed, his gaze flicking over the empty windows.

"Didn't Iveta write down her address?"

Donovan shoved a hand into his pocket, searching. A folded piece of paper caught between his fingers and he pulled it from his coat. Read the inscription. Swore under his breath.

"Is it her apartment?" Christensen frowned as Donovan marched around the car, heading for the buildings' entrance. "... I take that as a yes."

A muscle fluttered irately in Donovan's jaw.

Adalinda had deliberately kept information from him. He had suspected she was involved but he had not considered this. Everywhere he looked, everything he found seemed to lead back to *her*.

And the fact that she had left the gallery so quickly...

Donovan shoved the paper back into his pocket as he crossed the street and stepped up to the door of Adalinda's apartment building. He rammed his fist into the wood, the strikes echoing hollowly inside.

A heartbeat passed.

Then another.

The door to the building swung open, revealing a stout woman with greying hair. She glared at Donovan, dark eyes fuming, swearing and spitting ferociously in a foreign language.

The crease between Donovan's brows deepened as he pushed through the door. "I need to speak with Adalinda."

The woman grabbed Donovan's sleeve, squeezing her fist around the fabric as he started up the stairs. "What do you want with her?"

"To talk." Donovan ground the words through clenched teeth, pulling his sleeve away from the woman and continuing his ascent.

Christensen cringed, dancing around the woman as she followed on Donovan's heels. "I'm Detective Christensen, he's Detective

Donovan. We believe Adalinda has information about a murder that she has been keeping from us."

The woman stopped, tugging her dressing gown firmly around her waist. "I already confirmed her alibi last night. What more could you possibly want to talk to her about?"

"We… have reason to believe she's involved. We apologise for the intrusion." Christensen rubbed a palm across the back of his neck, his pace slowing as he passed the woman who was watching Donovan count the doors. "I assume you're her landlady?"

The woman dipped her chin in confirmation. "Diana." She lifted her slippered foot to the next step, arms wrapping around her waist. "I was about to take Adalinda some tea when *he* started pounding on my door." She gestured curtly at Donovan, who blew out an irate breath, halting at Adalinda's door.

Donovan felt Christensen's wince as he lifted a fist to knock, anger sweeping through him, heating his muscles, burning his veins.

He lowered his knuckles to the door.

Striking.

Softly.

There was no answer.

The air began to thicken, becoming heavy around Donovan's skin.

Again he struck the door.

Again, no answer.

Donovan sucked in a furious breath. He turned to Diana, her attention glued to his hovering fist. "Is there a spare key?"

Diana pursed her lips, preparing to shake her head.

When the door released a faint click and swung open.

Chapter Eight

ADALINDA STARTLED AT THE knocks which split the quiet, stomach twisting, ears ringing. Her head swam. The page on the mirror was a weight, pressing her down, its' scrawled words echoing in her head.

Don't you remember?

The memories came in waves, tapering off, then surging.

They hadn't been this bad in years. She thought they might have let her go, released her from their torturous grip, a grip of knives and thorns which woke her screaming, tears streaming down her face, clothing soaked with sweat.

Sobbing.

But no, how could a memory leave?

It didn't.

It simply waited to strike, waited until the mind was weak, until the walls built around it crumbled and it was unleashed in a darkly shrieking ambush.

The knocking stopped.

Adalinda stood, staggering slightly as the blood rushed back to her face. She stepped out of the bathroom, drifted through the bedroom, her movements vacant, empty.

Hollow.

Warm sand sifted through her fingers, drifting in an unbroken stream.

Adalinda swallowed the strain in her throat, trying to dislodge the memory. Her tattoo flashed with the sway of her wrist, pearlescent ink gleaming above her stammering pulse. She did not bother concealing it as she reached for the door, still submerged in her remembered terror, surface shining above, depthless black below. Something had her by the ankle and was slowly dragging her down.

Down.

The door swung open.

And Adalinda was met with the cold rage of a crashing storm.

Donovan marched into her apartment, towering over her like death in an alley, dark as midnight, radiant as the stars. His voice rumbled like thunder from his chest. "You've been hiding information from us."

Adalinda stumbled back, eyes growing wide as her scalp renewed its' prickling.

She glanced at the scratched trail marking her door.

And her heart faltered.

"The murdered woman lives *across the road from you.* You're connected to this murder, Adalinda."

Adalinda's calves collided with her coffee-table. She felt her balance slip. Her body tilted back.

Donovan caught her with one arm around her waist, his muscled chest heaving as he leaned over and growled. "Start. Talking."

Adalinda's stare flicked over the hard line of Donovan's mouth, the fluttering muscle of his jaw. His breath was the ghost of a fevered kiss on her skin.

Her hollowness fled.

Replaced with something *far* worse.

His lips lowered to her neck, bared teeth grazing her skin, his touch feather-light and gently scraping.

Until he bit down.

Fire ignited in Adalinda's core. An inaudible curse pitched across her tongue as she shoved the delusion aside. She narrowed her eyes, gathering herself as she realised she was still suspended by Donovan's arm, draped as if she were nothing more than a swooning, infatuated child. "*Excuse* me?" Adalinda straightened, regaining her balance, her traitorous heart sinking when Donovan's hand fell from her waist. "You just *assumed* that I knew she lived across the street?" Adalinda stalked forward, poking a finger into the dense muscle of the detective's chest and pushing him back towards the door. "Do *you* know *your* neighbours?"

"Yes."

Adalinda's fuming glare flicked to Christensen.

"Lovely old couple. They occasionally bake me cookies."

Donovan arched a chocolate brow, looking sidelong at Christensen.

"I mean..." Christensen cleared his throat, lowered his voice to a melodic base. "They're very polite and say hello sometimes." He rolled his shoulders, uncomfortable. "You don't talk to your neighbours?"

Donovan gritted his teeth. "No."

"And *you* accuse *me* of not knowing the woman *across the street?*" Adalinda crossed her arms, tucking her painted wrist beneath her elbow and ignoring the tingles Donovan's presence evoked beneath her skin.

Donovan tilted his head, his expression calm though anger still simmered beneath his eyes. "I'm not in the building most of the time."

Adalinda forced herself to look at Christensen, dragging her attention away from Donovan, away from the heat radiating from his skin. "I'm only here to eat and sleep. Mostly, I'm either at the gallery or in my studio—"

"What's that?"

Adalinda stopped. Stiffened.

Donovan was staring over her shoulder, a frown tugging the corners of his mouth.

She cursed under her breath, realising her mistake. Her back was turned to her bedroom door, exposing the gash scraping through the wood.

Donovan stepped forward and Adalinda reached out to bar his path, the cuff of her sleeve slipping down her wrist.

Unveiling her gleaming, pearlescent tattoo.

Christensen blanched. "Is that—?"

"The murdered woman's tattoo." Donovan seized her hand, his grip gentle despite his temper, despite the frown darkening his face. "When were you going to tell us about this?"

Adalinda wrenched her wrist from the detective's grasp, feeling the heat of his touch spread beneath her skin. She stepped back, desperate to distance herself from him, his presence like a thread, tugging on her soul. "If you'd be *quiet* for a moment, maybe I'd be able to *explain.*"

Donovan met her eyes. Expectant. Waiting.

Adalinda stroked her thumb across the faint extrusions of ink on her skin. The quiet stretched, growing heavy and tense. Fear danced over her bones, shivering beneath her scarf, as her chest expanded with a deep, shuddering breath. "I don't remember getting the tattoo. I have trouble with my memories..." Adalinda glanced at Diana, finding comfort in the woman's presence. "I came home and found the marks scratched into the wall. It leads to the bathroom..."

Donovan was stepping around her before she had finished speaking, his looming form disappearing through her bedroom door.

She watched numbly as Christensen followed.

Diana walked into the kitchen and calmly began to boil the kettle. She moved to the cupboard, retrieving a marble-patterned mug. "Tea or hot chocolate, Adalinda?"

Donovan's curse slapped the air, harsh and furious.

Adalinda trailed her fingers over the rustling fabric of her scarf, her reply absent as she stared at the entrance of her bedroom. "... Tea..."

"Thought so." Diana nodded, dropping a teabag into the mug and adding a teaspoon of honey. "Would you like to talk about it?"

Adalinda shook her head, slowly wandering towards the kitchen as a leaden hush drifted through the walls. "No."

"Thought not."

Adalinda lowered herself onto one of the kitchen stools, her golden eyes still pinned to the empty doorway as Diana waited for the kettle to boil, then poured the hot water into the waiting mug.

"Drink this. I doubt you've had anything to eat since yesterday. I'll find you some food and come right back." Diana reached over and cupped Adalinda's cheek in her palm, her thumb grazing the delicate skin of Adalinda's temple. "Don't blame yourself. It's not your fault, dear."

Her fault.

Adalinda barely registered Diana leave, barely registered the destructive hole the other woman left when she strode from the apartment. She raised the steaming mug to her lips, taking a mouthful of the scalding liquid. The sweet taste of tea and honey settled on her tongue, burning and smothering the fear still gripping her stomach. She squeezed her eyes shut, picturing the transparent lenses she had yet to remove, yet to replace.

Monster.

Adalinda stayed there, perched atop the stool, drowning and suffocating in her own injurious thoughts. Thoughts of thirst and terror, of darkness and death, of the scorching desert sand beneath her hopelessly naked feet.

A shudder charged across Adalinda's scalp and she raised a hand to her scarf, calming the fabric which seemed to shift beneath her fingers, rippling like spilled blood beneath a breeze. She stared at the vapour rising from her tea, listening as her instincts screamed at her to run, to hide somewhere no one could ever find her.

She ignored them.

She knew what it was to have nothing and no one.

She knew what it was to be alone.

She would not know that again.

So she stayed in the kitchen, perched on her stool, and waited.

Chapter Nine

... DON'T... YOU... REMEMBER...?

Donovan stood as if on a cliff, the toes of his boots hanging over the edge, fragments of stone and clouds of dust plunging into the abyss below. His reflection rose before him, broken and fragmented beneath the etching of a snake, his heart and sternum erased by the paper impaled on glass. Its' curling script blacked-out and bleeding. Its' disconnected words echoing through him like the unabating sting of a backhanded slap.

Don't you remember?

The world became muted by his pulse, by his drowned memories struggling for breath.

His burning lungs contracted, spent air bursting from his mouth in a swarm of parasitic bubbles.

A curse rasped through Donovan's lips, its' iced edges banishing the whisper of unwanted memory as he focused on Christensen's voice, barking into the speaker of his phone for a team of forensics, for Clarke.

Donovan stormed from the bathroom and through Adalinda's bedroom, his fingers hanging deceptively loose, tingling mounds rising on the skin of his arms.

Adalinda was cradling a mug of steaming tea in her palms, its' base planted on the kitchen bench. She stared at the ripples on its' surface, her features blank, absent.

Donovan stopped by her side, silent as the void beyond the sky, a flutter of concern plucking his heart as if it were laced with strings. "...You are under my protection effective immediately."

Adalinda's lips twitched in a nigh imperceptible frown as she glared up at him. "Am I just?"

"You've been threatened by a murderer. You're a target. You don't have a choice."

Adalinda's grip tightened on her mug. "Why don't you find someone who actually *needs* protection? Or, better yet, why don't you find whoever *killed* that *woman!* If you had found the damned place that she was *murdered—*" Adalinda stopped, her limbs becoming impossibly still. She pulled her hands away from the mug and flew to the window, the morning sun streaming over her form. She stared at the street below, her eyes flicking between the corner of an abandoned street and Rosenberg's apartment building. "You said the murdered woman lived across the street."

Donovan felt himself trailing Adalinda, unable to discern exactly when his boots had begun to move across the floor.

"Detective..." Adalinda turned from the window, he could see the pulse throbbing in her neck, the flash of urgency sparking in her stare. He understood what she was going to say before the words began to shape on her lips. "I know where she was murdered."

The front door swung open, revealing Diana balancing a plate of pastries in one hand as she shuffled through the door.

Donovan called for Christensen, striding across the room and catching the door before it could swing closed. He glanced over his shoulder, narrowing his eyes at Adalinda as she moved to follow. "Show me."

Adalinda nodded, sweeping past Diana and plucking a pastry from the woman's plate. She brushed the whisper of a kiss across Diana's cheek. "Thank you."

Diana grabbed the cuff of Adalinda's shirt before she could move any further. "You'll need two."

Adalinda stared at the plate, considering, then lifted her shoulder in a shrug and slipped her fingers around a second pastry as Christensen emerged from her bedroom.

"Clarke said she was a bit busy. Not her exact words. I won't repeat them as they were *slightly* expletive. She's sending the forensics soon... What did you want?"

Diana shifted the plate, holding it out to Christensen and he paused, inspecting the pastries, then looked at her as if in question.

She smiled. Nodded.

Christensen's mouth split in a beaming grin as he reached out, grabbing two pastries. He stuffed an entire pastry into his mouth and briefly paused, glancing at Diana again, before swiping another from the plate.

Donovan pulled the door wide, watching the shift in Adalinda's mood as she tore part of her pastry and delicately placed it on her tongue. "Adalinda believes she knows where Rosenberg was murdered."

Christensen's attention snapped to Donovan, a mist of powdered sugar dusting his chin as he spoke around the partially chewed mouthful. "How?"

"Broken glass." Adalinda took another bite of pastry, ignoring the flakes which drifted to the floor. She shot Diana an appreciative smile then stole past Donovan. A tremor of electricity trickled through him as her hand brushed his own, the movement deliberate, precise. She swallowed her mouthful and spoke in a low murmur, the second pastry hanging from the fingers of her other hand. "And

I'm *not* under your protection."

Donovan leaned close, his lips a breath above Adalinda's ear. His voice was a low rumble, dripping heated honey. "You don't have a choice."

Adalinda peered at him sidelong, the corner of her lip curling up in challenge. "I think you'll find I do."

Chapter Ten

ADALINDA STOOD STOICALLY beside Donovan, nervous tension braiding her bones, her arms protectively crossed over her chest. Her fingers tapped an anxious rhythm on the sleeve of her arm as a shiver swept over her scalp, trickling across her shoulders and down her back. The winter-morning chill seeped through her skin like tongues of frost through forest. She could feel part of her scarf beginning to slip, gradually falling loose. Like pebbles before an avalanche.

She needed to remove it.

Replace it.

They had been waiting for hours, watching as the forensics meticulously searched for evidence in her apartment, watching as they scanned the divides between cobblestones like hounds on the hunt.

They had been waiting for hours and the forensics had found nothing. Not a hint of how the murderer might have entered Adalinda's apartment. Not a drop of blood amongst the shattered glass littering the corner of the street. No proof that it might have belonged to Leena.

Nothing to provide any trace, any trail, which might lead them to the murderer.

All of it had been removed by the previous nights' rain.

Adalinda glanced at her fingers, the tips pale and beginning to ache from the cold. She could feel Donovan's burning gaze, see the muscles twitching in his jaw as another shiver raked through her.

She hoped he didn't see her fear, the anxiety which hid in the space between her breaths, squeezed inside the transient pause of one heartbeat and the next.

She hoped he didn't see. Hoped he *couldn't* see.

Her fault.

Monster.

Donovan stepped closer, softening his voice as his fingers began to deftly unfasten the top buttons of his coat. "You're shivering."

The cold.

He saw the cold.

Not the fear.

Relief softened the pursed line of Adalinda's lips, the corners quirking in a whispering smirk. "You're watching too closely, Detective. I still don't need protection."

A rumbling chuckle reverberated in Donovan's chest, the sound causing a prickling wave to surge beneath her scarf. "You still don't have a choice."

Adalinda couldn't choke the flutter of her pulse as she met his gaze, couldn't keep the slight hitch from her breath as she considered the man before her. So foreign. Yet so familiar.

She gestured with a hand towards his coat, his fingers unfastening the buttons at his chest. "You need that. I'll go back to my apartment and find something warmer." Adalinda pivoted on her heel, wet cobblestones glittering beneath her boots, thoughts snapping to her loosening scarf as her scalp began to prickle.

Donovan released his coat and turned to follow, casually shoving his hands into his pockets.

Adalinda came to a halt in the middle of the street. She could feel his pursuit, the heat of his form breaking the cold as a sun breaks the dark. "I don't need an escort, Detective." Her hand lifted of its' own accord, stopping just below the loosened fabric of her scarf as she remembered herself, temper flaring. She lowered her palm very deliberately, tucking it into her side. "It's my own damned apartment."

Donovan moved to obstruct her path, casual and graceful and towering. "A murderer left a threat on your bathroom mirror without any evidence of how he got inside. You may not need an escort but I won't leave it to chance."

Adalinda blew out a sharp breath, steam curling from her lips. Fatigue was beginning to plague her, tangling her mood into complex knots. A tingle crawled down her neck. "Let me lay this out for you, clearly and precisely. I did not sleep last night because the face of a murdered woman was floating in the dark every time I closed my eyes. I worked in my studio until sunrise, trying to get the echo of death out of my head. All I want is to go inside, get warm and have a *really long shower*. And if you, or anyone else, prevent me from doing so you will find out *just* how difficult I can be. I'll stay with Diana and if I need you I *will call*."

"Donovan."

Donovan refused to move his stare from Adalinda, his eyes calculating, his hands still buried in his pockets as Christensen called again.

"*Donovan*. Chief's on the phone."

Donovan pursed his lips, glancing at Christensen, then back at Adalinda. He withdrew his hands from his pockets, fingers curling and flexing as he came to a decision. "You will call immediately if you so much as see a *shadow* move incorrectly. And you will stay with Diana, *not* in your own apartment."

Adalinda bowed her chin in a confirming nod, the frozen breeze biting at her cheeks. She tensed involuntarily as Donovan shifted closer, feeling the warmth pouring from him as if the cold dare not touch him, as if he controlled the very air itself.

"If you don't answer a call from either Christensen or myself on the first ring, I will assume you're dying and *you* will find out just how difficult I can be."

Again, Adalinda lowered her chin, her shoulders rolling in an attempt to avert another shiver. "Fine."

"Fine." Donovan stepped around her, elegant as the ocean, steady as a storm. His arm brushed her shoulder as he murmured. "You may not need protection but I will drop whatever I'm doing and run here if I have to."

He did not wait for her response.

He simply walked away.

ADALINDA'S HAND SLID ACROSS the fogged surface of Diana's bathroom mirror, beads of moisture dripping erratic trails down the glass. She stared at herself, at the flushed and glistening skin of her naked form, at the unnatural glow seeping from her golden eyes.

Monster.

She sucked a breath of steam into her lungs, breasts rising, hand reaching for the creamy scarf which hung beside her towel.

She tied it around her head, her movements practised and precise.

She retrieved her contact lenses, delicately placing them on the curve of each eye.

She dried and dressed, silk and wool slipping over smooth, gleaming skin.

Adalinda stared at herself, at the fabric coiled around her scalp, at the pale, insulating clothing draped over her graceful form.

Don't you remember?

She brushed the tips of her fingers across her concealed head, listening to the rustle of the scarf as she ensured it would not slip.

She left the bathroom without a backward glance, closing the door as the steam began to settle, began to dissipate, and finally, began to disappear.

Chapter Eleven

A HIGH-PITCHED CHIME PIERCED the air as the elevator doors slid leisurely open and Donovan stormed through, his coat rippling behind him in a furious wave.

The chief had summoned them with nought but a call and like dogs to a whistle they had come.

Donovan clenched his teeth, the pressure singing in his ears, his breath pouring through his chest. He should not have left Adalinda. He should have convinced her to accompany them, should never have left her side.

Christensen jogged to catch up as the elevator doors slid closed. "Donovan, slow down."

A growl bubbled in Donovan's throat. His glare narrowed at the plaque on the door at the end of the hall, its' metal glinting the chief's name.

Akilah Wise.

"Donovan." Christensen threw himself into Donovan's path, flinging his arms wide and barring Donovan's view of the chief's door. "*Calm the hell down."*

Donovan's nostrils flared as he inhaled, his voice grinding through his teeth. "... I am calm."

Christensen raised his brows, gesturing to Donovan's rigid form with both hands. "I beg to differ."

"Are you going to *move?*" Donovan stepped forward, a current of heat seething through his bones.

Christensen crossed his arms, stubbornly planting his boots on the ash carpet. "Not until you grace me with the cause of your infernal temper."

Donovan waited a moment, the heat in his veins fading, the hum beneath his skin abating. He dragged his fingers through the dark waves of his hair, releasing a frustrated breath. "I left her."

Christensen's arms fell to his sides, his jaw going slack. "*This is* about Adalinda?" He stared, emerald eyes wide, as Donovan pressed his lips in a thin line.

"She was just threatened by a murderer..."

Christensen swore under his breath. "I've had to put up with this shit for *an hour* because you're feeling *guilty?*"

Donovan flexed his fingers, deliberately opening his white-knuckled fists. "She was just *threatened* by a *murderer.*"

"Doesn't matter how many times you say it, you're still angry because you feel—"

The elevators chime cut Christensen off as the doors sighed open. He peered around Donovan's shoulder, mouth curling down in confusion.

Donovan turned, watching as a woman glided from the elevator, hair streaming over her shoulders in a fiery river of ginger. She froze in the hall, her copper eyes flicking between the detectives as if their presence was unexpected.

"... Iveta?" Christensen stepped around Donovan. "What are you doing here?"

Iveta parted her lips, blinked. "I... spoke to Chief Wise in the gallery yesterday and she asked me to let her know if I found anything." The woman combed her fingers through her hair, clearing her throat. "I was watching the security footage and I have a list of the guests who spoke to the woman who was—" Iveta faltered, eyes guttering. She shook her head and scraped her hair over a single shoulder. "Anyway, I found three in particular who spoke to her for extended periods of time. There was a rather stunning man dressed in black, I couldn't find his name, I'm *sure* I would've remembered if I had it... But there were two other women who spoke to her and I misplaced your card so I thought I'd come here personally to give Wise their names and addresses." Iveta shifted her weight on her feet, her smile returning to her face with a vengeance. "I clearly had *perfect* timing because the secretary informed me that you had just arrived and were heading into the chief's office." She spread her arms, gesturing to herself, to the hall and elevator. "So here I am."

A crease formed between Donovan's dark brows. His stare tracked Iveta as she strode towards them, shooting Christensen an endearing smile and brushing past with the grace of a floating cloud.

"No sense waiting out here, I'm sure Chief Wise will want to hear these names." Iveta pushed her way through the door, not bothering to knock, simply cooing melodically to announce her arrival. "Good morning, *Akilah*."

Donovan's features darkened, the air around him beginning to thicken, as he watched Christensen mouth a curse and scramble to follow the gallery owner. Donovan's boots moved silently across the carpet, his skin beginning to tingle, the scent of a looming storm spilling into the hall.

He blocked the door with his boot before it could swing closed.

Chief Wise was sitting behind a walnut desk, a set of antique balancing-scales perched amid a mass of paperwork on its' surface. The bronze scale's were dull, scratched, and the chains suspending its' shallow dishes softly creaked as the chief pressed down, then released.

A hum churned in her throat, a billowing battle of snow and steel, as she watched the oscillating dishes with eyes of stunning silver, sharp as knives, strong as stone, and impossibly, magnificently cunning. "Iveta." The chief lifted her gaze, bronzed skin gleaming in the sunlight which poured through the office windows, head tilting in a fluid motion that almost appeared avian. "I presume you found those names I asked for."

Iveta glanced at Donovan, his boot still wedged against the door, before reaching into her coat and retrieving a meticulously folded sheet of paper. "Asim Nazari and Anja Anand, I spoke to both of them at the exhibition. Asim mentioned that she was a teacher. Private classes in the afternoon. I've written down the address that was on the business card she gave me." She placed the page next to the balancing-scales, smiling sweetly. "Anja comes into the gallery regularly to practice sketching, she's a member so I had her address on file."

"Wonderful." Wise settled her elbows on the desk, interlacing her fingers and gifting Iveta a rare smile before shifting her focus to Donovan. "What did you find this morning? Christensen mentioned a threatening message when I called."

Iveta tensed, copper eyes sparking. "A threatening message? Who received a threatening message? Was it *Adalinda*?"

A frown tugged at Donovan's mouth as Christensen cleared his throat. "With all due respect, Chief, I would rather discuss this in private."

"But—"

Wise raised a hand and Iveta fell quiet. "Iveta, I'm sure you're exhausted after such a traumatic experience. I appreciate your assistance, but you deserve a rest." The Chief unfurled from her seat, rising and carefully stepping around her desk. "Did you find a hotel to stay in until the forensics are finished with your gallery?"

Iveta nodded reluctantly, her hair slipping with the movement.

"Then my secretary will find you an escort to take you there, if you feel that is necessary."

Iveta tucked her escaping strands of hair behind her ear. "... Thank you." She turned, quietly sweeping into the hall, apparently unwilling to argue with Wise any further.

Donovan released a breath, letting the door swing shut and striding into the room. "Miss Veil was threatened by the murderer."

Wise frowned. "This is the woman whose sculpture was beneath the victim?"

"Yes." Donovan crossed his arms, forcing his rising anger to cool. "There was a note on her bathroom mirror, a page from a journal covered in black ink. The only words that had not been covered were 'don't,' 'you' and 'remember' all spaced on separate lines, in that order."

Wise leaned back against her desk. She tapped a dish on the scales, listening to the chains gently creak. "Did she say if those words had a significance?"

"No."

"... She also has a tattoo..." Christensen added. "On her wrist. The same as what was inked on the murdered woman."

Wise released a dissatisfied hum. "I want you to watch her. Miss Veil seems to be directly involved with this case and I want to know why. Do not leave her side until you find out." The Chief plucked Iveta's folded paper from her desk and handed it to Donovan. "Question these women first, I want to know the name of the man in that security footage."

Donovan slid the paper into his pocket, meeting the Chief's stare and dipping his chin in a brief nod. "We'll call if we find anything."

CHAPTER TWELVE

SHE MOVED LIKE A HURRICANE. Lean muscles rippling beneath toffee skin, lithe body gleaming with sweat. Beaded braids flashed gold as they swept about her head like a crown of furious, swarming bees.

Christensen swore under his breath, staring at the woman on the raised platform as she released a harsh cry.

Her giant opponent crashed to the floor before he even registered being hit.

Donovan scanned the room, his gaze settling on a pair of women leaning against the far wall, calmly discussing strategies.

The woman on the platform peered down at the great, wheezing man, still coming to terms with his proximity to the floor, and raised a raven brow. "What was *that*?"

The man glared at her, his frustrated scowl bleaching a scar which connected his hairline to his chin, the mutilated skin streaking over an eye of pale, sightless white. He sucked in a deep breath which clogged in his throat and launched him into a coughing fit.

One of the women leaning against the wall released a sharp laugh. "These men fight like tortoise. Slow. *Stupid.*" The accent poured from her rose and thorn lips, dense as forest foliage. "Better to fight woman. Move like viper."

Donovan frowned, dismissing the faint, suspicious recognition rising in response to the woman's voice.

A laugh of spring and wildflowers escaped the woman with the beaded braids. "That is *exactly* the right analogy, Vera." She placed a calloused hand on the rope bordering the platform, vaulting over it and landing with leonine grace on the wooden floor.

The woman leaning against the wall beside Vera smirked, her dark-chocolate lips twitching, her obsidian gaze flicking momentarily towards Donovan.

"I don't know what is *analogy*..." Vera narrowed her ice blue eyes at the woman of toffee and gold. "But what I say is truth." Her lips curved in a predators smile as she pushed off the wall, her tail of champagne hair swinging across her back. "This time I will fight. You will lose."

The woman flicked a beaded braid from her face, her gaze of burning umber glistened with delight. A smile of challenge lit her slim, toffee features. "Bring it on, Russian."

Donovan cleared his throat, stepping forward before the women could begin another fight. "Asim Nazari?"

Three sets of eyes snapped to him.

The woman beside Vera pushed away from the wall, her movements slow and suspicious. "Who are you?"

"Detectives Christensen and Donovan." Christensen plucked a photograph of Leena Rosenberg from his pocket. "This woman was found murdered yesterday morning in the Mirror Gallery. Miss Nazari was seen speaking with her at the exhibition two nights ago. We have some questions, if you don't mind?"

The woman with the obsidian eyes nodded sharply, her short, pitch and soot curls shifting as they floated in a dense cloud around her head. "Asim." She beckoned to the woman of toffee and gold. "Come."

"Don't summon me, Aisha." Asim glowered as she straightened, walking towards them. The flame in her burning umber eyes extinguished as her gaze fell on the photograph of Leena. "... She's dead?"

Donovan lowered his head in confirmation. "She was seen with a man. Did you speak with him?"

Asim's expression hardened as Christensen retrieved a photograph of the suspect, a caption from the security footage. "Yes, I spoke to him. Was he responsible?"

"He's a suspect. We have yet to find any evidence, but he left the exhibition shortly after Rosenberg." Christensen returned the photographs to his pocket. "Can you tell us anything about him?"

Asim studied Donovan, a frown momentarily shadowing her features before she turned back to Christensen. "His name is Theodore. Leena introduced us but I didn't speak to him much. I had only met her that night so I'm afraid I don't have that much information for you."

Donovan's dark brows narrowed at Asim's glinting beads. He flexed his fingers, ignoring the heat of unease shifting in his veins. "The security footage showed you leaving the exhibition two hours after Rosenberg. Did you go straight home?"

Asim's stunning features shimmered with sweat as she peered up at Donovan. "I share an apartment with Aisha, she can vouch that I was home by one in the morning."

Aisha bowed her head in a nod. "She was relatively loud."

Asim brushed invisible dust from her closely fitted singlet as she let out a huff. "I am *not* loud." She glanced at Vera who had walked over, her ice blue eyes assessing Donovan. "I don't know where Theodore is, but if you find him... And he killed her..." Asim pursed her lips, meeting Donovan's gaze. "*Don't let him get away.*"

Vera placed a comforting hand on Asim's shoulder, squeezing gently. Her rough accent softened as she spoke, dragging her eyes from Donovan. "We fight now."

Asim nodded, her beaded braids swinging, and followed Vera to the raised platform. "If I remember anything else I'll call. Leave your details with Aisha."

A sigh spilled from Aisha's dark lips as she watched Vera and Asim mount the platform, the giant having recovered and removed himself. "There's no excuse for murder." She turned, pinning her intense gaze on Donovan. "Find whoever did this and when you do, show him no mercy."

Donovan rolled his shoulders, loosening his muscles as if preparing for a fight. "I wasn't planning on it."

Asim and Vera began to circle one another, prowling with feline agility.

"Good." Aisha peered over her shoulder, watching the platform.

Asim struck first.

Christensen pulled a calling card from his pocket, absently holding it out for Aisha as he watched the women attack and defend, striking and feinting as if fighting were breath and they were simply breathing.

Aisha took the card and Christensen reluctantly peeled his gaze away from the women. "I wish I could move like that."

The corner of Donovan's mouth twitched, amusement momentarily lighting his features. "Perhaps you should ask them to train you."

Christensen glanced at the giant Asim had knocked to the floor, his bare fists slamming into a punching bag. The man was studying the women, observing their fight as it became a blurred battle of champagne and ivory, toffee and gold.

Christensen swallowed and shook his head. "They'd *kill* me."

A soft chuckle rose in Donovan's throat as he strode towards the exit, silent as the moon drifting across the sky. "Only if they wanted to."

EYES OF PALE CERULEAN FOCUSED on the black spot in the centre of the target. The girl's elaborately braided hair whipped in the frigid breeze, the loose ends cascading down her back like the graceful tendrils of an ebony waterfall. She flicked a pair of knives in her caramel fingers, ignoring the bow which leaned against her leg and the leather quiver mounted over her slim, athletic shoulders.

She threw the first knife.

Its' razor edge glinted as it carved through the air, reflecting the sunlight which struggled to pierce a layer of storm-scented clouds, their bruised and lingering mass threatening to hail.

The blade struck its' mark.

And the girl's mouth split in a triumphant grin, sweet as a daisy in bloom.

The smile faded from her lips as Donovan and Christensen approached across the flat rooftop of her apartment building. She turned to examine the towering men, adjusting her grip on the remaining knife and throwing it without looking at the target.

The blade struck the first knife.

Clattered to the ground.

"How'd you get up here?"

Donovan considered the target, frowning softly as the girl waited for his reply. "We took the stairs."

"Really?" Humour glinted in the girl's pale eyes. She pressed her lips together to hide her laugh. "I thought you might've flown."

"Unfortunately, we lack the wings." Donovan lifted his shoulders in an indifferent shrug, a memory waking in his mind as his ocean gaze skimmed the girl, her slim frame and youthful cheeks too young to be considered an adult.

The girl allowed her smile to creep back onto her face, the expression making her appear childish. Innocent. "What'd you come for? I'm not in the business of talking to strangers." She gestured to the target and the steel of her thrown blades. "Hence the knives."

"I'm Detective Christensen and this is Detective Donovan." Christensen extracted the photograph of Leena Rosenberg from his pocket. "Are you Anja?"

The girl paused, nodded.

"You were at an exhibition two nights ago, we wanted to ask you about a woman who was there, Leena Rosenberg, and the man she was with."

Anja's ebony brows furrowed, her smile abruptly doused. "She's the one who was murdered, isn't she? I heard someone talking about it in the street…" She caught her lip between her teeth, sorrow lining her eyes. "I spoke to her at the exhibition."

Christensen stepped towards the girl, curling his shoulders to make himself appear less imposing. "We wanted to ask you some questions. Is that okay?"

Anja sniffed and wiped her eyes with the edge of her sleeve. "I didn't kill her." Her fingers curled around the bow still leaning against her leg, the weapon balanced precariously yet still standing. "I've never killed anyone, I swear. This is just for fun."

Donovan strode to the target, pulling the knife from its' mark then stooping to retrieve the second blade from the ground. He paused, examining the weapons as he felt the tug of a vague familiarity. The metal was of silver and bronze, the shades seeming to shift like mist against glass but never to merge, remaining impossibly separate.

Donovan looked back at Anja whose chin was beginning to tremble. "We believe you." He swallowed the ache beginning to throb in his temples as he walked to the girl's side and handed her the strangely captivating knives. "What did you speak to Leena about?"

"Sketching." Anja accepted the blades, sliding the fingertips of her other hand along the string of her bow. "The man with her didn't say anything much to me. He was more interested in Leena."

Donovan frowned. "What did Leena say?"

"Not much. I showed her some of my sketches. Iveta had invited me to the exhibition because she thought it'd be good to socialise with other artists. I didn't really want to so I brought my book to sketch in. I was doing that when Leena stopped to talk to me." Anja stared at her knives, the edges glinting sharply. "She liked my work, said I was talented…" The girl sniffed again. Shrugged. "She mentioned that the man she was with was a doctor and that art was more of a hobby."

Christensen ran his fingers along the fold of the photograph before slipping it back into his pocket. "Did she say where he worked?"

"No." Anja shook her head, ebony hair rustling in the breeze. "I asked but he wouldn't give any specifics. He just said that he worked in the city. After that I went home, I think that was around ten." She threw the knives again, both at once, narrowly missing the mark. "I like to get up early so I can practice."

Donovan arched his neck, stretching in an attempt to banish the rising headache. He blew out a sigh and straightened, turning towards the stairwell. "Let us know if you remember anything else about the man, he's a suspect and we'd like to find him."

"You can call on this number." Christensen retrieved a calling card from his jacket and held it out to Anja. "Any time, day or night."

Anja nodded, trapping the card between two fingers and lifting it in a mock salute. "Will do."

"Good." Christensen smiled, his eyes skimming over the knives in the target. He turned to follow Donovan into the stairwell before shooting over his shoulder. "Keep practicing."

Anja scrunched her nose and poked out her tongue. She wandered over to remove her knives from the target as the detective's strode towards the stairwell, her pale, cerulean eyes tracking them until they disappeared.

Christensen followed Donovan down the steps, pausing as a vibration began to rise from his pocket. He shoved a hand into his jacket, searching for his phone and glancing at Donovan's back. "What do you think?"

Donovan clenched his hands into fists, the vibrations of Christensen's phone beginning to pluck at the persistent ache which had spread to the base of his skull. "I think she's a child."

Christensen nodded, brows knitting as he finally managed to wrest the phone from his pocket and answer the call. "... Clarke. Have you found anything?"

"*Hi Christensen, lovely day we're having, how was your morning? Good? Mine was nice. Productive. A little bloody.*" Clarke's voice streamed from the speaker, echoing mildly around the stairwell as the detective's descended. "*You know... the usual.*"

Christensen looked at Donovan, his emerald eyes gleaming. "You found something."

"*It wouldn't kill you to make some conversation, would it? I mean, I enjoy chatting up dead people but the back and forth's a little bland.*" The distant clatter of metal on metal resonated behind a short, manic laugh. "*And of course I found something.*"

Donovan lifted his fingers to gently massaging the crease from his brow. "What did you find, Clarke?"

"*Paint.*" Clarke's ecstatic grin was audible through the speaker as more metal rattled in the background. "*I found paint.*"

Christensen stared at the phone, his expression incredulous as he paused on the stairs. "What?"

"*To be specific, I found thermochromic paint. I was finishing up with the autopsy which, by the way, showed just how healthy that girl was.*" Footsteps echoed, accompanied by more metallic sounds. Metal tools clattering against a metal tray. "*I mean really healthy. Her stomach contents consisted of only vegetables, fruit and meat. If she hadn't been killed she would have lived for a long time. I can't find anything wrong with her... Other than the great big smile slashed across her throat.*"

Christensen's face contorted in a grimace. "Clarke, *how* did you find the paint?"

"*A heat-light. Obviously. Thermochromic paint reacts to heat.*"

Donovan cleared his throat, his ocean eyes sparking with his flaring headache. "You're sure it's paint?"

"*No, it's fucking chocolate cake. Who do you think I am?*" Mechanical doors hissed, an elevator chime echoing through the speakers. "*Look, I'm going to the gallery now to take a closer look at the crime scene. Chief said she'd tag along. I think she's getting bored of all that paperwork.*" Clarke released a snort. "*Who can blame her? Paperwork sucks! Anyway, there's some residue of the thermochromic paint on one of the victim's hands so I want to find out where it came from.*"

Donovan stared at the phone in Christensen's hand, dropping his fingers from his brow, shoulders tensing. "The crime scene was *already* examined. How was this *missed?*"

"*I was kind of focused on the dead woman hanging from the ceiling.*" Clarke's boots clicked against concrete as she exited the elevator, her voice hollow and reverberating through the basement carpark. "*Fuck knows what the other forensics were doing, I specialise in dead people not art. I'm guessing the paint came from one of the pieces in the gallery, presumably something close to the victim's corpse. The forensics probably took the 'do not touch' signs literally.*" A click sounded as she unlocked a car.

Christensen pursed his lips at Donovan's scowl as they continued descending the stairs. "Can you take a '*do not touch*' sign any way *other* than literally?"

A metal door opened and a noise akin to an audible shrug escaped Clarke's mouth as she slid into her car. "*Doubt it.*" She turned a key in the ignition, the car rumbling to life. "*I'd better be a good girl and hang up, talking on the phone while driving is apparently against the law...*"

"Clarke."

"*... Fucking politicians. I can sing while driving, bitch. Try making that illegal.*"

"*Clarke.* We'll meet you—" Christensen stared at the screen as it released a beep. "... She hung up."

Donovan rolled his shoulders, inhaling deeply as he emerged onto the ground floor.

"How could we have *missed* this?" Christensen dragged his fingers across his forehead, staring at the floor and following Donovan into the entry hall.

"You tell me." Donovan crossed the floor and shoved through the building's exit. "Because I sure as hell don't know."

Christensen dropped his phone into his pocket, barely evading the ricocheting door as he leapt onto the pavement. He muttered a curse, oblivious to the muscles dancing in Donovan's neck, the veins throbbing in Donovan's fists.

Don't you remember?

Donovan held his breath, suffocating the echo of the note in Adalinda's apartment, drowning the memories which seethed beneath it like writhing limbs of shadow and thunder.

He held his breath as he strode across the street, his ocean eyes pinned to his ink-black car.

He held his breath until his lungs began to ache, until his blood began to scream, until the simple need for air obliterated the whispering surge of his thoughts.

When, finally, Donovan deigned to draw breath, the stain of his memories was all but erased.

He flexed his fingers and twisted his neck, unlocking the car and sliding inside.

He didn't know how they could have missed the paint residue, nor how the murderer could leave a message in Adalinda's apartment and remain unseen. But they would find out soon enough.

All Donovan needed to do was wait.

Chapter Thirteen

THE GALLERY WAS DARK. The curtains had been drawn in a shield against the furious hail outside and the lights were subdued, muted, banishing the walls decorated with vividly painted canvases to shadow.

Adalinda's statue leaned in a frozen dance, the curve of her body appearing suspended by air, as if at any moment she might fall, fracturing and shattering against the gallery floor.

"What, exactly, are they doing?" Iveta hovered beside Adalinda, her fingers nervously braiding the length of her ginger hair. She stared with wide eyes as Clarke finished connecting cables to the heat-lights and black-lights flanking Adalinda's sculpture. "That *woman* just wandered around with a light in her hand for half an hour after telling me to unlock the gallery and wait."

"If I knew, I wouldn't be waiting *with* you." Adalinda swallowed her rising discomfort, ignoring the faint itch beneath her scarf, hands hanging loosely by her sides in feigned calm. "... But I'd say she found something."

Iveta chewed her lower lip, shifted her weight and dragged her fingers deftly through her braid. "They're just *standing* there." Her stare flicked over the detectives. The chief stood between them, her auburn hair twisted in a strangled knot, her cloud grey coat falling about her knees. "It's making me nervous."

Clarke tucked a stray lock of lavender hair behind her ear as she turned to Chief Wise. "It's ready."

Wise lowered her chin in the barest hint of a nod, pressing her lips and clasping her hands behind her back. "Turn it on."

Clarke flipped a switch.

The warmth of the heat-lights spread in an amber flood across the cold, gallery floor, gliding like a summer breeze over the smooth limbs of Adalinda's sculpture, over the stone dancer's reaching arms and tilted head and back arched like a bow.

For a moment, nothing happened. The heat simply soaked into the sculpture's naked form.

Until the pale skin of the marble began to fade.

The ivory surface retracted from the heat as if it were diseased, sliding up the arms, drifting up the legs, disappearing to reveal a figure made entirely of crystalline glass.

Adalinda's stomach dropped.

The blood drained from her cheeks, leaving her skin pallid, her flesh tingling.

Her voice was nothing more than a whisper, a breath caught on barbed wire. "That's not my sculpture."

Clarke snapped her gaping mouth shut, her eyes alight with glittering awe. "It's the *thermochromic paint*." She trailed a gloved finger over the sculptures' arm, her grin expanding as she admired the moulded glass. "Invisible when heated and—" She stopped, leaned closer to the glass, teeth chewing the side of her cheek, eyes pinned on something transparent floating inside. "*Shit*." She scrambled across to the heat-lights, the globes standing guard beside the still inactive black-lights. Clarke immediately extinguished them, squinting into the residual cloud of heated darkness. She fumbled for the black-light's switch. Turned it on. Winced as the globe erupted in a deep, rich blue.

Adalinda barely registered Iveta's gasp, the noise impossibly loud in the absolute quiet. Iveta clung to Adalinda's shoulder with a grip of choking iron, struggling to hold herself steady on a pair of trembling knees.

Nausea shredded Adalinda's stomach.

Her pulse thundered in her ears.

The glass dancer glowed from within, a phosphorescent blue illuminated by black-light, the hollow tubes of her skeleton shining the colour of the sky. Her light poured like a beacon through the gallery, bathing Clarke's bewildered face, drowning Donovan's furrowed brows.

Adalinda could feel the blood abandoning her extremities, her fingers bleaching, tingling, as she stared at the dancers' glowing sternum.

At the flaming, crimson heart suspended beneath the glass.

Red light dribbled down the sculptures' spine as if the vertebrae were painted in blood. It merged with the cerulean light of her ribs, creating violet, soft and menacing.

And scrawled across the dancers' stomach, in the same shade as her burning heart, was a single, bleeding sentence.

I know what you are.

Dark tendrils crept across Adalinda's vision.

Monster.

The breath shuddered into her lungs.

A whimper hitched in Iveta's throat, her fingers digging into Adalinda's shoulder. "How... how did this *happen*? I thought this sculpture was *yours*, Adalinda."

Her fault.

Adalinda shoved her nails into her palms, the pain snapping at her memories, at the fragments fighting to surface. She blinked, clearing her vision. Shook her head to calm her prickling scalp. "It was…"

"Then how was it replaced with this?"

Adalinda met Wise's sceptical stare, the chief's silver eyes stinging like a blade. "… I don't know."

Wise stepped forward, head softly tilting as she contemplated Adalinda. "You didn't suspect the sculpture wasn't yours?"

"No."

"Surely, it would have to be different. It can't possibly be *indistinguishable* from your own."

Adalinda refused to retreat as Wise continued forward, boots silent as sleep, head still vaguely tilted. "There was a murdered woman hanging from the ceiling when I was here last, I wasn't exactly focused on my own sculpture."

Wise stopped, her lips minutely twitching. "Where's the original?"

"I don't know."

"Why is the tattoo on your wrist identical to the victims?"

Adalinda glanced at her wrist, the sleeve dutifully obscuring her skin. "I don't know."

Wise released a frustrated breath, neglecting to remove her gaze from Adalinda as she spoke over her shoulder. "Find me some answers." She turned, her attention skimming over Christensen and landing on Donovan. "And don't let her out of your sight until you've proven her innocent."

Donovan's frown deepened as he looked away from the sculpture, broad shoulders tensed, fingers curled in fists. His ocean stare tore into Adalinda, flaring and brutal as blistering steel. "I wasn't planning on it."

Wise inclined her chin, her silver eyes glinting with the movement. "While you're at it, find out how the murderer got inside." She gestured to the sculpture. "He's creative and highly intelligent which makes him unpredictable. I want him incarcerated before anyone else gets hurt. Clear?"

Donovan rolled his shoulders, relaxing his white-knuckled fists. "Crystal."

"Clear as glass." Clarke piped up, still staring admiringly at the sculpture.

"Good." The chief raised a brow at Iveta who had lowered herself to the floor at Adalinda's feet, her coat spilling around her thighs, her eyes staring vacantly at the sculpture. "Iveta."

Iveta's pale lashes fluttered as she looked up at Wise.

"Perhaps you should find a cup of tea."

Iveta shook her head, her freckles stark against her already pale features. "I... I don't think I could keep it down, quite honestly."

"I'm sure you could. Why don't you come with me, I'd like to avoid doing any more paperwork this afternoon and I have a feeling you could use the fresh air."

Iveta swallowed and pushed herself to her feet, swaying slightly. "I have to lock up."

Adalinda caught Iveta's shoulders, ignoring Donovan's unrelenting stare and the shiver creeping down her spine. "I'm sure I can manage that."

Iveta remained quiet for a moment, considering, before reaching into her pocket and handing the keys to Adalinda. "The security code is the year I bought the gallery."

Adalinda nodded, dropping the keys into her cloak and forcing a reassuring smile to curve the corners of her mouth. "Go and relax, we'll be fine."

Iveta nodded, pausing as if about to speak before deciding against it and following Wise out the gallery door and into the hailing street.

Chapter Fourteen

"HOLY SHIT, I THOUGHT SHE wasn't going to *leave*." Clarke threw her head back, blowing out a harsh breath and bouncing on her toes. "I need to swear *profusely*. It's like holding in a breath for too long and suddenly feeling like you're going to fall over."

"Clarke, I don't think—"

"... *Holy.* Mother..."

"—That's really—"

"... Fucking. *Shit!*"

"—Necessary." Christensen rubbed the bridge of his nose, a sigh hissing through his teeth.

Clarke squealed, gesturing to the sculpture with fast, frantic movements. "This is *literally* the best thing I have seen. *Ever.*"

Adalinda pinched the back of her hand, sucking in a deep breath as Donovan strode to her side, his towering form moving with lethal grace.

"'I know what you are.'"

Adalinda tensed, staring at the words on the sculpture as Donovan's hushed voice dripped from his lips, raising mounds on her arms, sending shivers over her scalp.

"Do you know what it means?"

Adalinda shook her head. "No." She watched Clarke inspect the sculpture, scraping particles of dried paint into tubes, searching for something, anything, to find a link to the murderer.

Donovan shifted, the heat of his presence dancing across Adalinda's skin. "Adalinda, I can't find whoever did this if you aren't honest with me."

Adalinda kept her voice calm, even, despite the knots twisting in her stomach, the fear clouding her senses.

Monster.

"I don't know what it means." Adalinda felt Donovan's gaze as if it were a lead weight, dragging her down, constricting her lungs. She waited a moment. Took a breath. Forced herself to meet his eyes. Anchored and unflinching. "I don't *know* what it *means.*"

Donovan stared down at her, his breath kissing her cheeks, his nostrils softly flaring. She clenched her teeth, refusing to look away, refusing to retreat until his shoulders began to relax, until he blinked and sighed in resignation. "How did the murderer switch the sculptures, then?"

Clarke placed her sample in a bag behind the heat-lights as Adalinda rubbed her temples, searching for an explanation. "He would've needed a mould of the original and it was in the gallery as soon as I finished it. This looks as if it took weeks, possibly *months* to create. My sculpture has only been in the gallery for a few *days.*"

Donovan raked a hand through his hair, the dark waves gleaming in the pale gallery light, his skin lit by the sculptures' glowing bones. "We need to find out how the murderer got inside."

Adalinda hauled her gaze from Donovan's striking features as a spark of heat flared in her core. "There are six floors, including the gallery, and then there's the basement."

Christensen walked to Donovan's side, staring resolutely at the ceiling as he moved. "Does Iveta own all six floors?"

"Yes. She uses two as personal galleries, they're filled with art she's inherited and collected over the years, and her apartment consists of the two top floors." Adalinda gestured around them. "The first two floors are the gallery." She pointed to the floor. "And the basement is below."

A creased formed between Donovan's brows. "What's in the basement?"

"Any art that hasn't been sold or is in rotation and the artists have asked for them to be kept in the building."

Donovan grunted, the air thickening with his frustration. "There has to be something we aren't considering."

"I don't—" Adalinda fell quiet as the pocket of Christensen's jacket began to vibrate. The detective grabbed his phone, fumbling with it as he marched to the windows. He answered the call, pulling the curtains apart and peering outside. Soft light bled into the gallery around him, the evening sky obscured by hailing clouds. He spoke quietly, asked a few gentle questions, then hung up.

Donovan watched expectantly as Christensen released the curtain. "That was Anja."

The detective's lips curled down almost imperceptibly.

"We have a lead." Christensen turned away from the window, his bright eyes shadowed against his ebony skin. "Clarke, do you need us to wait?"

Clarke nodded, platinum and lavender hair sighing as it shifted around her ears. "Possibly. I have a feeling there's nothing on this sculpture except paint but I need to be certain." She turned to Christensen, letting her arms drop from where she had been scraping at the painted words on the sculpture's chest. "An hour, maybe? And then I need a drink."

Christensen slid his phone back into his pocket. "Good, because we're going to a bar." He glanced at the gallery entrance. "And I really didn't feel like braving that hail."

Chapter Fifteen

A BITING WIND HOWLED THROUGH the desolate streets, snapping at Donovan's heels, spitting at his cheeks, feral as a starved wolf mourning its' frozen pup. Pellets of ice hissed malice as they flew across the pavement, torn from beds of hail which littered the road. Streetlights flickered, rattled by the bitter squall and plunging the street into momentary darkness.

The bar crouched, vigilant, on the corner of the street, a few blocks shy of the gallery. Warm light poured from its' windows to spread over the road, the amber glow reflecting off the pavement.

"Well, this is about as pleasant as being a *fucking* cadaver in an icebox." Clarke shoved her hands further into her pockets. "It's cold as hell and I can't feel my fingers."

Donovan tipped his head back, peering into the black above. His eyes narrowed as he glimpsed a faint shift in the sky. The scattered stars winked out, fleetingly cloaked by a dark form which drifted between the buildings. The silhouette of an owl, its' vast wings extended, the whisper of its' passing muted by the wind.

Christensen tugged his jacket tighter, grumbling as he stepped off the path and onto the road. His boots slid on a sheet of black ice and he cursed, managing to catch himself on Clarke's slim shoulder.

She stumbled, then shot him a malicious glare.

"I'm going to die of hypothermia before we find the murderer." Adalinda clutched the collar of her cloak, curling her shoulders against the wind. Her nose and cheeks had become flushed from the cold and her lips were softly trembling, pressed in a thin line to stifle her chattering teeth.

Donovan peeled his gaze from the gliding owl, a frown curling his lips.

"I'm seriously considering returning to my car." Longing dripped from Clarke's features as she glanced over her shoulder and pouted in the direction of the vehicle. "I bet it would still be warm... Regular *body temperature* would be warm compared to this."

Adalinda nodded her agreement as Donovan moved closer to her, his elbow brushed her shivering arm.

"It'll be warm inside."

"Good." A weak smile flickered across Adalinda's stunning features. "I'm starting to think your protection will be the death of me."

Donovan's breath clouded, a low chuckle rolling from his lips, as he stepped up to the entrance of the bar. He shoved the door open and leaned against it, holding it open for Adalinda. Air rushed out in a heated gust as she slipped inside, her arm inadvertently grazing his stomach. His muscles tensed at her touch, his breath hitching softly, his ocean gaze trailing the graceful sway of her hips.

Donovan followed Adalinda into the enclosed space, leaving Christensen to catch the door behind him. He inhaled the dense heat of the bar, the heavy air flooding him with the scent of smoke and spiced liquor. Men and women lounged in leather booths or perched on wooden stools, painted lips laughing, teeth flashing smiles, immersed in fluent and varying conversation.

A tremendous stone fireplace stood against the far wall, its' blazing flames dancing over charring logs. The heat that poured from its' yawning mouth was visible, almost rippling.

Clarke unleashed an appreciative sigh, stepping around Donovan with a feline grace. She paused beside Adalinda, listening to the music which streamed from a live band, the musician's fingers flitting over strings and over keys. "... I need absinthe."

Christensen shook his head, moving in the direction of an unoccupied bench beside the fire. "There is something *fundamentally* wrong with you, Clarke." He loosened his posture, leading the group through the crowded tables until they reached the blazing hearth. "Though I can't say I'm surprised, given your chosen occupation." He pulled out a stool and gestured for Clarke to sit.

Clarke flashed him a brilliant grin. "What can I say?" She lowered herself onto the stool, tucking a strand of short hair behind her ear. "The dead speak my language."

Adalinda hummed under her breath, her shivering gradually beginning to subside as Donovan guided her to the seat closest to the fire. She blinked up at him, her golden eyes reflecting the hearth's dancing flames, and he weighed the urge to step a little closer, to find out if her skin was as soft as it looked...

A bellowing laugh speared through the room.

Adalinda turned, ripping her focus from Donovan. He felt something jerk in his chest, sensed an emptiness cleaving the space between his lungs, as she stared across the room at a group of hulking men, their enormous figures slouched around a wooden table near the bar.

One of them was staring back.

Donovan frowned, examining the scar which split the staring man's face from hairline to chin, the eye beneath it a pale, sightless white, his skin a rich, dark bronze. Donovan remembered him crashing to the floor, remembered Asim standing above the man as he wheezed.

He was studying Adalinda through the crowd.

Adalinda's brow creased softly and Donovan moved around her, smoothly blocking the scarred man's view. He glanced over his shoulder as one of the men grabbed at a nervous serving girl, the girl narrowly avoiding his reaching arm, her skirt brushing his smear of tattoos. The man hissed at her, his spittle flying onto her shirt as her cheeks flushed scarlet and she hurried away.

Heat began to trickle beneath Donovan's skin, fluid and tingling. He rolled his shoulders, aware of Adalinda lowering herself to her seat, and leashed his surge of annoyance.

The serving girl ducked around the bar, a tall woman behind it already reaching to pour her a drink. The woman glared at the tattooed man, her hazel eyes sparking malice, her hair falling over her shoulders in silken, brunette waves.

Donovan set his jaw, removing his coat and draping it over the back of a stool. "I'll get the drinks."

"I'll go with you." Adalinda curled her fingers over the edge of the table, beginning to rise from her seat. "I could use a whisky after today."

"Absinthe, please and thank you." Clarke smiled sweetly, moving a hand to catch Adalinda's wrist as she stepped away from her seat.

Adalinda paused, looking at the medical examiner in silent question.

"I'd stay here, if I were you." Clarke spoke softly, managing to keep the smile pasted on her face as she jutted her chin towards the tattooed men. Two of them were sneering at women around the bar while the third, with the scar, stared through the constantly shifting crowd, his ink-black eye pinned on Adalinda.

Donovan swore he felt Adalinda shudder.

Clarke tilted her head, gesturing to Donovan's simmering features, her murmur almost inaudible. "That man does not need a reason to fight and if you go up there, he'll just get *more* edgy."

Christensen nudged Donovan with an elbow, dragging his attention away from the women. "Anja was adamant the suspect mentioned this bar. The manager might know something."

Donovan gave a slight nod, his dark hair rustling past his temples as he glanced at Adalinda. She lowered herself back to her seat, deliberately looking away from the scarred man who had leaned forward and braced his arm on the table, stare shifting to Donovan.

Donovan met the scarred man's gaze and frowned, clenching his teeth, before turning away and forcing himself to follow Christensen to the bar. He felt an urge to turn back as the scarred man's attention drifted again to Adalinda, his dark eye intense, focused and calculating.

... As if he knew her...

Donovan shook his head, shouldering his way through the crowd. The scarred man hadn't been at the gallery on the night of the murder and Donovan doubted he was directly involved. Merely coincidental.

Donovan shoved his feeling of suspicion aside, dismissing a thorn of lingering doubt as he came to a stop beside Christensen, set his jaw, and asked to speak with the manager.

THE MANAGER LEANED FORWARD, placing the bucket of ice she was holding to one side as she rested her elbows on the bar, brunette waves falling around her angular face. The nervous serving girl lingered close by. Her hands trembled softly as she finished her drink, then walked back out into the room.

"Who'd you say you were, again?"

"Detectives." Christensen pulled his phone from his pocket, unlocked it. "I'm Christensen, this is Donovan. We'd like to ask you about a suspect in a murder investigation, Miss...?"

"Lorelei." The manager watched the screen of Christensen's phone as he opened the photograph taken from the gallery's surveillance footage. She frowned, the curve of her lips soft and flickering. "... I've seen him. He comes here on occasion, mostly sits over there." Lorelei nodded to the group of hulking men still slouched around their wooden table. Her hazel gaze lingered on the one who had tried to grope her serving girl, his bloated features bordering on grotesque. He was eyeing the girl as she began collecting empty glasses, giving his table a wide berth. "He never really spoke to anyone. Always came in alone."

Christensen nodded, placing his phone back into his jacket. "Did you or any of your employees manage to catch his name?"

"No." Lorelei shook her head, removing an elastic band from her wrist and securing her hair in a tail. "He was careful not to mention it, and he always paid in cash, but I'll ask around…" The manager's words trailed off as her attention shifted to the serving girl. The girl had just plucked a glass off the table behind the bloated man and was placing it on her tray, straightening to leave.

The bloated man shoved his chair backwards, its' legs screeching against the floor, and reached out to grab her.

His stubby fingers locked around the serving girl's thigh.

She gasped.

Lost her balance.

The empty glasses toppled from her tray and smashed across the floor. She yanked herself out of the bloated man's grip and began to back away, tray held aloft as if she could use it as a weapon.

A transient silence engulfed the room, all eyes levelling on the girl.

Donovan flexed his fingers, loosening fists he hadn't consciously closed.

Lorelei watching the bloated man stand. She tensed as he lumbered forward, following the serving girl's retreat to the bar, her tray still raised and aimed at the hideous smile slashing his face.

The girl ducked around Donovan and the bloated man snarled, baring a set of teeth stained yellow. "You think you can hide, you little bitch? Come out and stop playing games."

The crowd dispersed slightly, the music cutting off.

Donovan lifted an arm onto the bar, his features hardening as he turned to observe the brute's bulging stomach, the skin dangling beneath his chin. "Leave her be." He glanced at the serving girl over his shoulder, then looked at Lorelei in silent command.

Lorelei nodded, ushering the girl behind the bar as Adalinda quietly rose from her chair across the room, cautiously watching.

"You hear me, bitch?" The bloated man stepped forward, glaring at the serving girl as she pressed her back against the wall of liquor behind the bar. "I said *stop playing—*"

"She heard you." Lorelei growled softly, moving to block the man's view of the girl. "And you've just outstayed your welcome." She crossed her arms over her chest, a sharp glint of challenge lighting her glare. "I suggest you leave."

Across the room, Adalinda slid from her table, her golden eyes alight.

"This is of no concern to you, woman." The bloated man bared his teeth, clenching his pudgy hands into fists by his sides. "Stay out of this."

"Stay out of this?" Lorelei barked a laugh. "Stay *out of this*? This is *my* bar, you ungrateful piece of—"

"I think that's enough."

The room became motionless as Adalinda wove through the last of the dispersing crowd. She stopped in front of the bloated man, her back facing the bar, her slim figure dwarfed by the bulk of the fuming brute. Chin held high. Fingers brushing the base of her scarf.

A furrow creased Donovan's brow as he turned to look at her.

And the bloated man's lips spread in a leering smile. Stale breath leached off his tongue, the stench of rancid beer and creatures long dead clinging to the air around him. His eyes roamed over Adalinda's calm features, over the curve of her waist which peaked through the split in her cloak. Alluring. Enticing. "Well, aren't *you* a treat."

Adalinda glanced at the skeletal birds inked over the bloated man's hands. A frown played at the edge of her mouth as Clarke crossed the bar and stopped beside Christensen. "I believe you were told to get out."

The smile fell from the bloated man's face. "You don't want to pick a fight with me, woman. I could snap your bones like a twig."

An indelicate snort burst from Lorelei and she lifted a hand to cover her mouth as the stares of wary patrons flicked towards her.

Adalinda met the bloated man's glare, smirked. "I'd like to see you try."

Donovan rumbled a warning growl.

The bloated man leaned forward, his tattooed hands rising, preparing to seize Adalinda.

Donovan lunged, shoving himself between them to shield her as heat and anger flared in his veins. "Don't touch her." His fingers began to burn, the air around him thickening as he spoke to Adalinda under his breath. "Go stand with Clarke."

"Thanks for your concern, Detective." Adalinda shifted to step around Donovan, her words grinding between her teeth. "But I'm perfectly capable of throwing a punch."

The bloated man grinned, lifting his painted fists. "I've been itching for a fight all day. Bring it on."

One of the brutes from the bloated man's table abruptly stood. His boots crunched over the broken glass as he shoved his way through the crowd, his bald head gleaming in the electric light.

The scarred man leaned back in his chair, watching quietly.

Lorelei scowled, her hazel glare spearing both of the men. "Leave." She stood impressively still beneath the responding snarls, her nose scrunching irritably as the bald man spat on her floor. "I don't care that your boss owns this building. You tell Shade that this is *my* damned bar and if I see even *one* of his 'guards' here again *bones* are *going* to get *broken*." Lorelei brought her fist down on the counter, the thud echoing through the whisper-quiet room. "Get. Out."

Donovan tensed, glancing over his shoulder at the manager. "Shade?" His expression darkened, the heat beneath his skin flaring until it began to sting. An echo of the bruised girl from the orphanage flashed behind his eyes.

The bloated man cracked his neck, lifted his fists a little higher.

"What do you know about Shade?"

"These bastards have been in here every night for the past week, insulting my employees and threatening my customers because that *fucking* politician decided—"

The bloated man threw a punch.

Donovan felt the shift in the air, the brute's tattooed knuckles ploughing towards his exposed jaw.

Adalinda shied back.

A menacing snarl erupted from Lorelei.

Donovan's hand snapped up, catching the bloated man's fist in his palm and shoving it away from his cheek.

The brute shrieked, saliva spewing from his thin lips as the bones of his hand broke beneath Donovan's grip, snapping with a sickeningly audible *crack*.

Slowly, Donovan turned his head back to the bloated man, lifting a finger and wiping the spittle from his face. He watched as moisture began to collect in the brute's eyes, his breath shuddering through clenched teeth, his corpulent features contorted with pain.

Again, the bruised orphan flashed behind Donovan's eyes.

His anger surged, urging him to crush the bloated man, to shatter his bones and leave him limp on the floor. Donovan tightened his grip further on the tattooed fist, his ocean eyes thunderous, his brows deeply creased. He could feel the man's bones pressing through his tattooed skin, the splintered tips pricking his own palm.

The bloated man's howl cut through the whispering crowd like a knife through rotting flesh.

Christensen swore.

Clarke's eyes sparked with morbid delight.

Adalinda set her hand on Donovan's arm, a shiver driving through him at her touch. "Detective." Her voice was a cool breeze waking him from sleep. "We have an audience."

Donovan hesitated, then dropped the brute's shattered fist, swallowing the fire still burning through his veins, smothering a flash of disappointment as the man cradled his hand against his heaving chest, body trembling in shock. "I suggest you listen to the manager and leave." Donovan glanced at Adalinda, inhaled a calming breath. He dropped his hand, quivers coursing beneath his skin as Adalinda's fingers brushed his wrist.

The bloated man withered, curling in on himself as the bald man from his table bared his teeth.

"Before I change my mind." Donovan turned back to the bar, his unprotected back facing the brutes. He dragged a palm over his mouth, skin rasping over stubble.

Lorelei raised her brows.

"Whisky. Fill the glass."

The manager nodded, plucking a bottle from the shelf and pouring Donovan a drink. She placed the glass by his hand, watching as he lifted it to his lips, swallowed. "That's quite the grip you have."

Donovan grunted a non-comital response, setting the partially drained glass on the bar. He felt the air shift again, the humidity dancing across his skin.

He could almost sense the bodies at his back.

"They're not leaving."

Lorelei pressed her mouth in a line. "No. They're not."

Donovan blew out a sigh, flexing his fingers against the tingle of warmth still lingering in his veins. He turned. Brows furrowed. Shoulders taut.

And froze as the bald man raised a gun, aiming the barrel at Adalinda's head.

CHAPTER SIXTEEN

THE BAR ERUPTED, THE CROWD screaming and crying out, drinks crashing to the floor, glass shattering and spilling over skin and clothing. People ducked behind tables or cowered behind chairs, their trembling arms bent in useless shields above their heads.

Christensen hauled his own gun from beneath his jacket and aimed at the bald man's head. "*Drop it. Now!*"

Adalinda tried to move but found her knees locked, fear spilling through her muscles in cold, shivering waves.

Monster.

Her eyes flicked between the bald man and his gun.

She would not be shot.

She *could* not be shot.

Not here.

Not now.

Donovan's fingers curled into fists, the knuckles white against his tanned skin. The air vibrated with the fury of his growl. "Lower the gun."

The bald man grabbed Adalinda's arm and twisted her around,

pinning her wrist behind her back, pulling her closer to his gut. He glanced at the bloated man still cradling his fist. *"You broke his fucking hand!"*

The stench of beer and stale sweat seized Adalinda's lungs. Her scalp prickled violently as the bald man pressed the barrel of his gun against her temple. Cold steel kissed her skin. For a moment she pictured the bullet as it ripped through her temple, through tissue and bone, exploding in a cloud of shattered, blood-soaked death from the other side of her head.

Adalinda's muscles locked. She winced as the bald man tightened his grip on her arm, holding it twisted against her back.

She would not be shot.

Adalinda lifted her gaze to Donovan.

She would *not* be *shot*.

Donovan's eyes locked with hers, barely contained wrath blazing in their depths. She felt it pulse, like the thundering of her heart, as if his anger were a tangible mass. *"Lower the gun."*

The bald man placed his thumb threateningly on the hammer, pinning his dark eyes on Christensen. "Put the gun on the floor or I pull the trigger."

Adalinda pursed her lips.

Christensen bent down, placed his gun onto the floor.

"Kick it aside."

Christensen hesitated and the bald man leaned forward. He smiled, pressing his gun further into Adalinda's temple and pushing her head to the side. Adalinda shuddered as his breath caressed her neck, his grip tightening further on her arm, threatening to cut off the circulation. "I *will* shoot her."

Christensen nudged the gun with his boot.

Adalinda's nostrils flared delicately as she forced herself to breathe, pulse throbbing in her neck, hands squeezed in tight fists to stop the trembling. She kept her gaze on Donovan, shaking her head almost imperceptibly as his furious eyes flicked over Christensen's gun, the storm of his rage scarcely contained by her feigned calm.

Adalinda set her jaw, listening to the quiet whimpers which choked the crowded room.

Her eyes flicked to the bald man's gun.

Donovan stepped forward.

The bald man glanced at him.

Adalinda took her chance.

She dipped her chin and dropped, tearing her head away from the gun, wrenching her wrist out of his hand, pivoting her hips to throw the bald man off balance. Adalinda reached back, instinct drowning thought, blood pounding through her. She seized the man's arm, the gun still clutched precariously in his fingers, and threw him.

Forward.

Twisting and flipping him onto the ground.

The bald man bellowed as his weight crashed violently to the floor, his chest emptied by the impact, his body sprawling at her feet.

He was still clutching the gun.

Gasping and coughing.

Blood trickling from the corner of his mouth, from the wound he had bitten in his tongue.

The bald man's hand flew up, grabbing for the back of Adalinda's bowed head. His fingers grazed her scarf, missing by a hair before latching around the back of her neck. He held her down so her face hovered above his own.

Adalinda's heart stuttered wildly, terror wrenching her stomach. The man's hold constricted and she strangled a gasp as he dragged her further down, his rancid breath stinging her nose, making tears gather in her eyes.

The bald man swore, lifting his gun back towards her head. "*God damn—*"

Adalinda's fingers caught his wrist before he could cock the hammer.

She ripped his hand from the back of her neck. Hauled herself up. And drove her boot into the soft flesh of his cheek.

The bald man loosed a howl of pain. He rolled onto his side, the gun falling from his hand, his body curling in on itself as if he were deflating.

Adalinda sucked in a shuddering breath and stepped around him, forcing her limbs to cease their shaking as Donovan rushed forward, immediately placing himself between her and the man on the floor. "Are you alright?" He leaned over her shoulder to examine the back of her neck, his heated breath softly brushing her ear, causing a shiver to sprinkle over her skin.

Adalinda lowered her chin in a confirming nod, breathing Donovan in, his scent of woodsmoke and rain relaxing her muscles, his open collar exposing a gleaming stretch of skin. Warmth spread through her core as his fingers grazed the nape of her neck, searching for the beginnings of a bruise that would never come. His thumb brushed against her scarf.

And her scalp began to prickle.

Monster.

Adalinda choked and lurched backward, her body protesting as Donovan straightened, his mouth lowering in a concerned frown. For a moment the detective refused to move, his eyes sweeping over her scarf.

Her heart stopped.

Her stomach twisted.

She raised a hand, checking the scarf was still secure, before met Donovan's eyes. "I'm fine."

Hesitantly, Donovan let go of Adalinda's shoulder and turned towards the bald and bloated men, one clutching his broken hand, the other curled in a ball on the floor. "You were told to leave."

Adalinda's fingers dropped away from her scarf.

The bald man pushed himself off the floor and dragged the back of his arm across his bleeding mouth, reaching to grab his fallen gun.

He rose. Aimed the barrel at Donovan's chest.

Lorelei swore and ducked, dragging the serving girl with her.

Christensen grabbed Clarke and hauled her away from the bar, her arm catching the bucket of ice still on its surface and flinging over the edge. The bucket crashed to the floor, soaking the wood beneath Donovan's feet, shattered ice sliding in all directions.

A snarl curled the bald man's lip.

He pulled the trigger.

Adalinda launched herself at Donovan, a strangled cry shredding her throat. She crashed into his side, knocking him off his feet as the bullet drove into his shoulder and he fell to the saturated floor.

Adalinda lay over the detective, partially melted ice soaking her clothes, frozen blocks pressing into her skin. She stared at the shredded hole in his shirt, his chest rising beneath her palms in a quaking breath. Her voice cracked, the sound rusted, stricken. "*Clarke*."

Clarke was sliding across the floor before Adalinda had finished calling. She fell to her knees beside Donovan, steady hands parting his torn shirt and searching for the wound.

"Where is it?" Clarke frantically moved her hand over Donovan's skin, beneath the still-clean fabric. "*Where is it?*"

Adalinda pushed herself up, arms quivering beneath her weight, as she noticed a crumpled piece of metal glinting amongst the shards of ice on the floor. "Clarke..."

"Adalinda, there's *no wound*..." Clarke's hands grabbed at the hole in Donovan's shirt, hauling it open to expose unmarred skin. "There's no *bullet wound! How is there no fucking bullet wound?*"

"Clarke." Adalinda reached out an unsteady hand, her fingers gently plucking the crushed bullet from the floor.

It was still warm from the shot.

Clarke's fraught stare fell on the metal in Adalinda's hand. Confusion warped her features. Her jade and topaz eyes darted between the bullet and Donovan's shoulder, between his smooth, tanned skin and the ripped, woollen shirt.

Her hands fell to the floor, ice sliding away from her skin.

Her lips parted.

Shaped a word.

Stopped.

"... But... I saw the bullet *hit* him..."

THE FROZEN LAKE

TEN YEARS AGO

THE COLD BURNED LIKE FROZEN FIRE. *Numbing his limbs. Carving his bones.*

He felt nothing through the mindless ice, no weight, no ground, no up nor down. His mind was an abyss. Empty. Devoid of all except darkness, eternal and unending.

His lungs ached. His temples throbbed, starving blood screaming for air.

The fear crept up on him, out of the depths of his subconscious like a monstrous beast, a dark mass of writhing limbs, of curling bodies, seeping through his chest and swallowing the flesh of his erratically beating heart.

Icy liquid nudged against his bloodless lips, urging him to open his mouth, pleading with him to suck in breath.

In the darkness of his empty mind he knew drowning was a terrible way to die.

He was not ready.

He clenched his fists, choking on a grunt as searing pain shot through his contracting muscles, his lethargic blood beginning to wake.

He forced his eyelids open, irises flashing blue.

The cold struck him.

Indistinct, white light scorched his eyes.

Freezing water sank serrated teeth into his flesh.

He bit down on an agonised roar, the pain flaring bright as sunlight through his cells.

Skull shrieking.

Pulse pounding.

His body floated above a bed of stones, skin bleached of blood, fingers white as bone, dark hair drifting around his temples in a fluidly shifting mass.

His memories were a starless void, empty as the mind of a babe and drained as the eyes of the dead.

He had no idea how long it took for his eyes to adjust, to identify the light which stretched across the surface, opaque beams reaching towards the river's shadowed floor. For a moment he simply stared, admiring the clear water, the shifting light, the quiet whisper of the current as it flowed around his ears. He could almost feel the liquid pausing as it brushed against his skin.

His brows creased, a frown curling his mouth as he shook his head, dismissing the thought.

The cold was leaching his sanity.

He began to swim, driving his dazed legs to kick, urging his numb arms to haul his body towards the blinding surface. He squinted at the sunlight, shards of it pouring through a dense sheet of solid ice, the frozen length marred with cracks.

He launched himself up, muscles screaming, skin stinging.

He drove a fist into the ice, listening to the chilling echo as it fractured, as it broke. His desperate lungs contracted, spent air bursting through his teeth in a swarm of parasitic bubbles.

He tore through the ice, flinging translucent wedges into the depths.

His head broke the surface.

Spasms splintered his chest as he gasped, spluttered, the early morning air warm in his hopelessly frosted lungs. His breath came in straining pants, a groan climbed his throat as he dragged himself from the frozen river, pitching forward and collapsing on the ice.

He lay there, his body shivering with the cold, erratic clouds of breath flitting from his bloodless lips.

He had to move. Had to get up.

A grimace contorted his features. He groaned as he planted his palms on the ice, muscles convulsing, struggling to shove his lethargic body upright.

He lurched forward, urging his legs to take his weight.

He slipped across the frozen river, stare spearing the ice beneath his naked feet.

He did not see the cliff until he was immersed in its' shadow.

The stone surged from the water's depths, rising to tower above him, its' surface cold and worn smooth with time.

A deep breath shuddered into his lungs. He cursed. Slipped. Collapsed. Head crashing into the ice.

His incessant shivering slowed until it ceased. His breath became more inconstant, more shallow as he fell in and out of consciousness.

A dusting of snowflakes began to tumble from the sky, swirling and settling on the dripping waves of his dark hair, on his curling lashes and ashen cheeks.

His heavy eyelids fluttered...

The crunch of boots hitting snow dragged him from darkness, the sound almost drowned by the pitch of wolfish howls.

The snow had collected on his naked back, draped like a blanket over his motionless form.

The crunching quieted as a pair of leather boots stopped beside him.

A toe nudged his arm.

"... He's alive."

Strong hands grabbed his shoulders, hauling him to his feet.

He groaned as his numb limbs caved beneath his own weight.

The grip on his shoulders tightened. "Damn it, he is heavy. Are you going to actually help or just stand there watching?"

He lifted his bleary gaze, his ocean eyes flitting across a sled, the dogs strapped to its' head shuffling and impatient, their dark shapes obscured by the falling snow.

"How—?" His voice croaked harshly, scraping across his tongue as he fought his exhausted legs, taking a cautious step on the ice.

"How did we find you?" The woman grunted, slinging his arm over her shoulders as another figure came to her aid. "Luck." He glimpsed a braid of long, champagne hair peaking out from under the woman's fur hood. She peered at him through eyes consumed by a pair of reflective snow goggles. "And if luck does not run out you will not die before we find you shelter."

Chapter Seventeen

DONOVAN TORE HIS HAND FROM the spilled ice, muscles faintly aching, breath vaguely hitching as he inhaled and focused on the pair of yawning, golden eyes staring at him. He could feel Adalinda's fingers tangled in his shirt, feel the edges of her knuckles as they pressed against his chest.

Adalinda leaned back, abruptly releasing her fists. She glanced at the torn fabric of his shoulder, a frown flickering across her features as she tugged her cloak tighter around her shoulders and stood, dropping the bead of crumpled metal into Clarke's slack palm.

"... I may be more insane that I thought..." Clarke blinked between Donovan and the mangled bullet as Lorelei stood and leaned over the bar, staring in stunned silence. "Is no one going to *question* this?"

Christensen shook his head, clearing the confusion from his gaze as it swept between the bald man and his gun, still laying where he had kicked it across the ageing, wooden floor. "No, Clarke." His voice was almost lost beneath the pinched whispers of the bar's guests, their cowering figures still cautiously peering through gaps between the furniture. "In case you've forgotten, there's a *gun* still pointed at us."

"And *he's fucking bulletproof!*" Clarke flung her hands towards Donovan in an emphatic gesture, melted ice spraying his trousers. "Just use him as a *god-damned shield!*"

Donovan pursed his lips, a muscle dancing in his jaw as he pushed himself up. He strangled the memories trailing through his mind, their touch the kiss of poisoned silk. He ignored the humid air clinging to his skin, caressing the smooth flesh beneath the hole in his shirt, as he looked directly at Clarke and spoke in a low, resolute rumble. "The bullet missed."

Clarke stared at him, her eyes wide, incredulous. "*Bullshit.* I saw it *hit* you. There's a fucking *tear* in your *shirt.*"

Donovan's responding growl was gravel, ground through teeth. His shadowed form rose in a mountain above Clarke, back straightening, muscles tensing. Heat rippled beneath his skin in a faultless, pulsing current. His glare simmered, daring Clarke to argue as it pinned her to the floor. "You saw nothing."

The melted ice surrounding Clarke began to inexplicably shake. The medical examiner narrowed her eyes, jade and topaz irises glinting, her platinum and lavender hair sweeping into her face. She met Donovan's stare. Lowered her single, empty hand to the floor. And threw a block of ice at him.

It hit him in the side.

Bounced and disappeared beneath a chair.

"I hope your lying tongue gets frozen to a pole." She grumbled, dropping the bullet into her pocket and shoving herself off the floor. "I need some bloody absinthe."

Donovan watched Clarke slide to the bar.

Fire lit his blood as the air began to shift, as the bald man armed his gun.

"Stop moving."

Adalinda turned her glare on the bald man. She stepped forward, only partially aware of the bloated man as he stood in her peripheral, his eyes still watering, his broken fist still cradled against his chest. He took a step back as the bald man spat a snarl, levelling the barrel of his gun at the base of Adalinda's throat.

Adalinda lifted her chin in defiance, drifting towards Christensen's gun and disregarding Donovan's warning growl as the bald man's barrel tracked her graceful form. She watched for a twitch of the bald man's finger, listened for a shot.

The bald man held his ground, glancing at Donovan uncertainly.

"I hope you understand what you just did." Adalinda's smile was shards of broken glass as she tilted her head towards the bald man, gesturing for Donovan to move. "Because if you don't, you're about to find out."

Adalinda snatched Christensen's gun from the floor and flung it to the detective.

Donovan instantly lunged, the air thickening around him in a cloak of mist and nightmares. The moisture shimmered in the electric light, softly blurring his movements.

A bullet exploded from the bald man's barrel, carving past Donovan's head.

Glass shattered behind the bar.

The serving girl shrieked from her place on the floor.

Lorelei cursed, spitting fury.

Adalinda leaped aside, another shot slashing the floorboards by her boots, as Donovan seized the meaty flesh of the bald man's neck and *lifted*. Cutting off his air.

The gun slipped from the bald man's hand as he fought to pry Donovan's fingers from his throat, as he choked, as he struggled.

Finally, the scarred man deigned to move. His chair scraped the floor and he rose from the table, his single, dark eye sweeping over Adalinda.

Christensen pointed his gun at the man's chest. "Don't even *think* about trying anything."

The scarred man kept his expression blank, rising to his full height, almost as tall as Donovan. He stopped where he was and waited, observing the bald man as he dangled from Donovan's hand, as if he were content to wait for the man to suffocate.

The bald man thrashed and gagged and kicked.

Donovan frowned, muscles barely tensing. "Why are you here?"

The bald man's boot slammed into Donovan's shin, glanced off like a stone skipping water.

Donovan's fingers sank deeper into the man's throat. "I won't repeat myself."

The scarred man eyed Christensen's gun, his bronze fingers carefully rotating a near-empty glass of beer on the table. "They're hired muscle. They don't ask questions."

"They?"

The scarred man gestured to the bald man, and the bloated man, with a calm flick of his hand. "They."

The bald man gurgled, his thrashing limbs falling slack as his eyes began to roll. Donovan growled, releasing him and waiting impatiently as the bald man crashed to the floor, gasping, wet coughs racking through him. "Why are you here?"

"We were..." The bald man swallowed thickly, his voice rasping. "... told to watch."

Donovan lifted a boot onto the bald man's chest, leaning forward and softly applying pressure. "I'm going to need you to be more specific."

"*That's all.*" The bald man wheezed as Donovan slowly pressed his boot further into the man's sternum. "I *swear.* We were told to *watch.*"

"For what?"

"For information. For a way to blackmail that woman into letting Shade buy the bar." The bald man looked at Lorelei, who snarled at him.

"Why does Shade want this bar?"

"I don't know." The bald man shrank back as Donovan leaned forward. "I *swear*."

Donovan watched the bald man's wide, dark eyes, his bulging body tensed and anxiously waiting. After a moment, Donovan released a frustrated sigh and removed his boot from the bald man's chest. The moisture in the air around him began to dissipate. He dragged his fingers through the waves of his hair as the bald man scramble away, hauling himself across the floor. Donovan turned to the scarred man. "What about you?"

The scarred man met Donovan's hard gaze, waiting.

"You were with Asim. You were the man she was fighting."

The scarred man shrugged, his mouth twitching down as Christensen adjusted his grip on the gun.

Donovan rolled his shoulders and stepped forward, brow creasing. "Who are you?"

"Kaleth." Again, the scarred man looked at Adalinda, his white eye gleaming in the light of the bar. "I was also asked to watch." His gaze flicked over the cowering crowd, a few of them edging out the door.

The crease between Donovan's brows deepened. "*Who* were you asked to watch?"

Kaleth smiled grimly, the skin around his scar bleaching white. He nodded to the bald man and the bloated man, both of them scrambling for the door. "Them." Kaleth reached down and grabbed his jacket from his chair, calmly drawing a gun from it and aiming the barrel at Christensen. "And unlike them, I don't miss. Do not follow." He nodded to Lorelei, finished his beer and left, shrugging on his jacket as he disappeared through the door and marched after the tattooed men.

DEEP MUD AND MOSS EYES watched from a hidden space at the back of the bar. The events which had unfolded were unexpected.

He had anticipated a fight. *That* was *not* a fight.

It was barely a conflict.

Theodore pushed his hands deeper into his pockets, moving unseen through the bar and following the scarred man out into the cold. He made sure to use the shadows to hide as he slipped into a side street. And found Kaleth waiting there to escort him.

Theodore extracted his hands from his pockets and flipped the collar of his coat against the wind. He met the scarred man's cryptic stare and smirked, the expression crooked and brimming with arrogance. "You, my friend, are a *very* smooth liar."

Chapter Eighteen

FIRELIGHT GILDED ADALINDA with an amber glow, her golden gaze pinned on the crumpled bullet which had been placed in the centre of the table. Christensen and Clarke sat on either side of her, Christensen staring at Donovan, Clarke staring at the bullet, her chin planted flat on the table, her eyes narrowed to slits. She kept opening her mouth as if to speak, air escaping in frustrated sighs.

She was swinging her feet like a child through the legs of her stool.

The bar was empty, save Lorelei, who had sent everyone home. Now she stood behind the counter, her back turned to the group, mopping spilled alcohol and polishing washed glasses.

Christensen snatched the bullet from the table and shook it in front of Donovan's nose, the metal glinting wickedly in the firelight. "Explain."

Adalinda's eyes snapped up, a flurry of nerves shifting in her stomach as she noticed Donovan examining her, his focus fixed on her scarf.

"Explain."

Donovan glared at Christensen's hand, raised his glass of whisky to his lips.

Christensen shook the bullet as if it were a snow globe. "*Explain*."

Donovan pursed his lips and swallowed his drink, a smouldering ferocity building in his glare. "It. Missed." Christensen lowered the bullet, irately quiet, as Donovan took another mouthful of whisky and placed the glass on the table before him. He stared at the firelight dancing across its' surface, beautiful and exotic, reflecting in his haunted eyes. "There's no other explanation." Donovan's fingers closed into fists beside his drink, an extensive breath filling his lungs, and Adalinda could not tell if he spoke the words to Christensen or to himself, admonishing something that might be the cause of that haunted gaze.

"We should experiment on you."

Adalinda blinked at Clarke, the long side of the woman's hair was pooling on the table. She had not lifted her chin, nor looked away from the bullet. Though she did as Donovan grabbed his glass and drained the rest of his whisky.

Adalinda nudged Clarke's leg beneath the table.

"*What?*"

"You're not experimenting on him." Adalinda glanced at Donovan, the shadows on his jaw shifting with the flame of the fire. Her back was to the hearth and she felt its' heat through the fabric of her shirt, slowly sinking through her skin, warming the marrow of her bones now that she had removed her cloak. "No one is experimenting on Donovan."

An exasperated breath burst from Clarke's lungs and she shoved herself off the table, flicking her hand towards the bullet in Christensen's fingers. "Why doesn't this *bother* you? He was *shot* and there's *no blood*. There's *no wound!*"

Donovan's hand contracted around his glass, a muscle tweaking in his neck.

Adalinda froze as the glass fractured, pale webs splintering across its' surface.

Donovan's eyes widened. "Damn it." He moved to place the glass down.

It shattered in his hand.

Ice and glass spilled over the table, sliding across the sticky wood. "*Damn* it."

Clarke slapped a hand over her mouth, struggling to hide her laugh.

Christensen rolled the bullet in his fingers, raising a brow as Donovan plucked a handkerchief from his pocket, pushing the glass and ice into away from the table's edge. "Does this happen a lot?"

Donovan grumbled a curse under his breath and Christensen chuckled, watching him attempt to dry his hands with the now-soaking cloth. "Apparently so."

Donovan threw the handkerchief onto the table and stood, his chair scraping against the floorboards. "I am *not* bullet-proof, I will *not* be used as a shield and I will *not* be experimented on." He grabbed his coat and glanced at Adalinda, sending shivers skittering over her scalp. "You're coming with me."

Adalinda crossed her arms, leaning back in her chair. "Am I just?"

Donovan stopped, one arm into his coat. He released a tired sigh, the breath deflating him. His shoulders drooped, his chin fell almost to his chest. He pulled on the rest of his coat and lifted his fingers his temples, massaging an ache that looked to be soul-deep. "*Please.*" His voice was soft and warm as honey. And Adalinda found herself on her feet, quietly drifting around the table to stand before him as she draped her cloak over her shoulders. She carefully pried his hand away from his face, her heart stuttering as she saw the hollowness of his gaze, breathed his scent of woodsmoke and rain.

"Come." Adalinda hooked her arm through Donovan's as she turned to Christensen and Clarke. "I think we all need some rest before tomorrow, anyway."

Lorelei set a polished glass on the counter. She paused in her work to watch them leave.

Chapter Nineteen

ADALINDA LAY ATOP A SPARE BED in Donovan's apartment, her arms tucked under the pillow, her eyes staring at a vast, wooden bookshelf spread across an off-white wall.

Not moving.

Not sleeping.

The memory of Donovan being shot kept looping through her mind. Replaying like a nightmare. Constant and unending.

She threw herself at him.

He fell to the floor.

And every time the memory replayed she felt a lurch of inexplicable terror. It seized her bones and trapped her limbs. It gripped her with obsidian talons, sinking like knives through her flesh.

Her fear was not her own, though it felt leaden in her gut. It had erupted from the veil rippling in her mind, from the unnatural absence of memory, like the maw of a great, grinning beast.

It had not disappeared.

Not yet.

Not yet.

Don't you remember?

Adalinda closed her eyes, feeling a shudder beneath her scarf.

Nausea roiled through her.

Her fingers trembled as she clutched the pillow.

The words had been a taunt, suspended on her mirror. A reflection of her self, of her heart, of her mind. All of it empty. Bereft. As if stolen.

Adalinda sucked a breath through her teeth, the air hissing as she opened her eyes. She focused on the quiet, on the feel of Donovan's presence as it lingered down the hall, calling to her yet making no sound, as if his fingers had found a thread and tugged, unravelling part of her soul.

So she lay atop the bed, arms tucked beneath the pillow, staring at the shelf of books, waiting for the sun to rise. And she clung to that invisible thread as if Donovan's presence were driftwood, keeping her afloat while she fought the raging storm of nightmarish terrors playing through her mind.

DONOVAN SAT ON THE EDGE of his bed, his head in his hands, staring at the floor.

Not moving.

Not sleeping.

The memory of being shot looped through his mind. Replaying like a nightmare. Constant and unending.

Adalinda had thrown herself at him, as if her life meant less than his. Her gaping eyes as she lay atop him had left him with a lurch of inexplicable terror. It seized his bones and trapped his limbs. It gripped him with obsidian talons, sinking like knives through his flesh.

His fear was not his own, though it felt leaden in his gut. It had erupted from the veil drowning his mind, from the unnatural absence of memory, like the maw of a great, grinning beast.

It had not disappeared.

Not yet.

Not yet.

Don't you remember?

Donovan closed his eyes, feeling a prickle of heat beneath his skin.

He could feel Adalinda's presence like a wraith down the hall, as if a thread connected them, as if she called to him, though he knew she made no sound.

He wanted to go to her, to check if she was asleep, to lay himself beside her, wrap an arm around her waist and breathe her in and feel her warmth and trace his lips along her neck.

Donovan stiffened, face still buried in his palms.

He lowered his hands.

Peered at the wall.

Felt the flutter of a muscle as he tightly clenched his jaw.

He shoved the thought aside and pressed his fingers to his shoulder, to the skin the bullet had hit.

There was no pain.

No bruise.

A wisp of breath flowed from him as he leaned his elbows on his knees and clasped his hands, dark brows knitting, muscles smoothly shifting, lips shaping words from the air, without sound.

"The bullet missed. The bullet missed."

Donovan shook his head, chocolate hair rustling.

"The bullet missed. The bullet missed."

Because he could not accept. He could not explain.

The bullet had hit and not left a mark.

And he knew that he could bleed.

He knew that he could bleed.

Donovan's ocean eyes lifted to stare at the wall. Hollow and empty as an urn awaiting ashes. Reliving memories he wished he could forget.

He knew that he could bleed.

He had seen it.

He had *felt* it.

Donovan blinked as a buzz dragged him from his head. Bright light blared from his phone, the metal device vibrating on the table beside his bed. A cloud shadowed his face as he answered the call. He frowned as the hollowness dispersed, replaced by something far worse.

Donovan was on his feet and down the hall before he realised he was moving.

He found Adalinda standing outside her door, eyes tired and wide with dread, as if she knew what he would say before he opened his mouth to tell her.

... As if she had expected it.

Chapter Twenty

THE ORPHANAGE WAS SLEEPING, the children all dispersed in their rooms. The doors were locked, the howling had stopped, and Shade had left.

In the blackest hour of night.

Only one orphan was awake, still sniffling, still shaking, in the corner of her windowless room. River's neck was bruised, her stomach ached, her bloodshot stare was sightless. Her arms were locked around her knees and her face was stained with tears of terror.

All she could see was Shade's anger as he hurled her at the floor, shoving a cloth into her mouth and driving his boot into her stomach, the back of his hand striking her face. His anger was erratic, destructive and unpredictable. Sometimes he wouldn't come for days, sometimes weeks. At first she had relished his absence, certain that he would stop, but he always came back. And she learned, very quickly, that the days he did not come were like the clockwork rotations of a wind-up toy, the mechanics getting tighter, becoming strained, until it either breaks or is explosively released.

Shade never broke.

River froze as a shadow passed outside, its' presence barely a blink in the sliver of light beneath her door. She watched it disappear, chewing at her lip and thinking. It could have been Anna, the orphan caretaker, but she made noise when she walked, her trousers rustled, her feet tapped and, if she kept very quiet, River could hear her sighing breaths. The shadow had emitted no sound, not even a creak had been pressed from the floorboards.

River crawled across the room, curiosity surpassing her fear. She ignored the ache of her muscles and the screaming of her fresh bruises, ignored the spit-soaked cloth discarded on the floor.

She never broke, either.

River quietly stood, lifting her fingers to her door. Like a thief she twisted the handle and slipped into the hall, her eyes catching the shadows' edge just as it disappeared up the stairs.

Above River's head, in the furthest room of the orphanage, Anna was lost in her work. Her amber eyes were lowered to a microscope, her wire-rimmed glasses set aside. The orphans had been asleep for hours, and for hours Anna had worked.

She had not heard Shade arrive.

She had not heard him leave.

If she had known, she might have stopped him.

But she did not. And she had not.

Anna worked, oblivious, in a secluded, converted suite. It had been empty, so she had taken it, neglecting her own bed which was downstairs amid the orphan's rooms. Her suite was filled with empty flasks, extinguished burners, glass thermometers and stoppered vials, all of them clean and gleaming and waiting, just as she was, for her client to finally arrive.

A scaled body wound its' way up the length of Anna's arm, a forked tongue darting from its' mouth as it lazily coiled around her neck. And began to squeeze.

Anna's eyes lifted from the microscope, her lips tugging in a frown. "*Pretzel.* I've told you a million times, stop with the constricting. It's uncomfortable." Anna turned to look at her python, the snake's head smoothly reaching down her arm, to her wrist, its' thick middle pinching around Anna's neck. "We'll be here for awhile so you might as well explore." Anna lifted Pretzel, carefully unravelling the python and setting her on the bench. Pretzel hissed irritably as Anna turned, glancing at her door, held open by a rubber wedge.

The hall beyond was empty, as it had been all night.

Anna pursed her thin lips and checked her phone for a message.

The screen was blank.

The client was late.

Anna mumbled to herself, shifting uncomfortably. She had chosen to work in the orphanage, minding the children in the afternoon, working in her room at night. Always at night. And always in secret. As she had been asked.

The orphanage was private and undisturbed. No one ever asked what she did.

She was a chemist.

Not that anyone cared.

Anna rubbed an ache in her chest. Leena hadn't cared and she was dead. *Murdered.* Anna kept seeing the dripping faces of those detectives, asking her questions as the rain drowned the streets, as if the sky itself mourned Leena's death.

Anna was sure it did.

Pretzel's tongue flicked out as she slowly began to extend her immense body, slithering along the table and onto the wooden floor.

"That's a good girl." The corners of Anna's mouth flickered in an attempted smile as she leaned back into the microscope, examining the drop of sunshine-gold liquid she had placed on the slide. Anna had distilled it, as requested, and provided it for testing. She had been given jars and vials and a recipe, none of which were labelled correctly in an effort to obscure the ingredients. Anna had been told not to analyse it. She was to make it and forget it. Not that she could. She was far too curious for that. She had to know what it was. Anna had assumed it was a kind of active vaccine, perhaps a new anti-venom. In a way, she had been right, though she had never seen its' like before. This was something new. Something different.

Anna glanced at her tray of vials, all filled with sunshine-gold, the liquid seeming luminescent in the warm, electric light. She had an idea of what it was. She had called her client to get answers.

Anna flinched as a gentle knock startled her. Her head jolted forward, her eye colliding with the microscope. She yelped and muttered a string of curses, lifting a hand to rub her eye.

Pretzel hissed as she slipped onto the floor.

Anna waited a moment for her vision to clear, then turned from her work to assess the figure standing in the open door.

Anna relaxed her bunched shoulders. "Oh, it's you." She forced herself to smile as she stepped over Pretzel, the python having slithered in front of her feet. "You gave me a *heart attack*, I was expecting you to call so I could let you in."

Disgust flickered across the figure's face, the features masculine even beneath the shadow of his hood. He glanced at the python as he quietly stepped into the room. "I let myself in, I hope you don't mind."

Anna paused, brow creasing. "How? The door was locked."

"Was it?" The figure shrugged, drifting through Anna's laboratory and brushing gloved fingers over her burners and flasks. He stopped before the tray of vials, plucking one from its' place and tilting his hooded head. "I thought I asked you to stop making these."

"I know, I know, but you wouldn't tell me what it was and I've never seen anything like it!" Anna gestured to the microscope on her desk, reached for her wire-rimmed glasses and slid them onto her precipitous nose. "The genetic structure is *astonishing*! I had to study it and I think I know what it is."

The figure gently replaced the vial, his shadowed eyes scanning the tray. "Trust me. You don't."

"I have an idea... My tests suggest—"

"You *tested* it?" The figure tensed, his cloak swishing with the sudden lack of movement. "On who?"

Pretzel hissed, winding around Anna's feet. She shushed the snake before returning her attention to her guest. "On myself. Well, at first on a mouse or two so I could look for any changes in their bodies or behaviours but after that, on myself. There seems to be a shift in cell structure almost immediately after the substance is injected, I've never seen anything work that fast in my life!" Anna paused, leaning forward as she squinted at the figure's clenching jaw. "... Why didn't you do it yourself, if you didn't want anyone to know what it was?"

The figure stepped around the table, a single gloved hand reaching beneath his obsidian cloak. "You'll find that when you do something too many times it becomes tedious. I've been occupied with other, more important, tasks and you happened to be available when it was convenient." The figure stopped in front of Anna, hand still beneath his cloak. "I had hoped you would be more receptive to my requests."

Cold dread began to crawl through Anna's blood. Her eyes widened, the white edges stark against her amber irises, her wire-rimmed glasses flashing as they caught the room's light. "I *was*. I didn't tell anyone what I was doing, I only experimented on myself. I called you here because I wanted to tell you that whatever is in those vials is a leap forward in science! If I could just find a colleague, someone to *help* me—"

The figure released a long-suffering sigh and pulled his gloved hand from his cloak.

Anna stepped back, eyeing his palm. It was empty. As if he had decided he wasn't going to need whatever was hiding in his cloak.

The figure tugged at the fingers of one glove, sliding the fabric from his hand.

Anna frowned, her thick brows sloping to form a crease. "... What are you doing?"

The figure lifted his bare hand and tucked the glove into his cloak. "Fixing a problem."

Anna took another step back, watching the figure's index finger as it began to lengthen, the tip stretching, curving, shifting, into a glinting, obsidian talon.

Anna's breath was barely audible, her words like sand sifting through air. "... *What the hell...?*" She stumbled backwards, knocking one of her tables, the flasks and vials precariously clinking.

A specimen of a cobra's head fell from her desk, ethanol exploding from the jar as the glass shattered. The decapitated head rolled across the floor, its' lifeless eyes clouded and staring.

Pretzel hissed a warning.

"You really shouldn't tangle with things you don't understand." The figure rotated his hand, electric light winking over the tip of his talon. "*Especially* when you don't know who it is you're working for."

Anna launched herself at the door, fear scything a gash in her last thread of calm. The beat of her heart was deafening. The breath shuddered through her chest.

She did not see the figure move.

He blocked the doorway, his back to the hall, his hooded gaze like a barb through her stomach. "You can't run. That's not how this works."

A terrified bleat shattered Anna's throat, panic trapping her scream. She scrambled back into her room, leaping over her python, searching for a weapon, or a way to escape.

"... Anna?"

Anna froze.

That voice. She knew that voice.

Anna turned as the figure stepped aside, revealing a child standing in the hall. Her left eye was swollen shut, bruises spread across her cheeks, blackened welts stretched up her arms and across her neck.

"Anna… Who's this?" River dragged a mass of dark, tangled hair from her non-swollen eye, peering up at the figure in his obsidian cloak with his indiscernible face and his imperceptible frown.

The figure looked down at the child, hiding his talon in the folds of his cloak and examining her bruised and swollen face. "Who did that to you?"

River awkwardly chewed her lip. She could feel Shade's name like poison on her tongue. She could see him threatening to hurt the others.

She didn't want him to hurt the others.

The figure bent in a crouch, the corners of his mouth tugging further towards his chin. "Shade did this, didn't he."

River's eyes widened, her swollen skin shrieking with the movement.

Anna grabbed a flask from the table and stepped forward.

"Perhaps you should go back to bed. Let the adults finish their conversation." The figure stood, turning just as Anna hid the flask behind her back.

River glanced at Anna.

Anna shook her head.

The girl looked back at the figure in the cloak, her hands fidgeting with the hem of her nightshirt. "No… I'm thirsty."

"You're thirsty?" The figure released a huff, almost like a laugh. "Is *that* why you followed me up here?" With his gloved hand he reached into his cloak and retrieved a vial stoppered with a cork. He tipped it, liquid as clear as water sloshing up the tube. "Here, why don't you drink this? You'll feel much better. You might even forget how you got your bruises."

River took the vial, her face contorting in a frown. She kept her eyes down, away from Anna as the woman crept around her desk, flask raised above her head. "What is it?"

"It's very special water, from a very special river." The figure reached down and pulled the cork from the vial. "It's magic."

River's eyes narrowed, sceptical, aware of Anna stepping over Pretzel, almost close enough, almost to the door. "Magic isn't real."

"How do you know that?"

River lifted her dark, depthless eyes. She saw a flash of emotion, perhaps sorrow, perhaps kindness, dart across the figure's shadowed face. "If magic were real, I wouldn't have bruises."

The figure tapped the vial in River's hand. "What if magic were simply hiding, waiting for you to find it?"

River felt the ache of her bruises, the throb of her swollen eye, the phantom strike of Shade's backhand.

She *wished* that magic were real. It would be *so* convenient.

But she couldn't leave the children. Not with *him*.

"I can't." River shook her head. "The others—"

"The others will be protected." The figure lifted a hand, carefully brushing his knuckle against the orphan's bruised cheek. "I swear to you, they will be safe. Now, drink."

River hesitated. She knew the figure was telling the truth. She could feel it in her soul. So she raised the vial to her lips, tipped it and swallowed. The water was sweet and cool as it flowed over her tongue.

Anna released a furious shriek, slamming the glass flask over the figure's head.

He didn't even flinch.

He simply turned.

Sighed.

And sliced his talon through the flesh of Anna's neck.

Anna pitched forward, gurgling and grasping at her sliced throat. She crashed to her knees. The broken flask slashed her shins, sinking into her flesh as she fell to the floor, hands still clutching her severed throat.

Pretzel hissed, curling beneath the desk as blood spread across the carpet.

"Was that so bad?" The figure clucked his tongue and turned to River as the light seeped from Anna's eyes. He crouched before the child, his talon retracting until it was simply another finger. He slid his glove back on and took the vial from River's drooping fingers.

She blinked, lashes fluttering, and delicately rubbed her eyes.

"... Where... am I?" River looked up at him, her tangled hair falling into her face. "... Who are you?"

The figure smiled, gently turning the child by the shoulders and nudging her into the hall. "What do you remember?"

River's eyes lost focus, as if she were thinking, very hard. "I remember... an orphanage... A *new* one." She blinked again, a spark lighting her face. "We moved a few days ago! I have my own bed!" Her mouth split in a grin, her teeth gleaming as she beamed up at him. "It's *huge!*"

"Do you remember Shade?" The figure reached out and brushed a gloved finger across the girl's bruised cheek.

River winced despite his light touch, looking confused. She shook her head and lifted a hand to her swollen eye, pressing her palm into the bruise, frowning at the flare of pain.

The figure dropped his hand and watched as River examined the bruises on her arms. "You fell down the stairs. It'll hurt for awhile but you'll heal." He tapped his fingers against his knee, his expression hidden beneath his hood. He was quiet for a moment, thinking before he spoke. "... You got overexcited when you heard you were going to be adopted."

River's mouth fell slack, her bruises forgotten. She stared up at him, hope and awe swimming in her eyes. "I'm going to be *adopted?*"

The figure nodded, feeling the beginnings of a smile falter on his face. "Just as soon as I clean something up, okay?" He gently squeezed River's shoulder and turned to Anna's door. "Why don't you go down to the kitchen and find something to eat."

River grinned and nodded. He watched her run down the stairs, hair flying, clothes flapping. Her excited squeal followed him as he walked back into Anna's room, the sound filling the morbid scene with a child's innocent joy.

It was an hour before he was finished.

An hour before he had cleared away Anna's work and swung the woman's corpse over his shoulder, her body wrapped in a sheet, her neck strapped with torn bits of towel.

An hour before he found River asleep on the kitchen floor, a jar of half-eaten cookies in her lap.

The figure woke her gently, smiling as the girl took hold of his hand. Then he lead the orphan through the lobby and out into the frozen night, humming a haunting song as he walked. With a corpse over his shoulder. And bruised little girl skipping at his side.

CHAPTER TWENTY - ONE

ADALINDA STOOD IN THE DARK before dawn, the hem of her cloak clutched tight to her breast. Her eyes were locked on Donovan as he stepped into the hall, the white-brightness of his phone brushing the contours of his jaw, his gaze darkened by shadows of bruised and battered black.

She didn't move.

She didn't breathe.

Her shoulder pressed against the doorframe, stomach sick with a sense of dread.

She knew, somehow, in the depths of her soul. She knew what he was going to say.

It was why she now stood in the hall.

Donovan hesitated and slipped his phone into his pocket. It would have taken him a heartbeat to close the distance, to wrap her in his arms and hold her to his chest. She could almost feel his lips murmuring comforts in her ear.

Instead his lips carved a knife of words.

And plunged it through her heart.

"... There's been another murder."

Adalinda's voice caught in her throat, the choked breath barely a whisper, nothing more than the velvet flutter of a moth's broken wing. "Where?"

Donovan stepped forward, one hand reaching towards her. Only to stop, his fingers a breath from her cheek. "Adalinda—"

"*Where?*"

She knew.

Somehow.

She knew.

But she had to hear him say it.

It wasn't real until *he* said it.

Donovan pursed his lips, sorrow pooling in his ocean stare. It was an eternity until he spoke, until his voice crushed the silence like honeyed grit between teeth. "Your apartment." He paused, outstretched fingers curling in a loose fist. "... Diana found the body."

There was a moment of shocked quiet, a moment in which Adalinda couldn't think, her pulse stopped, her eyes grew vacant, a pitching wail built in her ears.

Her fault.

Adalinda heaved a fragmented breath.

Chest shuddering.

Shoulders curling.

Her fault. Her fault. Her fault.

Donovan caught her as she sank down the wall, knees buckling, head ringing.

Her fault. Her fault. Her fault.

Adalinda froze as Donovan pulled her into him, the warmth of his arms wrapping around her form, his hands massaging circles over the ridges of her spine.

As if he had held her a million times before.

As if he would a million more.

A stricken sob clawed up Adalinda's throat. She buried her face in Donovan's chest, her eyes clenched shut, tears pooling in her lashes.

Her fault. Her fault. Her fault.

She hadn't realised the words were passing her lips, muffled as she pressed her tear-stained face into him, as she felt the steady throb of his heart against her skin. "It's *my fault. It's my fault.*"

Donovan shushed her, the sound like wind through dying leaves, the warmth of his breath kissing the bare skin of her neck. He didn't speak. He didn't console. He simply held her. As if he knew that was all she would need.

Adalinda stood in his arms, tears spilling down her cheeks, sobs slowly beginning to subside. She took a deep breath, his scent of woodsmoke and rain flooding her senses, his hands still massaging circles into her back.

She didn't want to move. She couldn't *bring* herself to move. She wanted to hide in Donovan's embrace, ignoring the sun as it waited below the horizon, ignoring the death and the pain and the hollow, blackened void where her memories should have been. She just wanted *him*. His breath on her neck, his arms holding her close, the warmth of his presence. Calm and solid and strong.

She wanted the beat of his heart beneath her cheek as she slept.

She wanted his arms holding her close.

His smile against her skin.

Donovan drew back, tucking his fingers beneath Adalinda's chin and lifting her face to look into his. He brushed the tears from her cheeks with a stroke of his thumb, sending shivers over her skin, over her scalp, beneath her scarf.

Monster.

Adalinda stepped away, cold air seeping into the space she had torn between them. Her throat felt raw. Salt burned in her eyes. Her body cried a silent complaint as she swallowed, her fingers brushing the base of her scarf. "We should go."

Adalinda felt Donovan's eyes trailing her as she began to walk down the hall, as if his gaze were made of lead, anchor-heavy and nigh immovable.

"It's not your fault."

Adalinda stopped, head turning slightly until she could see his silhouette lingering by the bedroom door. She curled her fingers into fists, willing the tightness in her throat to loosen, the stinging in her eyes to pass. "You can't know that."

Donovan was quiet as she stepped out of the hall, passing his open kitchen and entering the vast, spacious lounge. The fireplace glowed scarlet with dying embers, red light spilling over the stone hearth and onto the floor.

She did not she see his troubled frown. Nor did she hear his murmur as he glanced at his hands, still warm from massaging circles into her back. "No. I shouldn't know that." Donovan dropped his hands to his sides. "Nevertheless, I do."

ADALINDA SAT ON THE DOORSTEP of her home, staring at the murdered woman, at the frost coating her lashes, at the bluish tinge of her thin and bloodless lips. The dark-haired corpse knelt on the pavement before her, almost reverent. Shrouded in a burnt-orange dress. Surrounded by a littering of shredded, time-worn paper.

"… There's been another murder."

Her fault.

Adalinda ran a chilled finger over the pearlescent surface of her tattoo, shivering as a frozen breeze sent the torn pages fluttering. She could almost see the page-less book in her vault, its' spine stripped bare, a message written in her own hand on the inside of the cover.

Find — The man who holds the ocean in his eyes.

I hope that will be enough for you to remember.

Adalinda glanced at Donovan who stood beside the murdered

woman, a sliver of paper clasped between his fingers, a frown darkening his face.

His presence changed nothing.

No recollections of him stirred in her mind. If anything, the veil choking her memories seemed to thicken...

Clarke cursed, scrambling across the pavement as she fought to catch handfuls of torn paper. A fragment caught on Adalinda's boot and she looked down. She reached for it, fingers shaking. A single word had been written, in her hand, on its' surface. She forced herself to read it, though her eyes kept fading in their focus, making the word appear to shift and change like shadows in the night.

... monster.

The paper slipped from Adalinda's fingers, catching on her cloak.

The word leached the life from her, just as the note on her mirror had.

She couldn't feel her fingers.

Couldn't feel the cold.

Didn't blink or shiver or hear or breathe.

There was just the echo of Donovan's voice, followed by her own accusatory thoughts.

"... There's been another murder."

Monster.

Adalinda forced herself again to look at the body, at the sallow, bloodless corpse. The murdered woman was positioned on her knees, hands resting on thighs, chin tilted up and staring at the door, at Adalinda.

Her amber eyes were glazed. Sightless.

Lifeless.

And Diana had found her.

The remaining heat leached from Adalinda's face, leaving her skin cold, her flesh tingling. A destructive trembling swallowed her whole. She curled her hands into shaking fists, knuckles screaming against the pressure, frozen air attacking her skin.

A collar bound the murdered woman's throat, the metal black and cold as it rested on her skin. Shackles circled her wrists and captured the ankles hidden beneath her burnt-orange dress.

Memories fluttered behind Adalinda's eyes.

She lifted a hand to the base of her scarf.

Monster.

Her body shuddered in a continual, vicious wave while the figures around her shifted, while the torn pages were blown down the street.

The paper on her cloak slid free, following the rest into the paling dark. Towards a cloaked figure, observing from the corner of an abandoned street, his face hidden in shadow, a knife-smile curving his lips.

For a moment streetlight dusted the edge of his hood, gilding him amber and grey.

An incessant shiver spread across Adalinda's scalp, creeping down her neck and echoing down her spine. She glanced over the murdered woman's shoulder. To find the street empty. The figure gone.

Adalinda frowned, her eyes drifting back to the murdered woman, to the burnt-orange dress fluttering against the pavement. She blinked and, in the darkness behind her eyes, saw a desert. Felt the scorching heat on her skin. The burning sand beneath her feet. The fear. Of death.

When the memories clawed into her mind she did not have the will to stop them.

Nor the strength.

She simply lowered her head and let them attack.

Singing Sands

Ten Years Ago

AIR RIPPLED OVER THE HORIZON like a sheer mass of shimmering fabric, strung from the heavens and draped across the sand. The woman scanned her surroundings, her golden eyes dry and full of grit. Sand stung her shins as it blew across the dune. Her throat was raw, her parched lips cracked, her skin was covered in dust and sweat and a shoulder of her dress was beginning to fray.

A shadow swept across her face as she lifted a hand, exposing her palm to block the path of the endlessly burning sun.

Her skin was beginning to turn a violent shade of scarlet.

It hurt to move.

It hurt to breathe.

Sand crunched between her teeth despite the edge of her scarf, secured across her nose and mouth. She blinked, grimacing as a sliver of searing light slipped through a gap between her fingers, momentarily splitting the shade on her face. Blinding her. Her pupils contracting. Pain stabbing her temples as she turned in a slow, hesitant circle.

The sun hung at its' peak in the sky, its' steady blaze eliminating all traces of shade.

She forced herself to walk, instincts tugging her towards the dune's peak, feeling as if she were eternally scaling the mountains of roasting sand. She headed for the dawn horizon, following the rising sun, and when the sun had passed its' peak she followed the direction of her own shadow.

She had lost track of time.

She had survived a night, more, nearly freezing in the bitter cold.

She should have been dead many times over.

But still she walked, the soles of her feet scraped and blistered, the skin burned and cracked and bloody, the ruptured wounds now filling with sand. She groaned and the sound was nothing but a croak. She swallowed and her throat ached, tongue rough and swollen against the roof of her mouth. Pools rippled in the distance, taunting, teasing. She could almost feel water trickling over her hands, clean and cold and gleaming.

Hallucinations and heatstroke.

She shook her head, lowering her hand to brush the dirt from her burnt-orange dress. Its' tattered hem thrashed about her knees as she reached the dune's curving peak, stared out over dawn's pale horizon.

And saw a shadow.

Flanking a stunted dune.

The heat flickered around her and the shadowed silhouettes danced like flames in a hellish pit. Tall, thin trunks rising from the sand. Angular structures of sandy stone.

Palms.

Buildings.

She forgot her dehydration and leaped down the face of the dune, launching herself across the sand. She slid downwards, sand scratching and spreading around her wounded feet.

A low, thronging hum sliced the surrounding quiet.

She turned to glance over her shoulder, looking for the source of the single, inhuman note flowing on the wind.

Her brows rose, her eyes growing wide as she realised her mistake.

The surface of the dune had been unstable.

The side of it was collapsing.

Sand surged towards her, streaming down the dune's slip-face, the granules humming a haunted cry of war.

She had started an avalanche.

Black tendrils of dread pitched through her stomach. She swore under her breath, foot catching on the dune, sand slipping between her legs.

She tripped on her skirt and lurched forward.

Her arms flew up to cover her face.

The gushing sand followed her as she tumbled down the dune, the hum rising, swelling.

She collided with the ground, pain shooting through her as she rolled to an abrupt halt. Her scarf ripped from her nose. She breathed in a mouthful of sand. Choked, coughed, gasped.

Gingerly, she lifted her arms, exposing her eyes to the blinding sun. Her body sang of agony, burned skin flaring, limbs grazed and weeping. She lay on her back, flat against the ground, with her stomach exposed to the unforgiving sky. And the mountain of sand pouring towards her. Still humming. Still surging.

If she didn't move she would be buried.

Suffocated.

She panicked, rolling onto her stomach and scrambling across the ground. Sand spilled from her dress. Her arms shook with the effort, her limbs exhausted, her muscles howling. She clenched her jaw and forced herself to push onto her knees, grabbing the loose end of her scarf and shoving it over her mouth. She took a deep breath. Desperately clambering forward. Deafened by the avalanche's hum.

As it struck.

And the sand swallowed her whole.

CHAPTER TWENTY - TWO

DONOVAN FROWNED AT THE TORN fragment of paper caught between his gloved fingers. It was worn, crinkled and browned, as if forgotten and left to age over time. For years. Perhaps decades. He recognised the script, the swirls of ink, slightly faded, with an edge of panic to the otherwise flowing letters. Perfectly matching the page that had been impaled on Adalinda's shattered, bathroom mirror.

Don't you remember?

A muscle fluttered in Donovan's jaw, soft as the vane of a feather hiding irately clenched teeth. His grip tightened on the paper, a piece the length of his palm with an incomplete sentence repeated down its' length, as if someone had been trying to remove a ruinous thought by gouging it through the surface.

I'm—

I'm not—

I'm not a—

Donovan lifted his eyes to Adalinda, still sitting on her doorstep with her eyes squeezed shut. Her brow was creased and twitching and her hands were softly trembling, as if she were trapped in a chasm of drifting terrors.

He had asked her to go inside, to sit with Christensen as he questioned Diana, but Adalinda had refused, seeming to think it necessary to punish herself by staring at the murdered woman. As if she truly believed it was her fault.

Donovan dragged his attention from Adalinda as Clarke crouched beside the kneeling corpse, the dead woman's skin appearing a colourless grey in the early morning light.

Clarke looked up at him, saw the fragment of paper in his hand. "I spend a quarter hour chasing those fucking pieces of torn paper and you retrieve *one? Seriously?*" Clarke snatched the paper from Donovan's hand and shoved it into her collection bag. "I would say thanks but you provided *zero* assistance."

Donovan raised a brow, his eyes flicking towards Christensen as the man walked out of the building and stepped around Adalinda.

"Oh, no apology necessary." Clarke tucked the collection bag in the pocket of her coat, grumbling to herself as she began to examine the murdered woman. "I *enjoy* crawling over the icy cobblestones, it's actually a *sport* in some countries."

Christensen stopped beside Donovan, frowning deeply. "Diana didn't see the murderer."

Donovan pressed his lips together, fingers methodically tapping the side of his thigh. "She didn't hear anything?"

"No."

Donovan stopped tapping and lifted a hand to drag it through his dark hair. He took a long breath, the scent of baking bread wafting into his lungs, then glanced at Christensen, a question in his eyes.

"Diana's cooking." Christensen shrugged. "She's stressed. She's making pastries." He stepped around Clarke to assess the murdered woman, her eyes a glazed amber, her lips a thin line, her nose sharp and precipitous. After a moment, his gaze shifted back to Donovan.

"... This is the woman we spoke to at the orphanage. Anna Winter, wasn't it?"

Donovan hummed confirmation, a spark of fire flaring through him as an echo of the bruised orphan flickered behind his eyes.

Two women dead.

A child *beaten.*

Bruised and broken and terrified.

Donovan's focus drifted to Adalinda, her trembling hands now violently shaking, her eyes clenched tightly shut. Her lips were moving, though no words escaped.

Clarke cleared her throat and looked up at the detectives. "I'd guess this woman hasn't been dead more than a few hours." She lifted the burnt-orange skirt, eyes narrowing. "Something cut her shins, possibly broken glass..." She replaced the skirt and gently lifted the dead woman's right hand, turning the stiffened muscles of the delicate wrist and pushing the shackle up to reveal the faintly smeared surface of a pearlescent tattoo. An exact replica of Adalinda's. Clarke pressed her gloved finger against the dead woman's shackle. "This is exactly the same as the tattoo on Leena Rosenberg." She replaced the woman's wrist and reached for the collar around her pallid neck. "... What are the chances her throat was cut?"

Donovan crossed his arms as Clarke lifted the collar. She leaned back on her heels, nodding to herself as she examined the lethal wound in the dead woman's throat. The flesh smoothly sliced. The gash professionally stitched.

"Two women killed within days of one another, both with a sliced throat, both with the same tattoo, and both working in Shade's orphanage." Christensen turned to Donovan. "We need to find out where she was murdered."

Donovan nodded. "Call Wise and tell her to meet us at the orphanage. Let's hope there's someone who saw something useful."

Christensen looked back at Anna's bloodless face. "Assuming Clarke doesn't find any evidence here connecting the murders to Shade."

Clarke released a snort, rising from her crouch and brushing her gloved hands against her trousers. "I'm flattered you have such a high opinion of me, Detective, but trust me, I won't find anything. Not unless the murderer wants to be found. Even the woman's *fingernails* have been cleaned. No dirt. No blood. No incriminating skin. *Nothing*. There's absolutely fucking *nothing*. And based on the first murder, there isn't *going* to be anything." Clarke lifted the bag of paper fragments from her pocket. "Aside from these..." She shook the bag, listening intently. "... *They whisper secrets.*"

Adalinda's eyes snapped open.

She gasped, scrambling backwards, her spine thudding against the door, her golden eyes wide with dread and locked on the murdered woman's corpse.

"... Adalinda...?" Clarke glanced at Donovan as he took a step forward. "You okay?"

Adalinda blinked, brows narrowing as if she were trying to remember where she was.

"You don't *look* okay..."

Donovan moved to stand before the corpse, blocking Adalinda's view. She lowered her face to her hand, exhaling a long, fragile breath.

Clarke slid the bag of shredded paper back into her pocket. "... Adalinda?"

Adalinda opened her eyes and looked up at them through the gaps in her fingers, her gaze of pure anguish and despair.

Donovan's breath caught in his throat. Her expression shattered him, like an axe shatters glass. He felt raw, flayed by the flash of terror he had seen on her face. A perfect reflection of what he had felt, waking in that frozen river, fear creeping from his subconscious like a hungry, monstrous beast.

Adalinda dropped her hand to her side, lowering those haunted eyes to stare at the ground. She curled her arms around her waist, a shudder ploughing through her. "It's... the memories..."

Donovan forced himself not to flinch, forced his own memories aside, slamming down a wall and locking them in place. His hand quivered, ever so slightly. "We all have memories."

Adalinda slowly shook her head. "You don't know—"

"I do."

Clarke and Christensen looked at each other as Donovan met Adalinda's gaze, trying to make her understand, trying to convey his thoughts through the intensity of his stare. He couldn't explain. Not here. Not now. But he needed her to understand. Inexplicably. Inescapably.

Adalinda searched his eyes, her brow softly creasing as if she could see through him. As if she saw what he had seen, had been through it and survived. As if she knew...

But how could she know?

She couldn't.

She didn't.

Adalinda lifted her fingers to brush the base of her scarf. She stiffened as her skin met the fabric, dropped her hand and peered around Donovan at the murdered woman still kneeling on the pavement.

Donovan felt something snap inside his chest as he watched Adalinda's features become blank. Emotionless.

"Did you find anything?"

Donovan flexed his fingers, willing Adalinda to look at him again. She didn't.

Her focus simply drifted to Clarke and Christensen, waiting for an answer.

"... She has the tattoo." Donovan watched the blood drain from Adalinda's face as she fought not to look at him. He closed his fingers into fists, burying the urge to walk over and sit beside her. "I need you to tell me where you got yours. Who knows you have it?"

Adalinda shook her head. "I told you this before. I don't remember."

"I need you to tell me the truth, Adalinda. I can't find the murderer if I don't have any information."

"I don't *remember*." Adalinda wrenched her golden eyes from the corpse to stare up at him, anger and desperation surging from her in great, seething waves. "You think I would *lie*? I have no memories of *anything* before I woke a decade ago in a *desert*—" Her eyes widened and she pressed her lips together, cutting off the words as if she hadn't meant to speak them.

Donovan almost reached out to steady himself against the wall, the strength in his muscles momentarily lapsing.

Icy liquid nudged against his bloodless lips, urging him to open his mouth, pleading with him to suck in breath.

"... You woke in a desert?"

Again, Clarke glanced at Christensen.

Adalinda's nostrils flared. She shook her head, pressing her fingers into the stone beneath her. She was scared of remembering. He felt her terror pulsing through his veins as if it belonged to him, as if it were part of him.

He wouldn't force her to tell him.

Donovan swallowed the fear, driving the memories aside. "What about the shredded papers? Do you have any idea what they are?"

Adalinda closed her eyes. She seemed to be warring with herself, her lips parting only to close against the building words.

The corners of Donovan's mouth lowered in a frown. "Adalinda—"

"It's mine."

"What?"

Adalinda opened her eyes to stare at the ground. "I have a journal in my studio, all of the pages are torn out. The cover has been in my vault for nearly a decade and I've never seen the actual pages, but the writing..." She clasped her hands in her lap, the tips of her fingers bleached, almost blue. "The writing matches my own."

Christensen moved towards Adalinda. "You saw the page on your mirror and you didn't say anything."

Adalinda's throat bobbed as she swallowed. "… I didn't trust you."

"And now?"

"I…" Adalinda looked at Donovan's hands and tilted her head, as if his question were a puzzle, something that required extended consideration. "… don't know."

Donovan's sigh burst from him in a frustrated gust. "Adalinda, we can't find the murderer if we don't know the *details*."

"I'm *well aware* of this." Adalinda lifted her chin, golden flames burning in her stare. She pushed herself to her feet and planted her boots on the pavement. "But I can't *give* you details I don't *have*."

They glared at each other, both refusing to retreat.

Christensen's phone rang and he cursed, pulling it from his jacket and walking away.

Finally, Adalinda let her gaze soften and shifted it to Anna's corpse. "Who was she?"

Donovan turned to face the murdered woman. He dragged his fingers through his hair, some of the waves catching on his knuckles. "Her name was Anna Winter, she was a carer at Shade's orphanage, as was Leena Rosenberg."

"Shade's involved, then." Adalinda didn't question it, she simply watched Clarke as the woman returned to examining Anna's body.

"That seems to be the case, though we have no evidence."

"I'm sure the population at large wouldn't mind if we simply *removed* him."

"*Removed* him?" Donovan felt himself involuntarily tense as Clarke looked up, her eyes gleaming.

"I've heard the rumours. Shade is cruel. Greedy." Adalinda lifted her shoulders in a delicate shrug. "A knife would solve a lot of problems."

Donovan stared at Adalinda as she stepped away from the door, astonished. This woman had wept in his arms, had broken at the thought of an innocent being murdered, had been overcome moments ago by anguish and terror and despair. She looked at him now with pure brutality. Her fragility evanesced. "I'm going to pretend you didn't just say that to a *detective* investigating a *murder*."

"Are you suggesting you wouldn't — if you could — stab that man through the throat and hang him over the ledge of his balcony by his own tie?"

Clarke barked a laugh. "I would *definitely* do that."

Donovan's fingers curled into fists, the ghosted memory of the bruised and terrified orphan flaring through his mind. "I didn't say that."

An appreciative hum reverberated in Adalinda's throat, the corner of her mouth curving towards a smile. "I thought not."

Donovan swore he saw something in her eyes, for a moment, something dark and strong and stained with blood. He saw her shift, saw her hands and arms drenched in crimson, her face hard, cruel yet beautiful, coated in the sorrowful victory of a fight.

He blinked and the vision was gone.

Replaced with the inconceivable glow of pride where caution and confusion should have been.

Donovan forced himself to release his fists. The pride faded. Leaving him concerned for his sanity and unsure if it had finally begun to shatter, after a decade of fracturing, of splintering.

Adalinda watched him, her lips set in a soft frown, her eyes devoid of the darkness he thought he had seen.

Donovan exhaled. "You don't strike me as the murderous type."

"Is it my innocent face or the fact that I had a lapse of control in your apartment this morning." Adalinda crossed her arms, a muscle tweaking in her temple. "A few tears and a woman is immediately deemed harmless."

Clarke smirked to herself, studying the shackles around the murdered woman's wrists.

"I did *not* say you were harmless. I said you weren't murderous. There's a difference."

"And what difference is that?"

"One ends with a man incapacitated on the floor of a bar. The other ends with a dead body."

Adalinda laughed, a sweet drizzle of acid laced syrup flowing from her lips. "That brute in the bar underestimated me." She paused and Donovan watched the humour leak from her eyes. "I should've taken his gun. I didn't think... I nearly got you killed."

Donovan pressed his fingers against his ribs, where the bullet had hit and the wound should have been.

Where the bullet had hit.

Donovan closed his eyes.

The bullet had *not* hit him.

It had missed.

"Donovan...?"

Adalinda stepped closer, he could feel her movements shifting the air.

She placed a hand on his arm.

Donovan looked down, watching her fingers press into his coat. He thrilled at her touch, as if fireflies danced beneath his skin, though her own was cold as ice. He allowed himself a heartbeat to consider her, to feel her presence before he replied. "The bullet missed."

Adalinda opened her mouth to argue, he could see it in her, a flash of defiance, a determination in her stance. It melted as he met her eyes and she saw the desperation in his face.

She couldn't question.

If she did he would have to provide answers.

Adalinda pulled her hand back and Donovan felt the loss like a punch to the stomach. "It missed. Of course it missed." She looked back at the murdered woman, her face darkening. "If it hit there would have been blood."

"*Or* it *did* hit him..."

Donovan turned to glare at Clarke as the woman flipped her platinum and lavender braid over one shoulder, the short side of her hair rustling in the wind.

"And he's a Manshield. Ha! Get it? Because you're a man and you're bullet—"

Donovan growled.

"—proof." Clarke rolled her eyes, planting her hands on her hips and scrunching her nose. "Oh, go stick your tongue to a pole you stubborn, humourless ass." She slid her gaze to Adalinda. "*You* think I'm funny, don't you?"

Adalinda pressed her lips together, hiding the smile which tugged at her mouth. She calmed her expression, lowering her lids over her golden irises and managing to look enormously unimpressed. "You're about as funny as a surprise slap to the face."

A delighted grin lit Clarke's features. She pointed it at Donovan. "See? I'm *hilarious*! I am the *definition* of hilarity."

Donovan stepped forward and Adalinda grabbed his wrist, pulling him towards her. "Clarke, stop tormenting him. Why don't you use your superior intellect for good instead?"

Donovan rumbled under his breath, glancing at Adalinda whose fingers remained curled around his wrist. "Superior intellect?"

Adalinda gently tightened her grip, gesturing towards Clarke with her other hand.

The woman was blushing.

"We need to find out where Miss Winter was murdered. There isn't anything on the body that I can find, and we all know I'm good. *Really* good. So this murderer has got to be really, *really* good to be able to avoid leaving incriminating evidence. There's *always* incriminating evidence."

On the other side of the street, Christensen lowered his phone and dropped it into his pocket before striding over to join them.

"Wise said she'd meet us at the orphanage. She's sending someone to collect the body for us. Said she wants us there immediately."

"She's bored." Clarke smiled knowingly. "That woman *hates* paperwork."

Christensen frowned. "Does *anyone* like paperwork?"

"Morons." Clarke kept the smile pasted on her face. "*Morons* like paperwork."

Adalinda let her fingers fall from Donovan's wrist.

Again, he felt the loss of her touch. As if it were a physical pain.

Clarke waved a hand dismissively. "Why don't you all go on ahead? I'll be along shortly. I need to wait for whoever Wise has sent to collect the body."

Christensen nodded, turning and moving towards Donovan's car.

Donovan glanced one last time at the lifeless Anna Winter kneeling on the stark pavement, her wrists and ankles bound in iron, her neck choked by a dull, blackened collar, her figure shrouded in a burnt-orange dress. This was calculated, deliberate. Everything had been placed for a reason, like the steady choices in a rigged game. And all of it was connected to Adalinda, whether she was a participant or a target.

Donovan walked across the road to his car, opening the door and waiting for Adalinda to ease inside. She sat, swinging her legs in and clasping her hands in her lap. The careful wall she placed over her emotions flickered, that terrified look returning to her eyes.

And Donovan frowned. He doubted Adalinda was a participant. Every bone in his body wanted to believe she was simply a target.

... But he had been wrong before...

BURIED

TEN YEARS AGO

BLACK.

Suffocating, incessant dark.

She couldn't breathe.

She could barely move.

Sand filled her mouth and choked her nose despite her hand and scarf. Piling and pushing and pressing her down. The weight was beginning to compress her lungs.

Fear became a stone in her throat.

She squeezed her fists, forearms caught beneath her chest, and shoved.

The sand above her shifted, particles of glittering rock hissing as they moved, as the avalanche above trickled to a languid halt.

Again she shoved. Wriggling her legs, her shoulders, her back. Trying to loosen the densely packed sand.

Again the sand above her shifted, falling in a hissing stream.

She clawed her way up.

Her head broke the surface.

She scrambled out of the hole, managing to tear the final, fraying strands which had been holding the left strap of her dress. It fell, exposing her breast, as she hauled herself into the dry desert air. Hacking and spluttering. Spitting sand from her mouth. Choking on particles that caught in her throat as she wheezed, and she gasped.

She bent forward, lowering her head to the sand, back curved, knees bent, terror shaking her bones. Her head swam and her stomach lurched.

She was lost, in the desert.

Stranded and alone.

No food.

No water.

Burned and then frozen as day turned to night.

And now buried.

Alive.

The corners of her mouth split as she released a terrible, trembling scream.

She screamed at the sand and the sun and the sky.

She screamed at herself and the empty afternoon air.

She screamed until her voice shattered, her throat dry and full of dust.

Her fear evaporated.

She rolled onto her back, a groan scraping from her lips as she tried to open her eyes and found the sun glaring. Always white. Always blinding.

Her lids slid closed.

She felt drained. Exhausted. Her arms were limp, her legs quivered, her throat and lips were so dry they felt torn. She lay in the sand, just barely alive, and wishing she were dead. The darkness of death would surely be kinder than this.

She groaned, rolling her head to the side and gingerly peering into the hole her body had wrenched in the sand. It was rapidly being refilled, the dry granules sliding to its' base.

She frowned.

She had survived a fall from the sky. Days and nights spent in the brutal expanse of the desert. Burned then frozen then buried.

She wanted to die.

She felt like she could die, if she remained in her place and simply made the choice.

The choice of death.

The choice of death over the instinct to survive.

The choice to face the darkness rather than to seek the cost of light.

A shadow darted overhead, claws tucked in, wings spread wide, earth and ochre feathers rustling as it flew.

She wanted to die.

How could she want death? An assumption of peace based on nothing but blind faith.

A screech broke the wind like a stone breaking water.

She groaned, struggling to lift her arm, to fling it across her face. Her sunburn flared as the owl continued to circle.

An owl.

In the desert.

She cracked open a golden eye, her voice a grating husk. "Can I not die in peace?"

The owl swooped, claws extended, and tore a row of gashes in her raised arm.

Pain.

Blood.

She shouted and scrambled back, gasping, coughing, sand hissing as her naked feet shoved it aside. The owl's feathers beat against her face, wrenching her from her debilitated daze. The owl pinned her with a moonbeam stare and screeched in her face before flying over a dune, in the direction of the shadows she had seen before she fell.

The palms.

And the buildings.

A thread of hope banished her morbid desolation.

She pushed herself to her feet, blood trickling from the wounds in her arm, the broken strap of her dress exposing her breast to the desert heat. Her features contorted in a wince as she took a step forward and her blistered soles began to shriek. Her legs trembled. Bright light clouded her vision. Her mind reeled with vertigo as she fought to keep her balance, fought to keep from fainting.

She flinched as a hum echoed in the distance.

Another avalanche.

She shook her head, trying to clear her mind as she took another step, tucking the end of her scarf over her mouth, inhaling the stench of stale sweat and sand. And blood. Her blood, trailing down her arm and dripping from her fingers as she forced herself forward, up the side of the next dune. Her limbs objected with every step. She slipped on the sand and fell to her knees, gritted her teeth and shoved herself up, determined to reach the top so she could search for the lingering shadows.

They were waiting, the palms and buildings, still shimmering in the distance.

A pellucid thread of hope tied itself to her pulse.

This time she tread carefully down the face of the dune, making sure not to aggravate the sand, making sure none was already loose. As she walked the shadows of the sun moved across the sand, licking over the dunes, elongating and shifting as the blazing disk floated across the pale-blue sky.

It was almost dusk when she crested the final dune, numb to thirst and hunger, her steps a stumbling mess. The beat of her heart was a hummingbird flutter, erratic and barely there.

In the fading evening light the wind released a sigh, the heat callously drained as the horizon swallowed the sun. She shivered, her scarf rustling imperceptibly as she slid down the dune, bloodied arm cradled against her chest. She stumbled until she found herself standing before a darkened shape, her golden eyes staring resolutely at the ground.

Her hope sputtered.

She lifted her gaze, trailing the trunk of a looming, shadowed palm.

A whimpering croak bled from her lips.

The palm stood bare, starved and lifeless, rising like a severed finger from the endless desert sands. Behind the palm lay a single building, its' walls of stone in ruins, worn smooth by sand and time. A tomb amidst dead palms and a brutally boundless desert.

A low moan bubbled in her chest as she fell to her knees, her eyes stinging with unshed tears.

There was no water.

There was no food.

There was nothing.

Nothing.

Her whine was so soft it disappeared before reaching her ears. "I'm going to die..." The realisation struck her as she pressed her bloodied fingers to the sand. "I'm going to die and I don't even know where I am." The last of her strength abandoned her. She knew that if she allowed herself to rest she would never get up. She would never wake up.

She closed her eyes.

She was so tired of walking.

Of moving.

Of surviving.

She lowered herself to the sand as the moon crested the horizon and an owl hooted in the night.

She made her choice.

She let herself sleep.

Not knowing if she would wake to see the dawn.

CHAPTER TWENTY - THREE

Adalinda could hear the voice, strong and sure as snow and steel, flowing like a melodic chant through the lobby of the orphanage.

She heard children gasp.

Heard the shuffling of clothes.

She stepped away from Donovan, aware of his eyes tracking her movements. She did not hear him begin to follow but she felt him, as if he were a rift luring the moisture out of the air. She felt him like she felt his gaze, like the heat of sunlight on her skin.

"... So the man sat by the river. Watching. Waiting. Listening for the approach of the monstrous beast."

Adalinda arrived at a door and peered inside. Children sat on pillows and blankets, all of them sprawled across a tiled, dining room floor. Tables had been dragged to the sides of the room, opening an enormous space decorated with paintings and mosaics and glittering crystal chandeliers.

A woman sat alone on a high-backed chair, her auburn waves

strangled in a knot atop her head, her silver-eyes almost appearing to glow like stars despite the sunlight streaming through the windows.

Wise curled her lips in a honed smile, sharp as a crescent moon's grin. "But the beast was cunning, she knew what awaited her and so she changed."

Adalinda felt a shiver crawl over her scalp as the children released a series of enthralled murmurs, some scooting forward, others plucking fruit and bread off plates which had been set on the floor among them. Donovan was peering over her shoulder, frowning and scanning the children, as if looking for someone.

"The beasts scaled, gruesome hide became soft, pale skin. Her razor-edged fangs shrank to smooth ivory teeth. Her long, snarling maw became a faintly sloped nose above rose-petal lips and a sweet, slender neck." Wise leaned forward, resting her elbows on the arms of her chair. Her eyes sparked as she inspected the children. "The beast walked into the clearing in the shape of a woman. She smiled at the man and batted her eyes... And do you know what happened next?"

A boy, lounging at the back of the room with legs crossed released an indignant huff, popping a grape into his mouth. "She killed him."

"She did not!" A fair-haired girl threw a roll of bread at the boy's face. "He fell in love with her, *obviously*."

Wise sat back, arching a brow. "No. And no." She tilted her head, calm, almost avian. "She stole him."

The boy swallowed his grape and scoffed. "You can't *steal* a *man*."

Wise glanced at Adalinda and unfurled from her seat. She looked back at the boy. "Believe me, you can." Wise stepped between the children, passing a woman who sat among them, gently holding a youngling in her arms. "I'll leave them with you, Tzali'ka."

Tzali'ka looked up, her ebony features decorated with tattoos and tribal scars, a perfect, serene smile softening the intensity of her face. Tzali'ka nodded and stood, walking over to the chair and cooing to the youngling in her arms as she went.

Adalinda frowned. She had seen the woman before... Before she had entered the gallery. Before she had seen the murdered woman hanging from the ceiling.

Tzali'ka had been standing guard outside.

Wise swept from the dining room and gracefully closed the door, blocking Adalinda's view of Tzali'ka just as the woman lowered herself into Wise's empty chair and began another story. "The orphans were chaotic when we arrived, with no one to mind them. A story and some breakfast seems to have helped."

"There's one missing."

Wise turned towards Donovan, blinked.

"A girl named River." Donovan's frown deepened. "She's dark haired, dark eyed. When I saw her last she was covered in bruises." He stared at Wise, the intensity of his eyes enough to raise the hairs on Adalinda's arms. "Have you seen her?"

"No." Wise shook her head. "But I'll check with a few of the children later, perhaps one of them knows." She barely spared a glance for Christensen, hovering at Donovan's side, as she asked. "Did you find anything on the body of the murdered woman?"

Donovan shook his head, clasping his hands behind his back. "The woman's body was kneeling in the street below Adalinda's apartment, she was surrounded by pages that had been torn from a journal and shredded. She had shackles on her wrists and ankles and a collar around her neck, hiding a sliced throat and a tattoo matching that of the first victim."

"Do we know the significance of the torn pages?"

Donovan glanced at Adalinda. "We have an idea..."

Adalinda swallowed, feeling her heart begin to flutter, feeling the prickling of her scalp spread down her neck. Donovan didn't speak, he simply waited, as if the choice to tell Wise was hers and hers alone. She took a breath and raised her chin, projecting a confidence she did not feel. "I believe they're from a journal in my studio. I've never seen the interior pages but I recognised the writing as my own."

Wise's silver eyes narrowed. "You've never seen the interior pages of your own journal…?"

Adalinda reached for her scarf. Stopped. "… No." She let her hand drop to her side. "I haven't."

Wise hummed, studying Adalinda, dispassionate cynicism pouring from her like wind from a storm. "And you believed this, Donovan?"

"I'm inclined to, considering the second woman was murdered last night and Adalinda happened to be under my watch." Donovan didn't move as Wise focused on him, leaving Adalinda feeling like a mountain had been heaved from her chest. "She has nothing to gain by lying."

Wise frowned, her features clouding. She watched Donovan for a moment, arms folded across her chest, fingers methodically tapping her arm. Finally, she released a breath through her nose. "And you found nothing incriminating?"

Donovan shook his head. "The woman's body had been cleaned, thoroughly, before being placed."

"We were hoping there might be something here to give us more information." Christensen rubbed the back of his neck, grimacing as Wise pursed her lips.

"I had one of the orphans show me the dead woman's room, according to him Anna made sure the children were asleep and then disappeared upstairs to work." Wise strode towards the staircase at the back of the orphanage, frowning at a portrait of a man as she passed.

Ink-black hair slicked smoothly back, a crooked smile which failed to reach the man's cunning stare.

Below the canvas rested a steel plaque bearing the painted man's name.

Wyatt Shade.

Adalinda watched Donovan's hands form crippling fists as he

followed Wise, his teeth clenching, his eyes becoming shadowed as they bled a terrible darkness. A broken, shattered darkness. A darkness rivalling that which hid in the depths of Adalinda's mind.

She reached for him, her fingers slipping through the orphanage air until they were a breath from his arm. She paused, frowning.

The air around him was cold.

Wet.

Adalinda pulled her hand back, staring at the faint sheen of moisture which had collected on her fingers. She slowed to a stop partway up the stairs.

"Adalinda?"

Adalinda blinked, lifting her eyes to Donovan who had stopped to look back. She wiped her hand on her cloak, brushing the moisture from her skin. "I'm fine, I just thought I heard something."

Christensen rounded them, glancing at Donovan curiously as he followed Wise's unhindered steps.

"You heard someth—"

The orphanage entrance burst open, a tangle of curses shattering the quiet of the hall. "I swear, if I have to drive behind another *asshole* who doesn't *indicate*—" Clarke looked up, slamming the door and striding across the lobby as she scraped strands of asymmetric hair out of her face. "Oh. Hello, Wise, have you been enjoying your paperwork?"

Wise turned to pin Clarke with a flat, wooden stare. "Morons enjoy paperwork, Clarke. I endure it."

Clarke froze, the echo of her boots on the tiles falling silent. Her mouth fell open. "That's what I said!" She grinned, scrambling forward and mounting the stairs. Her shoulder brushed Christensen as she climbed past. "Isn't that what I said, Christensen?" She reached the top and leaned in to Wise conspiratorially. "I've always liked you. This proves that my taste is, in fact, impeccable."

Wise raised a brow as Christensen turned to Adalinda.

"You must have *ridiculously* good hearing."

"What?" Adalinda lifted a foot, placing it on the next step.

"You said you heard something."

"Oh... Right." Adalinda stifled the urge to reach for Donovan again as he released his fists, no longer holding them behind his back. She moved past him, her focus on the damp still lingering in the air, her questions trapped and buried beneath her tongue.

"The woman you sent to take the body arrived quickly."

Adalinda lifted her head at the sound of Clarke's voice. The woman was smiling, trailing Wise as she continued down a hall.

"She probably ran a few red lights." Wise stopped before a service elevator, discretely set aside for the converted hotel's staff, and pressed the button to summon it. "She tends to do that."

"She was pretty. Very intense."

Wise watched as the numbers above the elevator began to count down. "She takes her job seriously."

"Do you think she likes women?"

The elevator doors slid open, a chime ringing through the hall as Adalinda stepped up beside Clarke.

"I doubt it."

Clarke mumbled a curse. "I was *sure* she was flirting back. People are so hard to *read*."

"That's because they aren't covered in words, Clarke."

Clarke blinked, mouth falling slack. "Was that a *quip*?"

"Oh, don't look so surprised." Wise stepped through the elevator doors as Clarke skipped in after her, Adalinda, Donovan and Christensen following close behind.

"You realise that you've set a standard now and you'll have to keep being witty."

Wise pressed the button for the top floor. The doors slid closed. "I think you'll find that less is more, in this instance."

Clarke pouted, crossing her arms. "Less is *not* more when it comes to quips. Humour is the essence of life."

"Humour is appreciated in small quantities but can become vexatious if overused."

Christensen cleared his throat, hiding a laugh at the look of shock on Clarke's face. "*Humour* is like *chocolate*. There can *never* be too much chocolate."

"Chocolate is an exception. If an entire conversation were humorous, where would the progression be?"

Clarke's brows pinched as she considered, tapping a finger on her lips.

The elevator chimed.

The doors slid open.

"Damn, I can't find a hole in that... You *are* wise."

The corner of Wise's lips twitched in a hidden smile as she stepped out of the elevator.

Clarke leaned closer to Adalinda, holding a hand to her mouth in a stage whisper. "I want to be like her when I grow up."

Adalinda raised her brows, then strode from the elevator a few paces behind Clarke as the woman trotted after Wise. Donovan's presence heated Adalinda's back, his motions shifting the air as he and Christensen moved into the hall. Adalinda pictured the sheen of water that had been on her hand, considering how Donovan would be able to sift the moisture from the air. Surely that was impossible. Though, the bullet was also impossible.

"The bullet missed."

Donovan had *insisted* the bullet had missed. But what if it hadn't...?

Adalinda repressed the urge to shake her head. If the bullet had hit Donovan then there would have been a wound. Yet there *was* no wound. She brushed her fingers along the base of her scarf, the silken fabric like breath on her skin, like the whisper of her thoughts sighing 'monster.'

The bullet had missed. That was the only explanation.

And Adalinda had imagined the moisture on her hand.

"Here."

Adalinda almost collided with Clarke as Wise stopped before a door, halfway down the hall, hanging open on its' hinges. The lights inside were off, abandoning the room to a darkness devoid of windows.

Clarke pulled an elastic tie from her wrist and began to twist her long plait into a knot. "Well, that's ominous..." She stopped, fingers tangled in her braid. Squinted into the black. Took a step forward. "I think I just saw something *move*."

A crease formed between Adalinda's brows. Her golden eyes sparked as a long, dark shape shifted beneath a table.

"Oh my God. It's a *snake!*" Clarke lunged towards the dark room, a gleeful grin spreading across her face as she dropped her partially coiled braid.

Christensen cursed, grabbing her around the waist and hauling her away from the door. "Clarke, are you *crazy*? Who runs *towards* a *snake*?"

"They're so *pretty!*" Clarke squirmed in Christensen's grip, drawing the attention of both Wise and Donovan as she struggled to tear herself free.

A breath filled Adalinda's chest. Her fingers twitched softly as she made an impulsive decision and slipped through the door. She felt for the light-switch on the wall, winced as the darkness abruptly vanished and she saw what the shadows had been hiding.

Blood.

Congealing on the floor.

Shattered glass spread through the crimson pool and across the wooden boards. The stench of spilled ethanol hung densely in the stagnant air. And a python curled around the legs of an emptied table.

Adalinda lifted a hand to her mouth, staring at the blood. A fire ignited in her throat, the muscles tightening painfully as she pictured the murdered woman lying there. Desperate and dying.

The ethanol fumes stung her eyes, causing a flood of moisture to collect on her lower lids. She held a hand beneath her nose, stepped over the pool of blood. And found the decapitated head of a cobra discarded in the corner.

Adalinda's scalp began to prickle, a wave of nausea warping her stomach.

"Adalinda." Donovan stepped into the room, careful to avoid stepping in the blood. "Come back to the hall. You don't need to see this."

A hiss slid through the room.

Adalinda waved Donovan away, holding in a cough as the fumes lodged in her throat. The python's dark body slithered beneath the table. She lowered herself to a crouch and held out a hand, palm submissively facing the ceiling.

Donovan stepped forward, opening his mouth to dissuade her.

The python slid onto Adalinda's arm and over her shoulder. She stood, allowing it to shift the collar of her coat and press itself into the warmth of her neck, its' cool, polished scales sliding against her skin. Adalinda smiled, stroking its' body with a gentle touch. "Poor thing. So cold and tired..." She turned, passing Donovan as she stepped back over the blood and returned to the hall.

Donovan followed her out, watching the python carefully. The weight of the snake pressed into her bones, draped like a living, breathing shawl as she looked to Christensen and Clarke.

"You can go in now."

Christensen swore, releasing Clarke and slamming his back against the wall as the woman loosed a delighted squeal, grinning ecstatically beside the eternally composed Wise.

Donovan held out a hand to brush his knuckles along the snake's scaled back. The python twitched but did not move away. "... It seems relatively docile." Donovan lifted his gaze to Adalinda. His expression hardened as he lowered his hand. "Don't do that again."

Adalinda batted at the python as it lifted its' head, tongue flicking beneath her scarf. "They're harmless." She gently took it by the neck and pulled it away. "Besides, Christensen clearly wasn't going to go in there with the snake."

Christensen shuddered, grimacing as he inched away. "I *hate* snakes."

"Don't be silly." Clarke leaned in until she was nose to nose with the python, staring at it with wide, admiring eyes. "Adalinda said it was harmless."

Donovan grunted, the corner of his mouth curling as he turned for the door, muscled arm brushing Adalinda's shoulder. "Christensen, stop having a panic attack, we need to actually do some work."

"I'm not having a panic attack." Christensen glared at Donovan, deliberately diverting his attention from the snake. "And you can't just *tell* someone to stop having a panic attack. It doesn't *work like that.*" Christensen's knuckles paled as he clenched his fists and edged around Adalinda, careful not to touch the python. A violent shudder shook him as Clarke kissed its' scaled nose. "God, I hate snakes."

Clarke patted the python on the head. "You can stay out here for moral support. I'm going to solve a murder." She winked at Adalinda, then followed Wise into the room.

Adalinda sighed, adjusting the snake on her neck and loosening its' body which had begun to constrict, tightening around her throat. She didn't enter the room again, knowing she would simply be a distraction, knowing that cobra's head lay on the floor, surrounded by spilled ethanol and shattered glass.

Adalinda shuddered, her crawling scalp sending shivers down her spine. She lowered herself to the floor of the hall, leaned her head against the wall, closed her eyes, took a breath. She focused on the python around her neck, the scales gently grazing her skin, the tongue flicking in and out like a feather brushing her cheek.

The veil over her memories fluttered.

She forced a memory aside.

They were getting worse, affecting her more than they had. She thought they had started to fade over the last few years, not nearly as terrible as they had been, not nearly as real. If she let herself remember she could almost feel the sand on her skin, the blisters on her feet.

Adalinda opened her eyes, swallowed.

They were worse.

And she had a feeling they would only become more so.

Donovan's honeyed voice flowed into the hall, edged in steel as he spoke with Wise. Adalinda clung to the sound, holding herself above the memories like driftwood in a tempest, remembering the feel of his arms around her as she sobbed in his apartment, his breath on her neck, his hands massaging circles over the ridges of her spine.

She clung to him, intuitively trusting that his presence would purge the terrors lurking behind her eyes as she sat in the hall and settled in to wait.

Chapter Twenty - Four

THE CRACK OF SPLINTERING WOOD broke the quiet of Donovan's apartment. Adalinda knelt before the hearth, gilded blue and gold, the fire warming her back, the cool light of dusk bleeding through the window at her side. Tearing the legs from Donovan's wooden coffee-table.

She had needed something to do.

A distraction.

Since the authorities had impounded the murdered woman's snake.

Her features hardened, teeth bared, eyes glistening, struggling to keep the memories at bay. They were closing in. Surrounding. Overwhelming.

Adalinda slammed her fist into the middle of the coffee-table.

The wood ruptured.

The table collapsed.

A bead of sweat dripped down her temple. Her hands were beginning to ache, but she kept working, kept focusing and destroying.

They had found nothing other than blood and ethanol in the dead woman's room, nothing to provide direction, nothing to point to a murderer. Clarke had left just before sunset, frustrated and grumbling under her breath. She had returned to her mortuary, stubbornly declaring that she *would* find evidence, if it wasn't on the body then she would search through the torn fragments of Adalinda's journal. Every. Single. One.

Adalinda glanced at the kitchen bench, at the empty cover of her journal. Donovan had asked her to retrieve it, thinking it might provide some inexplicable lead.

It hadn't.

It sat on the bench and taunted, the knotted snake on its' cover wickedly glinting.

Adalinda hissed through her teeth.

Another *crack.*

She tossed the table's third leg to the side, as if the wood were fragile, as if the strength required to tear it apart was negligible, insignificant.

She felt the protesting cry of her muscles but refused to stop.

The memories would come if she stopped.

Adalinda wiped the sweat from her brow, moving to the final leg.

Crack.

She held the wooden length in her lap, staring at it for a moment before standing and striding to the kitchen, grabbing one of Donovan's knives, and lowering herself onto a the leather cushion of a stool which was held aloft by antlers of antique, twisted iron.

Donovan's apartment was beautiful, all brick and steel and wood, vast, open and warm. Contrasted by contradicting surfaces, rough and smooth, shadowed and light.

It felt safe.

... Like Diana felt safe...

Adalinda ran the knife down the ruined table-leg, letting a shaving curl over the steel and fall to the floor. She could hear water gushing through pipes in the walls, the fire crackling in its' hearth.

The entire apartment smelled of Donovan, of woodsmoke and pouring rain.

Adalinda let herself relax, methodically scraping the knife over the wood, trimming and coaxing a shape from the grain.

Wings.

Feathers.

… An owl.

She was carving an owl.

Adalinda stopped, shoulders becoming stiff as she glanced at the empty cover of her journal, still perched on the kitchen bench.

Hide from the owls.

A tumbling shudder consumed her, a seed of dread planting itself inside, deep in the shadows of her soul, buried beneath the unknowable and the lost.

Her fault.

Adalinda's face contorted in a wince as pain lanced through her temples, something pressing against the veil which smothered her memories, something dark, something urgent.

She released a long breath, flinching as the door swung open and Christensen stalked inside, a brown paper bag grasped tightly in the crook of his arm. His eyes flicked over the pile of dismembered wood before the hearth, the length of it in Adalinda's hand, the knife.

"What…?" The bag rustled as Christensen shifted his grip, his face contorting in a confused frown at the slab of partially sculpted wood in Adalinda's palm. "Is that Donovan's *coffee-table*?"

Adalinda lowered the knife to the wood, calmly watching the shaving as it leisurely curled and dropped to join the others beneath her boots. "… It was."

Christensen was silent for a moment while he scanned the pile of wood. "But… why?"

"I needed a distraction."

The apartment door whispered quietly as it swung closed and

Christensen stomped forward. "Just because you need a *distraction* doesn't mean you should *destroy* a *table*."

Adalinda's golden eyes glinted as they flicked to Christensen. "I didn't *destroy* it." She returned her attention to the carving. "I introduced the beginnings of a form of metamorphosis."

"You're justifying this based on the fact that a caterpillar can turn into a butterfly." Christensen grumbled a curse as he entered the kitchen.

Adalinda lifted her shoulders in a shrug, finishing a cut and watching the shaving drop through the air like a dead moth. "In essence."

Christensen muttered under his breath. "I leave you alone for *two seconds...*" He dumped his bag on the counter, searching the apartment. "Where's Donovan?"

"In the shower." Adalinda tilted her head, gesturing vaguely behind her, listening to the gushing, groaning pipes. "Can you not hear the water?"

"*We* are supposed to be protecting *you* and you're sitting in the kitchen with a *knife*." Christensen pulled a box of steaming food from the bag and placed in beside Adalinda's elbow. "Eat. I haven't seen you touch anything all day."

A chorus of creaks echoed through the pipes as the water cut off.

Adalinda breathed in, the scent of meat and spices flowing from the boxes of food as Christensen continued to pluck them from his bag.

The bathroom door groaned open.

Adalinda kept her eyes on her carving, aware of Donovan emerging from the hall. His voice of melted honey raised the hairs on her arms as he padded towards the kitchen. "What did you get for dinner?"

Adalinda looked up, turning to face him.

She nearly dropped her knife.

Steam curled off Donovan's exposed skin, tenderly caressing the air. Water dripped reluctantly from his dark hair, trickling over his freshly shaven jaw, tracing sparkling lines down his long, muscular neck. A hand webbed with heated veins rested against the burgundy towel he had slung low over his hips, exposing a trail of hair reaching towards his navel.

The threatening memories which had been circling Adalinda evaporated.

Her teeth scraped across his dripping skin, breath hitching, lashes fluttering closed.

Adalinda's fingers tightened around the handle of the knife as she swallowed the noise bubbling in her throat. She shook her head, clearing it of the lingering vision.

And found herself staring at Donovan's chiselled stomach.

Heat flared in her core.

A blush climbed her neck.

"Noodles."

Adalinda tore her eyes from Donovan, planting them on Christensen as he finished removing food from the bag and shot a glare at Donovan.

"You left her sitting here *alone.*"

Donovan closed the distance between them, muscles rippling as he reached over the counter and plucked an apple from a bowl of fruit on the bench. His teeth sank into its' flesh, tongue adeptly catching the escaped juice as his ocean eyes drifted over his ruined coffee-table and the knife gripped in Adalinda's hand. "She's suitably armed and capable."

Christensen rolled his eyes, turning to pour himself a glass of water as Adalinda shivered. She could feel the heat streaming from Donovan in waves as he caught her gaze, a single brow arching, the corner of his mouth lifting. He took another bite of his apple, some of the juice escaping down his chin. "You owe me a new table." He turned and strode back towards the bathroom.

Adalinda dropped the knife onto the kitchen bench, her fingers suddenly limp. She stared at the muscles shifting in Donovan's back, pulse throbbing in her veins, hunger blooming deep in her core, coiling vines of heat reaching up her neck. She blew out a frustrated breath, shaping a curse and fighting not to throw one of the remaining apples after him as his still steaming form disappeared into a dark room. "Bastard."

Christensen set a fork on the bench and gestured to the box of noodles in front of her. "Eat, you're going to need the energy."

Adalinda pursed her lips but took the fork, feeling the memories return to their incessant circling as she placed her carving on the bench. "Have you heard anything from Clarke?"

Christensen shook his head. "Still waiting."

Adalinda opened the box of noodles. "... What happens if she doesn't find anything?"

"We start from the beginning. Go back to the gallery." Christensen speared his fork into the noodles, twisting them around the metal. "Let's hope it doesn't come to that."

"Why?"

Christensen lifted his noodles, staring at them with darkness in his eyes. He looked up at Adalinda, watching as she grew tense, as her scalp began to prickle. "Because if we don't find something soon either the murderer is going to escape or another person is going to die... And we'll have no way to stop him."

Adalinda lifted her fingers to brush her scarf, enduring the ache which had begun to strain her throat.

If another woman were to die...

Her fault.

Monster.

Adalinda's teeth sank into the flesh of her cheek, the pain of it chasing the stinging from her eyes.

She would not let another woman die.

She couldn't.

It would break her.

As surely as thunder breaks a storm.

CHAPTER TWENTY - FIVE

THE OVERSIZED, BRONZE MIRROR rose above Donovan, reflecting his form as he leaned over the sink, the steel bowl resting inside a split-log bench. A handle creaked as he turned it, cold water erupting from the tap, cupped hands splashing his face.

Her golden eyes glinted beneath her partially lowered lids, fanned lashes fluttering, pupils dilating. She leaned forward. Laboured breaths curled from their near touching mouths, gently caressing lust-parted lips...

Donovan blinked the delusion from his mind, shivering as he reached for a hand towel and patted it against his dripping face. He had heard Adalinda breaking his coffee-table, had peered out the door to check that she was alright and left her because he understood. She needed to do something, to distract herself. Donovan glanced to the side, at the core of his apple sitting atop the polished bench, seeing the repeated memory of Adalinda glancing at his chest, at his stomach.

Donovan lowered the hand towel and gripped the bench, fingers digging into the rough bark which marred its' curved underbelly.

The bare soles of his feet pressed against the stone floor, its' rugged surface cool, grounding.

That woman was going to drive him insane.

He could still feel her leaning against him, sobbing into his chest. He could still feel his arms around her, his hands massaging her back, his breath kissing her neck... As if he had held her a million times before. As if he would a million more.

Donovan grunted, frustrated and confused. He felt like he *knew* Adalinda, like he could trace the curves of her face in his mind and every detail would be exactly as she was. The spark in her eyes, the slope of her nose, the angle of her mouth, her lips.

Her lips...

Donovan cursed, squeezing his eyes shut.

He had to find a *murderer*. Instead, he was imagining the feel of Adalinda's hands sliding down his chest, her kiss against his skin, her eyes as she shoved him away from the bullet.

Donovan's eyes snapped open.

He lifted a hand, pressed his fingers to the inside of his shoulder.

The place the bullet had hit.

He felt no pain.

No bruising.

No sign at all that anything had touched his skin.

The bullet had missed.

The bullet had *missed*.

A wisp of breath flowed from him as he reached down and removed the towel from his hips, lifting it to rub his still dripping hair. His brows knitted together as he drew the towel across his body, muscles shifting smoothly beneath his skin.

"The bullet missed." He said it like a prayer, like a plea, like a whisper. He lifted the towel, hanging it from a steel hook and turning to his bronze reflection. His piercing, ocean eyes stared at their sepia imitations, questions and memories flicking through them, erratic and covered in blood. He shook his head, damp hair rustling, and stepped forward to plant his palms on the wood surrounding the sink. "It missed."

He saw the lie in his face, his stare dull and shadowed with pain.

If the bullet had missed it would have embedded itself in the bar. Or hit Adalinda. It would not have been a sphere of crumpled metal discarded with the ice on the floor.

Donovan clenched his fists, dismissing his thoughts like water down a drain.

He turned from the mirror, shunning the questions and the memories as he began to dress.

Hypothermia

Ten Years Ago

Steaming water cascaded from the shower head, spilling over his tightly wound muscles still numb from the frozen lake. His ocean eyes were squeezed shut, his jaw clenched against the screaming, biting sting. The heat burned, sending needles of pain through him with each drop that collided with his half-frozen skin. He could feel the rough massage of hands, harsh and aggressive, coaxing the blood to return to his extremities.

He drew in a shuddering breath, heavy mist clearing his lungs, the water singing to him, soothing him with its' relentless patter as it poured over his body and streamed onto the tiled floor. His head was beginning to clear, his thoughts returning from the frostbitten fog which had been congesting his mind. He opened his eyes to find a woman bowed over him, her eyes consumed by a pair of snow goggles, a braid of long, champagne hair peaking out from beneath her fur hood. He could see sweat beading on her forehead and trickling down her cheeks.

He recognised her.

The woman who had saved him.

She hadn't stopped to remove her clothing, she had simply dragged him into the house, into the shower, and had immediately shoved him under the scalding water.

The woman growled, tearing the watertight gloves from her hands and throwing them aside. She muttered under her breath as she drove her fingers into his muscles, her accent dense through lips of rose and thorn. "Stupid man. You must move yourself. I cannot fix you like this. Is too hard."

He groaned, managing to bend his aching fingers.

"Move, Donovan."

His dark brows furrowed, a frown carving his features. He croaked, spitting a mouthful of hot water. "Who's Donovan?"

The woman stiffened, pursed her lips. "... Is you." Her hands returned to aggressively rubbing his muscles.

"You know my name?"

"No." The woman shook her head. "Dark-haired man. Is Donovan." She grunted, heaving Donovan up until he sat beneath the pouring water. "... This name was given by friend."

"Your friend?"

She nodded, grabbing his hands and kneading the muscles. "He left. Is unreliable, but finds good names."

Donovan gritted his teeth as his fingers began to burn, the blood returning to their pallid tips. He watched as the woman stood, stepping back and eyeing him through the clouding surface of her snow goggles. She wiped a hand across their reflective exterior, grabbed a towel and began drying her hands, the water rolling off the sleeves of her jacket in gleaming beads.

"You can do rest. Food is in kitchen." She turned, snatching up her gloves and stomping to the closed bathroom door. "This is empty house, for travellers. Stay here long as you like."

Donovan groaned, pushing himself to his feet but staying beneath the pouring, steaming water. "Where are you going?"

"Out." The woman frowned, taking the handle of the door and pushing it open. "I will not be back."

Donovan blinked, dragging his soaked hair away from his face. "You're leaving?"

"Yes."

"At least tell me where I am."

The woman stared at him through her goggles, her expression flat, irritated. "Small town in mountains. Why are men so needy? I saved your life. That is enough." She walked out and closed the door.

Donovan listened to her boots stomping across floorboards, listened to the door slamming as she left. He gritted his teeth, dismissing a flutter of unease, and concentrated on the water spreading across his back, coursing over his shoulders and chest, clinging to the spattering of hairs trailing down his stomach. His skin was still burning, though it had begun to fade.

A few of his fingers remained numb.

He stood in the shower, staring at the door. Processing. Trying to understand.

Finally, Donovan twisted the taps and the last of the water spattered to the floor, leaking from the shower head in a tapering stream as he stepped out and into the bathroom. Steam floated around wooden walls, obscuring the glass of the mirror and hanging in the air around his face.

He peeled the soaking trousers from his hips, dried himself with a towel and moved silently into the lounge. He crossed the room in a few, short strides, plucked a shirt and caramel trousers from where they hung on a rack in the corner of the room and slipped them on.

... They were his size.

Donovan glanced at the fading light outside, wondering what had happened to him and considering his next actions. His heart began to feel like a stone in his chest, his bare shoulders sinking as if being weighed down.

The woman had left him.

After finding him in a frozen river, almost dead.

Donovan cursed under his breath, stalking past the crackling hearth and searching through the kitchen for food.

He found a curry, simmering in the oven.

Donovan closed the oven door and straightened, his frustration slowly replaced by a dawning uncertainty. He looked down at the clothes, perfectly fitted and appearing vaguely worn. He looked at the burning hearth, the pot of curry, the bowl and cutlery which had been set on the dining table in the centre of the room.

The woman had said this was a house for travellers, that he could stay as long as he liked.

It felt wrong.

Too simple.

Predetermined.

Donovan took a steadying breath, a feeling of dread settling in his stomach.

He had nowhere to go.

No idea who he was.

No idea where he was.

Waking in the frozen lake kept replaying in his mind. The pain a haunting echo of aching lungs and throbbing temples. Icy water nudging his lips. Numbness spreading through his limbs.

The fear crept up on him, out of the depths of his subconscious like a monstrous beast, a dark mass of writhing limbs, of curling bodies, seeping through his chest and swallowing the flesh of his thrashing heart.

Donovan's fingers clawed through his damp hair, scraping his scalp. He raised his forearms to shield his head. Anger and desperation bubbled up his throat; a growl spilled through his clenched teeth, swelling until it became a sharp, frustrated bellow. He wrestled with the absence of his memories, reaching for a name, for a face, for anything.

There was nothing.

Nothing but an innate sense of dread and his waking beneath the ice.

Nothing but panic.

And confusion.

How was he alive? Would he not have drowned? Or died of hypothermia?

Donovan sucked a breath through flaring nostrils, sinking to the floor beside the oven, staring at the wall with wide, ocean eyes. He was terrified. Exhausted. Angry and aching and alone.

Alone.

So alone he felt hollow.

As if a piece of him were missing. Not simply his memories but something more, something vital, like a beating heart or a breathing lung, like a sky without its' moon or a snowy night without a fire.

Donovan shuddered, taunted by the scent of curry and spice, assaulted by a combination of hunger and nausea.

He was on the floor. And he was splintering.

Donovan set his jaw, snarling at himself. He let his anger overcome his fear. He stood, turned the oven off and walked to the fire, watching the flames until he began to settle, until the dancing tongues became glowing coals.

It was dark by the time he moved, not a single light beyond the windows of the cabin, no sign of life, no sound save the wind.

Donovan threw more wood onto the fire, lit a few lamps and walked to the oven. He ate a spoonful of curry and waited, not trusting the food, unsure if it was poisoned. There was no reason it would be, since that woman had saved his life. Still, he waited. And when he was sure it was not poisoned, he ate. Then dragged a cushioned chair in front of the fire and slept. Fitfully. Through dreams of golden eyes and wicked smiles. Through visions of a weapon carved with ancient text and embellished with shards of pearl and shell and bone.

Through memories which fled at the wake of dawn.

Leaving a hollow, empty nothing.

Chapter Twenty - Six

"A thing like that doesn't just happen." Christensen leaned on the table, arms crossed, fingers tapping. He jutted his chin towards the knife in Adalinda's hand, pushing his empty box of noodles aside. "I bet that knife would bounce right off Donovan, just like the bullet."

Adalinda's mouth twisted in a frown as she looked up from her carving, brows furrowed. "You want to throw a knife... at Donovan."

Christensen lowered his chin in a nod, fingers moving to rhythmically tap the counter. "That bullet hit him. Clarke saw it. I saw it. *You* saw it."

Adalinda gently placed the partially carved wood on the bench and lifted the knife. Naked bulbs dangled from the roof in cages of blackened steel, their warm light glinting off its' polished blade. "Why are you bringing this up *now*?"

"I need to know what you saw." Christensen stared Adalinda down until she released a resigned sigh.

"I don't know what I saw. And I'm not going to throw a knife at Donovan to find out."

Christensen walked around the bench to stand beside Adalinda.

"He's hiding something. I thought I *knew* him. Why would he hide this from me? If he really is bullet-proof, shouldn't I *know*?"

"Can't you just trust him?" Adalinda twisted the blade in her hand, staring intently at the steel. "If a bullet hit you and didn't leave a mark, would you want *him* to throw a knife at *you* to find out why?"

"... No. But I wouldn't *lie* about it."

"If he didn't lie to you, he wouldn't be able to lie to himself..." Adalinda placed the knife on the bench, understanding flooding through her. She brushed the base of her scarf, still staring at the blade. "He's scared, Christensen. He won't tell you because he's scared. Just like I didn't tell you about the tattoo. Just like I didn't tell you about the journal. Because I was scared."

Christensen shot her a flat look. "You think *Donovan* is scared." He looked up as the door Donovan had disappeared through swung open.

Adalinda grabbed the knife, frowning at her empty box of noodles. "I know he is." She stood and walked to the couch, stepping over the ruined coffee-table and folding herself onto the cushions. She watched the fire for a moment, listening to Donovan as he sat at the bench and began to eat.

"Donovan."

Donovan grunted, lifting a fork of noodles into his mouth. He didn't look at Christensen.

"We need to talk about the bullet—"

"I thought we established that it missed."

"*You* established that it missed. You avoided my questions."

"The bullet missed, Christensen."

"You're just lying because you're scared—"

Donovan's stool scraped across the floor. He rose to his full height, voice grinding through his teeth. "*The bullet missed, Christensen.*"

Adalinda stopped carving.

She looked up.

Donovan's nostrils flared. His fists began to tremble. "I said it missed and it missed. If it hit, why is there not a wound?"

Christensen dropped onto the stool beside Donovan, grumbling. "Maybe it *healed* really quickly."

"There was no blood."

"Maybe you can't bleed."

"Maybe I can't bleed?" Donovan crossed his arms, raising a brow. "What the hell do you think my heart is pumping? Stardust?"

Christensen narrowed his eyes. "*Star* dust...?"

"My point is, there's no explanation for why the bullet didn't leave a wound. Therefore, it missed." Donovan sat down and returned to his food. "I'm done with this conversation."

"Adalinda said you were scared."

Donovan growled, digging noodles from his box. "Adalinda needs to continue carving the wreckage of my coffee-table and stop analysing my emotions."

Adalinda pressed her lips together and looked back at her carving, trying to hide her smile. She began to etch feathers into the wings, slowly, deliberately.

"Have you heard from Clarke?"

Christensen shook his head, pulling his phone from the pocket of his jacket and setting it on the bench. "Not even a message."

Donovan took a mouthful, chewing with a frown. He swallowed. "If she hasn't found anything yet, she isn't going to."

"I know."

"We'll go back to the gallery tomorrow, we still haven't found out how the murderer got into the building in the first place."

Christensen sighed, pushing himself up. "I'm going to have a shower." He glanced at Adalinda, still etching feathers while perched on the couch. "This time stay with her, if I come out and she's alone with only a knife to protect herself I'm going to shove that noodle box down your throat."

Donovan chuckled and Adalinda found herself smiling.

"I mean it."

Donovan turned on his stool, holding the box of noodles to his chest and pointedly staring at Adalinda. "I won't let her out of my sight."

Christensen glared as Donovan kept eating, his eyes locked on Adalinda, an expression of stern determination on his face.

Adalinda focused on the knife in her hand, the tip slicing through wood. She felt Donovan's gaze as Christensen left, as he finished eating, as he stood, cleared the bench and poured himself a drink.

"... You think I'm scared?"

Adalinda started, her grip tightening on the knife. Donovan had moved without making a sound, walking from the kitchen to the hearth before her in perfect silence.

She lifted her eyes to meet those of stunning ocean, desirous wings fluttering in her stomach, an appreciative shiver flourishing beneath her scarf. "Aren't you?"

Donovan didn't answer. He grabbed a leg of the coffee-table from the floor, the wood as thick as his forearm, and snapped it in half as if it were nothing more than a stick. He threw it onto the fire. "No questions?" He watched as a cloud of glowing ash burst from the embers, darting around his hand like wandering fireflies. "You haven't asked any."

"You haven't answered any."

The comforting scent of woodsmoke clung to Donovan as he turned to her. "That doesn't mean I won't."

Adalinda twisted the knife in her hand, unconsciously inhaling as he moved closer. "I don't need to ask questions, I don't need to be watched, and you need to sleep. I doubt you slept at all last night and despite the shower you can't hide the fatigue in your eyes."

Donovan lowered himself onto the couch beside Adalinda, his broad back reclining on the opposite armrest. "I've been finding it difficult to sleep as of late."

Adalinda released an understanding hum as she lowered her knife to shape the final details of the wooden owl, choosing not to discuss the subject further. She tensed as Donovan shifted, a breath of warmth whispering as his knee grazed her thigh, awareness prickling across her skin like stroking fingers. She pressed the blade into the wood and waited impatiently for Donovan to speak.

He sat quietly for a moment, fastidiously observing as she used the tip of the knife to softly outline the base of the beak. His gaze flicked to her face, to her scarf, examining her in the light of the fire, as if she were something worth studying. "I left a clean towel in the bathroom, if you decide to take a shower."

Adalinda paused as she met his gaze, allowing herself to absorb the intensity of it, the hunger which echoed her own. She fought the urge to smooth her scarf, feeling the shiver from her scalp dance down the length of her spine. "Thank you." She rotated the knife handle in her palm as she trailed her gaze across his face, admiring the strong edge of his jaw, the stunning shadows of his cheeks, the tempting curve of his mouth. Adalinda stared at the bursts of turquoise and sapphire in his irises, wondering why she was ignoring the flames blooming in her core. The warm glow of the fire kissed his features as he lounged on the end of the couch, his expression calm, his gaze molten, smouldering, admiring. If she just leaned forward...

Adalinda dragged her attention back to the carving, smothering the flush of heat which crept up her neck as she noticed the sprinkle of dark hair disappearing beneath his robe. The exquisite, midnight fabric flowed elegantly over his figure, deep burgundy embroidery spreading across the collar and cuffs in flourishes of thorned vines. It was beautiful.

He was beautiful.

Adalinda sucked in a breath through clenched teeth and lowered the knife to the wood.

"I have a second robe if you're so inclined." Donovan's enticing lips curled when she kept her eyes on her project, deliberately ignoring the heat which was rising through her veins. "If you don't mind it being oversized."

The knife in Adalinda's hand escaped slightly as her concentration slipped. "I don't need a robe." She leaned forward, placing the knife and the carving on the floor beside the pile of wooden shavings. "And Christensen is in the shower."

"There's a second bathroom."

"Fine." Adalinda stood, brushing her gaze over Donovan's devastating smile and smothering the longing which twisted her stomach. She wanted him to hold her, as he had the other night...

Adalinda pressed her fingernails into her palms. "Where is the second bathroom?"

Donovan rested against the arm of the couch, his smile curving wickedly. "The ensuite of my bedroom. You'll find it easily enough."

Adalinda swallowed, forcing herself to step away and slip past the window. Her steps were silent as breaths across the floor, her golden eyes fixed on the hall, desperately ignoring the hunger in her veins, the want spreading through her core.

And oblivious to the dark silhouette which lingered in the street below, lurking in the night's cold shadows.

A man. With eyes of mud and moss.

Staring intently up at her as she moved past the window of Donovan's apartment.

Stoically watching.

Impatiently waiting.

Cursing in the winter cold as Adalinda disappeared from his sight.

Chapter Twenty - Seven

Donovan near choked on his drink as Adalinda appeared in the lounge, her graceful figure shrouded in the oversized dressing gown she had dismissed earlier. He had hung it outside the bathroom door once she was in the shower, in case she changed her mind.

He cleared his throat, fist thumping once against the solid surface of his chest. "You decided to wear it."

Adalinda brushed her fingers over the fabric, admiration lighting her golden eyes as she studied the cerulean embroidery, the fabric dark against her smooth, pale skin.

"It suits you." Donovan tracked her steps around the ruined coffee-table as she returned to her place on the couch, the smooth skin of her ankles peeking through the floor-length hem. She lowered herself to the cushions, tugging the fabric over her chest as it began to slip, momentarily exposing the soft flesh beneath.

"It's a work of art." Adalinda looked up from admiring the fabric, a demure smile on her lips despite the edge of sadness apparent in her features. She swept her thumb over the tattoo on her wrist, the pearlescent ink shimmering in the firelight, and her smile withered. "I keep thinking about the women, the blood in the orphanage, the murderer…"

Donovan's heart skipped a beat in his chest. He shifted closer, gingerly reaching out to take her hand. The crackling fire abruptly silenced, inaudible beneath the hum resonating through him as his fingers brushed her own. "We'll find him."

Adalinda looked down at their hands, her eyes sparking sorrow. "What if we don't? What if he does it again?"

"He won't."

"Did you hear from Clarke?" Adalinda shifted her fingers over Donovan's skin, heated sparks shooting from the contact. "Did she find something?"

"She swore profusely at Christensen and told him to go to bed. She apparently can't concentrate when he keeps messaging her." Donovan smiled, watching the sorrow begin to leak from Adalinda's face. "Christensen is sulking in his room, reading."

Adalinda breathed a laugh, her gaze like the remnants of a kiss as it swept over him.

"We'll find him and there will be no more murders." Donovan squeezed her hand, gently stroking with his thumb. "Even if I have to remove him myself." Adalinda narrowed her eyes as Donovan smiled. "You said yourself a knife can solve a lot of problems."

"Yes, but I wasn't expecting you to *agree* with me."

Donovan's smile widened as he leaned back a little, adjusting his grasp on her hand, satisfied that he had temporarily displaced her sadness.

He ignored the urge to move closer, to hold her against him.

Adalinda tucked her legs beneath her, a curious spark in her golden eyes. She raised a hand to brush her ever-present scarf as she tilted her head curiously, assessing him. "You're becoming more and more interesting by the minute, Detective."

Donovan released her hand, a feeling of familiarity tugging at him as he watched her form shift in the flickering light of the fire. "As are you." His gaze lingered on her for a moment, on the bruised circles beginning to darken around her eyes, on the deflated curve of her shoulders. She was hiding it well, the fatigue, the fear, but he could see it weighing on her, like a cliff beginning to crumble. What would happen if she broke? If she couldn't hide it any more and she snapped?

Donovan frowned, twisting to look at the antique clock suspended on the kitchen wall, its' hands moving steadily through the fourth quarter of its' face. "It's getting late, you should try to get some rest..."

"You say that as if I'll sleep." Adalinda gracefully uncurled and stood, taking the knife and her carving from the floor and handing them to him as she rose. The owl stared at him, unblinking. "That's a little difficult when dead women lurk behind my eyes."

Donovan began to stand, dropping the carving and the knife to the couch.

Adalinda lifted a hand, gesturing for him to stay. "I'll try, nonetheless. If I can't sleep I'll come back out." She smiled at him and it failed to reach her eyes. "Goodnight, Donovan."

Donovan smothered the frown threatening his features as her lips shaped his name, a name which felt impossibly wrong coming from her. It had felt the same in the bar, after he had been shot. An innate sense of wrongness, of something amiss...

Donovan forced a reassuring smile onto his face, watching as Adalinda crossed the room and disappeared down the dimly lit hall. His ocean eyes darkened once she was gone, her hips swaying beneath his oversized robe.

How could a name feel hollow as it did when she spoke?

How could a bullet hit and leave no wound?

How could he hear the rain whisper as it fell? As if it had a voice. As if it were alive.

Donovan plucked the knife from the cushion at his side, turning the blade in his hand as he stared at the fire and waited for Clarke to call.

He sat there for an hour.

Two.

No call.

Donovan growled, pushing himself off the couch. He took the knife and Adalinda's carving to the kitchen and poured himself another drink.

The whisky burned as he tipped the glass, swallowed the contents and poured another.

He had a feeling it was going to be a long night.

Chapter Twenty - Eight

ADALINDA COULDN'T SLEEP. She rested on a couch before the windows of her room, curled around a book of mythos which lay open in her lap. Not reading. She stared at the words, finding the lines of black text incomprehensible, her mind unable to cling to their meaning, her thoughts wandering like a river around a bend.

She kept seeing Donovan snap the coffee-table leg. Muscles barely straining. Throwing it onto the fire.

Adalinda looked up at the sheet of amber light creeping through her windows, the streetlight kissing the glass, the warmth of a reading lamp breathing on her neck.

She did have questions, but questions were like secrets, they were for trading, one in exchange for another. She knew what he would ask, if he had the chance, and she would not be able to answer it. Not truthfully. So she kept her questions to herself, hoarding them like a dragon and feeling them begin to gather weight.

Adalinda released a tired sigh, fingers brushing her scarf as her scalp began to prickle, her gaze returning to the book in her lap.

Outside her window, something moved.

Adalinda paused, looked up.

Wrong.

Something was wrong.

She closed the book, placing it on the couch. She doused her reading light and walked to the window, feeling sick to her stomach.

The sky beyond was deepest black, the streetlights like oversized lanterns beneath the scant breadth of her balcony, illuminating the street with a bright glow that rose almost as high as the rooves and bathed the glistening cobblestones in pools of brilliant light.

The street was silent. Deserted, save the shadows abiding in the scattered recesses of doors. Her body relaxed as she convinced herself the street was empty, that her nerves were simply making her skittish.

She was waiting for another murder, despite what Donovan had said.

She knew there would be another.

Adalinda moved back to the couch, sat down, opened the book.

Stared at it in the dark without really wanting to read it.

Her eyes began to blur.

Adalinda spat a curse, the words flowing from her bowed lips like deadly venom. She slammed the book shut in her lap, her hands pressing on the covers with unnecessary force. She breathed deeply, the air heaving into her lungs as she stood, the book of mythos falling back to the couch with a gentle thud.

She began to pace, her steps silent on the wooden floor, her eyes sweeping over the street outside as she pivoted and approached the windows. Every cell in her body told her to move, to run, to fight, to hide, to *do* something.

She didn't want to break.

She could feel herself fracturing.

Her fault.

Monster.

Adalinda halted in her tracks, her golden eyes glowing like a cats in the dark as she looked past her reflection in the window.

Feathers rustled.

An owl swooped from the roof.

Adalinda watched, waited. Poised like a predator ready to pounce. Peering through the woven iron of her balcony's railing, at the opposite side of the street.

The owl hooted.

Something moved, in the street below, in the shadows of a doorway.

Time seemed to stretch, each beat of her heart loudly drumming in her ears.

Her scalp began to crawl.

She lifted a hand to her scarf.

... Perhaps she had been wrong.

The shadow moved, skirting the street-lights before slipping into the darkness of another doorway.

A man. Dressed in a flowing cloak so black it seemed a shadow, as if it were made of woven darkness and a chasms abyss. He was watching the apartment, the brightly lit lounge where Donovan was still awake.

The murderer.

It had to be.

Adalinda cursed herself a fool as she unlatched the window, glancing at Donovan's dressing gown still wrapped around her form. She took it off and threw it onto her bed, revealing her own clothes, a woollen shirt and loose, flowing pants. She had put them back on when she had left the warmth of the lounge, when she had started shivering.

Adalinda leaned into the window frame and swung it open. Winter burst inside. Freezing. Numbing. She paused, looking out, staring over the balcony at the drop to the pavement below. "What are you doing?" Bumps rose on her skin and she sucked in the frigid night air, cursing quietly at herself. "It might not be him..."

But what if it was...?

Adalinda took another breath, feeling the cold move through her lungs. She turned back, looking at the wall in the direction of the lounge, where Donovan was.

What if it was the murderer?

What if she could catch him?

... She should go to Donovan...

Adalinda shook her head, turning back to the street. The figure was watching the lounge. If she left to find Donovan then she would be giving him a chance to escape.

And she was not feeling that generous.

There would be no more deaths.

No more murders.

Adalinda knew it was him, just as she had known there had been a second murder.

Trusting her instincts, she stole onto the balcony, climbed over the railing.

And dropped off the edge.

Chapter Twenty - Nine

Theodore

THEODORE RAN A HAND THROUGH his thick, brunette hair, his mud and moss eyes peering up at the illuminated lounge. He could see Donovan pacing, brushing past the windows, his eyes no doubt dark and staring at the floor.

Theodore shivered.

It was cold.

Too bloody cold.

He felt like he was being punished. Made to wait in the middle of the night.

He should just go home-

An owl hooted.

Theodore slammed his back against the door, the hood falling from his face as he buried himself in shadows. The owl dove from the roof above Adalinda's darkened room and Theodore moved to the next doorway, closer to the window Donovan was pacing across.

He watched quietly, shivering. Until a figure stepped out of Adalinda's room and dropped from balcony to balcony, passing four sets of windows, as quiet and delicate as a leaf on the wind. Adalinda's clothing flapped as she caught the balustrades with pale fingers, occasionally slipping on the iced iron, and made her way to the ground.

Theodore breathed a curse, his eyes growing wide as Adalinda hit the pavement, a grimace painting her face when the force made her stumble. She looked up and her gaze seemed to glow, like stars in darkness, like the depths of a burning hell.

Theodore shuddered, feeling a spike of fear. If he stayed in the shadows she would find him. If he ran, she would chase him, but he might be able to make it to his car before she caught him and began beating answers out of him. In fact, she would probably beat the life out of him for good measure. Just because she could.

Theodore clenched his teeth and drew in a deep breath.

Running it was, then. Cowardly, but effective. He liked his face too much for it to be beaten anyway.

Self-preservation was key.

The owl disappeared over a rooftop.

Adalinda stepped forward.

Theodore launched himself out of the doorway and into the street, sprinting over the slick pavement, cursing himself for parking further away than was absolutely necessary. He swore a rainbow as he slid on a layer of ice, frantically regaining his balance and hurtling around the next building, into the next street.

He could see his silver car parked in the amber pool of a street light.

Theodore pushed himself to run faster, gaining on the vehicle, fishing in his pockets for the keys. Front, back, left, right.

Where the *fuck* were his *keys*?

Jacket.

They were in his jacket.

The hazard lights blinked, the car unlocking as he stabbed the keys' button.

He could hear footsteps at his back.

Close.

Too close.

Panic took him in a vice grip as he thrust himself the last few steps to the car.

His boots collided with ice.

A yell of desperation escaped Theodore as he plummeted to the cobblestones, sliding on his side past the car, the rough ground slicing his cloak.

He clawed for something to stop him. His hand caught the front tire and his shoulder wrenched as he hauled himself up from the awkward position.

Adalinda was a few steps away, her eyes fierce with fiery hatred.

Theodore grabbed the door handle and yanked it open, leaping inside and fumbling with the keys. He slammed the door closed with his free hand. Locked it.

Adalinda reached the car, teeth bared. She grabbed the door and pulled at it, fighting to get inside as her boots skidded on the ice.

The metal handle buckled.

"You *killed them!*" Adalinda's hiss tore through him, the venom in it raising the hairs on his arms. "You *bastard!*"

Theodore felt the key slide into place and he turned the ignition. The engine sputtered but didn't catch. A string of curses flew from him as he tried again. "Come on. *Come on.*" He winced as Adalinda raised her fist, moisture collecting in her glowing eyes.

Her fist began to move.

Theodore tightened his grip on the key, tried the ignition once more.

The engine roared to life and Theodore accelerated, wheels screeching on the road as Adalinda's fist broke through the driver's side window. She managed to grab the collar of his cloak, running to keep up with the car, one hand gripping the door handle.

"*Damn it!*" Theodore grabbed at the mad-woman's hand. He pried her fist open, forcing it back through the hole she'd broken in the window while struggling to keep his attention on the road. The ruined glass tore Adalinda's skin, slashing her sleeve and forearm to ribbons. She fell from the moving vehicle, her shoulder colliding with the ground, the breath bursting from her lungs and cutting off her scream of pain.

Theodore glanced in the rearview mirror and immediately regretted it. Adalinda's eyes were still glowing, her body bathed in the crimson of his tail-light as she lay on the pavement like a furious, broken doll.

A numbing chill seeped into the marrow of Theodore's bones as Adalinda released an infuriated scream, her face crumpling, tears from the cold dripping down her cheeks.

She pushed herself upright, struggling to stand, shoulders curling as she clutched her wounded arm to her side. Dark blood streamed down her wrist, staining her white shirt and dripping onto the pavement.

Theodore turned back to the road, the image of her seared into his mind. He sucked in a trembling breath, trying to stop his hands from shaking, trying to slow the thunderous drum of his pulse.

Too close.

Too close.

That had been *too damned close.*

He swore, shuddering, and turned the corner. His stomach churned. His muscles were *vibrating* and he could see it *through his clothes.*

The owl appeared overhead and Theodore swore at it, losing his voice to the freezing winter wind lashing through his desecrated window.

The bird narrowed its' moonbeam eyes and disappeared over a roof.

Theodore took a deep breath.

The shaking did not stop.

CHAPTER THIRTY

A FURIOUS SCREAM FLOODED the lounge, drowning out the crackling fire and paralysing Donovan like a fox in torchlight. His hands fell limply to his sides. The destructive sound tore through him, splintering him with savage malice, draining the blood from his face.

He moved to the window, his eyes darting over the empty street, bypassing his stark reflection in the glass, feverishly searching for the source of the cry.

Christensen emerged from the hall with bloodshot eyes and a face marked by the folds of his pillow. He mumbled an indistinct question, standing and listening, before a wave of recognition swept over him and he charged for Adalinda's room.

The cry stopped abruptly, leaving Donovan feeling cold. He shook his head, attempting to clear it, the unbearable sound replaced by a consistent, high-pitched whine.

A dark streak shot through the reflection in the window, Christensen bolting for the door, his shirt only half tucked in. His yell hit Donovan as a muted, contorted jumble.

The ringing in Donovan's ears faded and he turned to look at Christensen who had flung himself out the door, the man's yell finally taking form, the urgency of the words hitting Donovan with the force of a Herculean blow. "*Adalinda's gone.*"

Donovan began to move, the powerful muscles in his legs throwing him out the door, down the hall, into the stairwell. He lunged towards the stairs, winding down multiple flights, ignoring half of the steps beneath him as he ran. Adrenaline pulsed through him as he passed Christensen, the heat of it fuelling his rising panic. He flung himself down the last of the stairs, the handle of the entrance collapsing beneath his palms as he shoved with unnatural strength and burst into the street.

The door swung outward, crashing against the wall before ricocheting back into place.

Donovan was already halfway down the street by the time Christensen exited the building, his brows furrowing at the crushed handle of the door.

Donovan skidded to a stop at an intersection, his panic-stricken eyes falling on Adalinda's back. She stood in the middle of the road with an arm braced by her side. Shivering. Her shoulders curled and shaking.

"Adalinda..." Donovan's voice broke as it trickled into the stillness, as its' cloud dissolved in the frozen night air.

Adalinda turned, chin trembling, tears from the cold leaking down her cheeks.

Donovan inched towards her, approaching her as he would an injured animal. "It's alright." He opened his hands, arms outstretched. "Just tell me what happened." He could hear Christensen's heavy breathing behind him, unaccompanied by footsteps on the pavement. The man had stopped and was watching.

Adalinda stared at Donovan, not quite seeing. "... I lost him..." Her voice was the husk of a whisper as she pressed her arm further into her side, crimson spreading in morbid flowers across the ivory fabric of her clothes.

She was hurt.

Donovan cursed, forgetting his caution and marching to her side. "Christensen, find some bandages, she's bleeding."

Christensen darted back across the street, disappearing into Donovan's building.

Donovan took Adalinda's wrist, lifting the bloodied skin and scanning the torn flesh of her forearm. He removed the belt of his robe and began to wrap the fabric around her arm, feeling her relax slightly at his touch. "Who did you lose?"

"The murderer." Adalinda ground it through her teeth, her eyes meeting his, her anger and despair locked in a glowing battle.

Donovan paused, fighting to smother a burst of rage as he finished tying the makeshift bandage and gently grasped her shoulders. "You saw the *murderer* outside and you didn't come to *get me*?"

"If I'd come to *get you* he would have *disappeared*." Adalinda growled, her nose crinkling. "I climbed down the balconies. I nearly caught him but..." She trailed off, her eyes lowering to Donovan's chest. "He got into his car... I broke the window and tried to grab him but he pushed me out and escaped." Her shoulders tensed beneath his grip, the fingers of her uninjured hand squeezing into a dangerous fist. "I *lost* him."

Donovan rubbed his hands along Adalinda's arms, feeling the cold skin beneath her shirt, keeping his anger on a leash. He drew in a long breath of frosted air, calming himself before he decided to track that murderer down and tear him limb from limb.

He would deal with the fact that Adalinda had climbed out a *window* in pursuit of him later.

Donovan unclenched his jaw, using Adalinda's presence to ground himself. "Can you describe the car?"

"Silver."

"Model?"

Adalinda's breath stretched from her mouth in swirling bursts of steam. She shook her head. "I don't know. It's dark. I couldn't see."

Donovan stepped around Adalinda, holding her shoulders and guiding her back to his apartment. "Next time, let *me* chase the murderer."

"You didn't see him."

"That doesn't mean you should *throw* yourself out a *window*."

Adalinda clenched her teeth. "Next time I'll invite him in for tea, shall I?"

"How about just asking for my help?"

Adalinda stopped, her muscles growing taut. After a moment, she sucked in a calming breath and continued walking. "You know what? You're right, it was foolish. I just... I needed to *do something*. I feel like I'm waiting for a storm to hit and I'm hiding in a lace tent."

Donovan opened the door to his building, waiting for Adalinda to step inside. He glanced at the doors' crushed handle, winced. "It *was* foolish and you won't do it again."

Adalinda stepped inside, cradling her wounded arm against her chest and starting up the stairs. "Don't treat me like a child."

"Then don't *act* like one." Donovan let the door swing shut, he could see Christensen's silhouette above, racing to his apartment. "How did you climb down the balconies? There's no ladder."

"I dropped."

"... You dropped." Donovan raised a sceptical brow.

Adalinda stubbornly lifted her chin. "You were shot and you didn't bleed. Don't ask questions if you're not going to answer in turn."

Donovan stopped, his hands falling to his sides. "*Now* you use that?"

"What? You thought I didn't have questions?"

"Damn it, woman, you're *infuriating*."

"I'm also bleeding and angry. Don't push me." Adalinda stomped up the stairs, her boots remaining silent.

Donovan growled and stormed after her, his fingers flexing in and out of fists. "Can't you just—"

"*I will bring up the leg of the coffee-table!*" Adalinda span on him, pained and furious. "You snapped it like a twig," she snarled. "*I said don't push me.*"

Donovan felt his heart stutter, staring at her untempered fury. She stood a few steps above him, her face level with his own, leaning forward until their breaths began to mingle, her teeth bared, her glare on fire.

He knew that fury. It was the fury of lost control, of remorse and guilt beneath the weight of constant stress. She was terrified and hurt and she was hiding it beneath her anger, like cornered prey.

Donovan raised his hand, brushing his thumb across the curve of her cheek. "You aren't mad at me, Adalinda. Not really."

Adalinda's fury fled like the flame of a blown candle.

"You're scared and angry."

She squeezed her eyes shut.

"You feel defenceless, but you're not. You're strong. You're just hurt and tired."

Adalinda's chin began to tremble.

Donovan nearly leaned in.

He nearly pulled her into him.

Nearly pressed his lips against her own.

"I'm sorry." Adalinda whispered, opening her eyes, the fury gone, leaving her vulnerable, hurting. "I thought—" She swallowed. "I thought I could catch him."

Donovan let his hand slide from her cheek and dragged it through his hair. Stars, she was stunning. "You did what you thought was right." He began to climb the stairs, carefully stepping around her as she turned to follow. "We'll take a look at your arm and I'll run you a bath. I'm sure I have scented oils hiding somewhere... Possibly bubbles."

"Bubbles?" Adalinda rubbed a hand over her face, cradling her wounded arm against her chest. "*You* have *bubbles*?"

Donovan lifted his shoulders in a shrug. "I might."

"Can I have both?"

"A little indulgent, aren't we?"

Adalinda smiled, her golden eyes softly glinting. "Only after chasing a murderer down an abandoned street in the middle of the night."

Donovan echoed Adalinda's smile. "Infuriating woman."

Adalinda hummed a laugh, nudging him with her shoulder as they reached the top of the stairs.

They walked the rest of the way to his apartment in silence, Adalinda cradling her bleeding arm, Donovan hovering at her side. She should have been faint, stumbling from blood-loss, he had only glanced at her wound but her forearm looked as if it were torn to ribbons. She acted as if it were simply a scratch.

Donovan opened the door to his apartment, watching Adalinda walk inside. "Let me see your arm."

She shook her head. "It's fine."

Donovan let the door swing shut, levelling a flat stare at her. "It's bleeding through my belt."

"I just need a bath."

"You need stitches."

"I do not."

"Adalinda—"

"No. I'll make a deal with you. You don't ask questions, I won't ask questions. If I say my arm is fine, then it's fine. If you snap a coffee-table leg like it's nothing, or get shot and don't bleed, I'll stay quiet." Adalinda held up a hand as Donovan opened his mouth to cut in. "This is non-negotiable, Detective."

Donovan closed his mouth, frowning. He watched Adalinda for a moment, lifting his gaze when Christensen appeared with a box of bandages. A frustrated growl rolled deep in Donovan's chest. He walked over to Christensen and took a bandage from the box. "I'm drawing her a bath."

"What about—"

"The wound isn't bad, just a few scratches. It looks worse than it is."

Christensen narrowed his eyes but kept his mouth shut, watching as Adalinda followed Donovan into the bathroom and Donovan closed the door behind them.

Chapter Thirty - One

Steam curled around Adalinda, lapping indulgently at the hollows of her collarbones as she lay submerged in the bath, her elegant legs spread beneath the surface, her fingers tapping and teasing the ripples in an attempt to distract herself.

She had stopped shivering. Finally. She had never been able to cope with cold, it seemed to leach the warmth from her blood, instead of simply slowing her circulation.

Liquid beads like sparkling glass trickled down her skin as she lifted her forearm from the water, examining it with a furrowed brow, the edges of her mouth tilted towards her chin. The lacerations had diminished to broken slivers of pink, trailing from her inner elbow to her wrist.

Lethal wounds.

At least, they should have been.

A few glass fragments were discarded in the bin beside the sink, still coated in blood, atop the remnants of her slashed and blood-soaked shirt.

Adalinda's frown deepened. She had seen people with cuts and grazes on the street. Rough, black scabs protecting raw, unhealed skin.

She was not like them.

She was something else…

A knock on the door dragged Adalinda from her thoughts. She pushed herself to the edge of the bath, shoulders rising over the cool edge in a cloud of steam. She pushed her healing arm under the water. "Yes?"

The door swung open and a strong arm reached through to place a pile of folded fabric on the wooden bench of the sink. "I found the robe on your bed."

Adalinda felt her lips soften in an unintentional smile as she assessed Donovan's deliberately turned face.

He cleared his throat. "How are you feeling?"

"Better."

"And your arm?"

Adalinda narrowed her eyes. "My arm is fine."

Donovan frowned, scanning the bathroom, no doubt looking for blood.

"If you start asking questions—"

Donovan grunted, shooting her a glare before immediately looking away. "Do you need anything?"

Adalinda sighed, watching as Donovan's fingers flexed and folded into fists. She could see he was anxious, worried, no doubt picturing the skin of her arm still torn and covered in blood. "Where's Christensen?"

"I told him to get some more sleep."

Adalinda remained quiet for a moment, glancing at the stiffness of Donovan's shoulders, then at the healing wounds on her arm. "Donovan… why don't you step in here and close the door?"

Donovan hesitated, then pushed the door further open and slipped inside, his ocean eyes fixed on the sink.

"I'm going to need you to look at me."

Again, Donovan hesitated.

Adalinda rolled her eyes, lifted her healing arm from the water. "No questions. I'm just showing you that my arm is alright so you'll stop standing there making me feel nervous."

Donovan turned. His eyes fell on her steaming arm.

Her heart began to flutter.

Donovan's brow twitched, almost imperceptibly, as he walked further into the bathroom. "... It healed..."

"Yes."

He hummed, deep and low, like a rumble of distant thunder.

Adalinda pulled her arm back into the bath. "Satisfied?"

Donovan raised his eyes to hers, to her scarf.

Her scalp began to prickle, the tingle shooting down her neck and over her shoulders, heat flaring in her core.

Donovan shook his head. "Not in the least." He turned and strode purposefully back towards the door, shoulders stiff as a length of steel.

Adalinda stared at his back, the intensity of her expression flickering.

He paused by the door, one hand on the doorknob. "You didn't take my robe when you decided to leap out of the window."

"I didn't want to ruin it."

Donovan glanced at the folded pile of fabric on the wooden bench of the sink. "So you decided to freeze?"

"Do I *look* frozen to you?"

Donovan pressed his lips in a line. "I'm not going to answer that."

Adalinda smiled, watching him close the door. She laid her head back and closed her eyes, water quietly sloshing against her skin, against the edge of her scarf.

Monster.

Her teeth clenched as the murdered women flashed behind her eyes.

Her fault.

Adalinda cursed and pushed herself from the bath. She was exhausted. Her eyes were beginning to itch. Her head beginning to ache.

She needed to sleep, though she wasn't sure she could without seeing blood and death in the dark of her room. So she found a towel, dried herself and slipped into the Detective's robe before padding into the lounge and curling on the couch beside Donovan. She settled her head on her arms and closed her eyes.

Donovan's gaze skimmed over her before returning to the fire. He remained quiet, not questioning her presence, as if unwilling to disturb her, content to watch the flames as she drifted into sleep.

His scent of woodsmoke and rain kept her memories at bay.

Until he left.

And she woke.

Screaming.

CHAPTER THIRTY - TWO

THEODORE

THEODORE SAT ON THE EDGE of the desk in the Mirror Gallery, impatiently waiting. His lean legs dangled over the polished marble floor, his agitated fingers tapped the white surface of the desk. He was surrounded by art, sculptures and paintings, one fake and made of glass.

He kept seeing the gallery filled with people, kept seeing Leena flirting, laughing.

He had liked her, the distraction of her beauty and intelligence... And now she was dead.

Theodore forced an exasperated sigh, his mud and moss eyes staring at the ceiling.

Typical.

He had spent hours calming down after his escape from Adalinda, ages waiting, attempting to perfect his greeting as he moved from his sprawled position on the couch to the rotating chair behind the gallery desk. He had grudgingly decided to do as asked, as usual. Honestly, it would probably get him killed. Though he always felt like something would get killed, and he always ran before that happened.

Theodore had planned to sit in the chair with its' back facing the door and slowly swing himself around to view his guests when they arrived.

He always appreciated a good cliché.

He had spun in the chair so many times he had begun to feel sick, swinging his legs and staring at the paintings as they blurred colourfully on the walls. He'd had to take his place on the desk until the world stopped spinning.

Theodore turned his head, trailing his moss flecked gaze from the ceiling to the chair, and felt his insides cramp as a wave of revolving nausea swept over him.

His eyes snapped back to the ceiling.

The nausea began to subside.

Apparently, the chair was no longer an option.

CHAPTER THIRTY - THREE

ADALINDA WOKE SCREAMING. Thrashing and gasping. Tears streaming down her cheeks.

She remembered blood and pain, *so much pain*. But it had not been hers. No. If it had been hers, it would not have left her feeling as if a chainsaw had slaughtered her heart, shredding flesh and crushing bone to a cloud of crimson mist.

The dream fled. Gone in an instant. So terrible it left her shaking with a savage, inescapable dread.

Adalinda sat up, gripping one of the couch cushions to her chest, breathing heavily. She rocked back and forth until her pulse calmed, until the shaking stopped, until she noticed Christensen staring at her with eyes so wide they almost fell from his head.

Adalinda's hand flew to her scarf.

It was still there, the fabric was still tight and unmoving.

She released a fractured breath and wiped the tears from her cheeks. "Where's Donovan?"

"... Uh... He went to get breakfast..." Christensen stared at her, her arms still clinging to the cushion, her body still faintly rocking. "Are you... alright? You were... screaming..."

Adalinda forced herself to replace the pillow, to stand and walk into the kitchen. "It was a dream. It happens."

"Yes, but *that*—" Christensen glanced between Adalinda and the couch, flicking his hand in a frantic gesture. "That was *not normal*."

Adalinda poured herself a glass of water, raised it to her lips and took an unsteady mouthful. She swallowed before she spoke. "Let me ask you, Christensen. What, exactly, about me looks normal?"

"I feel like that's a trick question and it's going to get me slapped..."

Adalinda frowned, lifting the glass again and emptying it. She wiped a hand across her mouth. "Smarter than he looks."

Christensen stalked forward, pointing his finger at her accusingly. "I don't know what your game is, Adalinda, but ever since you arrived Donovan hasn't been himself."

"And you think that's my fault?"

"Yes."

"You don't think the *murders* might be a factor?"

"No. It's definitely you."

Adalinda set her glass down, turning to lean her elbows on the bench. "Explain to me what I have done to disconnect Donovan from himself."

Christensen narrowed his eyes.

"Are you going to answer or just glare at me, Detective?"

"Your arm isn't bandaged."

Adalinda looked down at her arm, covered by the sleeve of Donovan's robe. "It wasn't as bad as it looked."

"Your eyes glow in the dark."

"So do a cats."

"You never remove your scarf."

Monster.

Adalinda flinched, a flicker in her calm, almost indiscernible. She tapped her fingers on the bench and sucked in a breath. "Did Clarke find anything?"

"No, she's going to meet us at the gallery after breakfast."

Adalinda straightened, pulling Donovan's robe tighter around her waist. "I'm going to get changed." She walked around the bench, heading towards her bedroom, but paused in front of Christensen. "I didn't do anything to Donovan. If you want to know why he's changed then I suggest asking him yourself instead of taking it out on me." She kept moving before he could answer, teeth clenched tight, still flustered from her dream. She could taste the salt of her tears, despite having wiped them away.

When she closed her eyes, all she could see was blood.

She walked into her bedroom to find a torrent of sunlight flooding over the balconies, reaching past the windows and spilling onto the floor. She removed Donovan's robe, draped it over the bed and padded to the set of drawers where she had a change of clothes.

She pulled the clothes on while staring at the bed, fingers uncontrollably trembling, deaf to the sounds of the apartment door closing and Christensen's irritable grumbling.

She just saw the blood.

It was everywhere.

And nowhere.

It was on her hands, on her face, on the floor.

It was not hers.

And it was.

Adalinda lowered herself to the bed, scalp crawling. How could blood both belong to her and not?

She dropped her face into her hands, rubbing her eyes, massaging her temples. The dream must have come through the veil, through the darkness smothering her memories. She had no other explanation. It had been too real.

Though all dreams felt real to a dreamer. Small, indisputable truths which clung to the subconscious.

Adalinda grabbed her cloak and stood, leaving the quiet room to find Donovan standing in the kitchen with breakfast. Steaming apple muffins, pastries and fruit. He handed her a muffin, his ocean eyes concerned. Christensen must have told him what had happened when she woke.

"How are you feeling?"

"Angry, tired and hungry." Adalinda tore at her muffin, placing a chunk into her mouth and hanging her cloak on a stool. "I may be the flesh equivalent of hell this morning."

Donovan arched a brow at Christensen, who shrugged and glared at his pastry. "I guess you'll be wanting this then." He pulled a chocolate tart from the bag on the bench.

Adalinda stared at the tart, chewing another bite of her muffin. She looked up at Donovan. "That's for me?"

He smiled and she felt herself melt.

Adalinda set her muffin aside and took the tart, considering it. "This is *not* morning food, you do realise."

"Then eat it this afternoon when we get back from the gallery."

Adalinda set the tart back down, staring at the assorted berries on its' surface as she retrieved her muffin, a feeling of inexplicable fragility coupling with her lingering dread. She sat down at the bench and continued eating, trying to dislodge the tightness in her throat as she looked back up at Donovan. "You'll have to share it with me."

He nodded, taking the tart and placing it in the fridge.

Christensen shot Adalinda a dark look as she took another bite of her muffin. "We need to go, Clarke will be leaving soon." He stood, walking to the door and shrugging on his leather jacket. "I called Iveta to ask if she could meet us there, since she's the only one with a set of keys."

Donovan nodded, taking one of the muffins, a pastry and an apple. "Let's hope we find something." He took a bite of the muffin, his eyes shifting to Adalinda as he chewed, swallowed, then turned to follow Christensen.

Adalinda took her cloak and the rest of her muffin and followed them out the door.

Chapter Thirty - Four

Adalinda stood by the gallery entrance, peering through a window. A man was sitting on the desk inside, swinging his legs as he stared at the ceiling. Completely oblivious to her presence.

Iveta grabbed Adalinda's arm and hauled her away from the glass. "Is that the *murderer*?"

Adalinda nodded, feeling her pulse thundering through her veins, throbbing in her ears.

"What is the *murderer* doing here?"

Adalinda lifted a finger to her lips, narrowing her eyes, signalling for Iveta to be quiet. The woman pursed her lips but made no further comment as she retrieved a set of keys from her coat and stepped up to the gallery entrance.

Beside her, Clarke snuck forward, squinting through the windows to get a better look.

Iveta unlocked the door and retreated.

Donovan glanced at Christensen, jutting his chin towards the door as he drew his gun. The firearm glinted in his hand, matching the anger in his eyes. Christensen lowered his chin in a confirming nod and they moved, storming inside. The door swung viciously on its' hinges, slamming open and ricocheting back.

"*Get on the floor!*"

Theodore released a startled cry. He scrambled backwards, tipped over the edge of the desk and fell. Heavily. Adalinda heard a string of violent curses as Donovan and Christensen crossed the room. She stole a deep breath, the air seeming thick as it travelled down her throat, released her fists and strode towards the door.

"Wait." Iveta hissed. "What if he has a gun?"

Murderer.

Adalinda stiffened, pausing only a moment before slipping into the gallery.

Theodore lay sprawled beside the desk, his back planted on the marble floor, his legs partially caught on the white surface, feet in the air.

Fire ripped through Adalinda as Theodore untangled himself and stood, brushing his hands on his thighs, the simple act taunting her as she imagined those hands holding a knife to a delicate throat.

"Well." Theodore straightened and ran a hand through his dishevelled hair. "*Finally.*" He shook his head and moved around the desk, ignoring the aimed gun-barrels as he crossed his arms. "I was beginning to think you weren't coming." His mud and moss eyes flicked over the Detectives' before settling on Adalinda. "I was getting *so bored.* You don't really understand how bored you can get until you sit and wait for someone to arrive." He let his arms fall to his sides and took a step forward, speaking to Christensen as the man flinched. "I hope you don't have an itchy trigger finger. I hadn't planned on being *shot* today."

Donovan raised a dark brow. "We have a few questions for you."

Theodore glanced at the Detective, then returned his attention to Adalinda. "You look rather lovely today, Adalinda. New cloak?"

Adalinda forced herself not to flinch as he examined her clothing. "I like the boots and leather pants." He smiled, revealing perfectly aligned, ivory teeth. "Elegant but tough."

Donovan's muscles locked as a threatening growl escaped his throat. "Do not address her."

Adalinda tightened her fists, vaguely aware of Iveta and Clarke stealing into the gallery.

Theodore stood calmly, his lips lifted in a comfortable smile as he leisurely dragged his gaze over Adalinda again, pausing when he reached the curve of her slim waist.

Donovan's eyes narrowed, sparking viciously. He took a step forward.

"Calm down, I'm only looking." Theodore raised his hands defensively, turning to meet Donovan's cold stare. "I came because I have information."

A groove formed in Christensen's brow. "If you have information, why were you watching the apartment last night?"

"I was just passing through?"

Donovan adjusted his grip on the gun.

"... I have my reasons." Theodore shrugged and looked back at Adalinda. "You're fucking terrifying, by the way."

Adalinda straightened her back, fists constricting beneath her cloak. "You have *no* idea." Theodore smirked and she went rigid as she struggled to keep herself steady. She forced words through her clamped teeth, seething and boiling beneath her draping cloak. "You *murdered* those women."

Theodore huffed. "I did not."

Adalinda's glare sparked venomously. Her fists opened into claws and the heel of her boot lifted as she shifted her weight, preparing to tear Theodore's face from his skull.

A rumble of warning scaled Donovan's throat.

"You're supposed to reply with 'did too' and then we can have a verbal fight until Donovan gets angry and starts growling." Theodore smiled at Adalinda, slight dimples appearing on his smooth cheeks as he waited for her to take the bait. He was playing with her, like a child. He *wanted* her to react.

Adalinda flexed her fingers and bared her teeth, but didn't move.

Theodore watched her for a moment, waiting. His smile began to wilt, shoulders drooping. He rolled his head back on his neck and stared at the ceiling. "Oh, *come on!*" He tilted his head down to stare at her with widened eyes. "*Nothing?* I give you the perfect opportunity for a slap and you choose to do *nothing?*"

Adalinda slid her glare to Donovan. He shook his head and she let out an exasperated breath, spinning on her heel and stalking across the room.

"Like a dog on a leash." Theodore sighed, shoving his hands into his pockets and returning his focus to Donovan. "Well, *she's* in a bad mood." He leaned back against the desk, quirking the corner of his mouth, his brows climbing suggestively. "Not getting any yet?"

Donovan marched forward and planted the barrel of his gun in Theodore's hair, his ocean eyes simmering.

Theodore winced. "I take that as a *no.*"

Donovan gritted his teeth. "Start talking."

Theodore removed his hands from his pockets and tugged at the cuffs of his tweed jacket, leaning away from Donovan's gun. "Honestly, I thought you were going to find me much more quickly. You detectives are getting *slow.*" Theodore quirked a brow as Donovan clamped his jaw, a muscle in his neck twitching irritably. "You know, the last time I was held at gunpoint it was *very* different. It was a plastic gun, you know? Less talking and more..." Theodore smiled. "Well, we know it's not what *you're* getting."

Donovan shoved the barrel of his gun further into Theodore's temple, pushing the man until his face was pressed against the surface of the desk, cheek flattened. "Don't press me, pretty boy."

"You think I'm pretty?" Theodore forced a smile, his eyes seeking out Adalinda around the edge of Donovan's hip. "You're not just saying that are you? Because that would be really mean if you said it and didn't *believe* it—"

"Keep talking, Theodore. We'll see how far I can push this gun into your skull."

"Now that *is* mean." Theodore's smile fell from his face as Donovan shifted the weight on his gun, pressing it yet further into the man's hairline. "Stop. *Stop!* You're going to leave a bruise! I didn't *kill* anyone, okay? Do I *look* like a murderer to you?"

Christensen pursed his lips as he regarded Theodore, the man's face still wedged against the desk. "*Seriously?*"

Donovan stared at Theodore, considering the man's uncovered hands, his mussed and tousled hair.

Adalinda narrowed her eyes.

"He didn't kill anyone. Look at him, he's not wearing gloves, he's leaving fingerprints everywhere." Donovan pulled the gun away from Theodore's head. "If anything, he's a distraction."

Theodore straightened, rubbing a hand against his cheek. "*Exactly.*" He slid his gaze over Iveta and Clarke, lifting a hand in a condensed wave, fingers wiggling. He smiled and Iveta blushed.

Christensen stepped forward to take Donovan's place. "What do you know?"

Theodore shrugged, watching as Adalinda continued pacing through the gallery, her steps silent on the marble floor, her fingers lifting to brush the fabric around her head. "What's under the scarf, Adalinda?"

Adalinda stiffened. She turned, her eyes blazing fire.

"If you aren't going to answer, why don't you get me a glass of water? I'm thirsty."

Christensen swore under his breath and grabbed Theodore by the collar. "Maybe if you would *shut up* for a second your saliva would have time to refill *your mouth* and you wouldn't be so *fucking thirsty.*"

Theodore gasped, his gaze snapping to Christensen. "I will *not* shut up. My saliva has *nothing* to do with my *dehydration*. And I *like* to talk." The smirk returned to his lips as Christensen gritted his teeth. "My voice is damned angelic."

Christensen's fists tightened on Theodore's collar. "Answer the question."

Theodore's smirk widened, facetious as it spread across his face. "What was the question, again? Honestly, I wasn't listening."

Christensen dragged in a deep, deliberate breath, forcing himself to calm. His hands dropped from Theodore's collar. "What do you know?"

"I know a lot of things. You're going to have to be more specific."

Adalinda stopped before the glass imitation of her sculpture, staring at the swirls of painted marble decorating its' surface. She frowned, reaching out to brush the figure's arm with the tips of her fingers. "How did the murderer get in?"

Theodore stood and moved away from Christensen. "How do you *think* he got in?"

"He didn't come from the street, not through Iveta's windows or through the gallery entrance. The only alternative is the basement..." Adalinda's brows narrowed as she turned, her gaze falling on Theodore. "But how did he get *into* the basement?"

"Now *that* is a specific question." Theodore brushed the sleeve of his jacket, inspecting it for non-existent lint. He wove around Donovan, still moving towards Adalinda. "He used the stairs. Obviously."

"The stairs?" Donovan closed a hand over Theodore's shoulder, stopping the man in his tracks. "Where are the stairs?"

"Call me 'pretty boy' again and I might tell you."

Donovan began to lift his gun.

Theodore rolled his eyes, ducking away from Donovan. "The stairs are behind a shelf. Where *else* would stairs be in a basement? *Good Lord.* Use your *imagination.*"

"Um... I have a question..." Clarke cleared her throat, stepping away from Iveta who was methodically braiding and unbraiding her hair. She trailed her eyes over Theodore. "If you aren't the murderer then who the fuck are you and why were you *waiting* for us to *arrive*? You realise that's creepy, right?"

"I..." Theodore smiled, straightening his jacket. "Am God's gift. Literally. The name Theodore originates from the Latin name Theodorus, meaning 'God's gift.' In this case it isn't really *God's* gift so much as—"

Clarke held up a hand, cutting him off. "I'm sorry, you're going to need to start again because I got distracted by your *face*." She scratched her head, knitting her brows. "I mean, realistically, *who is that pretty?* I keep thinking you're going to *blind* me, you know, like when you stare into the sun and you get dots in your vision? I'm going to have little versions of Theodore just hovering there like bursts of inverted sunlight... or *lightning.*" Clarke stalked over to Theodore and began lifting his arms, twisting his shoulders, squeezing his face with deft fingers and pushing at the flesh as if she were moulding clay. "... Is there an *off-switch* somewhere...?"

Theodore took Clarke by the wrists and pulled her hands away from his face. He stared at her, his expression darkening. "What?"

"No off-switch then?"

"... I honestly don't know what to say to you."

Adalinda closed her eyes, pressing her fingers to the bridge of her nose. She stopped listening and focused on her breathing, on the passage of air in and out of her lungs, the soft crawling prickle beneath the fabric of her scarf, the scent of woodsmoke and pouring rain...

"Are you alright?"

Adalinda turned to find Donovan looming at her back, his eyes searching, his lips pressing in a firm, tempting line.

"We need to find those stairs."

Donovan nodded, then brushed past Adalinda and strode towards the basement entrance. "Christensen, bring Theodore, we'll need him. Clarke, see if you can find anything the murderer might have left behind. Iveta." Donovan paused, glancing over his shoulder. "... Wait here."

"What?" Iveta looked up, her fingers locking mid-braid. "No, there's no *way* I'm doing that. There's a *murderer* out there killing young, beautiful women..." Her wide eyes drifted to Christensen. "*I'm* a young, beautiful woman!"

Theodore grumbled under his breath. "I'm beautiful too... No one's worried about *my* safety."

Iveta exhaled a piqued breath. "Are *you* a *woman?*"

"I could be."

Iveta presented Theodore with a look as flat as a salt plain.

Theodore bristled. "*You* don't know."

"He's a man." Clarke pointed at Theodore's crotch. "There's a bulge."

Christensen coughed, hiding a laugh.

"See?" Iveta lifted her chin, triumphant. "Told you. Can we go into the basement now, please? I don't want to get *murdered.*"

"Well, there's a sentence I never thought I'd hear." Clarke ran a hand through the short side of her hair, tucking it behind her ear and moving to follow Donovan. "Let's go into the ominously dark basement so we *don't* get murdered."

Adalinda stopped before the door at the back of the gallery, fingers curling, scalp crawling.

It creaked as Donovan pushed it open.

"Oh look, the door squeaks, that's fucking marvellous." Clarke slipped between Donovan and Adalinda, tromping down the concrete stairs into darkness. Her voice echoed into the gallery. "Guess I'll be the first to die. If I start screaming, back the fuck up."

Adalinda looked at Donovan, damping the fear rising in her stomach. She stepped through the door, edging her way down the stairs, one hand on the cold, stone wall. She bit her cheek, fighting the memories and trying to ignore the hollow footsteps following her down.

Something clicked.

Light flared. Bright and brutal.

Iveta planted her hands on her hips. "You forgot the lights. Who walks into a basement without checking for a light switch?"

"I do." Clarke shrugged, turning a corner and reaching the bottom of the stairs. She stepped out into a maze of shelves, cabinets and paintings hung from walls of wire mesh. "I'm just badass like that."

Adalinda crossed her arms over her chest, keeping her hands away from her scarf. She drifted into the basement and glanced over her shoulder at Theodore. "You said the stairs were behind a shelf."

Theodore shook Christensen's hand from his shoulder and gestured into the maze, spread beneath the gallery and back towards the street. "It's on the far wall. Looks like everything else."

"How do you know this?" Clarke frowned, waiting for Theodore to take the lead.

Theodore was quiet for a moment. He lifted a hand to rub the back of his neck. "I accidentally stumbled across it..."

"Well that's *clearly* a lie."

"The first murder was a girl I was courting, okay? I wanted to find out why she was murdered so I went looking." Theodore pursed his lips, glaring at the ground. "I received an anonymous message the night before last, creepy as all hell, a note slipped under my door telling me to take a look at a shelf at the back of the gallery's basement." Theodore stopped walking. "I don't actually know what it looks like, I only know what I was told."

Christensen glanced at Donovan, then back at Theodore. "Where's the note?"

Theodore pulled a crumpled piece of paper from the pocket of his jacket, handing it to Christensen.

Christensen held it up, staring at the blacked out words, the dripping ink, the swirling script. "It looks like the torn paper we found scattered around Anna's body."

Adalinda shuddered, her fingers tightening around her crossed arms as Donovan placed a comforting hand on the back of her shoulder.

Theodore kept moving, leading the group further into the basement. He reached the end.

Turned the corner.

Stopped.

A wooden cabinet stood on an angle, its' glass doors shielding a collection of intricate, bronze castings and a single, painted vase. It appeared to have been partially pulled away from the wall, revealing a sliver of darkness beyond.

Theodore stepped back. "... It's open..."

Clarke crept forward, peering into the cabinet. "There's something in the vase..." She reached forward and opened the glass door, gently pulling a note from the vase's neck. She paused. Reading. "Um... Not to ruin anyone's fun but I think we should turn around and go home. Let the murderer go. He's clearly a psychopath. Maybe he'll walk in front of a car and we'll be rid of him."

Donovan rumbled a growl, stepping closer to Adalinda and nudging her behind him. "What does it say, Clarke?"

Clarke pursed her lips, as if she didn't want to speak the words. She looked up at Donovan. "It says 'Let the hunt begin'..."

Donovan flinched, recoiling.

"*Fuck* that." Christensen shuddered, shaking his head and turning to go. "I'm not playing chicken with a murderer." He stalked over and grabbed Clarke by the arm, dragging her away from the open cabinet. "Let's go. No one's dying today."

Iveta brushed her woollen skirt, the thick fabric draping to her ankles, her heeled boots clicking on the floor as she shifted her weight. "You're supposed to be a detective. Isn't this your *job*?"

"There's a limit." Christensen pointed at the note. "And *that* just crossed it."

"... We know he's in there."

Christensen paused and turned towards Donovan. "That doesn't make it any better."

"We have to go in. If we don't we might lose him."

Christensen grumbled a curse, continuing to walk back through the shelves.

"If we lose him there'll be another murder."

Christensen stopped. He stared at the wall, still clinging to Clarke.

"We have weapons. I'll go first."

Christensen dragged a hand over his face, looked over his shoulder. "If we die, it's your fault."

Donovan nodded, his gaze drifting to Adalinda. "You're staying here."

Adalinda raised a brow, her golden eyes glinting challenge.

Donovan sighed, drawing his gun and stalking towards the cabinet, towards the sliver of darkness, the cavity between the makeshift door and the concrete wall. "Fine. Then at least stay behind me."

Iveta pressed her lips, lifted her chin and began to follow, Clarke at her side.

"I'm going to stay up here, if it's all the same to you." Theodore lifted his hand in a nonchalant wave. "Have fun being murdered." He disappeared into the shelves.

Christensen swore under his breath, seeming conflicted as to whether or not he should follow.

Donovan curled his fingers around the edge of the cabinet, pulling it further away from the wall. It glided back, smooth and quiet, revealing a winding, concrete staircase. "Leave him. If you hear a gunshot, I want you to run. Do *not* wait for me." He began to move into the stairwell, then stopped. "Iveta, go back upstairs. And take Clarke."

Clarke released a humourless laugh. "I'm not going anywhere. If there's a gunshot I'll just hide behind you... you know, because you're basically a shield."

Adalinda placed a cool hand on Donovan's arm as his muscles grew rigid. She leaned in, breathing his scent of woodsmoke and rain, feeling the warmth drifting from him in waves. She spoke in a soft murmur so as not to be overheard. "If something happens I'll get them out. You saw the wounds on my arm, I'm not that easy to kill. This is not going to end with another death."

Donovan set his jaw, glancing back at her. "Infuriating woman."

Adalinda forced a reassuring smile, squeezing his arm and stepping back.

Donovan moved forward and she followed him down the stairs.

Smoke and Scarlet

Ten Years Ago

DONOVAN SCANNED THE FROZEN LAKE, *vainly seeking answers among the layers of crystalline ice. He could see the lakebed through patches in the snow, an unbroken layer of stones beneath water, some smooth, others rough, some as large as boulders.*

It had been easy to find.

Too easy.

The sun had just begun its' ascent over the horizon as he departed the cabin, wandering the streets while the soft hues of morning kissed the sky. He had ignored the wooden buildings and quiet roads, lost in thought until he found himself staring out over the solid expanse of iced-over water.

He could almost feel the liquid pausing as it brushed against his skin.

Donovan frowned and repressed the memory, focusing on the gusting wind as it tousled the waves of his hair, ceaselessly nipping at the exposed skin of his cheeks, rough with stubble he had neglected to shave. His stomach twisted, gloved fingers twitching as he scoured his empty mind for answers. He found nothing but a billowing veil, unreachable memories which twirled on the edge of his consciousness, leaving him with an infuriatingly vague impression of something important, something lost and irretrievable.

Icy liquid nudged against his bloodless lips.

Donovan pressed his mouth in a hard line as he turned from the lake, his long, charcoal coat snapping at his shins.

An incoherent whisper brushed over him. Full of longing. Brimming with pleas.

Donovan paused, brows furrowing as he turned towards the sound. His skin heated in response.

The water of the lake sighed beneath the ice. Calling. Begging.

A sound that should have been silent.

Donovan turned away, shoving his gloved hands into his pockets and leaving the lake, his long strides carrying him back to the small mountain village. The furrow between his brows deepened, his ocean eyes lifting to the pale, cerulean sky in response to a faint scent of burning wood, wafting down the snowed-over path. He shook his head, shoving his fists further into his pockets as he dismissed the smell.

It was winter.

People lit fires.

He stared vacantly at the snow depressing beneath his boots, compacting silently as if afraid to interrupt his ruminating quiet. He drifted into the village like a shadowed wraith, fuming over the loss of his memories. The dissipated scent of smoke increased as he moved, curling around him in condensing threads until they became whirling tentacles, pirouetting with the occasional, fevered breath of heated air.

Donovan blinked as a flake of soot drifted to settle on the snow before him, snapping his concentration and plucking the self-imposed shield from his senses.

The muffled roar of a raging fire poured from above, ceaseless in its' savage melody.

Donovan drifted to a stop, glancing up at the chalet across the street, at the flames which ravenously lashed against the tarnishing windows of the second floor.

People were crowding from their homes, staring at the flames, pointing and screaming.

Donovan adjusted his shoulders beneath his charcoal coat, ocean eyes tearing from the flames as he stepped forward, his boot crushing the flake of soot into the snow. He stepped around the people spilling from the building, narrowly avoiding a graceful man in a scarlet coat.

The chorus of shrieks and cries scraped over him, grating against his decision to leave.

There was nothing he could do.

He would not endanger his life for an empty, burning building.

"Is that a child?"

Donovan stopped, tensed.

The man in scarlet pointed a slender finger at the smoke-veiled window of the third floor. "My God, it's a little boy!"

Donovan swore, the curse tumbling from his lips as he pivoted, searching for the child's location. Third floor apartment. Furthest window. Donovan shoved through the crowd, crashing through the door of the burning chalet and flying up the charring, wooden stairs. Clouds of smoke rippled in the air, plunging into his lungs as he rushed past the second floor, the exquisite kitchen-lounge consumed by flames, the bedroom doors hanging open. He grabbed the bannister and hauled himself around a bend in the stairs, billowing heat clinging to him, seeping through the heavy fabric of his coat. He bounded upwards, the smoke thickening as he climbed, the taste of burning wood collecting on his tongue.

Donovan squared his shoulders and lunged up the final steps, bursting onto the third floor in a cloud of soot and ash. The apartment's lounge beyond was silent, perfectly calm aside from the groaning wood of the floorboards and the burning scent which hung like death in the air.

"Hello?" Donovan's voice melted through the walls, its' honey mixing with the smoke as he jogged to the furthest room, all too aware of the flames eating through the ceiling in the apartment below.

He twisted the doorknob at the far end of the chalet, rattling it when he realised it was jammed. A whimper seeped through the door and Donovan drove his shoulder into the wood, splintering the lock and striding inside.

The boy stood at the window, pyjamas hanging loosely on his stricken frame. He stared down at the fire which had burst through the glass in the apartment below, his white knuckled fingers gripping the window frame.

"We need to go." Donovan moved smoothly across the room, careful to keep his voice low and calm. "It's not safe here. Is there anyone else?"

Wide, dark eyes turned to him. The boy pursed his lips and shook his head.

Donovan crouched before the child, lowering one knee to the ground so he seemed less imposing. "I'm going to carry you down, alright?"

The boy dipped his chin in a mute nod as Donovan plucked him from the floor and strode for the door, moving towards the stairwell. "You need to cover your eyes."

The boy lifted his hands to his face, sucking in a ragged breath. Donovan started down the stairs. Smoke spewed from the lower floor like a black hand, its' fingers curling around them both.

The boy began to cough uncontrollably and Donovan cursed under his breath, lunging back to the third floor. If he took the boy down there the child would suffocate.

Another silent curse sharpened his lips and he turned, moving back along the hall and glancing through the open doors at the empty windows.

Each window lead to a balcony, though he doubted he could climb past the fire.

The boy gingerly parted his fingers, peeking through them at Donovan's furrowed expression. Donovan's eyes flicked to him, momentarily softening as the boy stared. He forced his mouth to curl in a reassuring smile as he strode to the boy's room and disappeared inside. He paused, his grip on the boy tightening as a hissing interrupted the persistent growl of the fire.

Donovan glanced at the gas heater, his heart thundering in his chest, ocean eyes widening.

The flames were eating through the pipes.

Donovan made the decision instantly, instinctively, launching across the room and curling himself protectively around the boy as he flung himself against the window.

Glass shattered, shards glinting in the morning light, reflecting the boy's gaping mouth as a blood curdling shriek wrenched from his throat.

Flames burst through the room, parts of the heater exploding and embedding themselves in the walls. Fire shot through the third floor, the gas causing consecutive explosions, smashing through walls with impossible force.

A great plume of blazing flame spewed from the windows, the shockwave colliding with Donovan's back and flinging him through the air, away from the building. He tightened his grip on the boy as debris sprayed around them, glass and splintered wood showering the pavement.

Donovan fought the panic rising in his throat, the deafening pulse crashing through his veins, as he twisted and plummeted, using himself as a shield between the boy and the ground.

Donovan squeezed his eyes shut.

Glass from the shattered windows detonated as they struck the road, the shards fracturing and sprawling across the street, glittering in the snow.

The ground thrust the breath from Donovan's lungs, pain lanced through his shoulders, down his spine, as his back slid across pavement. His coat tore beneath him, the wool catching on the uneven ground and ripping down the back.

The gutter caught him, the nape of his neck striking concrete.

A gasped breath filled his lungs, his chest heaving beneath the boy.

The boy.

Donovan peered down at the frail body cradled in his arms, like a toothpick between clenched teeth.

Immediately, Donovan released his grip and the boy coughed, gaping at Donovan as he planted his miniature hands on Donovan's chest and pushed himself up.

"Let's do that again!"

A relieved sigh blew from Donovan's lips and he collapsed, the back of his head striking the pavement. "Let's not." When he opened his eyes the boy was grinning at him, exposing a number of gaps where adult teeth were sprouting. "Where are your parents?"

"At work." The boy shrugged, content in his position sitting atop Donovan's muscled torso. "How did you do that?"

Donovan grunted as he pushed to his elbows, ocean eyes scanning the gathering crowd, the men and women hosing down the flames, most of them staring. "Do what?"

The boy tilted his head, his mop of blonde hair swinging in response. "Survive jumping from that height."

Donovan reached out and lifted the boy, depositing him on the cold ground. "I don't know."

"Why not?"

Donovan's nostrils flared as he let out an exasperated breath. "Because sometimes adults don't know." He set his hands into the snow and shoved himself upright, revelling in his lack of injuries. "Do you always ask so many questions?"

The boy chewed his lip, considering Donovan's question as a single doctor pushed through the murmuring crowd. "Yes." He lowered his chin in an exuberant nod. "I like questions."

Donovan removed his coat and glared at the doctor as she told him to sit back down. "Call the boy's parents. Let them know what happened." He flicked the debris from the ruined fabric of his coat. "And leave me alone."

The doctor bit her lip, blinking up at him with irritated, ice blue eyes, her hair hidden beneath a knitted cap. "Sir..."

A growl rumbled deep in Donovan's chest. "No." He turned to the boy who grinned up at him, dark eyes bright and unfazed. "Go with the doctor, she'll look after you for now."

The grin dropped from the boy's face as he watched Donovan stride through the crowd. He ignored the whispers and murmurs, inspecting his damaged coat and turning down an alley, leaving the fire to the villagers, needing a moment to think.

"That was quite the stunt you just pulled."

Donovan groaned, raising his eyes to the smoke filled sky. He wanted to be alone. He needed to be alone. "Go away."

"Hold on." A gloved hand grasped Donovan's shoulder, the accompanying voice fluid and impossibly familiar. "I have a question for you."

Donovan clenched his fists beneath the draping fabric of his ruined coat. "I don't have any answers." He turned, simmering as his glare landed on the graceful man in the scarlet coat. "And even if I did—"

"You wouldn't tell me?" Disturbingly violet eyes glinted in the dim light of the alley. "Oh, I didn't think you would." The man released Donovan's shoulder and stepped forward, exposing the glinting tip of a syringe, the metal shimmering like mist beneath glass. "I simply wanted to get your attention." The man plunged the syringe into Donovan's neck, the daffodil liquid inside disappearing into his artery.

Donovan lifted a hand, grabbing for the needle as the man withdrew it from his neck and stepped back, easily avoiding Donovan's reach.

"Have a lovely sleep." The violet-eyed man's smile was a knife's edge as he waved his fingers in Donovan's face. Donovan lethargically lifted his fists and stumbled, his coat slipping from his arm, his body collapsing against a wooden wall beside the burning building. A light laugh escaped the violet-eyed man, fluttering over Donovan like the wings of a dragonfly as his thoughts began to slip. "The paralysis won't last too long. I doubt it'll kill you, though you might have a slight headache on waking."

A violent curse slurred through Donovan's lips.

"Oh, don't be so tedious. You saved that boy from the fire, I'd say that was bordering on heroic." The man crouched beside Donovan, his figure nothing more than a scarlet blur. "If you're lucky, and I'm feeling generous, it might even earn you some answers."

Donovan groaned, feeling himself tip, crashing into the pavement.

The man dissolved into bright, white light.

CHAPTER THIRTY - FIVE

DONOVAN CLENCHED HIS EYES shut as he felt the world slip away, the dark echoing stairs, the rising temperature, the humid air. He lost himself, hearing the recurrence of Clarke's voice in his head, reading those words, that note.

"... *Let the hunt begin...*"

Donovan's hold on his memories slipped.

Violet eyes flashed like a shade through his mind.

Donovan gritted his teeth and shook himself, forcing the memories back. The muscles in his jaw hardened, he shifted his grip on the gun, scanning the stairwell. Light. There was light pouring up the steps. The temperature rose around him, clinging to him as if it were tangible, shifting around him as if it were alive. He pressed his back to the red-brick wall, gun aimed at the ground.

He peered around the corner.

Into blinding, heated light.

Donovan blinked, waiting for his eyes to adjust. He crept around the corner, down the last of the concrete steps.

And stopped.

Clarke moved forward, heels loudly connecting with the last step, jade and topaz eyes sweeping over his shoulder. Amazement poured over her elven features, freezing her expression. Her lips parted slightly. Her jaw dropped. "... Well, shit."

The stairwell descended into heaven.

The whisper of trickling water kissed Donovan's ears. A stream carved the room, weaving through emerald grass, gurgling beside a paved path of polished, ivory stones. The water slid between apple trees, pale blossoms thriving as light caressed their velvet petals, their intoxicating perfume wafting on a light breeze as the heated air rose to the cold storage room above.

Adalinda's shoulder grazed Donovan as she slid past, moving onto the grass, her boots sinking into the thick emerald blades as if it were a natural carpet. She drifted towards a patch of brilliant gold, reaching down to let her fingers brush the soft petals of vibrant daffodils.

Clarke glanced at Christensen, his expression bewildered as she stepped onto the path, moving across the grass to stare at the vines of white roses and violet wisteria scaling the steep, brick walls. "I live here now. Everyone get out."

Iveta wandered from the stairwell, passing Donovan, then Adalinda, as she moved towards a sculpture, a woman carved of marble partially hidden behind the slim trunk of a tree.

A leaning dancer, arms elegantly extended, unseeing eyes gazing eternally up.

"The sculpture..." Iveta inhaled a breath, long and deep. More sculptures were spread through the garden, placed between clay pots of decadent orchids, parts of their bodies cocooned in the possessive tendrils of vines, sweeping across naked hips, reaching over curvaceous legs. "All of these are remarkably similar to your style, Adalinda."

Adalinda straightened and returned to the path, her troubled gaze shifting over the contents of the room. "None of these are mine..."

"Aside from this one." Iveta murmured, still staring at the sculpted dancer, a perfect duplicate of the figure of painted glass which remained in the gallery above.

Donovan walked along the path, scanning the sculptures, the trees and vines, searching for shadows which might hide a murderer. He listened, past the gasps and murmurs, past the hushing brook, to the rumbling splash of falling water as the stream abruptly vanished, disappearing down the centre of a second stairwell of twisted, gleaming copper.

Donovan kept walking, tense as a mountain, with his gun aimed at the descending stairs.

The light of the basement below was dim, but Donovan could see the vague impression of a pool through the breaks in the steps, through the leaves and flowers cut into the copper. The stream fell through the hole created by the spiralling bannister, its' water whispering.

Calling.

Donovan's breath hitched, a hollow feeling stretching through his chest.

His skin began to tingle.

Warmth unfurled in his veins.

The moisture in the air began to thicken, collecting around his form.

Donovan began to edge down the stairs, eyes narrowed, brow creased. He glanced at the water falling at his side, its' mist slicking the copper steps. He could feel his heart dancing with his sternum, the pulse thudding through bone.

Christensen rushed down the path after Donovan, throwing an apprehensive look at the women and gesturing for them to wait.

Clarke's voice wafted with the plummeting stream, almost lost as Donovan rounded the stairs. "Well... Apparently we're doing that, then."

Donovan reached the bottom, finding himself in the heart of an inch deep pool, its' water somehow draining into the floor. Another path began at its' edge, black as polished obsidian, with sculptures guarding its' length as it stretch through a second garden; this one overgrown, wild, filled with tall grasses and beds of flowers, indigo and orange, scarlet as blood, their colours faded in the second basements dulled light.

Donovan knew they were all toxic.

He wasn't sure how.

"Keep your voices down. And don't touch the flowers." Donovan glanced at Christensen, back up the stairs towards Adalinda who was trailing her hand through the cascading water. The falling liquid almost muted his voice. "They're poisonous." He stepped into the shallow pool, feeling the water seep into his boots.

"The *flowers* are poisonous?" Christensen hissed, stretching his neck and lifting his gun. "Oh, alright. *No worries then.*"

Iveta trudged off the steps after Adalinda, her hands gripping the woollen fabric of her skirt. She cringed as she held it above the water. "What kind of sadistic maniac plants a toxic garden in a basement?"

Clarke's gaze sparked as she skipped past Iveta, splashing through the pool and grinning childishly. "I *definitely* would if I had the resources."

"Obviously." Christensen grumbled, watching Donovan as he moved out of the water and onto the obsidian path. "What else is to be expected of a person who cuts dead people open for a living."

Clarke beamed proudly, smiling up at the sculptures as she inspected them. "Yes. This is my home now."

Donovan sucked in a breath as Adalinda closed the distance between them, her shoulder brushing his arm. "There's another staircase." She gestured to the far end of the room, where a set of shadowed, concrete stairs disappeared beneath the floor.

Donovan grunted confirmation. The humidity here was more dense than upstairs, he could feel the moisture as he inhaled heavy breaths, sweat beginning to seep down his temples.

Adalinda removed her cloak and hung it from a sculpture.

"How do they pollenate the flowers?" Iveta whispered, frowning at a patch of tiny, white buds rising on thin stalks from the ground. "I don't hear any bees."

Clarke smiled as she turned her head to Iveta. "Maybe the bees are *silent.*"

Iveta flicked her manicured nails nervously, skirt still bunched in one hand.

Adalinda paused to peer at a ceramic pot filled with deadly nightshade, its' limbs spilling out over the edge. "... Why go to all this effort?"

"Someone must *really* dislike you." Clarke clicked her tongue and pivoted, spinning around before continuing as she had been before. "What did you *do* in your past life?"

Adalinda flinched, her elegant hands balling into white-knuckled fists. "... I don't know..." She murmured, rolling her shoulders and lifting a hand to her scarf. "But this seems... excessive."

A clearing spread before him, its' width a deep, jade gash splitting the flesh of the forest.

Donovan swallowed the memory, flexing his fingers and staring pointedly at the wall. The room was open, no trees or crevices, no places to hide...

"Ah..." Clarke paused mid-stride, her eyes falling on the concrete stairs at the end of the path. "We aren't going down *there*, are we?"

Donovan stopped as he reached the third staircase, the concrete disappearing into dense, humid black. "We are."

"Marvellous." Iveta grumbled under her breath. "And I suppose it leads to *another* garden."

Clarke wandered to Donovan's side, bending forward and peering down the steps. "I bet it's a garden full of dead bodies. Skeletons and screaming, decaying—"

"*Gross.*" Iveta span on her heel. "I am *not* going any further, that's just *asking* for trouble. I'll be upstairs if anyone needs me."

Adalinda stared into the darkness as if facing a beast, fear flickering in her eyes. She inhaled a determined breath and shoved a hand into the pocket of Donovan's coat. "Let's go." She pulled out his phone, activated the torch, and started down the stairs. The murderer knew they were coming. There was no sense in hiding their presence.

Donovan swore under his breath, glancing at Christensen and Clarke. "Stay here. I'll call when it's safe." He marched after Adalinda, grabbing her arm and hauling her behind him, the torch of his phone swinging through the dark. "Keep the light moving and stay behind me unless you have a death wish. Warn me if you see anything."

Adalinda nodded, holding the torch beneath his raised arm, angling herself so she could see around the side of his chest, below the gun he aimed at the dark.

Donovan kept her shielded against the wall, his heart a trapped hummingbird in his chest, his breaths as deep as chasms. His whisper was a breath as the darkness consumed them, as Adalinda became nothing more than a warm shadow at his back. "I'm not entirely convinced you *don't* have a death wish..." He could almost feel Adalinda's responding smile. Her shoulder grazed his side, sending shivers over his skin.

Until the torch shifted.

And a face appeared in the dark.

Chapter Thirty - Six

The breath burst from Adalinda's lungs as Donovan leaped back, slamming her against the concrete wall. The phone flew from her fingers and clattering against the stairs.

It shattered.

The torch went black. Plunging them into darkness.

Adalinda pressed her hands into Donovan's back, clinging to his coat, managing a shallow gasp. She could feel his furious pulse, thundering through his spine. A crashing, hammering reflection of her own.

They waited.

Tense.

As invisible to the face as it was to them.

Donovan held his breath, waiting for an attack.

Dread flitted through Adalinda veins.

Slowly, her eyes began to adjust. She blinked, frowning at the patches of cobalt and jade smeared across her vision. Blue and green.

Blurred.

Another garden.

This one *glowing*.

Adalinda shifted and Donovan leaned forward, allowing a shuddering breath to enter her lungs. She kept her voice low, so quiet only Donovan could hear. "What... What was that?"

Donovan shook his head, lowering one hand from his gun and reaching back to find her hand. She let it fall from his back and his fingers curled through hers. She could see them, eerily painted blue and green, faint as a forgotten memory, an apparition in the dark.

And then she looked up. To find the face. The figure. Standing beside the stairs.

Silently screaming.

The blood drained from Adalinda's cheeks, leaving her skin cold and tingling.

Her scalp began to crawl.

It was a sculpture. Hideous with fear. Locked in a nightmare. Hair fell over her cowering shoulders, her fingers were clawed and covering her eyes, their lids almost, but not quite, closed.

Adalinda swore she could see tonsils in the depths of the sculptures gaping mouth.

Donovan's grip tightened on Adalinda's hand and he continued forward, down the last of the steps, keeping her pressed against the concrete wall. The glowing smears began to form shapes, leaves and flowers, vines draping from the ceiling, moss and fungus spread across the floor, all of them luminescent as the stars on a moonless night.

All of them illuminating the screaming expressions of sculptures. Men and women and a single, abandoned child, its' diminutive form paralysed in a terrified ball on the grass, blank eyes gaping and staring into the dark.

Adalinda's teeth sank into her cheek.

The toe of her boot collided with Donovan's shattered phone, sending it skittering off the barely visible path and into a luminescent bush.

A tall, dark figure appeared at the top of the stairs, backlit and warped by the brightness above. Christensen, peering after them into the black.

"Fuck it." Clarke's whisper broke the quiet. "I'm going in." She stomped past Christensen's silhouette and began edging down the stairs, back to the wall, feeling her way as she stepped into the dark.

Christensen mouthed a curse.

Clarke's form rippled slightly in the shadows as she tripped, caught herself, quietly swore. "You're not dead are you?" She murmured. "Because that would *suck*."

"Not yet..." Adalinda let go of Donovan, stepping around him until she stood at his side, feeling the shift from concrete to earth as she departed the final stairs. She glanced at the gun in his hand as he inched forward, further into the luminescent garden, scanning the shadows for places to hide, ducking beneath a low-hanging vine.

"Holy shit." Clarke's boots thudded to a stop. "This is so *much better* than a garden full of dead bodies!"

Christensen aimed his gun, muttering into the dark. "You're not particularly good at *stealth*, are you Clarke?"

Clarke gestured offensively at him and poked out her tongue, her form softly lit by the radiant plants.

Adalinda followed Donovan as he moved deeper into the room, over the path of crumbling dirt, vines rustling and kissing his hair, searching for the murderer.

Stone features emerged from the gleaming foliage as they passed, arms clutching twisted bodies, hands grasping shoulders, fighting to shield themselves from the shadows as moss scaled their ankles, their thighs and stomachs and ribs.

A shudder drove through Adalinda as she passed a set of choking hands threatening to asphyxiate, the sculpted fingers stretching wide and curling like vicious talons, the sculptures lips stretched in a soundless, agonised scream.

Somewhere in the black, feathers impatiently rustled. And a pair of moonbeam eyes blinked.

Then disappeared.

Fear's iron claws squeezed Adalinda's heart as Donovan began to move ahead, scanning the dense curtain of vines hanging along the walls. They drooped over the ground, motionless and matted, concealing the cold stonework with waves of glowing jade.

Let the hunt begin.

Adalinda tilted her head, staring at the wall, dismissing the insistent crawl of warning consuming her scalp. She pictured the notes and desecrated pages of her journal, the warnings and the threats, the murders—

Adalinda's skin began to itch.

Something was watching her.

Her golden eyes snapped to the side.

A bush rippled almost imperceptibly, disturbed by a swooping breeze.

Concern crept over Adalinda's features as she watched the leaves, listened to their susurrate hush.

A moment passed and all was still.

The quiet became weighted.

Strained.

Adalinda turned to Donovan, the air around him cool and humid, as if he called to the moisture, as if it followed him. His back rose before her, gun still aimed and searching. He paused, ocean eyes staring at the wall further down the path, narrowing at a space below the vines. "Light..." His murmur was almost lost in the vast basement.

Adalinda shifted uneasily as Donovan stepped away, her instincts flaring, overwhelming her with a barrage of prickling skin. Her head began to ache. "Donovan..."

The vines on a sculpture fluttered.

A shadow extended across the wall, a figure of vacuous black spreading and growing before the glowing vines.

Adalinda's eyes widened. Her heart lurched in her chest. "*Donovan.*"

He was already moving towards the opposite wall. Away from her. Away from the shadow.

Adalinda took a step, her arm outstretched to grasp his shirt, her eyes pinned on the shadow as it shifted, drawing something from its' cloak.

Donovan turned, brows furrowing in confusion as he noticed her fingertips brushing his elbow, as his gaze trailed up her arm, over her face still staring at the wall...

Donovan froze. His eyes grew wide as he noticed the shadowed figure.

It raised its' arm, as if taking aim.

Donovan yelled, launching himself towards Adalinda, strong arms thrust out, fear like lightning flashing across his face.

Donovan lifted his gun.

Adalinda stepped back as a shot of thunder slammed through the room.

Short.

Sharp.

The air around Adalinda vibrated. The sound ricocheting off the stone walls. A high-pitched ringing rose in her ears, the piercing shriek drowning her, the chill of dread spreading down her back.

Her heart dropped to her stomach.

She couldn't breathe.

Couldn't think.

A vice grip tightened around her lungs, her sudden panic suffocating.

She gasped, unable to find air.

As the shadowed figure bled into the darkness and disappeared.

Chapter Thirty - Seven

THE SHOT OF COMPRESSED THUNDER split Donovan's ears. Pain lanced through his chest. His eyes locked on Adalinda, frantically searching for a wound, hoping she hadn't been hit.

She stood unmoving, a mimicry of the statues as she stared at the empty wall where the shadowed figure had been.

Donovan grimaced, stumbling back as the pain in his chest spread, molten, blazing.

His head began to ache.

He opened his mouth, attempting to breathe.

The air burned like liquid glass, catching in his throat.

Donovan choked, dropping his gun, fingers reaching for his chest.

Finding it wet.

Warm.

Leaking.

Donovan's eyes widened in shock.

The bullet hadn't hit Adalinda.

The gun hadn't been *aimed* at Adalinda.

Cold, undiluted panic surged through him.

The moisture in the air began to vibrate.

The world tilted and Donovan fell, light dancing in front of his eyes, a shuddering breath exiting his lungs. He collided with the ground, and found himself numb, muscles paralysed by shock, blood oozing through his shattered sternum, past the blazing metal bullet wedged inside his chest.

Familiar.

So familiar.

Adalinda's silhouette lingered above him, her edges faintly glowing, haloed by the walls of luminescent leaves, as if she were the stunning, shadowed remnants of a fallen star's heart.

She hadn't heard him fall.

She was still staring at the wall.

Deafened by a moment of dread.

And it had only been a moment.

The length of a few heartbeats.

A few breaths.

Perhaps one.

Adalinda blinked through her shock, terror visibly trembling through the muscles of her clenched fists.

His sense of familiarity returned.

Impossibly.

Indisputably.

She was the familiarity.

He remembered...

He knew—

Agony twisted in Donovan's chest, in his stomach, seizing with a grip that burst and spread through him, tearing apart his thoughts with savage ferocity.

He gasped. Hands clutching his chest. Muscles convulsing.

The spark of fire in his ocean gaze clouded. His eyes rolled back, disappearing behind fluttering lids as he fought the darkness, battled the fathomless silence threatening to take him.

A bellow wrenched through his mind as he slipped, his consciousness thrashing, desperate, terrified.

He would not die.

He would *not*.

He couldn't...

Part of him fractured as the shadows hauled him under, as he realised he had lost Adalinda, the woman with eyes of golden fire. His woman. *His* woman of stone and embers, infuriating and beautiful.

She was left in the depths of a basement with a *murderer*.

He was *deserting* her.

Donovan fought death with all he had. Clinging to the pain as it began to fade.

He would not die.

He would not *leave her*.

He would not die.

It became a plea as he felt himself slip.

As he felt his body surrender.

As he fell.

Into the dark abyss.

And disappeared into oblivion.

Part Two

The Permanence of Death

CHAPTER THIRTY - EIGHT

ADALINDA STOOD FROZEN IN PLACE, her body violently trembling as she stared at the wall, not daring to turn around as a shadow slipped through the door Donovan had been watching, the light outside muted by the mass of twisted vines.

Clarke and Christensen were yelling, their words panicked, tense, muffled by the pulse thundering in Adalinda's ears.

"Was that a *gun shot?*"

"I can't see anything. There are too many *god-damned statues!* Donovan, what happened?"

The muscles in Adalinda's throat burned as they tightened, a persistent sting shoving at the backs of her eyes.

"*Donovan!*" Christensen's bark was a whiplash through the basement.

The piercing ring in Adalinda's head grew insufferable as she turned to where Donovan had been standing, about to shove her from the path of the bullet. Her terrified gaze lowered, focusing on the tall, muscled figure lying motionless on the ground.

"... Donovan...?" Christensen's footsteps grew frantic as he launched into a run.

Adalinda's hands clamped over her mouth. A shuddering breath forced itself into her lungs. "No."

The word was raw, flayed.

Christensen skidded to a stop, white rings of dread surrounding his emerald eyes as he heard the soft trembling of Adalinda's voice, as he saw the body sprawled across the ground.

The world stopped. Consumed by silence. A silence drowned only by the panic-stricken thundering in Adalinda's chest. The screaming in her ears.

"No."

A ragged gasp shook her lungs.

Her legs crumpled, trembling violently as she crashed to her knees beside Donovan, hands frantically searching for the wound.

"No. No. No!" Claws seized Adalinda's heart, wrenching wickedly beneath her sternum. A despairing wail spilled from her mouth, drowning in the pain of a thousand tortured souls, as her fingers slipped on the warm, viscous liquid seeping from the wound torn in Donovan's chest.

Clarke grabbed her phone, stopping by Christensen's side.

The light of her flash swept over Donovan's unmoving body.

Christensen roared like a wounded animal.

The bright light illuminated the blood blooming across Donovan's chest, hungrily soaking the fabric of his shirt as it crept towards the ashen flesh beneath his collar.

Adalinda's shaking hands clamped over the wound, struggling to staunch the bleeding.

Donovan's eyes were rolled back in his head, his lashes fluttering, his brows deeply creased.

Silver tears breached Adalinda's pleading stare. A broken whimper scraped her throat as she watched the flinching muscle in his jaw release, the colour leach from his flesh, the life abandon him.

Adalinda pressed her hands more firmly against Donovan's chest, feeling shards of bone protruding from his shattered sternum. "You will not die." Her voice was a desperate plea as blood spread over her hands in a layer of heated crimson. "You won't…"

Beneath her fingers, Donovan's heart stopped.

The world shattered.

"No." The sharp tang of iron ambushed Adalinda's senses as she screamed at him, slamming her palms down, tears threatening to stream down her cheeks. "Breath. Breathe! *God-damn-it, Donovan, BREATHE!*"

"Adalinda." Clarke's voice was a broken murmur as she moved forward, her light intensifying on Adalinda's blood-soaked hands.

Adalinda's fingers locked over one another, attempting to stop the blood as she pumped them into his chest, blood pulsing from the wound with each ineffective push.

"His heart—" Clarke's voice broke as she stood above Adalinda. "The bullet pierced his heart."

Adalinda wrestled off her woollen shirt, exposing a sheer, cotton singlet, and forced the material against the wound. She pounded Donovan's chest. Fighting to restart his heart. Despite the bullet. Despite the futility.

Warm, dark liquid soaked into her fingers as panic shook her bones.

He was losing too much blood.

"*Fix him!*" Adalinda snapped her head to Clarke as she hissed through her teeth. "*Bring him back.*"

"I'm a medical examiner, not a surgeon!" But Clarke was already on her knees, her fingers desperately checking for a pulse to prove she had not been right, as Adalinda kept pumping her hands into Donovan's chest.

Christensen stood paralysed on the path, his hands shaking uncontrollably, still clasping his gun.

Desperation exploded through Adalinda with the intensity of an eruption. Her breaths shook. Her eyes burned.

She could save him.

She had to *save* him.

Adalinda gritted her teeth and slammed her hands into Donovan with renewed force, shoving the blood-soaked shirt into his chest, fighting the stinging ache behind her eyes.

"Adalinda."

The voice was a whisper. Nothing compared to the persistent ringing in Adalinda's ears. Nothing compared to the screaming of her mind.

"*Adalinda.*"

More intense now.

Urgent.

"Adalinda." The voice crumbled as cool hands gingerly covered Adalinda's, ignoring the blood that bathed them. "... He's gone."

Adalinda snarled, glaring at Clarke with such ferocious anger that the woman retracted her hands.

"He has no pulse. The bullet pierced his heart."

"No." Adalinda shook her head as she continued pumping. Her shoulders trembling with the burden of her dry and smothered sobs. "I can fix it. I can. I have to..."

"He's gone, Adalinda."

Christensen struck his fist into the sculpture at his side with a sickening thud.

"Adalinda."

Adalinda shook her head.

He was not dead.

There was no way he could be.

Another sickening thud as Christensen struck the sculpture again, a sob wracking through him.

Adalinda was still shaking her head.

Donovan would be alright.

He would wake up.

If she just kept *pumping*.

Adalinda stared at her bloodied hands and knew she was lying to herself, just as she always had, just as she always would.

A soft hand gripped Adalinda's shoulder, Clarke's bloodied palm leaving a mark on her exposed skin. Adalinda shook her head. Her heart convulsed in her chest, abruptly snapping as she lifted her trembling hands from Donovan's chest and gradually sank back on her heels.

Donovan lay motionless before her, his stunning features ashen, his ocean eyes closed.

Dead.

Murdered.

Adalinda lifted her crimson hands to her face, smearing her features with Donovan's blood. She took an unsteady breath, lowered her hands and stood, fingers curling into furious, shaking fists. Her anger detonated. She turned her flaming glare on the stone woman Christensen had punched, the marble hands reaching out to choke.

Adalinda attacked the sculpture, seizing its' shoulders and releasing a brutal, agonised scream that drowned the darkness in her despair.

She flung the statue at the wall.

It shattered. Marble head rolling across the grass.

Adalinda span and stormed to the next sculpture, gripping its' waist and flinging it across the room. Her strength inhuman. Her rage a furnace.

Another scream flew from her in a swarm of darkness and fire.

How *dare* he die.

How dare he.

She flew on silent feet to the wall Donovan had been watching, to the hidden door the shadow had disappeared through when she had been too shocked to follow. She ripped at the vines concealing the metal, dropping them to the ground in a mass of glowing leaves to reveal a steel lock near a gap in the wall.

No handle.

No key.

Adalinda flexed her trembling fingers. Dragged in a deep breath. Lifted her fist.

Plunged it into the metal lock.

A wicked, broken smile twisted her blood-stained lips as she heard the steel crumple.

And the door swung open.

Chapter Thirty - Nine

THE DOOR SWUNG ON SOUNDLESS hinges beneath the force of Adalinda's fist, as if terrified even a sigh would wake the perilous force of her wrath.

Incapacitating light flooded the basement, spewing through the tangled vines, pale as bone, cold as frostbite. And illuminating the blood-soaked shirt covering Donovan's ruined chest.

Adalinda surged through the open door like a bitter, seething storm. She emerged at the end of a hallway, its' arched, concrete walls lined with heavy, steel doors. With guards. Towering and tattooed. Dressed in black. And armed with guns.

Clarke cried out, seeing the men through the gaping door. She shoved herself off the blood-stained grass, leaping around Donovan's corpse and grabbing Christensen by the arm. The detective didn't move. Tears streamed down his cheeks as he stared at Donovan's body, his eyes haunted and unseeing.

The closest guard barked a warning, aiming his rifle at Adalinda's chest.

Clarke began screaming, begging Christensen to draw his gun.

Adalinda didn't slow her pace.

A wave of calm consumed her. Engulfing her in a song of silence.

Her eyes stung beneath the layer of blood, death a painted masterpiece smeared across her face. Her scalp prickled beneath her scarf. Her pupils contracted to pinheads amongst gold. The brightness stark and stabbing.

The guard barked at her to halt.

Adalinda couldn't bring herself to care.

She wanted payment.

Blood for blood.

She wasn't going to stop until the murderer's innards were plastered across the walls.

She strode down the hall, her boots almost soundless against the rough concrete floor, rage whistling through her veins in a swarm of poison and slaughter. She inhaled a breath, deep and slow.

The closest guard planted his feet, bracing himself. His finger squeezed the trigger.

Adalinda rotated her shoulders, a vicious smile creeping onto her bloodied lips as she felt the heat of the bullet singe past. Her eyes flicked along the walls, the hairs on her arms rising in anticipation as the rest of the guards aimed their rifles.

Another shot sliced the air, muted shouts echoing through the hall.

The rest of the guards began to move.

Adalinda stepped to the side and felt, rather than heard, the bullet hit the wall. A humourless laugh trickled from her as she glanced back at the crushed bullet. The guard was aiming to incapacitate, not kill. Whoever owned this place apparently wanted to question intruders rather than dispatch them.

Or perhaps he wanted them tortured...

The closest man's face contorted in a roar as he marched forward, a hail of bullets spewing from his firearm. The shots hissed past her flesh. Some burned gashes in her arms. Some grazed past her bones. Others missed entirely, crashing against walls and dropping onto the floor.

Adalinda didn't pause as her shoulder was shoved back, the force of a bullet splitting her skin, embedding in her flesh, snapping her collarbone. She glanced numbly at the wound, assessing the compact hole and feeling nothing. No pain. No shock. Her senses remained empty save her cold, malicious fury.

Adalinda looked up to find herself a breath from the closest guard, staring into grey-green eyes. She smiled, shoved the rifle out of his grip with her uninjured arm before he could fire another shot. The rifle fell, catching on its' strap as Adalinda locked her bloodied fingers around the soft flesh of the guard's neck.

And lifted.

Slamming him into a metal door.

The other guards paused.

"Where is he?" Adalinda snarled as the guard kicked her shins, his eyes bulging, his hands clawing hopelessly at her fingers. "Tell me where he went." She shoved her hand further into the guard's neck. He choked at her tightening grip, a gasp catching in his throat, his mouth flapping uselessly as he struggled to breathe. "*Where is he?*" Her scream reverberated through the hall, blazing across the walls like invisible wildfire.

"What... are... you—" The guard wheezed between the words, forcing them from his collapsing throat. "— *talking* about?"

Adalinda gestured sharply at the door to the basement with her chin. "Someone *else* came out of there. *Tell me where he went.*" She bared her teeth, primal rage pulsing through her veins. "And if you ask any more *god-damned* questions you will find your *intestines* in your *lap.*"

The guard narrowed his bloodshot eyes, a wet, cough raking through his throat. "Man in... black cloak."

Adalinda seethed, loosening her grip, trying to lift her wounded arm and feeling the bones of her broken collarbone begin to grind. She let the arm drop. "Where did he go?"

The guard glanced sidelong, gagging as the others began moving again, their barrels aimed and armed.

A muscle fluttered in Adalinda's jaw, her attention darting to the gun-barrels in her peripheral vision. "Fine." Her fingers dropped from the guard's neck. He gasped, boots hitting the floor, clutching at the bloody handprint branding his throat. Adalinda frowned at the near-empty magazine of his rifle, turned, stepped up to another guard and snatched the rifle from him before he could react, yanking its' strap over his head and flipping the gun.

She fired a shot, single handed, through the first guard's shoulder.

Exactly where he had shot her.

The first guard screamed, howling as his body shuddered, as he collapsed to the floor.

Adalinda hummed her approval, smiling down at the rifle.

Blood for blood.

Monster.

The wall of guards moved forward, the one she had stolen the rifle from staring at his empty hands.

"I just want to know where the cloaked man went."

The guards bared their teeth.

Adalinda kept her voice low. Calm and brutal. "Tell me which door the cloaked man went through." She raised the gun in her crimson-stained hand, tucking the shoulder-stock under her arm.

One woman holding a rifle against a barrier of armed men.

Donovan's blood climbed from her fingers like a butcher's slaughterous gloves. She could feel it congealing, beginning to crust beneath her nails, her lashes coated in viscous gore clinging together as she blinked. Blood leaked from the scrapes and grazes covering her body, soaking into her tattered singlet where the bullets hadn't quite missed. "Tell me and I promise I won't kill you."

"What the *hell* is going on?!"

The guards stiffened, glancing between themselves as they abruptly stepped aside, their bodies parting to form a path, their rifles remaining aimed at Adalinda.

An enormous, hulking woman marched through their ranks, her ink-dark clothes rustling, her hard, coal eyes glaring. She sneered at the guard slumped by Adalinda's boots, his breaths shuddering unevenly into his lungs.

The woman twisted her neck, bones popping audibly. She lifted her hands, cracking her knuckles, the skin of her exposed forearms inked with screaming bodies and thorny vines. Her glare skewered one of the guards like a spear through flesh.

The guard stepped forward, his tanned skin gleaming in the fluorescent light as the woman glanced at the blood covering Adalinda, at the bullet lodged in her shoulder, at the rifle still raised in her hands. "She came through the far door. Wants to know where the cloaked man went."

The woman sniffed. "Did she now?" She smirked, her pale lips stretching over a set of pristine teeth.

Adalinda glared at the woman, her golden eyes spitting fire, her features contorting in a savage snarl. Slowly, deliberately, she growled through her teeth. "Get out of my way. I don't want to hurt you, but I will."

The woman's jaw tightened, her narrow stare glinting. "Take her." She stepped back, turning to leave. "The boss with want her questioned."

Adalinda blinked.

Aimed the rifle.

Fired.

Giving no warning as she pulled the trigger.

The bullet collided with the back of the woman's shoulder. The metal crumpled, wedging its' tip into bone, and a savage shriek ripped from the woman's lips.

The guards' stared as the woman collapsed, her head slamming into the concrete floor.

Adalinda pointed the gun, her finger balancing on the trigger as the corners of her mouth twitched.

As the woman on the floor groaned.

As Christensen finally stepped out of the basement, his eyes red and swollen, tears staining his cheeks.

Donovan's ashen form flashed behind Adalinda's eyes.

Cold, unforgiving rage screamed through her.

She clenched her teeth and took aim.

Each bullet hit a guard in the shoulder, rupturing flesh and shattering bone, sending the men stumbling back. Each wound an exact replica of that which had been torn in Adalinda.

She pursed her lips beneath the layer of blood, tasting it on her tongue, crimson staining her teeth. "Get on the floor."

The guards lowered themselves to their knees, tears of pain welling in their eyes as they clutched their wounded shoulders.

"Lay down."

The guards obeyed, some trembling, others whimpering.

Adalinda paused as a guard lifted his gun, his muscles shuddering as he attempted to hold the weapon with his uninjured arm.

Adalinda gritted her teeth. Aimed her rifle. "Try anything and I'll shoot you somewhere it *really* hurts."

The guard groaned and retracting his hand.

Adalinda seized his rifle. She slung it over her neck, tossing the one she had snatched from the other guard aside, its' magazine devoid of bullets. She kept the firearm ready, waiting for a fight, as she began stepping around the guards.

None of them moved, though some watched.

She was grateful they didn't give her a reason to shoot. She didn't want to hurt them, she simply wanted the murderer.

Adalinda swallowed and glanced at her blood-soaked hands, one smearing crimson over the rifle, Donovan's blood shimmering oddly in the light. Confusion tipped the corners of Adalinda's mouth towards her chin. Her shoulder was beginning to howl, the numbness that had blocked out the pain beginning to subside. She wasn't sure how long it would take her snapped collarbone to heal but she didn't have time to wait, or question. If she wanted to catch the murderer, she needed to leave. Now.

She was already too far behind.

Most likely too late.

But she had to try.

Chapter Forty

Christensen stood behind Adalinda, gawking as he assessed the hall, assessed the guards whose forms almost overlapped one another as they lay on the floor. "You just shot *a dozen* men."

Adalinda shrugged her uninjured shoulder, reaching the lone woman, anger heating beneath her skin.

"Why?"

Adalinda deliberately lowered a boot to the woman's hand. "They refused to get out of my way and now we may have *lost* the *murderer*." She pressed down with her boot to emphasise her words, listening to the bones fracture in the woman's tattooed wrist.

The woman shrieked, curling in on herself.

"... Or have you forgotten what we came down here to do?"

Christensen cringed. "Theodore was right. You *are* fucking terrifying."

"Good." Adalinda turned to glare at Christensen over her bleeding shoulder, boiling rage spilling from her eyes, scalp prickling beneath her scarf. "I wouldn't want to give anyone the *wrong impression*."

"You have *got* to teach me how to shoot like that."

Adalinda's glare flicked to Clarke as the woman stepped into the hall, her eyes on the guards.

Christensen cursed. "Clarke, I told you to stay in the basement."

"But—"

"Get back inside." Christensen pointed at the entrance to the luminescent garden. "Do your best to bar the door in case any of these bastards get back up."

Clarke grumbled under her breath. She frowned, looking at Adalinda, at the rifle she was still holding. "What are you going to do?"

A haze of red swept across Adalinda's vision. "I'm going to find the murderer and I'm going to make death look like mercy."

Christensen's jaw fell slack. "... What?"

Adalinda turned and stepped over the remaining men. "Don't fall behind." She started to run towards the metal door at the end of the hall, not waiting for Christensen.

Christensen clenched his fists by his sides and followed, scanning the gleaming, metal doors lining the walls, all of them locked from the inside, with no visible handles. No one had bothered to emerge in wake of the gun shots and the place had become eerily silent. The guards still watched from the floor.

Adalinda could taste Donovan's blood on her lips, feel it cooling on her skin.

She felt sick.

She forced her chin to stop trembling, choking down a wave of sorrow and attempting to replace it with the anger she had felt. The shallow wounds in her flesh burned as she ran, brutal pain flaring from her shoulder. She could feel the bullet still in the wound, the blood dribbling down her shoulder, her arm, and mixing with the crimson already staining her skin.

Donovan's blood...

Adalinda bit down on the inside of her cheek, forcing herself to disregard the pain, the loss.

Christensen caught her as she reached the final door, a single, faintly glowing leaf resting at its' base.

This door had a handle.

Adalinda pressed the end of it, watching as it rotated. The door swung open on silent hinges to reveal a collection of steep, steel stairs ascending to a flat, concrete platform.

Adalinda launched herself up, taking two steps at once. She could hear Christensen following close behind, gun in hand, his features dark with determination. They reached the platform, turned a corner and continued up, passing another door, presumably leading to another hall.

Christensen sprinted furiously at her back, panting, sweat dripping from his brow.

They passed another door... And the staircase ended.

Abruptly.

With a final door standing to their right.

Heavier than the others.

Flood-proof.

Through it Adalinda could hear trickling water, along with a low, melodic hum.

Someone was singing.

Adalinda flung the flood-door open, lunging through it and finding herself in the stagnant gloom of a cavernous sewage tunnel, wider than the streets aboveground and high as a domed cathedral. Brick walls curved up to form a towering ceiling interspersed with the occasional grated gutter, their patches of threaded sunlight unable to reach an arms length into the shadowed murk. Smaller, arched tunnels appeared as gaps of darkness in the walls, their thresholds blacker than black and twenty paces apart, the stream of water from the main tunnel escaping in rivulets along their sunken floors.

A dark cloak fluttered in the distance. Almost indiscernible. The murderer was still humming his song, deep in his throat, the melody softly lilting as it bounded along the walls.

As he steadily climbed a rusting, spiral staircase, the steel partially hidden by an alcove in the wall.

Adalinda lifted a rifle.

Fired an impossible shot.

Missed.

The murderer disappeared through a hole in the ceiling, still humming.

A frustrated scream tore up Adalinda's throat. She hurled herself after him, sprinting along the tunnel's sloped edge, keeping away from the water's rushing path. She leaped over a trickling stream leading through one of the intersecting tunnels, landed on the other side and kept running.

Christensen bellowed at her to stop.

Adalinda tuned him out, lunging for the staircase, wounded and furious, barely out of breath. She hauled herself upwards using the rusted, metal handrail, gritting her teeth as her shoulder screamed, the rapidly healing muscle tearing around the bullet, the broken collarbone grinding.

She reached the top of the winding stairs. Grabbed the rim of the hole in the ceiling, bloody fingers meeting cold stone, letting the rifle drop to hang from her neck. She hauled herself through the hole, tears of pain welling in her eyes as she forced herself to use her wounded arm, unable to think through her throbbing, savage rage.

Adalinda dropped onto her stomach, gasping, hurting. She was in the corner of an enormous bathing room, showers lining the walls, steaming pools set into the floor. The water projected patterns across the ceiling, blue and grey and rippling.

Adalinda's rifle scraped the tiles as she searched for the murderer.

And found the room quiet.

Empty.

Adalinda shoved herself up, grimacing as Christensen climbed from the grate, its' circular cover discarded beside the opening, the metal intricately patterned and engraved.

The detective stepped forward, gun held high as he scanned the room. "Did you see where he went?"

"No." Adalinda lifted a hand to her bleeding shoulder, pressing against the wound, sucking air through her teeth.

There were three doors.

Two in the wall to their right.

One directly ahead.

"I'll check out there, you check those." Christensen stalked towards the single door ahead, leaving her to move for the others.

Adalinda crossed the room, forcing herself to push past the pain as she lifted the rifle and took aim. She stepped through the first door, into a room full of cupboards and toilets.

Soundless.

Vacant.

The second was the same.

A deep, excruciating pain settled into the shards of Adalinda's heart, into the marrow of her bones.

She'd lost him.

She'd lost the murderer.

Her limbs felt heavy, the hollow silence a burden as she fought the haunting, remnant images of Donovan's lifeless body, bleeding out on the overgrown grass. She held in a fractured whimper as she tightened her grip on the rifle. Hot tears shoved at the backs of her eyes, piercing the sensitive areas like salted needles.

A frustrated growl burst from Christensen as he stormed back into the bathing room. He had holstered his gun and was dragging a hand over his cropped hair. "I can't find him. He disappeared... But I know where we are..."

Adalinda inhaled a long breath, staring into the water of a heated pool. She stood for a moment, trying to ignore her failure, the echo of Donovan's death behind her eyes. Her hands shook as she pulled the rifle from her neck, setting it aside and kneeling on the floor.

She began washing the blood from her hands, again noticing the faintest shimmer amid the darkening crimson...

Christensen cleared his throat. "How are you... able to heal so fast?" His voice was tight, dry as it rasped through his lips. "Donovan—" The hoarse voice broke. Christensen swallowed past the pain, his emerald eyes, forcefully devoid of emotion, locking on her as he stopped by her side. "He wouldn't tell me about his past."

Adalinda shook her head. Her skin itched, crawling beneath Donovan's blood. She scratched at her arms beneath the water, blood dissolving in a cloud of dispersing crimson, tendrils of it curling beneath the surface. She had no explanation for Christensen. She only understood one thing about herself and she hid it, so well she occasionally forgot. "I have no answers for you." She winced as she moved her wounded shoulder. The torn muscle around the bullet had settled into a constant throb, the bone was beginning to reset itself, becoming less of a break and more of a fracture.

Christensen scanned Adalinda's rapidly disappearing wounds. In some places it was only her ripped and bloodied clothing that showed any sign of the gashes that had been left by the bullets. Though crimson was still streaming steadily from her shoulder. "Why isn't your shoulder healing like the rest of you?"

"It is." Adalinda winced, feeing her shoulder fighting to heal around the crumpled bullet. She new instinctively that she had to keep moving, to keep ripping the slowly healing muscle away from the metal. "I have to move my shoulder to interrupt the healing process, otherwise the skin and muscle will close around the bullet. But I can't remove the bullet myself without—"

"Reaching in to grab it?" Christensen grimaced. He crouched

beside her, examining the wound. "So you're not as infinitely tough as you seem."

Adalinda pursed her lips, lifting a hand from the water. It was still stained, flushed with marks from her scraping fingernails. She reached for her shoulder.

Christensen swore under his breath. "Hold on. I'll do it. Why didn't you just ask for my help?"

Adalinda stiffened as Donovan's voice echoed in her mind.

"How about just asking for my help?"

She swallowed past the ache in her throat. "I wasn't sure you would, after what you said this morning." She lifted a hand, gingerly touching the sensitive area surrounding the broken skin. She sucked in a breath as pain shot through her shoulder.

"Of course I would've helped. This morning..." Christensen closed his eyes and let out a tired sigh, rubbing his temples. "You woke screaming and I... I had a moment of lapsed judgement. I apologise. God, I feel like the mouse and the lion right now."

Adalinda smiled softly. "You're the mouse and I'm the lion with the thorn in my paw?" He nodded as she lowered her hand to her side and set her jaw. "How do we get it out?"

Christensen patted his pockets, pausing with one hand on his holstered pistol. "We could try shooting the bullet out."

"And shatter the one already in there?" Adalinda stared at him, turning back to the pool and splashing the water over her face. Donovan's blood leaked into her eyes, her mouth, down her shirt. "There's no way in hell."

Christensen lifted his shoulders in a shrug, standing and walking to find her a towel. "It was only a suggestion. I didn't say it was a *good* one."

"Don't you have a knife?" Adalinda wiped a hand over her eyes, clearing them of blood and water. Her brows furrowed as she peered into the pool.

"No." Christensen disappeared through one of the doors, returning to her side and handing her a towel.

Adalinda dipped the edge into the water and began scrubbing her face and neck, the handprint Clarke had left on her shoulder.

Christensen stared at the pool, his eyes distant. "There isn't really much point having a knife when a gun can maim from a considerable distance."

"There's a point when you need to remove a bullet from your own shoulder." Adalinda released a sigh, drying her skin and staring at the towel, the white fabric now stained pink.

"We should go back. Clarke will be able to remove it."

Adalinda nodded.

"We'll have to find you some clothes too." Christensen took the towel from her, scrubbing the wet edge over her forehead and cheeks, removing the blood she had missed. She sighed at the warmth against her rapidly cooling skin. "And you'll have to remove your scarf."

Adalinda recoiled, her expression becoming hard and unyielding as she glared at him, daring him to touch her scarf.

Christensen retracted the towel from her face. "Alright, we don't need to remove the scarf." Adalinda relaxed and he continued washing her face. "You're as bad as..." He trailed off, pain and grief clouding his features. He lowered the towel. "I can't believe he's..."

Adalinda lifted her hand to squeeze his shoulder, her lip wobbling slightly as she fought to keep control. "Don't say it."

Christensen swallowed, nodded.

Adalinda smiled softly, the expression hollow. She took the stained towel from him and patted her skin dry, staring at her stained hands when she had finished.

"We should go. Clarke may not have been able to barricade that door."

Adalinda uncoiled, long legs pushing her upright as she flung the blood-stained towel to Christensen. "Where do we put this?"

Christensen strode to the entrance of the mens toilet and disappeared. She listened as he shuffled about inside and then emerged, dusting his hands together.

"What did you do?" Adalinda raised an eyebrow and reached down to retrieve the rifle as he strode to the washroom exit.

"I put the towel in the rubbish." He paused as Adalinda moved after him, her eyes narrowing slightly, calculating the likelihood of the towel being found. "It's hidden beneath a bunch of paper towels."

"As if *that's* going to help."

"You'd be surprised." Christensen shrugged, reaching for the handle and pushing the door open. "People who aren't looking, don't see." They stepped into a painted, stone hall leading to a large, desolate lobby.

"Where is everyone?" Adalinda's murmur was softer than Christensen's footsteps as they moved into the open room. She frowned at the looming wooden door leading onto the street, pressing her hand into the wound in her shoulder to stop the bleeding. "Is this...?"

Christensen stopped, his gaze locking on a painting up the stairs. "Shade's orphanage."

Adalinda followed his eyes and sucked in a breath as she noticed the painting of Wyatt Shade. She felt her scalp begin to crawl beneath her scarf. "We should go." She grabbed Christensen by the arm and tugged him back towards the washroom as she began to shiver, the winter cold spilling into the lobby causing mounds to rise on skin. "It'll take less time if we go back the way we came."

"We can't, we told Clarke to bar the door." Christensen looked at Adalinda. "We'll go along the streets, where we're less likely to get shot." He removed his jacket, forcing her into the leather fabric, still possessing his warmth. "It'll take us awhile to get back to the gallery. Don't want you to freeze."

"But the blood—"

"Won't matter if you freeze to death."

Adalinda smiled gratefully, arms wrapping around herself, shifting her shoulder to reopen the wound.

"Keep the rifle hidden, will you?"

Adalinda tucked the rifle inside the jacket and followed Christensen as he walked out the door.

The cold slammed into her, a wall of burning ice wiping the smile from her face. She stared at the pavement as they began the long walk back to the gallery's basement, her skin still itching with the memory of Donovan's blood, his ashen face haunting the dark inside her lids.

The cold crept into her like a parasite, numbing her fingers, chilling her bones.

With each step, she felt herself fracture.

Felt the crushing loss of Donovan.

Her failure to catch the murderer.

The guards laying wounded on the floor.

Monster.

Adalinda took a breath and set her jaw. She forced herself to keep moving, to keep walking. Because if she didn't, she feared her strength would abandon her.

Just as the life had abandoned Donovan.

Chapter Forty - One

Leda

A SUPPRESSED KNOCK ON A wooden door announced the presence of a young secretary. She tucked a tumbling lock of brunette hair behind her ear and listened for the cursory grunt which permitted her entrance. Her wide, hazel eyes narrowed slightly as she pushed through the door, tightening her grip on the cream envelope clutched to her breast. Its' seal of crimson wax gleamed in the glaring light of the office like a shimmering mound of congealing blood.

She was met with the repulsive reek of mint and cigars. Her body convulsed in a strangled shudder, responding involuntarily to stench, as the stifling air caressed her skin with gaunt, dank fingers.

Disgust crept through the marrow of her bones.

Sallow.

Oozing.

She willed her breaths to shallow, a crease blooming between her dark brows.

Not long now.

She would leave this place soon enough, once her task was complete.

Hatred flourished in her stomach as her gaze swept over the office, as she sneered imperceptibly at the dark, wooden floorboards, the lavish, sable carpet. The walls loomed above her, black as ash, suffocating as smoke, overbearing masculinity seeping from every crevice.

"Don't push yourself too hard, Leda." The harsh accent rasped through the room, sliding over the secretary in an oil-soaked embrace. "You'll get a wrinkle."

Irritation sparked across Leda's features. Her glare slid to a man leaning over an enormous, oaken desk. A fountain pen dangled from his long, bony fingers, its' winking tip methodically beating a stunted mound of paperwork. "I beg your pardon?"

The man lifted his obsidian eyes to examine her. His gaze leisurely grazed her breasts and slid down her thighs, invoking a revolting flood of shivers which crept incessantly in its' wake. "Honey, we both know that head of yours is devoid of intelligence. Don't ruin that lovely face by trying to think."

Leda pursed her cupid-bow lips, her knuckles bleaching as she tightened her grip on the cream envelope. "A *package* arrived for you, *Mister Shade*." She trampled the urge to pitch the envelope at his face as a conniving smirk twisted his mouth like a hideous plague.

"On the desk, *sweetheart*." Shade's voice dripped derision, his piercing gaze lingered, hungrily consuming the alluring curve of the secretary's slender hips. His knuckles tapped the desk beside him, a silent command for her to relinquish the envelope as he returned to his paperwork.

Leda stepped forward, her heels an accusatory curse on the midnight carpet, a swarm of burning moths shrieking in her stomach as she fumed.

Forcing herself to calm, she placed the envelope on the desk. No doubt another illicit transaction in need of being discrete.

Not long now.

Leda tensed, revulsion sluicing her veins, as a cold hand smothered her own.

Shade gently rotated her palm. The pad of his thumb stroked the inside of her wrist in a scraping, vulgar massage, his obsidian stare frosted with obscene desire. His lips warped into the ravenous leer of a starved beast and Leda saw his want, his greed. It stained the air as he spoke. "Is there anything *else*?"

Leda snatched her hand away, her slender face momentarily contorting in disgust as Shade's leer withered, his desire drowned by a surge of annoyance. She cleared her throat, met his glare with that of stewing hazel. "Chief Wise called. Again. Another woman who worked at the orphanage is dead."

Shade combed his fingers through the thick, silver-streaked strands of his midnight hair. He leaned forward, his mint and cigar breath curling with her own, challenging her to aggravate him more than she already had, daring her to retreat like a scolded child. "A*nd?*"

The corner of Leda's mouth twitched as she shifted, distancing herself from his abhorrent presence. "A*nd*, she mentioned that she would like to pay you a visit, so she can speak with you *personally*."

Disdain curled Shade's features in a tempestuous sneer. He released an exasperated breath. "If you're not interested in providing a *decent* distraction..." Again, his glare flicked to her breasts. He arched a brow before raising his eyes to scowl in her face. "Then I have no more use for you." He flicked a hand redundantly, returning his attention to the documents on his desk. "Get out."

A muscle twitched in Leda's neck, rage crashed through her as she pivoted and stalked across the office.

Not long now.

She slipped out the door, hauled it closed behind her and vowed that the next time Shade touched her, he would *severely* regret it.

Chapter Forty - Two

ADALINDA SAT ON THE FLOOR of the luminescent basement, staring at Donovan's lifeless body, as Clarke dug the bullet from her shoulder with a pocket-knife; a small, silver blade she kept hidden in her coat. The blade sliced Adalinda's flesh, the torn muscle parting to reveal crushed pieces of metal scattered around rapidly healing bone. Blood streamed down Adalinda's shoulder to soak her cotton singlet, plastering the fabric to her body as if it were a second skin. She felt nothing. No pain. No sorrow. No despair. Nothing. As if the presence of Donovan's corpse were dulling her senses. She was unable to understand death. Unable to understand why she could not force Donovan to wake up, to open his eyes and smile at her, or frown, or growl. She didn't care what he did. She just wanted him to *wake up*.

So she waited.

And waited.

Her blood-stained fingers pressed into the moss-encrusted dirt, her pale face illuminated by the jade and cobalt leaves. She felt the knife as a vague nudge, carefully shifting beneath her skin.

Clarke's tongue periodically darted over her lips, concentration shadowing her features. She managed to pry the last piece of the bullet free and set it aside, then crossed her legs and leaned forward. "How long will it take to heal?"

Adalinda shrugged, vaguely aware of the pain which should have lanced through her shoulder. She was still staring at Donovan, at the crimson soaking his shirt, and her own, still bunched over the wound where she had tried to staunch the bleeding. Some of the blood had dribbled up his neck, leaking onto the ground.

And Adalinda felt nothing.

She was hollow.

Empty.

... Waiting.

Clarke raised her eyes to the vines which drooped from the ceiling. "We're going to have to call Wise, get her to bring reinforcements—"

"No." Christensen did not stop his pacing, roaming up and down the walls, occasionally glancing at Donovan's body. "Just... Not yet."

"Christensen, he's—"

"*Don't.*" Christensen tensed, shooting a glare at Clarke. He stood there a moment, setting his jaw, breath flaring through his nostrils in short, sharp gusts. Finally, he sighed, stepping over the head of the sculpture Adalinda had shattered, and kept pacing. "Don't say it."

"What are we going to do, then?" Clarke gestured to Donovan's body, his features appearing nauseatingly ashen, bathed in humid, preternatural light. "We can't just stay here. It's not like he's going to wake up."

"*You don't know that.*" Adalinda snapped, her scalp prickling as a surge of anger consumed her nothingness. It was gone as soon as her eyes returned to Donovan, replaced by emptiness, eternal and unending.

"Actually, I do. It's my job. People don't just wake up from death." Clarke stood, brushing her hands on her pants. "And even if they did—" She stopped abruptly. Shook her head. "Why am I *explaining* this to you? This is *ridiculous*." Clarke stepped around Donovan and knelt opposite Adalinda, peeling Adalinda's woollen shirt away from the wound.

Something tumbled from the fabric onto the ground.

Clarke muttered a curse under her breath, reaching into the moss and lifting a crumpled shard of bloody metal. A bullet. "What in Deaths' deep-blue eyes...?" She rotated it in her hand and Adalinda glimpsed a surface of silver and bronze, the colours seeming to swirl like trapped smoke, like mist beneath glass...

"Aegisium."

Clarke looked up from the bullet, her brows deeply furrowed. "What?"

Adalinda pursed her lips, trying to find the origin of the word. It had appeared on her tongue, slipped through the veil smothering her memories. "The name of the metal... It's Aegisium."

Clarke hummed, considering. She leaned forward and peered into Donovan's wound, pressed her fingers against the hole in his sternum. "But why is it not still in his chest...?"

Adalinda narrowed her eyes, studying Donovan's unmoving features, his pale skin.

Pale.

Not ashen.

"How in the hell is the bullet *not in the wound?*"

Adalinda's breath caught in her lungs.

Her heart stuttered.

Donovan's chest rose, almost imperceptibly.

"... Adalinda, are you alright?"

Adalinda opened her mouth to respond.

Donovan's lashes fluttered.

"*Holy Mother of*—" Clarke pressed her fingers against Donovan's neck, checking for a pulse. "... He's not dead."

Christensen snapped to attention.

"He has a pulse." Clarke scrambled back, grabbing Donovan's wrist and pressing her fingers into the skin. She concentrated for a moment, cursing under her breath. "He was shot in the *heart. He was dead and now he has a pulse!*"

Adalinda lifted a shaking hand to her throat, heart throbbing beneath her fingers.

Donovan gasped a deep, shuddering breath.

His eyes flew open.

Christensen yelled triumphantly, leaping towards them.

Donovan groaned and pushed up onto his elbow, head bowed, hair draping over his brow to obscure his face.

The wound in his chest began to close.

A relieved whimper trickled from Adalinda's throat.

"Bastard." Christensen whispered, his lips splitting in a grin, his teeth gleaming in the bioluminescent light. "You *fucking magnificent* BASTARD!"

Clarke shook her head. "How is he *alive?*"

"I don't care." Christensen danced on his toes, shifting his weight from one foot to the next. "I *knew* that bullet hit him in the bar. I *knew it.*"

Donovan abruptly stiffened, his free hand lifting to the hole in his shirt, gently touching the fiery mark of the healing wound. "... Was I *shot?*" Donovan looked up, his brows creased and shadowing his stunning, ocean eyes.

The feeling of nothing vanished.

Adalinda reached out, her fingers grazing the edge of his cheek.

He was warm.

He was *breathing.*

A fire lit in Adalinda's throat. His scent of woodsmoke and rain rose above the tang of blood, the humid air seeming to close in around them.

Adalinda lifted a hand to her mouth, tears stinging her eyes. "I thought you were *dead.*"

Donovan grunted, his arm visibly shaking as he held his own weight. His focus drifted, fading until his eyes were almost vacant, staring yet unseeing.

Adalinda's stomach tightened in a squirming knot. Gingerly, she brushed the hair from Donovan's brow, fingers shaking, her whisper woven of feathers and broken shells. "... Donovan?"

Donovan's face contorted in a grimace. He squeezed his eyes shut, clenched his teeth. "I'm fine."

"*You died.*"

Donovan opened his mouth to reply.

"Don't you *dare* tell me that bullet missed."

Donovan pressed his lips in a firm line, rolling until both elbows were planted in the dirt, his chest facing the ground. He began to push himself up, his muscles quivering, his brow knitting in focused determination.

Adalinda caught him as he collapsed.

She locked her arms around his shoulders and heaved him up until he knelt on the ground. "You need to rest..."

Donovan shook his head, slow, lethargic.

He slumped forward.

Adalinda caught him. She glanced at Christensen, grinding words through her teeth. "Are you going to *help*?"

Christensen had stopped hopping on his toes and was standing as if inert, his mind processing, lost in a trance. He shook himself and nodded, before lurching forward to grab Donovan's arm.

Adalinda shifted on her knees, pressing one hand into Donovan's chest, angling her shoulder under his arm and draping it around her neck. "He won't be able to walk. We'll have to lift him."

Again, Christensen nodded.

"Clarke, do you still have that bullet?"

Clarke closed her gaping mouth, her fingers forming a fist around the blood-stained, Aegisium bullet. "... I think this is what it feels like to lose one's mind..."

Adalinda shoved herself to her feet, groaning beneath Donovan's weight as Christensen ducked beneath Donovan's other arm.

"All those dead people I work on... What's keeping *them* from coming back...?"

Donovan's head sagged, knees buckling.

Christensen swore under his breath. "Clarke, this is not really the time for an existential crisis."

"What?" Clarke blinked, looking up at them from her place on the floor. "Oh, right." She shoved the bullet into her pocket and climbed to her feet, brushing herself off with blood-stained hands. "Sorry."

"We need to get him back to his apartment." Adalinda clung to Donovan, stepping forward, moving back towards the stairs, back towards the gallery. "Clarke, we managed to avoid Iveta when we came in but I'm going to need you to check where she is. If she sees Donovan..."

Clarke peered at the gaping hole in Donovan's shirt, the blood spread across his chest, his neck. Her eyes grew vacant. She shook her head. Started stomping towards the stairs. "If she's there, I'll distract her." She slid her bloodied hands into her pockets, one hand twisting the Aegisium bullet.

Aegisium...

The word tugged at Adalinda's mind, tethered to her lost memories.

She shifted Donovan's weight more evenly across her shoulders, her attention flicking towards his bowed head. He was trying to walk, stumbling forward with his hair hanging in his face and his eyes partially closed. His breaths were still uneven, his strength obviously drained.

And his skin remained pale as death.

Her fault.

Adalinda's grip tightened on Donovan's draping arm. Her scalp crawled beneath her scarf as she felt something move beneath the veil, in the darkness consuming her memories.

Monster.

She had been waiting for Donovan to wake.

She had not *known*, but she had been waiting. Unwilling to accept.

Donovan opened his eyes and peered at her through the sighing waves of his hair, unable to lift his head. "I know you... I know—" Donovan frowned, the murmur dying on his lips. "I knew..."

He knew?

Adalinda shuddered, angling her head until her scarf no longer touched his skin. Her scalp continued its' prickling. More constant. More insistent.

He was alive.

She could hear his breaths, feel his pulse. After a bullet had mutilated his heart. After his blood had poured from his chest.

Adalinda braced herself as they reached the stairs, looking up to find Clarke already disappearing into the second basement, deep in thought. She forced the questions from her mind, the fear that Donovan would collapse again, the terror that she was asleep and when she opened her eyes he would still be dead with that gaping hole ruining his chest.

Her fault.

He had saved her.

He had died *because of her*.

Adalinda glared at the steps, furious at herself, furious at *Donovan*. She felt like screaming at him, cursing and snarling. How dare he die for her?

For *her*?

The veil over her memories rippled like an ocean, as if stifling a beast rising from its' depths.

Adalinda closed her mind, fighting her anger and something deeper, something lurking in the darkness, whispering.

Monster.

Monster.

Adalinda focused on Donovan's weight, cleared her mind of thoughts, and began to climb.

Let The Hunt Begin

Ten Years Ago

HARSH, STONE WALLS SWAM BEFORE Donovan's eyes, unfamiliar and rippling. A rasping groan perforated the silence, echoing in his pounding head.

He felt broken.

Shattered.

His neck cramped irritably, punishing him for some obscure crime he had committed unconsciously.

Donovan shoved himself upright, instantly assaulted by a jarring slap of vertigo, an onslaught of nausea. He braced his taut arms against the cushioned surface beneath him and bowed forward, head reaching for his knees.

The room lurched violently, pitching like a ship butchered in a storm.

Inexorable pain lanced through his bones and he clenched his eyes shut, attempting to banish it.

The syringe glinted, plunging into the pulsing flesh of his exposed neck.

Donovan gasped, air streaming into his aching lungs at the memory of the daffodil liquid. He could feel the ghost of its' presence, surging, burning through his veins in an explosion of fire and liquid steel.

His limbs screamed as he shifted, the skin feeling raw, the surface stinging and flaring as if flayed.

Donovan opened his eyes, peering down at his arms to find the skin in place, the tanned surface smooth, unmarred. He sucked a steadying breath through his lips, tasting the stale air, laced with dust. Slowly, he lifted his bleak, ocean gaze to assess his surroundings, remaining otherwise motionless for fear of his stomach revolting, of his consciousness disintegrating. The mattress of an enormous four-post bed bowed beneath his weight, its' velvet curtains of deep maroon draping over carved, mahogany supports. He dragged his legs over the side, his bare feet landing on an opulent carpet, its' patterned surface suffused with dust. A groan rumbled from his chest and he reached for the carved post at the end of the bed, strong fingers locking around the wood. He hauled himself up, fighting to keep his fatigued legs beneath him as the blood drained from his face, leaving him pale, swaying, skin tingling.

The muscles of his naked back convulsed as he desperately clung to the post.

"I was wondering how long it would take you to wake."

Donovan froze, the wooden support beneath his palms creaking as his grip tightened.

"You recovered quickly. I had to inject you three times to get you here. You kept regaining consciousness." An exasperated sigh blew from the figure blocking the room's lone window. A light breeze billowed his scarlet coat, attacking the motes of dust in the air and sending them swirling uncontrollably. "Inconvenient, I must say. If you had just co-operated in the first place, perhaps you wouldn't be in this mess."

"Co-operated..." Donovan panted as he straightened, his warm, honey voice laced with malice. "Who are you?"

"I have many names." The man lifted his narrow shoulders in a nonchalant shrug, his disturbing, violet eyes shifting to land on Donovan. "Many faces too, if I so choose." He turned from the window, sunlight haloing his shock of cropped, onyx waves.

Donovan took a step forward. His fingers dropped from the post to curl by his sides, forming fists in response to the throbbing of his temples. "Who are you?"

"You're going to cling to that question?" The violet-eyed man tilted his head, his fascinated gaze glinting. "I would have thought the operative question was 'where am I?' Or perhaps 'where is she?' Though I don't suppose you remember her."

Something twisted deep in Donovan's stomach. It slithered towards the steady pump of his heart, sinking in toxic fangs, causing his pulse to stutter.

Velvet, rosebud lips curved in a smile behind his eyes.

Donovan lunged for the memory, for more than just a taunting whisper of his forgotten past, for some evidence to anchor him as he was dragged away by the suffocating current of confusion, of desperation.

The vision slipped like a startled moth, darting out of his grip and disappearing into the unattainable depths of his extinguished memories.

A satisfied smirk graced the other man's face as Donovan's expression settled into a lethal glare. "Well, in any case, you are here because I happen to like fighting and strategy. You provide the fight, I'll provide the strategy."

Donovan swallowed the dehydration in his throat. "What are you talking about?"

The man pressed his lips together impatiently. "Look, it's really very simple." He plucked a dagger from beneath his coat, the blade flashing in the light which streamed through the open window, its' kaleidoscopic surface of silver and bronze like the curl of mist beneath glass. "You will fight, or run, whichever you see fit, and I, along with some others..." The man's face lit with anticipation as he flipped the dagger in his palm. "...will hunt you down like a wild beast and incapacitate you."

Donovan smothered a wave of vertigo as he stepped forward again, flexing his fingers, his dark brows creasing above a scowl that bled hostility. "And if I refuse to participate?"

"I swear…" The man lifted his gloved fingers to his eyes, removing his piercing gaze from Donovan as he shook his head.

Donovan seized his chance and flung himself across the room, blood pounding through his veins in a stampede of thundering rage, purging him of his remaining vertigo and nausea. He could almost feel the limbs tearing from the violet-eyed man's body, see the breath catching beneath his choking grip.

He thrust the swell of rising apprehension aside as his fingers locked around the man's throat.

Violet eyes snapped open, gleaming delightedly as they peered up at Donovan. "That's the spirit."

Pain.

Blazing, white pain.

Donovan faltered. His ocean eyes lowered to stare at the other man's hand, locked around the hilt of the dagger, the base of its' bronze and silver blade protruding from between Donovan's ribs.

Donovan sucked in a shuddering breath, shock digging barbed claws into his stomach as his grip slackened and fell from the violet-eyed man's throat.

The dagger scraped brutally against bone, sucked against muscle as the man leisurely pried the bloodied blade from Donovan's chest.

A cavernous moan bubbled over Donovan's tongue. He collapsed, a cloud of dust spewing from the carpet as his head struck the floor, as pain exploded through his torn flesh.

The violet-eyed man lowered himself into a graceful crouch, his coat pooling around his leather boots. He wiped the blade on the rug, leaving a dark, crimson smear. "Next time, put up more of a fight." He straightened and stepped over Donovan's immobilised form, over the river of crimson spilling from his throbbing wound, and calmly walked through the great, wooden door.

He closed it behind him.

Leaving Donovan to drown in a sea of his own blood.

SOOTHING SUNLIGHT DRIFTED across floorboards smothered in dust, across the spreading, darkening blood defiling the carpet beneath Donovan's pallid form. Beams of warmth delicately caressed the barely shifting muscles of his naked chest, the sunlight exposing the rise and fall of lungs drawing shallow breath. His shoulders and knees were curled, cradling his draining wound, refusing to move for the torture of sliced skin and severed muscle. He lay there with blood seeping through his fingers, the coarse rug scratching the tender skin of his side, until the sun departed, revoking its' warmth and relinquishing him to the rapid approach of night.

Cautiously, Donovan lifted his blood-stained hand and watched as the last of the torn flesh knit itself together, the river of crimson congealing on his skin the only evidence of the now non-existent wound. He remained in his place on the floor, his impossible, ocean eyes staring and absent, as the birds sang the sun to sleep, as the wind began to howl.

Finally, he pressed his palms to the floor and forced himself upright, his muscles convulsing in muted protest. Long legs stepped up to the open window, his approach chasing an owl from its' perch on the sill. It hovered a moment in the air, blinking at him, its' eyes of captured moonbeams spilling intelligence, its' feathers of copper and ivory rustling in the breeze as it methodically beat its' wings.

A growl quaked within Donovan's chest. Deep-rooted anger surged through him, eddying as he struck the cool stone of the windowsill. The surface shattered like glass, fracturing and crumbling to litter the floor.

The owl released a piqued hoot and flapped onto the roof above, settling to peer at him over the edge.

Donovan snarled at the creature, his lips peeling back over ivory teeth, his glare forged of murderous ice and cruelest steel.

An innocent tilt of the owl's feathered head doused the fire in Donovan's veins. He lifted a hand from the ruined windowsill, dragging his blood crusted palm across the rough planes of his jaw and silently scolding himself for lashing out at a defenceless bird.

He leaned through the still-open window, feeling its' stone walls graze the curves of his broad shoulders. A breeze rustled the silken waves of his hair as he peered down, assessing the harrowing drop to the paved walkway far below. The soft light of dusk painted his surroundings in twisting shadows of sapphire and violet. Dark, silhouetted pines shot up through rolling mist which collected in cobweb clouds, its' phantom fingers licking the edges of the trees swaying limbs.

Donovan swallowed a bout of nausea. He turned back to the cylindrical room, raking a hand through his sweat-damp hair and releasing a pained-filled groan. He strode across the length of the chamber, his bare feet silent on the ageing floorboards and fraying carpet, his gaze sweeping over the giant, wooden beams supporting the roof.

Violet eyes flashed. The dagger sliced his flesh.

Donovan squeezed his eyes shut, shaking his head to dislodge the memory, to remove the confusion, the anxiety hurriedly blossoming into fear. He peered down at the smear of drying blood across his ribs, brows furrowing at the section of smooth skin where the wound should have been.

He had to find the violet-eyed man.

He needed answers.

Donovan's long strides slowed and he stopped by the stunted, wooden table set beside the bed. His eyes flicked between the table and the heavy, wooden door through which the violet-eyed man had disappeared. Through which he would follow.

But he could not follow unarmed.

Donovan seized the table and it splintered, its' leg snapping submissively beneath his unforgiving grip. He rotated the makeshift spear in his palm, considering the crooked tip, the threatening, fractured spike.

It would inflict a jagged wound.

Nothing so smooth and elegant as the dagger.

The corner of Donovan's lips curved sharply in a destructive smile, dark and deadly as the ocean's crushing depths. He marched towards the imposing door, the leg of the table poised and primed for a fight.

The door screamed as he hauled it open, its' rusted hinges piercing the inundating quiet.

It was unlocked.

Unguarded.

Suspicion hardened to lead, forming a gruelling weight inside him.

Beyond the wooden door, a desolate stairwell descended into darkness. A flickering lantern hung from a wall, fiercely battling the stagnant shadow as the flame ravenously consumed its' wick. Melted wax bled from its' candle, light seeping through the discoloured blemishes of its' glass.

Donovan plucked it from the wall, surrendering himself to instinct as he silently stalked down the stairs.

The violet-eyed man had poisoned him.

Stolen him.

Stabbed him.

An earth-shattering anger trampled Donovan's flutter of fear.

The lantern banished the stale darkness around him, casting the sharp angles of his furious expression in flittering amber. He set his jaw, teeth grinding aggressively, glare flashing with untameable violence.

The stairs sloped severely, coiling on themselves in an endless tunnel, the monotonous stone walls broken only by the occasional, slitted hollow; a window deprived of glass.

Donovan emerged from the stairwell in a glowing pool of light, expectant as he scanned the immaculate hall, the polished floorboards peaking out beneath a vivid length of scarlet carpet. Ancient paintings decorated the walls, their surfaces depicting vicious battles; wars atop writhing masses of broken bodies, blood spattered crimson over dying fields and splintering ships.

Donovan's frown deepened, shadowing his cheeks and hollowing his eyes. The paintings reached for him, tugging at the dark veil restricting his memories with cold, skeletal fingers. He suppressed a shiver of disgust and lengthened his strides until the paintings transformed into vague, smeared canvases, sweeping past his peripheral vision. His fingers tightened on the makeshift stake, the wood fracturing beneath the prison of his palm.

He unconsciously loosened his grip and came to an abrupt halt before a towering window.

Moonlight poured through the glass, caressing the dried smear of blood across his ribs.

The knife's hilt glinted, embedded in his flesh.

A soft, delighted laugh fluttered through the darkened hall, echoed by a chorus of glasses striking one another, their sharp chimes raising mounds of flesh on Donovan's arms. Listening past the raging of his pulse, he caught a breath of muffled music. The vivacious tune floated through the hulking, stone walls, its' whisper dancing to him along the length of scarlet carpet.

Donovan rolled his shoulders. The muscles of his back rippled, gilded by his glowing lantern and the silver moonlight streaming through the windows. He strode forward, converging with the music and laughter, the stake clutched by his side, imperious as a glinting spear. His fierce eyes narrowed at the flood of light spilling from an intersecting hall. He stormed towards it, then through it, his presence a commanding entity, his looming shadow shaving the floor, lurching in response to the flaming, iron torches secured to the labyrinthine walls. Their heat kissed Donovan's exposed skin. Blood pounded through his veins, thunderous in its' intensity, driven entirely by instinct and smothering rational thought.

His pace slowed as he reached the threshold of a vast, stone chamber. His steps were silent as he padded inside.

And found himself beneath a ceiling supported by tremendous, wooden beams and embellished with two identical iron chandeliers, their candles burning serenely.

At the far end of the room, a carved, stone fireplace restrained a beast of bellowing flames, its' powerful glow silhouetting several figures gathered around a long, rectangular table.

"Ah, the entertainment has arrived!"

Donovan bristled at the familiar voice, adjusting his grip on his stake and contemplating the damaging effects of a flung lantern as rage erupted deep in his core.

The violet-eyed man had removed his scarlet coat, revealing an ebony shirt which whispered around his slender shoulders as he stood. He left his position at the head of the table and raised a crystal glass of rich, butterscotch liquid. "I see you managed to acquire a weapon." The man lifted a brow at Donovan's stake, his disturbing gaze glinting derision. "How quaint." His lips curled in a barbed smirk. "Are you going to use it as a toothpick?"

A growl vibrated in Donovan's throat, his features shifting like a darkening storm. He shot a furtive glance at the table, registering the occupants all turned to peer at him, registering the single, empty chair, a plate poised before it, greased with the remnants of a meal.

The violet-eyed man settled back into his seat, sipping his drink and delicately crossing his ankles on the surface of the table. He gestured for the musicians to cease their song. They instantly lowered their instruments, eyes fixed expectantly on him. "The rules of the game are as follows..."

Donovan bared his teeth. "I'll not play your game."

The violet-eyed man set his glass beside his plate, flicking an elegant hand and absently dismissing Donovan's interjection. "You may fight with any weapons you can find."

A snarl spilled from Donovan. He began to stalk forward, muscles rigid, preparing to attack. He shot a glare at the figures surrounding the table, daring them to intercede. "I will not—"

"I would stay very still, if I were you." The murmur drifted over him, cool and sickly sweet, punctuated by the honed tip of an axe pressing against the lowest curve of Donovan's spine.

Cold steel grazed his skin.

Blood bellowed in his ears.

He froze beneath the promise of the pressure.

"Wouldn't want to foul the floorboards." Warm lips brushed his ear. He felt a woman's exhilarated smile against his skin. "Blood's a bitch to clean up."

Donovan's gaze flicked to the single, empty chair at the table, to the cutlery leaning against the plate, to the partially filled crystal glass, its' contents waiting patiently to be finished.

The violet-eyed man continued, deliberately ignoring the woman and her axe. "You have free reign of the castle and the forest. If you so choose you may run, or hide. There is fresh water and sufficient wildlife to survive, if you are able to evade us for long enough for that to be required." The light of the fire skimmed the flash of his razor grin, a challenge breaching his violet gaze. "And that is a substantial if."

Donovan choked his budding sense of panic, concentrating on the chill of the axe pressed against his spine, remembering the pain of the dagger, sliding between his ribs. He was no fool. And he was getting tired of being toyed with.

He twisted in the woman's grip, dropping his stake and reaching for her axe.

Her blade sliced his skin, a sliver of blood welling to the surface.

He swung the lantern, its' flickering walls gliding toward the axe-wielder's temple.

The woman leaped back, falling into a crouch.

The lantern carved through vacant air.

"When you are caught, you will be debilitated and returned to your starting position for the next round." The violet-eyed man lifted his hands to cradle the back of his head, spreading his elbows wide and leaning back in his chair.

He closed his eyes.

The axe-wielder's loose, brunette curls consumed her face, displaying only the delighted curve of her ecstatic grin. She launched herself at Donovan, the blade of her axe severing the lantern from its' handle. Glass shattered on the floor, molten wax spilling and solidifying in the shards.

Donovan dropped the handle and lunged, evading the woman's guard, driving a palm into her chest, slamming her into the floorboards.

The back of her skull crashed into the ground.

Her breath exploded from her parted lips.

A single, violet eye split open to peer at Donovan. The figures around the table began to whisper and murmur. "This is a game of combat and strategy." The man opened his other eye, his relaxed countenance swept aside like an insubstantial curtain, replaced with startlingly keen interest. "I expect you will provide a decent challenge. After all, the thrill of the hunt is in the chase."

Another woman uncurled from her position beside the man, her brunette curls matching those of the winded woman on the floor. A faint rasp echoed through the room as she drew a gleaming gun from her belt. And aimed the yawning barrel at Donovan's head.

"You have a ten minute head start." The violet-eyed man slid his boots from the table, elbows bracing on either side of his plate. He steepled his fingers as Donovan straightened, abandoning the woman lying at his feet.

The violet-eyed man tilted his head, the movement almost avian.

A smile crept over his face.

And when he spoke, a cold shiver rippled beneath Donovan's skin.

"Let the hunt begin."

The woman cocked the hammer of her gun with a taunting smile. Donovan ran.

Chapter Forty-Three

DONOVAN WOKE TO DARKNESS. A rasping groan scaled his throat. His head ached with an unabating throb. He felt broken. Shattered. His muscles cramped, punishing him for some obscure crime he had committed unconsciously.

Donovan shoved himself upright, instantly assaulted by a jarring slap of vertigo, an onslaught of nausea.

He had felt this before.

He had *done* this before.

Donovan reached to remove the blankets draped over his chest, but paused, eyes adjusting.

He was in his room. In his bed.

There was a weight leaning on the mattress at his side.

Adalinda.

She slept on the edge of a chair, her arms crossed on the bed, her cheek pressed into his blankets, her breaths soft and even.

Donovan settled back on his elbows, warmth spreading through his chest as he watched her lashes delicately flutter. The skin beneath her eyes seemed bruised, mildly swollen, it was barely visible in the dark, as if she had been struggling to stay awake and had finally succumbed to sleep.

Donovan pressed his fingers to his sternum, feeling the wraithlike memory of a mortal wound. The cleaved skin and shattered bone had healed, the surface of his chest now completely smooth. As if he hadn't been shot. As if he hadn't died.

As if he hadn't remembered.

He remembered the fury of an irrepressible tempest, the sorrow of a weeping sky. He had clung to the memories, seizing them with insubstantial fists, only to have them torn from him as he woke, stolen, again, leaving an empathic impression and a gaping, uninhabited abyss. A hollow chasm where the memories should have been.

Adalinda shifted in her sleep, humming gently and turning her head.

Donovan remembered her dragging him through the gallery basements, grunting when he stumbled, gritting her teeth when his consciousness lapsed. He remember Christensen on his other side, Clarke's figure traipsing ahead.

He remembered leaving the gallery.

Then nothing.

And now there was her. Sleeping at his side. Stunning as a night bloom and absent of her stubborn ferocity.

Familiar.

So familiar.

Donovan tentatively pushed himself up, sitting and reaching for the glass of water Adalinda must have left on his nightstand. He tried not to disturb her as he drank, as he set the glass back down and gently pushed aside the covers. He would get up, carry her to her room...

Adalinda moaned, rising and dragging her hands across her eyes. She sat back in the chair, brows furrowing when she noticing him. "... You died..."

Donovan didn't move.

Adalinda's gaze lowered to his chest, to the place the bullet wound had been. She was wearing a new scarf, dark as roasted chestnuts, her woollen shirt and trousers chosen to match.

"Your heart stopped."

Donovan waited for the questions, waited for the inevitable disbelief, the confusion, the inability to understand.

Adalinda leaned forward, her golden eyes alight as she released a seething, accusatory growl. "Don't you *ever* do that *again*." She bared her teeth, silver tears collecting on her lower lids. "I thought you were *gone*. I thought—" The anger fled from her expression. She took a composing breath and stood, stepping over to his nightstand and retrieving something from the table, along with a pair of spoons. She sat on the edge of his bed, the chocolate tart he had bought her cradled in one hand. She looked at him, her gaze enthralling, stubborn strength forming a barrier across an endless, fracturing despair. "I am *not* eating this alone."

Donovan smiled and slid aside, making room for her, and she set the tart on the sheets. She looked exhausted, fragile and drained, as if in a heartbeat she might break. "I seem to recall you mentioning this wasn't a morning food."

Adalinda handed him a spoon, gesturing to the curtains drawn across his windows. "It isn't morning, it's evening."

Donovan grunted, taking a spoonful of the tart. He chewed slowly, watching her.

Adalinda frowned at the assorted berries, spoon hovering in the air. "Did you know you would heal?"

"No." Donovan carved another chunk out of the tart, waiting for Adalinda to do the same. "... I wasn't sure."

"But you can heal."

"Yes."

She was quiet for a moment, staring at the tart. "Perhaps you're like me."

Donovan paused, then placed his spoon on the nightstand. "I don't know. That depends on what you are."

Adalinda's fingers moved to brush her scarf. She stopped, taking a bite of the tart and staring at the curtained window. When she swallowed and spoke, her voice was barely a murmur, faint as falling snow. "You don't want to know what I am."

Donovan brushed his fingers over Adalinda's hand, closing the space between them until he felt her breath on his lips. Her skin was cool beneath his, sending shivers up his arms. "Tell me."

Adalinda's gaze drifted to his mouth, lingering just enough to ignite a yearning flame, smouldering in the depths of his soul. He wanted her. He felt as if he knew her but he wanted to *feel* her, to know she was real beyond the occasional brush of their skin, he wanted to admire her delicate flesh, worship the soft sway of her curves, savour the taste of her lips against his, of her skin beneath his tongue.

Adalinda lifted her eyes back to his, the corner of her mouth twitching in a despondent smile. She slid her hand from beneath his, took the unfinished tart and rose. "You need to speak with Clarke and Christensen, they're waiting in the kitchen. We can finished this later."

Donovan felt himself crack.

Adalinda collected his spoon and walked to the door, pausing as she stepped into the hall. She turned her head, looking at him over her shoulder. "... I'm glad you're alright, Donovan."

Again, his name felt wrong on her lips, like drizzling syrup that tasted of ash, like sugared acid or a candied knife. He felt as if the name were not his, just as *she* was not his.

He was struggling to understand why.

Donovan trailed Adalinda's movements as she closed his door, listened for the sounds of her padding feet in the silence.

She did not make a sound. She simply slipped away.

Away from him.

Donovan lay back in his bed and released a low, wearied groan. Adalinda did not ask questions because she was hiding something. Clarke and Christensen would not be so accommodating. He had died and they would want answers. *Adalinda* wanted answers, despite her hiding the truth. He owed it to them, an explanation. He just wasn't sure that the explanation he was willing to give would be enough.

Chapter Forty - Four

an iced-over lake..."

Adalinda felt Donovan's eyes on her back as she stared out the window of his apartment, arms wrapped around her waist, chewing the inside of her lip. Christensen leaned on the windowsill at her side, his arms crossed over his chest, while Clarke perched on the floor, cross-legged and fiddling with the coffee-table Adalinda had dismembered.

"... I should have drowned."

Adalinda closed her eyes, feeling the memories of sand beginning to bury her, to suffocate her. She felt the warmth flowing from Donovan's fire, remembered the tangible heat rippling across the desert.

"I don't have any answers for you. I don't know why I'm able to heal. I don't know why the bullet in the bar didn't leave a wound. I've been avoiding and dismissing this for almost a decade because I don't want to become a weapon, or a tool." Donovan's eyes flicked to Clarke. "Or an *experiment*."

Clarke sighed. "Shame. You'd make an attractive experiment." She began arranging wooden splinters in a pattern on the floor, seeming to have overcome her initial shocked response to Donovan's resurrection. "Can't we just try to make a *tiny* incision to calculate your rate of healing?"

Donovan's expression became flat.

Clarke turned to Christensen, her fingers resting on wooden splinters. "Is that a 'no'?"

Christensen ignored her, keeping his eyes pinned on Donovan. "So you're saying that you're basically indestructible and you've been dead before."

Donovan frowned. "I'm not sure if I actually died..."

"Okay, so you *may* have been dead before but you decided, in your infinite wisdom, *not* to find out if you were immortal."

Donovan leaned forward to rest his elbows on his knees, brow creasing. "That would require an unwavering belief and a willingness for self-immolation, neither of which I possess."

"Adalinda said the metal was called 'Aegisium.'"

Donovan's eyes shot to Clarke.

"Do you know what that is?"

He pressed his lips in a line, a muscle quirking in his jaw. "No, but I've heard it before. I can't remember where..."

Adalinda raised a hand to her scarf, listening to Donovan's warm honey voice, watching his reflection in the night-darkened window. She kept having to remind herself that he was alive, that he had woken from death and this wasn't a simple taunting of her mind. She turned around, pressing her fingers into her palms to stop the shaking. She could still feel his blood on her skin, could still see the life draining from his face as his heart stopped beating.

Adalinda's throat tightened.

Donovan looked at her and his expression softened, like ice melting over a flame. He pushed himself off the couch and strode to her side. "You mentioned you woke in a desert ten years ago without memories, you heal quickly and I come back from death…"

Adalinda's breath hitched. She pressed her lips together, curled her hands into fists.

She knew what he was going to say.

"Perhaps the murders aren't just a threat to you, they're a message to *both* of us. You said it yourself, perhaps I am like you."

Adalinda's laugh barely contained her sob as she swallowed the tears stabbing at her eyes. "I was wrong. You have no idea how different we are. You're a miracle and I'm—" Adalinda shook her head. "You don't want to know what I am. *None* of you want to know what I am."

Monster.

She stepped around Donovan. "We need to find the murderer and the best place to look will be back in those tunnels." She raised her fingers to her shoulder, where Clarke had removed the bullet. "There's an entrance through Shade's orphanage."

Donovan's expression hardened. "What?"

Adalinda skirted around the broken coffee-table, feeling the air in the apartment begin to thicken as if the moisture in it were condensing. She felt Donovan's eyes on her as Christensen moved away from the window.

"We found a set of tunnels when you were…" Christensen paused, glanced at Clarke. "… Dead." He cleared his throat. "There were guards, like the one's in Lorelei's bar. Adalinda shot them."

Adalinda looked down at her hand, her skin was beginning to feel damp, as it had when she'd reached for Donovan in the orphanage.

A faint sheen of moisture began to glisten in the air.

Donovan rumbled a growl. "Who were the guards?"

"We aren't sure, we were too focused on following the murderer."

"You went after the murderer and *took Adalinda?*"

Adalinda's ears popped. The air began to smell of rain, of clouds and storms…

"*She* went after the murderer, I just followed! Why are you getting mad at *me*?"

"You were supposed to be *protecting* her."

"I *tried!* She ran into a barrage of bullets! You seriously think I was going to walk into that?"

Donovan went quiet. Adalinda could feel him fuming. His stillness *hummed.*

Her scalp began to prickle.

Adalinda took a humid breath and turned to find the air around Donovan dense and shimmering, the light of dusk refracting through it.

Clarke had stopped arranging fragments of the shattered coffee-table, her arms were limp at her sides, her eyes wide and glinting. "What. Is. *That?*"

Christensen reached out and the moisture collected on his hand as it brushed Donovan's arm. "*What the hell…?*" He breathed, rubbing his fingers together.

Donovan closed his eyes and inhaled an unsteady breath. "It happens when I get angry." He exhaled and the water disappeared, dispersing into the air. "I take it you didn't *find* the murderer."

Adalinda hugged her arms around her waist. "No, he escaped."

"I want to see the tunnels."

Christensen was still staring at his hand, the moisture gone, the skin inexplicably dry. He looked up at Donovan and let his hand fall to his side. "I haven't seen this happen before."

Donovan grunted. "Adalinda makes it worse."

A grin spread across Clarke's face as Adalinda dropped her arms and raised her brows.

Donovan dragged a hand over his face, a sheet of stubble darkening the smooth skin. He looked tired. Worn. "We have to find the murderer. There have been too many interferences and we can't afford to fall any further behind."

"What do you suggest we do?" Christensen crossed his arms. "Those tunnels are filled with guards, all of them armed with rifles."

Adalinda smiled softly. "I don't think that's going to be much of a problem."

Christensen narrowed his eyes and gestured to Clarke. "In case you haven't noticed, *some* of us are mortals incapable of immediate healing and resurrection."

"Speak for yourself." Clarke sniffed.

Christensen's fingers dug into his biceps. "You're not like them."

Clarke's lips curled in a wicked, razor tipped smile. "Have you *seen* me die?"

"No, but—"

"Then you can't possibly know, can you?" Clarke lifted her shoulders in a deliberate shrug as Donovan and Adalinda exchanged a look.

Christensen dropped his arms to his sides, a muscle flickering in his jaw. "I hate all of you."

"Deal with it, *mortal*." Clarke pushed herself off the floor, smirking.

The corner of Adalinda's lips twitched up in amusement. "I suggest we find some weapons... I left that rifle I stole in the basement." A shiver spread across her scalp, prickling as it trailed down her neck and her smile faded. "I'm not particularly optimistic about surviving those guards a second time, even *with* a living shield."

"Manshield." Clarke corrected.

Donovan released a weary sigh. "None of you are coming."

Adalinda's heart stuttered in her chest, irritation rising through her. "You don't get to choose."

"I'm not risking any more deaths." Donovan straightened his shoulders, lengthened his spine. "You're a target, Adalinda." His eyes grazed over Christensen and Clarke. "And you're both going to tell me where the entrance to the tunnel is and keep her here, because if you don't I swear to the stars and back that I will knock you all unconscious and secure you here myself."

"No. I may be a target but I saw the murderer in that tunnel and he didn't so much as *look* at me, even when I tried to shoot him." Adalinda marched back over the ruined coffee-table, stopping in front of Donovan and pressing a finger into his chest. "There's no way in the furthest reaches of *hell* that I am letting you go down there alone."

Donovan's shoulders tightened, a muscle flickered in his neck as he peered down into her simmering, golden glare. "You will because you won't have a choice, Adalinda."

Adalinda growled, masking the fear rising within her. Panic twisted her heart and clawed at her throat. She had seen him die and it replayed in her mind, over and over, his features ashen, his blood covering her skin. "I'm going with you." She gritted her teeth and glared up at Donovan. "I will not *lose you again!*"

A startled silence fell over the room, dense and brimming with tension.

Adalinda's finger dropped from Donovan's chest and she met his stunning ocean eyes, darkened by the barest impression of a frown. "You can threaten all you like but the only way you'll keep me from going into those tunnels is by leaving my cold, dead body with the remains of that damned coffee-table." She pointed at the shattered wood on the floor, then took a steadying breath and rolled her shoulders. "And even *that* might not stop me."

Clarke brought her hands together in a brusque, cutting clap. Her lips split in a grin. "*Damn right.*"

Christensen nodded his confirmation, eyeing Donovan's resolute stance, the severe line of his mouth. "What? Did you honestly think we would sit and stay like good little puppies while you got to go play hero?" Ebony skin gleamed as Christensen shook his head. "I don't think so. *Not* going to happen."

Donovan's fingers flexed and contracted into white-knuckled

fists. "Adalinda, may I have a word?" His warm, honey voice flowed over her, barely concealing the anger teeming beneath the surface as he wrapped his fingers around her arm and gently led her to the other side of the room.

A grimace twisted Clarke's face as she rose, words skipping over her tongue in a sweet chirp. "We're going to find weapons." She grabbed an oblivious Christensen and tugged him away, her quiet murmur barely audible as they slipped past the kitchen. "I'm not sure we want to be part of this."

Donovan watched them disappear down the hall. When they were gone he turned on Adalinda, looming over her with an expression of cold fire. "*What are you doing?*" He stepped forward, his chest heaving, sucking in furious breaths. "I'm trying to *protect* you."

Adalinda planted her feet, refusing to retreat. Instead, she matched him, moving forward and pressing her chest against his as the air began to thicken, as the water-pipes in the walls began to groan. "I have told you, I don't *need* your protection." She fumed as his scent of woodsmoke and rain caused shivers to brush up her spine, molten heat blooming in her core. "I am *not* some swooning damsel and I am *certainly* not going to sit here uselessly while *waiting* for *you*."

A growl rumbled through Donovan's chest. "I'm telling you to stay so I don't go out of my mind worrying that you'll get yourself *hurt* again. Did you even consider that maybe I wouldn't be able to concentrate with you in the *line of fire*?" Donovan blinked. The flames leaked from his eyes, the tension seeped from his shoulders. He lifted a hand, grazing his thumb over the curve of Adalinda's cheek. "I don't expect you to be anything less than what you are, Adalinda." She shivered as he bowed his head, closing his eyes and leaning his forehead against her own. His breath coiled with hers in a smouldering dance between their mouths. "I just don't want to see you hurt."

Adalinda inhaled, the air unsteady in her lungs. Her palms pressed against the hard planes of Donovan's stomach, relishing the sparks awakened by his touch. His lips called to her, the distance between them pleading to be closed as a hollow ache began to spread through her chest. "I can take care of myself."

"I know." Donovan's words were a whisper caressing her skin as his arm snaked around her waist, pulling her into him, banishing the air which separated them while his skilful fingers traced her jaw.

The pulse began to throb in her veins, heat flourishing in her core, tangling with an unbearable, aching *need*. Like the hunger of starvation. Like the thirst of dehydration. Profound and unreservedly vital. The invisible, crushing mass of gravity itself.

Donovan lowered his mouth.

A sigh bled from Adalinda, her exhaled breath pouring into Donovan's tantalisingly parted lips.

Her scalp began to prickle. Intense. Quivering.

Adalinda stiffened in Donovan's grip, plucked from her fervent haze. She raised a trembling hand to her scarf and wrenched herself away, stumbling back.

A flash of hurt and confusion darted across Donovan's face as he reached for her. "Adalinda..."

Adalinda tore her eyes from his, turning to hide the flush creeping over her cheeks, to hide the bout of panic eating at her stomach.

Monster.

"Adalinda." Donovan strode towards her, his features flooding with concern, his hand outstretched to close over her shoulder. "What's wrong?"

Adalinda pulled away from him, angling her shoulder so his hand hovered over empty air. She felt sick. Horrified. She had almost let him kiss her. Almost let him in. She couldn't. She couldn't tell him what was wrong. If he knew—

If he knew...

Monster.

Her fault.

"I'm sorry." Adalinda shook her head, wishing she was anything other than herself. "It's nothing."

"No, it's not." Donovan let his hand fall to his side. "Tell me."

Exhaustion settled over Adalinda in a heavy blanket. She was so tired of hiding, so tired of running from her own truth. If she told him, perhaps he would understand. Perhaps he wouldn't see her as what she clearly was. A monster. Adalinda opened her mouth, preparing to speak, the air curling on her tongue, about to form the terrible words. "I—"

Clarke barrelled out of the hall, startling Adalinda into silence. "Okay, so we have two guns, Christensen's and Donovan's, we found a paperweight and a stapler. *And* I remembered I have a crowbar in my car." She lifted the stapler in her hand, flicking it open and depressing it.

Nothing came out.

"God damn it, why does this not work?" Clarke twisted the stapler, inspecting the inside and grumbling under her breath. "... *That's such a let down.*"

"Damn it Clarke, put the stapler away." Christensen stomped in after her, gun in hand, narrowing his emerald eyes at the solid, glass paperweight and the stapler. "I swear, five minutes alone with you and I've thought of *a dozen* different ways to kill you."

Clarke raised a brow at him, the long side of her hair falling into her face, the piercing in her lip glinting. "Only a dozen? I would have expected—" She stopped abruptly, frowning at Donovan and Adalinda who stood frozen at the edge of the room, both of them staring at her. "... Did I interrupt something?"

Donovan's reply collided with Adalinda's. "Yes, actually."

"No." Adalinda shot Donovan a warning glare. "No, you didn't interrupt anything."

Clarke clucked her tongue, glancing between the two of them

before shrugging and moving to drop the stapler onto the kitchen bench with a loud *clunk*. "I don't know about you, but I want the paperweight."

An exasperated sigh blew from Christensen. "Clarke, you can't go into the tunnels armed with only a paperweight."

"Oh, *really*?" Clarke turned on him, challenge written in bold across her face. "Watch me."

Adalinda stepped away from Donovan, a hole forming between her lungs. "I'll just steal another gun from one of those guards... Perhaps I'll take the crowbar as well."

Clarke smiled triumphantly, crossing her arms and tucking the paperweight beneath her elbow. "I *told* you she'd want the crowbar."

Christensen scowled at the paperweight. "I think we're going to need more than two guns, a paperweight and a crowbar. They'll be alert after what we did this morning, they might have even replaced the guards."

Adalinda peered at Donovan, his features a mask of calm. "Clearly you haven't seen anyone fight with a crowbar."

"And you have?"

Adalinda shrugged. "I have a few ideas."

"We can send Manshield in first." Clarke grinned, nudging Christensen with her shoulder as Adalinda glanced out the window.

The moon was beginning to rise, a pale sliver in the cold darkness.

She crushed a flutter of anxiety, hoping they hadn't left the guards enough time to recover.

She was not eager to find out if they had.

CHAINS

TEN YEARS AGO

THE SILENCE LINGERED LIKE DEATH, thick and morose, crammed between the stale, viscous air and the cold which slithered over the walls and floor, reaching and leaching through shuddering flesh and aching bone.

A hollow drip split the leaden quiet, leaving her throbbing ears ringing with an endless, phantom scream.

Numb fingers twitched as her skin began to prickle, as the blood began to flow, creeping towards her hands strung from the ceiling by creaking chains. The cold steel of manacles bit into her drooping wrists, the ceaseless pressure marking her skin and threatening to rupture her flesh.

A disoriented moan dribbled from her dry and fractured lips, the noise accompanied by another resonating drip. Her lids felt weighted as she opened her eyes, blinking in sluggish confusion at the suffocating dark beneath her bowed head.

Her irises burned like golden flames, glowing eerily in the black.

She swallowed, her parched throat flexing, her skin scraping against the metal collar wedged beneath her chin. Her brows narrowed as she shifted, legs smarting violently in protest before reluctantly enduring her weight. Her muscles ached as she stood, relieving the pressure of the leather brace which supported her ribs, listening to the harsh clink of chains which accompanied her movements, softly tinkling, then savagely chanting.

Her legs convulsed.

Her knees collapsed.

The brace ploughed into her chest, shoving the air from her lungs. She gaped. Gasped. Coughed. The cracked flesh of her lips split. She tasted blood. And still she continued to cough, wrenching her exhausted muscles, gasping great breaths of the damp, sour air, wincing when her wrists and neck dug into the steel of her restraints. She fought the violent urge to be sick, to empty her cramping stomach and slick the stone floor with bile.

A desperate sob fell from her mouth, reverberating with the rattling of chains as she forced herself to still, to think through the panic and listen past her ragged breaths.

Another drip, hollow and metallic.

She clawed at her mind, struggling to remember where she was, how she had escaped the desert, only to find more gaps, more memories which slipped and shifted like sand beneath the wind.

She was draped across the back of a camel, burnt-orange dress torn and creased, arms and legs limply swinging on either side of the creature's stomach. Her wrists and ankles had been shackled to the saddle, chains clinking, metal burning, roasting beneath the blistering sun.

The camel grunted, ceaselessly plodding as she slid in and out of consciousness, so smoothly she barely noticed.

A frustrated moan reverberated in her chest as the memory slipped, as she fought to hold on.

She caught glimpses of a man riding ahead, nothing more than a silhouette wearing a scarf across his face. He turned and the sunlight flashed in his eyes, one of them a pale, sightless white.

She remembered a scar carving his face... and an owl, perched on his shoulder...

She shook her head and the steel collar scraped her neck, dragging her back to the darkness. "Hello?" The word was barely a croak, a scratching, whispered sound choked by dread in her sandpaper throat. She opened her mouth, preparing to speak past the pain, to smother the fear. "Someone?" The word escaped a husk. Barely a breath.

Futile.

She hauled herself upright, ignoring the grating chant of chains as her slender wrists took her weight, as her legs struggled to lock beneath her. She ignored the feeling of her splitting skin, blood seeping from the insides of her wrists, over her shackles and down her forearms. She ignored her desperate thirst, aggravated by the echoing drip of water and the irregular drip of her blood as it leaked from her elbows and collided with the floor.

A groan rasped through her throat, her teeth singing as she clenched her jaw, her golden eyes alight with anguish. She lifted her wrists, releasing the pressure from the manacles, and endured a bout of vertigo as the blood escaping in rivulets began to steadily flow.

She forced her cramping legs to move, grunting as she stumbled forward, the weight of chains dragging at her ankles and screeching across the damp, stone floor.

She recognised the pain, and fear, as she did her own shadow.

Something rippled beneath the veil imprisoning her memories.

She pursed her lips in an obstinate line. Took another step. The movement halting. Jarring.

Her muscles screamed a suicidal howl.

Her knees shrieked.

Then buckled.

She pitched forward.

And the collar snared her throat, the chain attached to it stopping her fall. She caught on the leather brace around her ribs and her body dropped, becoming limp, swinging like a marionette suspended by biting, metal strings.

Her scalp began to prickle.

The sensation brushed across her neck, echoing over her shoulders. Her numb arms began to throb, to heat, to burn. A torrent of pins and needles spread like wildfire, the returned feeling shredding her muscles. Her shoulders began to shake, trailed by a coarse, scraping sound which spread through the room like sand poured over steel. "I'm in hell." The noise took shape after those words, after a dam broke in her chest and her lips opened, curving up at the corners and spilling a deranged laugh. "I died in the desert and this is hell?" She lifted her head, the delusional laugh still pouring from her in waves. "What? No fire? No tempests? No demons?!" Her words spat at the walls in a tangle of languages, still harsh and dry but louder now, encouraged by her splintered sanity. "Where is the river of boiling blood and fire? The lake of frozen ice with its' drowning spirits? I find myself disappointed by your lack of creativity!" She shook her stinging arms in their chains, filling the pitch dark with a frenzied racket. "Why don't you try something new? Drown someone in their own blood. Or try a meat hook speared through the stomach. Now wouldn't that be brutal! Join the adults, you bastard! Why don't you try some damned barbed-wire?!"

A scraping beyond the room caused her to fall silent. She cocked her head in the thick darkness, her blazing eyes glowing like coals. This time, her voice was quiet, almost lilting. A beautiful, poisonous rasp as she sang through her scraping throat. "Come out, come out, wherever you are."

She was met with an all-consuming quiet.

The quiet of terror.

The quiet of frightened prey.

"I know you're out there." She cemented her bare feet on the crisp, stone floor, wriggling her toes and smiling into the black. The chains loosened as she straightened her spine with renewed strength, the smouldering reminder of pain all but forgotten.

Furious, indistinct shouts clawed through the walls and her gaze snapped up, focusing on the darkness which smothered the room before her.

The voices stopped, replaced by the grinding of steel hinges, engulfing the room in a flood of delicious noise.

The darkness parted. Amber light bled through the shadows, reflecting in her eyes, licking over her features like the tongue of a brutal flame.

The door swung open, whining as a dark silhouette stretched across the stone floor, haloed by the brilliant light.

A tight smile tugged at the corners of her parched lips.

She stepped towards the silhouette, the chain at the back of her neck growing taut. The prickling of her scalp increased, sweeping across her neck and down her spine in furious waves as another hollow drip resonated through the chamber. "I assume this isn't hell, then." She peered at the silhouette poised outside, lingering beneath the towering, steel frame of the door. "Won't you come in?"

The silhouette shifted, head softly tilting beneath the shadow of a hood.

She kept the smile on her lips, kept the fear buried, as she carefully watched the figure. Its' cloak was a pool on the floor, dark as deepest night. "Perhaps, you would like to tell my why I'm here."

The silhouette paused, glanced out the door, and retrieved a lantern from outside the threshold.

Its' steps were silent and graceful as it slowly drifted inside.

Chapter Forty - Five

Leda

Leda's agitated fingers tapped methodically at the wooden surface of the reception desk. She glared at the door to Shade's office, her hazel eyes hooded, the curve of her chin sinking into her palm. A bored grumble escaped her cupid-bow lips as she listened to the clock hanging precariously above a double-seated couch, the infernal ticking counting the hours she had been working.

The sun would soon vanish below the horizon, its' pale light dissipating into frozen dark.

Leda blew out a harsh breath, fluidly straightening her posture and reaching to pluck a book from the edge of her desk. Shade had ordered her to cancel all of his meetings for the afternoon, disappearing into his office to work while she preoccupied herself with reading, occasionally shooting steaming glares at either the clock or his door; she was unbiased as to which.

Her fingers peeled the pages apart while she lifted her lithe legs, propping her leather boots atop the desk and leaning back in her chair. She sucked her lip between her teeth, absently chewing as her gaze stroked the pages. A soft chuckle bubbled in her throat and she tucked a curling lock of brunette hair behind her ear, eyes sparking with amusement as she read. The methodic tick of the clock faded, the minutes stretching and merging.

Leda paused as a door slammed and heavy footfalls began tramping across the floorboards of the hall. A frown curved her mouth, her dark brows creasing as she reread the line.

As she reread the line *twice*.

Leda kept her eyes on the book, ignoring the hulking figure as it stomped into her peripheral vision.

"Where's Shade?"

Leda lifted a single finger, gesturing for the woman to wait, silently seething beneath the heated gusts of rancid breath that rustled her hair.

The woman leaned down, her face levelling with Leda's own, her breasts sagging heavily, neglected, as they strained against the stained fabric of her shirt. "Tell Shade I need to see him."

Leda's eyes snapped to the woman's snarling features, absorbing the hard, coal stare, the sooty, leather jacket and jeans stretched taut over a thick frame. The woman was cradling a tattooed hand against her chest. It was swollen, possibly broken. Leda snarled right back. "I'm nearly finished the page. Sit down and wait."

The woman struck Leda's desk with her unbroken fist, the thorned vines and screaming bodies inked on her forearm writhing in response to the impact.

Leda's computer rattled with the force. She looked back down to continue reading and the woman exhaled a sickening breath. Into Leda's face. "Fine. I'll find him myself."

Leda grumbled as the tattooed woman turned and stomped for Shade's office. "Hold on." She scanned the last sentence of the page and shifted her long legs off the desk, letting her boots drop to the floor before swiftly standing, flipping the book closed and pressing a button on the desk phone to call Shade. "You have a visitor."

"*I thought I told you to cancel all of my meetings.*"

Leda peered at the tattooed woman fuming by Shade's door, her coal eyes glinting in the artificial light. "... I did."

Shade's anger seeped from the speaker in a tangible mass, frothing and roiling through the air in an acidic curse. "*Honey, if you were half as smart as you are hot...*" He growled under his breath and Leda felt the blood begin to boil in her veins. "*Get rid of them.*"

Leda lifted her finger from the button, fury writhing beneath her skin, and plastered a spiteful smile onto her face. "Please, allow me to open that for you." The tattooed woman stepped aside as Leda slipped across the room with an assassins finesse. She placed her palm on the handle, electric malice thrumming inside her, and swung Shade's door open, carefully remaining concealed behind its' threshold.

"*What did I just—*" Shade froze, his obsidian eyes locking on his guest.

"*Suffer.*" The word was a poisoned breath directed at Shade as Leda gestured for the tattooed woman to enter. She waited until the woman had taken a step before moving into the doorway herself, her hazel eyes deliberately wide, blinking abashedly between Shade and the dark material stretched across the tattooed woman's back. "I'm sorry, she was insistent."

The tattooed woman shot Leda a look swimming in suspicion.

Shade straightened in his chair, his livid expression spilling into his steadily enunciated words as he spoke. "Step. Inside." His obsidian glare was a rotting blade, his fountain pen aggressively tapping his paperwork. "Shut. The. Door."

Leda hesitated, thrill flaring in response to his anger as she entered the office and quietly closed the door behind her.

Slowly, Shade rose from his leather seat, lengthening to his full height to glower at the intruding tattooed woman. He carefully placed his fountain pen beside his paperwork, aligning it to match the stack's perfect edge. "Sit down."

The tattooed woman rumbled, a feral sound bubbling from her throat. "A detective found the facility—"

"*Sit down.*" Shade fumed as the woman stomped across the carpet, barely contained rage revealing itself through the snarl which crept onto his lips as she took a seat. "Now, what is the rule?"

"Don't come here."

The woman winced as Shade leaned forward, slamming his palms onto the desk, paperwork crumpling beneath the force. "*Don't come here!*" He sucked a deep breath through his teeth and straightened to comb his fingers through his silver-streaked, midnight hair. "What is so *important* that you required an *audience?*"

"Sir... the facility was breached."

"Breached." Shade nodded, trailing a skeletal finger along the edge of his desk, slowly walking to its' corner. "You risk my reputation by coming here because someone *breached the facility?*"

The woman shifted uncomfortably in her chair, thorned vines constricting as she squeezed her fists. Her knuckles were pallid beneath the tattooed ink. "I thought—"

"No." The sound of Shade's teeth grinding sent a quiver along Leda's back. "You didn't think, because if you *had* thought you would have realised that by coming here *directly after a facility breach* you were LEADING THEM RIGHT TO ME!"

"... I wasn't followed."

"Oh?" Shade lifted his obsidian gaze to Leda, allowing his eyes to roam over her figure, lingering on her breasts. "What if someone checks the security cameras?"

"What?"

"The *security cameras.*" Shade reached down and smoothly pulled a drawer open in his desk, shooting a glare at the tattooed woman. "I suppose you avoided all of them while entering the building, because why would you come here, at this hour, parading in front of the *cameras*?"

The woman stood, her cropped hair rustling, the painted mouths of screaming bodies yawning wider as her solid arms flexed. "I came here to *warn* you—"

Shade snarled, retrieving a glinting object from the open drawer. "Consider me warned." He lifted his hand, the barrel of a bleak gun aimed at the woman's chest.

The silencer smothering the shot.

"Consider your employment terminated."

The woman gurgled as she collapsed, her coal eyes rimmed with a shock of white, blood seeping from the mortal wound to soak the charcoal fabric of her shirt.

Leda swore, trembling as she lifted a hand to cover her mouth. Her curling, brunette hair swept forward to form a shining curtain around her face. "You *shot* her!" She stumbled back, her free hand fumbling for the door handle. "You *murderer!*"

Shade watched blandly as the tattooed woman gasped, her muscles twitching horrifically. He threw the gun at the floor, the metal colliding with the woman's shin and looked at Leda. "Enough of the acting honey, I know you're working for someone else."

Leda glanced at the tattooed woman, at the crimson liquid trickling from the minute hole rupturing her chest, her aorta.

Leda drew in a long, smooth breath and lowered her hand from her mouth. "I was wondering how long it would take you to figure it out."

The corner of Shade's mouth curled in a cold smirk as he grazed his hungry eyes over her curves. "I was willing to allow you to stay awhile."

A wicked smile clawed its' way onto Leda's features, masking her irritation. "I think you underestimated me and you didn't notice."

On the floor, the tattooed woman's eyes lost focus, becoming glassy and vacant as they stared at the ceiling.

Shade lifted his angular shoulders in a dismissive shrug. "Get rid of the body and the gun. And find whoever broke into my tunnels. I'll deal with the security cameras."

Leda let her smile drop, her hazel eyes blazing as they narrowed. "I'm not your maid, do it yourself."

"What would your employer say if you were to lose your position as my secretary?" A soft rustle whispered through the room as Shade began to move, stalking towards her with predatory purpose.

"My *employer* would remind you to keep your nose out of bear traps." Leda stepped over the dead woman's head, her movements swift and fluid as a flowing rapid. She shuddered in disgust as Shade stopped before her, so close she could feel the heat of him seeping through her clothes. He dragged his knuckles over the curve of her hip, reaching around to sweep his palm over her backside.

Leda growled a warning, her lips twisting in distaste as Shade leaned towards her, his foul breath heating the curve of her neck.

Not long now.

Leda flinched at the scrape of rough, wet flesh against her skin. Shade's tongue, dragging over her pulse, sliding over her jaw, crawling along her cheek.

Leda tore herself from him, unmasked rage flaring across her face. The air raised mounds of revulsion on her skin. She could feel the repulsive trail of Shade's saliva growing cold.

Shade's lips split in a feral grin, his leer sparking challenge. He slammed his lips into hers, the stench of cigars and mint violating her senses, the warmth of his tongue driving between her teeth. One hand wrenched her hair. The other grabbed her breast. Pain flared as his fingers dug in, *crushing* her soft flesh.

Leda felt herself snap.

She lashed out, her teeth drawing blood as she mercilessly bit down on his tongue, her knee crashing brutally into his groin.

Shade howled a curse, doubling over and retching as he clutched himself.

Leda grabbed his collar, hauling him up as she spat the taste of him onto the floor, her spit flushed scarlet with his blood. She dragged her sleeve across her mouth and hissed into his pain-stricken face. "*You disgust me.*"

"How *dare* you." Shade bared his teeth, furious and steaming. "I could *ruin* you."

Leda shoved him back, taking pleasure in his gasp as he collided with his desk, hands scrabbling to catch himself before falling any further. "I highly doubt it." She glanced down at the paintings on the dead woman's forearms. Her hazel gaze locked on the coiling body of a snake, hidden amongst the thorns and bodies. She paused a moment, tapping a finger against her lips, considering the use of a murder as leverage. "Very well. I will remove your... *rubbish*. On one condition."

Shade furrowed his midnight brows, rage burning in his eyes. "You're not in a position to state conditions, *honey*."

A patronising smile curled Leda's mouth, sharp as any honed blade. "You know, guns sing a complex melody, if you have the ears to listen." She elegantly bent in a crouch, plucking the gun from the floor and checking its' magazine for bullets. "I can't decide whether it was moronic or incredibly intelligent to only have a single bullet in your gun, Shade." Leda replaced the empty magazine and flicked the firearm, eyes glittering as it twirled expertly around her finger. "Fortunately, if you are creative, like myself, you'll find that there are *many* more ways to use a gun than simply shooting." Leda uncoiled from her crouch, her movements a dancing blur as she swept across the floor. She hovered before Shade, his palms still planted on the desk, blood dripping through his crimson stained teeth and trickling down his chin. Her free hand caught his wrist in a destructive grip as he attempted to escape. "Move and I'll break it." She tapped the handle of the gun against his temple, smiling warmly as he stilled, as he registered the density of the gun, the pain it would cause. "Good, you understand." Leda met Shade's stare, watching a kernel of anxiety spread across his face. She had learned a lot about him in her time working as his secretary, including specific details about his more *felonious* endeavours. She felt a blooming satisfaction as she began to form her request, allowing the words to spill from her lips in a murmur, intimate and terminal. "Now, about that condition..."

Chapter Forty - Six

VELVET DARKNESS FLOATED above Shade's orphanage, its' façade
softly illuminated by the warm glow of the lamps standing sentinel
in the street. The moon hung in the bruised void above, a silver
crescent, sharp as a blade in the clear, frigid night, alone but for the
occasional burst of starlight.

The view would have been beautiful if Donovan had taken the time
to see it. It would have been serene in the quiet, ruminating shadow
the sun left upon the earth. But he did not see it, he did not notice
it. Because all he could see was her.

Adalinda stood in the street, chin tilted towards the sky, shining,
golden eyes staring at the moon as she inhaled a lingering breath.
Her cloak fluttered around her ankles, its' hood drawn and framing
the stunning features of her delicate face.

Her gloved hand tightened on the crowbar balanced across her
shoulder.

A steady stream of curses poured from Clarke's mouth in billowing
clouds as she tugged a fur hat lower over her ears and slammed the

car door closed. "*Satan's tight ass*, how is it so *cold*?"

Christensen stepped onto the footpath, his boots scuffing against the freezing pavement. "It's the middle of winter."

"Thanks, Captain Obvious." Clarke shoved her gloved hands into her coat and dramatically rolled her eyes. "Would you like to tell me why the sun has heat as well?"

Christensen frowned disapprovingly as he pressed a finger into the door bell of the orphanage. "You're grumpy this evening."

Clarke dug the glass paperweight from her pocket and held it up, threatening to throw it. "Don't make me use this."

Adalinda lowered her gaze from the moon and strode to the door. She angled her head slightly, listening to the metallic click of locks being turned inside.

The hinges groaned and the door opened to reveal a pair of bright, hazel eyes peering at them through the gap. "No visitors."

"We know." Christensen pressed a hand to the door, palm flattening against the wood. "We need to use your bathing room."

The hazel eyes narrowed, crinkling slightly at the corners as the woman repeated. "No visitors."

Donovan remained silent, his ocean eyes glued to Adalinda, as Christensen drew his identification from his pocket and held it out. "My name is Detective Christensen and we need to access the orphanage bathing room. We have reason to believe that it leads to the drainage tunnels underground."

A sceptical hum reverberated from the woman's throat. "Couldn't you just climb down a manhole?"

A crease formed in Donovan's brow as a lock of dark, curling hair fell into the woman's face and she brushed it aside.

"Climb down a manhole?" Christensen folded his identification and shoved it back into his pocket, turning to frown at Donovan.

"Why else would your friend have a crowbar?" The woman gestured to Adalinda who was holding the crowbar beside her leg as if it were a walking-stick.

Donovan quietly cleared his throat and Christensen stepped aside, raising his brows in question.

"Lorelei."

The woman's attention snapped to Donovan, her hazel eyes widening slightly at the mention of her name.

Donovan moved forward, his steps silent, his movements smooth and effortless on the frozen pavement. "You're the manager from the bar down the street."

"You're the one who was shot."

Donovan nodded.

Lorelei's expression softened slightly as her eyes roamed over him. "What are you doing here?"

"I volunteered." Lorelei tapped her fingers against the door. "I heard they had no one to look after the children."

Donovan lowered his chin in an appreciative nod, mouth curving in a soft smile. "We'd be grateful if you'd let us in." His arm brushed Adalinda's and he struggled not to flinch when she discretely pulled away. "We're in pursuit of a criminal and this is the easiest way to cut him off."

Lorelei tapped her fingers on the doorframe, her eyes flicking over Clarke and the paperweight still clutched in her gloved hand.

Clarke blanched and the paperweight disappeared into her pocket.

After a few moments, Lorelei lifted a shoulder in a noncommittal shrug and removed the chain from the door. "Alright, but don't wake the children."

"Thank you." Donovan watched as Adalinda slipped through the door first, swinging the crowbar back onto her shoulder and striding purposefully through the entrance hall, hips swinging beneath her cloak. Christensen and Clarke followed. "We can find the bathing room ourselves."

Lorelei closed the door behind Donovan and leaned into it, her shoulder taking her weight. "... I can see that." She crossed her arms and leaned her head back against the door, a smile tugging at the corner of her cupid-bow lips. "Let's hope you don't run into any trouble."

THE BATHING ROOM WALLS SEEMED to dance with undulating light, the steaming pools lit from below and glowing a crystalline blue. Adalinda saw herself as she washed Donovan's blood from her arms, the ghostly impression of a memory. She tightened her grip on the crowbar, glancing at Donovan in his billowing coat, his gaze locked on her. Her chest tightened and she tore her eyes from him, fighting the urge to shove him into the pool. He appeared so calm, so absolutely unchanged, after having been *killed*.

The crowbar twisted in her hand and dropped from her shoulder, heavily striking the steel grate, the metallic *clang* reverberating through the room.

Christensen tensed, abruptly shushing her as the sound faded, along with some of her frustration. "Are you *trying* to announce our arrival?"

Adalinda lowered herself to the grate, gently placing the crowbar beside it. There was a remnant smear of blood on the tiles, from when she had dragged herself from the sewer after the murderer. "It slipped."

Christensen grumbled under his breath, his dark emerald glare flashing in the rippling light.

"Next time it slips I'll bury it in something *softer*, shall I?" Adalinda looked pointedly at Christensen's abdomen before she slid her gloved fingers into the darkness below the grate and curled them around the patterned steel. A shallow breath flitted over her tongue as she pulled, the circle of metal smoothly sliding free of the stone floor.

Donovan's gloved hands darted out, helping Adalinda set the grate gently on the floor and she lifted her eyes to his, shoving aside the anticipatory flutter of butterflies.

Her gaze flitted to his lips.

She had nearly kissed him.

Monster.

Adalinda looked back at the grate.

Clarke held the paperweight up, occasionally adjusting her grip. "If something jumps out of that hole, I'm going to throw this and you'd better not be in the way."

"If you throw that you'll lose your only weapon." Christensen stepped forward and peered into the uncovered hole, his gun glinting menacingly in one hand. He dug a torch from his jacket and switched it on, illuminating the rusted stairs leading into the tunnel.

"Yes, but I'll have provided a distraction." A smug smile stretched across Clarke's face as she stepped closer to Christensen. She leaned in, raising a hand to the side of her mouth as if divulging a secret, then spoke in a staged murmur. "I throw, you shoot."

Donovan peered at Clarke, his expression unreadable.

"Well?" Clarke gestured to the uncovered grate. "Lead the way, *Manshield.*"

Donovan frowned but returned his attention to the hole, watching the stark light of Christensen's torch as it filtered through the grated, steel steps. He lowered himself down the spiralling staircase, neglecting to take the light from Christensen, one hand gripping his gun as he carefully scanned the shadows. Adalinda tensed as Donovan was swallowed by darkness, then cautiously followed, plucking the crowbar from its' place on the tiled floor. She climbed down with her fingers on the steel railing until she found Donovan standing on the tunnel's edge, watching her with a contemplative frown. He tucked his gun into his belt, took the crowbar from her and leaned it against the brick wall, then reached out to grip her waist and lift her down the last few steps. Donovan paused with Adalinda suspended in his arms, her boots dangling over the paved brick floor, her hands braced on his broad shoulders. She breathed him in subconsciously.

"Donovan?"

Donovan cleared his throat and gently placed Adalinda on the ground. His yawning pupils contracted as he snatched his gaze from her and looked up towards Christensen's voice and the torchlight pouring through the stairs.

"... You're not dead again, are you?"

"No." Donovan bowed his head to Adalinda, the heat of his breath seeping through her scarf and sending shivers over her scalp. He remained quiet for a moment, as if thinking, contemplating. "Earlier, you were going to tell me something. What was it?"

Adalinda stiffened but did not move. If she tore herself away from him again it would only make him question further. "Now isn't really the time for explanations."

Donovan stepped back, eyeing her. He handed her the crowbar and hummed under his breath, the sound a low, unsatisfied rumble. A muscle in his jaw twitched as Christensen hopped off the steps, torch sweeping the tunnel. The light flashed across the stream of water meandering through the subterranean dark, whispering of past storms and snow melt.

Christensen looked up as Clarke stepped through the hole. She leaned over the railing, head just below the opening, and peered down at them. "Should I replace the grate?"

Donovan shook his head. "No, leave it."

If they had to run it would become a hindrance and slow their escape.

Clarke shrugged and lowered herself the rest of the way down the stairs, running fingers over the smears of dried blood on the railing. "I take it this is Donovan's blood."

Adalinda shuddered, absently wiping her gloved hands on her cloak. "Yes..."

"Wonderful." Clarke leaped off the stairs and dusted her hands on her trousers. "I'll have to take a sample later."

Donovan dragged his fingers through his hair, searching the tunnel's dim depths before retrieving the gun from his belt. "Where's the entrance?"

Christensen shifted nervously as he gestured with his torch, its' beam sliding over the black arches of smaller tunnels, towards the door which would lead into the stairwell of the hidden hallways. "Let's hope the guards aren't still down there."

"I've a feeling they are." Adalinda moved forward, listening to the echo of steps as the others followed, listening to the hollow drip of water. Her memories began to stir. She felt the haunting bite of distant shackles and the blood draining from her wrists. Saw the murdered woman kneeling before her home... Adalinda ground her teeth and adjusted her grip on the crowbar, shoving the memories aside. "Let's just hope they aren't ready for a visit."

Donovan grunted, his voice reverberating as they walked past an intersecting tunnel, stepping over a stream of water and closing on the entrance to the halls hidden below.

Christensen's torch shifted over the paved ground beneath the door and Adalinda squinted her eyes. A pair of scuff-marks trailed into the shadows of the tunnel up ahead, faint as frost, barely a shade darker than the bricks. As if something had been dragged, leaving a streak of recently dried blood.

Adalinda stepped closer to the blood-trail, covering the marks with her cloak and looking up at Donovan. "Why don't you and Christensen check the stairwell? Clarke and I will wait up here until it's safe."

Donovan straightened, his features almost unrecognisable in the gloom. He stared at Adalinda, uncertain. "... You want to stay here."

"Yes." Adalinda nodded, aware of the damp cold which was creeping into her boots and lungs.

Donovan's mouth pulled into a frown as he adjusted his grip on his gun, still pointed at the ground. "Yes?"

Adalinda stepped closer, enough that a deep breath would cause her chest to graze his arms. "Is there something wrong with 'yes?'"

"Possibly." Donovan closed the distance, the contact momentarily erasing their surroundings. Adalinda's heart began to flutter, warming like bird wings in the midmorning sun. She forced herself to move back, brushing shoulders with Clarke.

The woman was scowling at her.

Christensen handed his torch to Clarke, the light spilling over the bricks and into the water. "The stairwell is lit, we won't need this." He shoved the door handle and stepped into the blinding light surging from inside, gun aimed down the steps. "Yell if you're attacked."

Donovan kept his eyes on Adalinda, reluctant to leave. She lowered her chin, gesturing for him to follow Christensen. Despite his deepening frown, he strode through the door and swung it shut.

"Um..." Clarke tapped the handle of the torch on her forearm, its' light swinging with the movement, glinting off the damp walls, paperweight clutched in her other hand. "What was that?"

Adalinda reached out almost blindly and plucked the torch from Clarke's grip. "What was what?"

"We'll wait up here?" Clarke stomped a solid boot on the brick floor, the noise echoing loudly through the tunnel. "*Why the hell would we want to wait up here?*"

Adalinda pointed the torch at the floor, its' circle of light illuminating the faint marks of dried blood on the bricks. "I thought, perhaps, we should do some research."

Clarke's eyes widened and she crouched to examine the trail, a veil of platinum hair falling into her face. She flicked it aside. "Blood." She raised her gaze to Adalinda, a smile curling her lips. "It's *blood.*"

"I say we follow it and find out where it leads. *Then* we follow the men. I'm sure they can survive without us for at least a few minutes."

Clarke's smile faltered, the gleam in her eyes fading as she turned to examine the stairwell door. "What if we're more than just a few minutes?"

"We'll give them ten." Adalinda watched as Clarke uncoiled from her crouch, tossing her paperweight and catching it with ease. "Then we return and rescue them from whatever disaster they've undoubtedly unleashed."

Clarke nodded and Adalinda began to move, striding quickly and silently as a wraith, crowbar balancing on her shoulder. Clarke's grin was blazing and ecstatic in the darkness of the tunnel as she caught up and Adalinda handed her the torch. She shone the light on the trail of blood, tightened her fingers around her paperweight, and spoke through smiling teeth.

"Bring it on."

CHAPTER FORTY - SEVEN

COLD LEACHED THROUGH THE back of Donovan's coat as he leaned against the concrete wall of the stairwell. He and Christensen stood beside the first steel door, two levels above where Adalinda had shot the guards, guns held aloft while they listened for any sounds of movement. The stairwell remained silent save for their unwavering breaths, the exhalations melting into the surrounding cold air and abruptly disappearing.

Donovan's ocean gaze flashed in the fluorescent light, his eyes glued to the trail of dried blood on the staircase platform as his feet. The marks began at the flood-proof door of the drainage tunnel above. They scuffed down the first set of stairs to the platform where he and Christensen stood, then disappeared down the second set of stairs, leading further below the ground. Donovan had noticed them outside the entrance before they had entered the stairwell, though he hadn't given it much more than a passing glance. There were more pressing matters at hand.

Donovan paused, a vision of Adalinda armed with only a crowbar flaring behind his lids. He pressed the fingers of his free hand to his brow, attempting to forcefully banish the image. "We left them in the dark with a *crowbar* and a *paperweight*." Donovan shoved off the wall, his boots silent as he began to move back to the stairs leading up to the drainage tunnel's flood-door. "I'm going back."

Christensen pursed his lips to form a tight line as he stared at the expanse of Donovan's back. "You'd prefer them to be down *here* with a crowbar and a paperweight?"

Donovan paused, his boot hovering over the first step, before releasing a grudging sigh.

"Trust me, anyone unlucky enough to sneak up on Adalinda will find themselves with a crowbar through the stomach." A line formed between Christensen's ebony brows. "And, quite possibly, a paperweight to the face from Clarke. Just for good measure."

Donovan peered over his shoulder, assessing Christensen's raised gun and gleaming, leather jacket. "Adalinda saw the trail of blood."

Christensen shrugged, seemingly unaffected by the concept. "So let's hope she didn't follow it." He paused, gaze becoming slightly empty as he lost himself to his thoughts. "I saw her heal from multiple bullet wounds and shoot a group of men with perfect precision." He blinked and returned to himself, dragging his fingers over the pillow of coiled hair atop his head. "Believe me, she's the last of our concerns right now."

Donovan looked up the stairs to the flood-door, his heart stuttered in his chest like the plucked strings of a violin. After a long moment, he expelled a frustrated breath, face lifting to the ceiling and exposing the muscles of his neck. His fingers tightened their grip on the gun, the steel groaning against the pressure. "How many halls are there?"

"Three. Do we check them all or go straight to the one Adalinda was shot in?"

Donovan angled his neck, listening to the bones crack, feeling the muscles stretch and release as he turned his back on the tunnel entrance, turned his back on Adalinda. "Check them all. I don't want to walk into a trap."

Christensen nodded and reached out with his free hand, grabbing the steel handle and pressing until the door began to swing inwards. He shoved and ducked behind the wall, blinking into the hall beyond. His brow furrowed, a frown tugging at the corners of his mouth.

Donovan strode into the path of the swinging door as it ricocheted back, blocking it with his boot.

Bright, fluorescent light reflected off the steel doors lining the hall, their surfaces devoid of handles and separated by rough, concrete walls. Donovan dropped his gun to his side as Christensen slipped past the threshold and slowed to a stop.

The hall was empty, utterly abandoned, not a soul standing guard, not a whisper to betray any presence.

"... There's no one here."

A curse blew from Donovan's lips as he moved inside, releasing the door and listening to it swing shut on oiled hinges. He strode smoothly to the first of the gleaming steel doors which lined the walls, pressing a finger to the recess of a keyhole. A keyhole. No electric locking mechanism. No security cameras. Nothing to connect it to the grid. "Clearly, someone wants to keep this place hidden."

Christensen grumbled as he began to walk further along the hall. "Shade."

Donovan loosed a confirming grunt, rapping his knuckles against the glinting metal of the door, listening past Christensen's footsteps for a response from inside.

Silence was his only answer.

Christensen kept walking, moving steadily and glaring towards the wall marking the end of the hall as if he expected it to open into a hidden maze. "This place is directly beneath Shade's orphanage, which is equipped with the perfect, unassuming entrance."

Donovan hummed his irritation through a tight frown, his ocean gaze examining the steel door before him. "You're referencing the grate."

"Yes, I'm referencing the *grate*." Christensen turned and marched back up the hall, palmed gun swinging by his side. "I don't like this."

"Fuck it." Donovan slammed his boot into the door, watching it burst open. His gun was poised instantly, the barrel sweeping over the interior. Automatic lights flickered in response to the movement, illuminating a cell, a chamber full of musty, discarded blankets piled on the floor and a single bucket. The stench of urine and excrement assaulted him, stale shit and mould and dust.

"... Of course you're able to kick through a fucking steel door." Christensen growled under his breath, his emerald eyes sweeping over the room. "Bastard."

Donovan raised a brow, the corner of his mouth curling slightly in response.

"This looks like a prison." Christensen leaned into the room, cupping a hand over his mouth and nose to impede the stench. "*Worse* than a prison. But why would Shade...?" Christensen glanced at Donovan.

Donovan clenched his jaw, listening for any sounds that might indicate someone hiding in one of the other rooms. He heard nothing. No shuffles or coughs. They didn't have time for him to kick in every door. "Let's check the other halls." He strode back to the stairwell entrance, pulling the door open and holding it until Christensen stepped through. "If we find the guards we may be able to get answers from them."

Christensen nodded. "Sounds like a plan."

Donovan let the door swing shut, his eyes clouding as they brushed over the marks of dried blood on the floor. He glanced at the door leading into the tunnels and sucked in a calming breath, forcing his gaze away from the exit. He began his descent, quiet as a breeze down the stairs, and hoped that Adalinda hadn't chosen to follow the trail of blood.

CHAPTER FORTY - EIGHT

"THIS TUNNEL IS A PLACE OF nightmares." Clarke grimaced, her mouth pulling taut around the silver ring piercing her lower lip. Her voice echoed through the tunnels, duplicating and returning a decayed husk. She lagged slightly behind Adalinda, sweeping the torch across the damp, brick floor, its' minimal beam barely able to penetrate the ominous dark.

Adalinda peered back at the other woman, her golden eyes pale in the light of the torch. She raised a brow in question.

"I saw a rat." Clarke tossed the paperweight she still held in her opposite hand. The glass glinted as it rose, then fell, returning to her gloved palm with a muffled *thud*.

Adalinda huffed a laugh, her mouth curving in amusement. "There are worse things than rats, Clarke."

Clarke frowned, dropping the paperweight into her pocket. She collected the long side of her hair and began twisting it around her fingers. "Adalinda, we're following a trail of blood through a sewer. I doubt there are many things worse than the filth we're stepping in."

Adalinda's smile splintered, the gleam dropping from her eyes as she turned back to the blood-trail. Her shadow loomed before her, shifting with the movement of Clarke's torch. "But there *are* worse things..."

"Like what?" Clarke dropped her hair, letting it uncoil and fall loosely around her cheek. "Provide me with an example."

A dense silence gripped the pair of them for an extended moment, broken only by Clarke's reverberating steps. Adalinda's scalp began to crawl beneath her scarf and she lifted a hand to calm the ruffles. "... An *army* of rats."

Clarke spat a sound of disgust, scrunched her nose. "You're right. That's *much* wors—"

Adalinda stopped. So abruptly that Clarke stumbled, nearly dropping the torch. A curse tripped over the woman's tongue as she attempted not to collide with the crowbar still balanced atop Adalinda's cloaked shoulder.

"What the *hell*, Ada? *Warn me* next time you're going to suddenly *stop* so I don't *impale* myself on your *crowbar*. Thanks. Much appreciated."

Adalinda shot Clarke an inscrutable look, before gesturing ahead. The light of Clarke's torch spread to an opening in the wall, similar to the smaller, intersecting tunnels they had already passed. Except this one housed a set of stairs. "The blood leads up there."

Clarke exhaled a breath, eyes trailing skyward to find a dim alcove part way up the tunnel wall, its edge guarded by a metal rail. She adjusted her grip on the torch and began stomping towards the stairs.

Adalinda followed on the woman's heels, moving through the threshold and climbing into darkness.

Thick, damp darkness.

Plucking at the memories circling the back of her mind.

Clarke's torch released an eerie flicker as they moved from the stairwell into the alcove.

And found an aged flood-door set into the wall, the trail of blood disappearing beneath it.

"… I'd say we found what we were looking for."

Clarke hit the torch against her hand, gritting her teeth until it stopped its' flickering. She stepped forward and pressed her ear to the door, the short side of her hair rustling against the metal as she listened, frowned. "I don't hear anything."

Adalinda reached out a gloved hand to rotate the rusted, metal handle. It released a groan of protest, then reluctantly twisted. "It's unlocked." Mild apprehension fluttered in her stomach as she glanced at Clarke, whose ear was still pressed to the door. "Shall we?"

Clarke nodded and pushed away from the metal surface. She lifted the glass paperweight from her pocket, took aim, flashed Adalinda a vivid grin. "Do it."

A quiet reflection of Clarke's smile graced Adalinda's lips and Clarke sucked in a breath, her jade and topaz eyes examining Adalinda's features with no small amount of appreciation. "Ready?"

"*Damn it* Ada, just open the door."

Adalinda leaned into it, wincing as it screeched on its' hinges and dim light began pouring into the alcove.

Clarke gasped a deep breath.

Shelves of glass bottles lined the brick walls inside, creating glittering, miniature alleys. A set of simple, wooden stairs beside them led to another door through which music and laughter merrily drifted.

Clarke released a delighted squeak, shoving the torch into Adalinda's hands as she danced into the cellar, examining the bottles. "*Alcohol!*" She plucked a bright bottle of absinthe from the shelf beside the stairs, the air bubble in its' green liquid floating across the glass as she turned it in her free hand, paperweight still poised in the other.

Adalinda blinked, her eyes flitting to the blaze of warm light filtering beneath the door above. She pressed her lips together, brows furrowing, considering the path they had taken beneath the street. "... I know where we are."

Lorelei's bar.

Adalinda tensed as footsteps thudded above. She hissed violently at Clarke. "Leave it, we need to go."

"But—" Clarke's eyes snapped up as the doorknob began to twist. She sprinted across the cellar, absinthe clutched protectively to her chest.

Adalinda hauled the flood-door closed behind Clarke, hinges screaming, hissing as it sealed. She switched the torch off and dragged the medical examiner into the stairwell, hiding their position in case they had been heard. Then glared at the stolen bottle of absinthe. "What are you going to do with that?"

Clarke stared at Adalinda, her bewildered look hidden in the dark. "... Drink it?"

Adalinda sighed through her nose. She tilted her head and listened for the sound of the door opening, listened for any signs of pursuit. After several bated breaths, she switched the torch back on and began to move down the stairs, returning the way they had come. "Let's hope the music and conversation was enough to drown out the hinges."

Clarke skipped along behind, absinthe cradled against her chest, paperweight still clutched in her other hand. "I don't think anyone heard."

Adalinda agreed, but still she quickened her pace. Adrenaline swelled in her veins as she calculated the distance between Lorelei's bar and the orphanage. The entrances were too close together, the trail of blood too easy to follow.

A thread of unease wove itself around her heart.

"We need to get back. I have a bad feeling."

Clarke worried her piercing between her teeth, hearing the change in Adalinda's tone as they darted from the stairwell. "What is it?"

"... I'm not sure..." Adalinda focused on following the trail of blood, backtracking through the sewage-tunnel, as she listened to the *shush* of the water across its' sunken floors. She could feel something heavy in the subterranean air, something beginning to weigh her down, like a cliff preparing to crumble, like an avalanche of burning sand. Adalinda took a steady breath and tightened her grip on the torch. "But I think we're about to find out."

CHAPTER FORTY - NINE

DONOVAN AND CHRISTENSEN stood on the threshold of the second hall, two levels below the drainage tunnel, backs facing the stairs. Their palmed guns hung loosely by their sides, suspicious frowns shading their features.

The doors of this hall were all propped open, save the entrance, which Donovan held with one broad shoulder.

"Okay, this is starting to feel like a bad idea." Christensen kept his voice low, quiet, as he raised his gun and walked to the first door.

A set of automatic lights flickered on when he stepped inside.

Donovan released a breath and followed, scanning the empty hall. The space brimmed with a mocking silence, creeping over the surfaces of concrete and steel as if it were a living beast, stealthily hunting its' prey.

A grunt burst from the room Christensen had disappeared into and Donovan launched himself through the door, gun poised before him, fingers burning to shoot.

Christensen's eyes widened, darting around the room as he searched for movement. "What? What happened?"

A muscle in Donovan's neck twitched and he lowered his gun. "I thought you were being attacked."

"Oh." Christensen grimaced, sheepishly gesturing at the floor. His boots were tangled in a blanket. "No... I tripped."

Donovan stared at Christensen a moment, expression flat. "You're holding a loaded gun."

"I didn't *fire* it." Christensen lifted the gun, shaking his boots to free them of the blanket. He rubbed the back of his neck. "The blanket was just lying in the doorway."

"You didn't see it?"

An exasperated huff blew from Christensen as he marched back into the hall. "I can see it *now*."

Donovan smirked despite their situation as he and Christensen moved further down the hall, checking all of the open steel doors, guns aimed and searching. Automatic lights flickered to illuminate the cells as they passed, the rooms beyond them appearing bleak and abandoned. The concrete floors were scattered with discarded blankets and a single bucket, stained with excrement, had been placed in the furthest corner of each.

They reached the end of the hall and turned, heading back towards the stairwell with Christensen stomping ahead, a bruised cloud of irritation hovering over him. He glanced at the first cell as they passed it, at the blanket he had tripped over.

The corner of Donovan's mouth twitched up almost imperceptibly.

"Shut up, Donovan." Christensen shot a sharp glare over his shoulder. "I can *feel* you enjoying this."

Donovan released a rumble that was almost a laugh and strode past Christensen. "Blame it on your lack of sleep."

Christensen mumbled a string of bitter curses as they returned to the stairwell and descended the last of the stairs, the invisible storm cloud expanding above his head. "You know what, Donovan?

You can just—" He cut off, his boot slipping then catching on the last step as Donovan came to an abrupt halt before the door leading to the lowest hall, where Adalinda had unleashed her fury at Donovan's ephemeral death. "... Oh hell."

The door was open.

Hulking guards barred the hall, some leaning against the walls, others simply standing. A dozen had bandaged shoulders, though a few appeared unwounded. And each had a rifle aimed at Donovan's head.

A man shoved his way through the bottle-necked horde. His features were creased in a frown, causing the blood to leach from the edges of his scar, the eye beneath it a pale, sightless white.

Donovan ground his teeth, raised his gun. "Kaleth."

"Detective." The scarred man nodded, appearing entirely unfazed as he came to a languid standstill between the last of the guards. "You didn't follow when I left the bar."

"A mistake I won't be making again." The air around Donovan began to thicken. "What did you do with those men?"

Kaleth lifted his shoulders in a dismissive shrug. "I let them go."

Christensen's brow creased, his fingers shifting on his gun. "You weren't there to watch them, were you?"

"No." The scarred man rubbed a hand across his stubbled chin. "I was there to watch Adalinda and Theodore, as I was asked."

Christensen ducked around Donovan before he could be stopped, his mouth spewing an impressively illicit string of curses. He aimed his gun at Kaleth as he lowered himself to the hall's concrete floor. "Tell us what the *hell* is going on."

"Something beyond your understanding." Kaleth pursed his lips. "This is not your fight."

"That's not your decision to make."

Somewhere amid the guards, a woman cleared her throat.

Kaleth glanced back as she stepped through the mob, stopping with her face hidden behind the shoulder of a guard. Kaleth leaned towards her and she murmured quietly, her voice so soft it was lost, soundless to all but him.

A smile flicked across Kaleth's scarred lips in response to the woman's muted words. "I was hoping you'd say that." He began moving towards Christensen, knuckles cracking audibly.

Donovan growled a warning.

Christensen stalked forward.

Fired his gun.

The bullet hit Kaleth square in the chest.

And the man kept walking.

Christensen's steps faltered as Kaleth pulled the collar of his shirt aside, revealing a bullet-proof vest. He smiled darkly as he reached the detective, grabbing him and driving an unforgiving fist into his stomach.

The breath burst from Christensen's lungs. He retched, doubling over, gun slipping from his grip as Kaleth shoved him to the floor and kicked the firearm aside.

It slid across the concrete.

Collided with the wall.

"The lady has informed me that if you won't accept this isn't your fight, I am to give you a taste of what's to come." Kaleth's smile fell from his face, his single, white eye gleaming beneath the streak of his brutal scar. "I hope you're ready for a beating."

Chapter Fifty

Clarke swore violently as she and Adalinda skidded to a halt, sliding across the stairwell platform, staring down the last of the steps towards Donovan and Christensen.

Christensen was on the floor with Kaleth looming above him. The scarred man's boot crashed into the detective's side, sending him sprawling across the concrete to the base of the stairwell.

Christensen coughed, blood misting the floor beneath his mouth. He pushed himself to his knees, arms near collapsing, then peered up at Adalinda and smiled, exposing ivory teeth stained crimson. "Welcome to the party." He spat to the side, clearing his mouth of saliva and blood.

A sound of disapproval crawled over Adalinda's tongue.

Donovan stepped around Christensen, shooting the other detective an accusatory glare. The barrel of his gun glinted in the fluorescent light. A visceral growl thundered in his chest.

Adalinda was at Donovan's side in a heartbeat, graceful as a breeze gliding down the stairs. Her shoulder grazed his ribs and his rigid muscles loosened, responding involuntarily to her touch. She tightened her grip on the crowbar still balanced on her shoulder. "We decide to let you come down here alone and Christensen ends up bleeding on the floor."

"Go back upstairs." Donovan shifted in front of Adalinda, keeping his eyes locked on the scarred man. "And for God's sake, take Christensen."

Adalinda's mouth twitched in a frown as she leaned around Donovan to stare at Kaleth. She had felt a faint sense of unease when she had seen him in Lorelei's bar, but she had been unable to explain it. Now, the vaguest memories were beginning to float to the surface.

She caught glimpses of a man riding ahead, nothing more than a silhouette wearing a scarf across his face. He turned and the sunlight flashed in his eyes, one of them a pale, sightless white.

She remembered a scar carving his face... and an owl, perched on his shoulder...

Adalinda lowered the crowbar, listening to the *crack* as its' curved end connected with the concrete floor. "... I *remember* you..." Recognition cleared Adalinda's features like smoke blown from the horizon. "You were the man in the desert. You had camels... and an *owl*..."

Kaleth's brows rose in surprise.

A muscle ticked in Donovan's jaw. "Adalinda, take Clarke and Christensen back to the tunnels." He kept his gun aimed at the scarred man, raising it to Kaleth's head.

Adalinda dipped around Donovan's stance, sweeping through the open door and into the hall. Her cloak whispered against her heels, her crowbar shrieked as she dragged it across the floor. She glared at Kaleth, the memory of pain and anger waking inside her. "Was it *you* who locked me in that *cell*?"

Kaleth stomped forward, his uneven gaze burning into Adalinda. "I did what I was asked."

"Adalinda." Donovan warned.

"You did what you were asked?" Adalinda blinked, brows creasing, eyes narrowing. "... Who asked you?"

Kaleth scowled.

Adalinda felt the heat of Donovan's presence, the shift in the air as he moved to her back. He slipped an arm around her waist, tugging her against his chest and holding his gun over her shoulder, still aimed at Kaleth.

"Adalinda, will you just *listen* to me?" Donovan's breath seeped through her scarf.

Her scalp began to prickle.

"Go back upstairs. I don't need you shot."

Adalinda ignored him. Her instincts screamed at her to fight, to find answers. She straightened in Donovan's grip, her chin held high and confident, feeling the cool metal of the crowbar as a steady weight in her palm. She lowered one hand to Donovan's forearm, still locked around her waist. "Who asked you, Kaleth?"

Kaleth glanced at Donovan's gun, at the scarf wrapped around Adalinda's head.

Monster.

She was tired of keeping her distance, tired of the caution and fear brought on by her prickling scalp. She would not be able to hide much longer and the knowledge made her sick, on edge, aware. Adalinda looked up at Donovan, his glare slicing into Kaleth. His grip was steel around her waist. He wasn't going to let go. She *needed* him to let go.

Adalinda turned in Donovan's grip, allowing herself to look at him, at the hardened planes of his face, the gleam of challenge in his eyes. She lifted her free hand, fingers drifting over his side. "Donovan—"

"No, Adalinda." Electricity sparked beneath Adalinda's skin as Donovan's gaze slid to her, furious and burning with hunger. "Whatever it is, the answer is no."

Adalinda's nostrils flared.

She exhaled a frustrated breath.

"Enough."

Kaleth looked over his shoulder, responding immediately to the disembodied voice.

"Argue on your own time."

The guards began to shift, moving to stand against the walls, clearing a path for the woman who had spoken, the one who had murmured earlier to Kaleth. Her tall, leather boots were planted beside a slumped figure, a corpse, the pale flesh of its' exposed forearms painted with thorned vines and screaming bodies. Adalinda recognised them, the tattoos, and the dead woman's face. It was the lone female guard. The one she had shot.

… But her shot had not been fatal…

A faint crease bloomed on Adalinda's brow.

She raised her eyes to the woman standing over the corpse as Donovan's grip on her faltered.

The warm weight of the Detective's arm dropped from Adalinda's waist as he recognised the woman standing above the dead guard. "… *Lorelei?*"

The woman blinked her hazel eyes, a cunning smile breaching the line of her cupid-bow lips. "Leda." She gestured behind Donovan with flourishing fingers. "*That* is Lorelei."

Both Adalinda and Donovan turned to look over their shoulders.

A woman with identical, hazel irises and tumbling, brunette curls grinned from a few steps above where Christensen had begun to push himself to his feet, still on the concrete floor outside the threshold of the hall. The woman's fingers clutched an exquisite, short-hafted axe, her practiced hold deceptively relaxed, her free hand hovering over a duplicate strapped to her thigh. An owl had been embellished on the weapon, the design stretching to disappear beneath her grip. Florescent light glinted off its' wings, the feathers extending to the edge of the axe's blade. The gleaming metal appeared to swirl like mist beneath glass.

Aegisium.

And its' blade was held against the supple flesh of Clarke's throat.

Lorelei smiled, pushing Clarke down a step, then two. She leaned forward and her breath soughed through the short side of Clarke's platinum and lavender hair as she spoke. "I think it's time you lowered your gun, *Donovan.*"

Chapter Fifty - One

EARLIER

LEDA GLARED AT THE PAIR OF crimson-soaked gloves staining the black leather of her passenger seat, her hostile scowl scorching the air. The boot of her car sagged slightly beneath the weight of the tattooed woman she had indelicately shoved inside. It had been relatively simple to drag the leaden corpse into Shade's private elevator, to haul the body through the garage and wrestle it into the car.

A quiet, disdainful smirk quirked Leda's lips as she pictured Shade returning from tampering with the security footage to find the smeared trail of blood she had left on his polished floorboards. He would be forced to hire a cleaner, if he could find one with the appropriate level of discretion.

Leda tapped impatiently on her steering wheel. The blazing scarlet of a traffic light gleamed in the dark, the methodic, amber flash of her indicator striking the darkened pavement. The night had proven heavy, the moon barely a sliver fighting desperately against an obsidian void as it attempted to climb above the buildings. The sun was not long gone, but its' remnant light had been thoroughly consumed.

A sigh, soft as bird's down, drifted from Leda's mouth in response to the shifting colours of the lights, as scarlet switched to blinding emerald, staining the frozen street.

She pressed a leather boot into the accelerator, listening to the wheels spin when their grip faltered, slipping briefly atop a layer of black ice.

Leda focused on the warm light spilling through the windows of a bar on the corner of the next street. She eased her car up to the curb, cutting the engine and jerking the handbrake, her eyes scanning the silent interior of the building. She had called ahead, knowing this was the sole place which would allow her to enter the tunnels without having to climb through a frustratingly inadequate grate to find a flight of tight, spiralling stairs.

A subconscious flick of her fingers extinguished the headlights, plunging the road before her into shadow, and she stepped out of the car, plucking the blood-soaked gloves from the passenger seat with fluid grace as she exited.

"You're late."

Leda shot a vicious glare at the figure stepping out of the bar. The woman's gleaming hair tumbled over one shoulder in undulating waves, the brunette curls appearing ink dark in the night. "Why don't *you* try shoving a whale of a woman into a boot half her size?" Leda stalked to the back of her car and hauled it open, grumbling at the partially coagulating blood still pooling from the wound in the tattooed woman's chest. "Just get over here and help, would you Lorelei?"

Lorelei's lips tilted in a smirk as she batted her hazel eyes at Leda. "Anything for my darling sister."

Leda raised her brows, glancing at Lorelei with features identical to her twin's. "You're stalling."

Lorelei rolled her eyes and twisted her long curls into a bun, securing it with an elastic tie which she constantly kept around her wrist. "You would too if you were clean and about to drag a dead woman into a drainage tunnel."

Leda tugged on her leather gloves, grimacing at the damp feeling of blood in the fabric. She seized the tattooed woman's arm and dragged her up, a curse tainting her lips as the corpse's head rolled limply on her thick neck. "Gods-damned thugs."

Lorelei appeared beside her a moment later, sleeves folded to the elbow despite the freezing cold. She reached out and grabbed the woman's opposite arm. "You know the Gods aren't listening."

Leda swept an expectant gaze over the street, lingering on the rooftops. "... You never can tell."

A clouded groan blew from Lorelei's mouth as she helped lift the corpse, hauling the body from the car and grudgingly draping a tattooed arm around her shoulder. "Let's go. I want to get out of this cold before I freeze."

Leda lifted a foot and slammed the boot shut with her heel, neglecting to lock the car. She grunted beneath the weight of the body, frowning at the blood-stains on the dead woman's clothes.

The blood was still wet, sticky.

"Ew." Lorelei glared at Leda over the corpse's sagging head as she shouldered through the door, leading them into the silent bar. The fire growled in the hearth, a steady warmth spilling from its' mouth and filling the room with a subtly smokey scent. "This is going to *ruin* my jacket." She pouted at the dark fabric of her shoulder as she stomped across the wooden floor, her boots clinging to the adhesive aftermath of spilled drinks.

Leda lifted one shoulder in a dismissive shrug. "Just rinse it and give it to a cleaner."

Lorelei sneered, the bridge of her nose scrunching irritably as she surveyed the dead woman's slack features. "I don't think this woman knew what a shower was. She smells like garbage."

"Stop complaining, you can have a bath at the orphanage."

The sneer instantly dropped from Lorelei's face. Her hazel eyes glinted like jewels as she sighed. "Gods, I love those baths. If I could live in a bath, I would."

"I know." Leda groaned as she reached for the handle of the door leading to the cellar. "What, exactly, did you say to clear the bar while we did this?"

Lorelei flashed a proud grin, stepping back as Leda dragged the door open. "Free drinks for the rest of the night if they leave and come back in an hour."

A laugh bubbled from Leda's throat, a smile gracing her features. "The same with the bartenders?"

Lorelei dipped her chin in a pleased nod. "Absolutely. They went to get a late dinner, I told them I wouldn't be back but I would leave the door open."

They hauled the body through the cellar door, listening to the dead woman's boots thump against the stairs as they struggled to keep their balance.

"What about the blood-stains on the floor?"

Lorelei blinked at Leda, then looked at the floor. The dead woman's bloodied boots had left scuff marks. "... Maybe I can tell them it's red wine?"

Leda narrowed her eyes, frowning.

Lorelei cursed under her breath. "They aren't going to believe it's wine, are they? ... Damn it, I'll have to clean it." She dropped the tattooed arm from her shoulders and launched back up the stairs.

Leda grunted, the sound tearing through her chest, as she fought against the dead weight. "*Lorelei.*"

"Just..." Lorelei flicked her gaze over the cellar, assessing the shelves of alcohol. Her eyes landed on the entrance to the drainage tunnels across the room. "... Drag her around to the tunnel entrance." She slipped through the door leading to the bar, snatching a mop and bucked from a recess beside the landing as she went. "I'll be *five minutes.*"

"I'm going to kill her." Leda growled, heaving the body to the tunnel door and releasing it. The corpse smacked to the floor in a pile of ashen limbs and blood-soaked clothing.

A relieved sigh poured from Leda, the cloud of her breath barely visible in the damp cold of the cellar, impervious to the fire in the bar above. She stepped over the dead woman, opening the tunnel door and dragging the body through by the collar. She leaped back over the threshold, allowing the door to catch on the dead woman's back as she peered at the crimson slowly oozing from the wound, the constant moving of the corpse wasn't allowing the blood to settle.

Leda waited for Lorelei, tapping her boot impatiently and watching as the congealing blood began to stain the floor of the alcove outside.

"Finished." Lorelei slipped back into the cellar with the grace of a cat, returning the bucket to the recess on the landing. "There's a bit of a stain but it should be fine." She scanned the trail of bloody marks down the stairs, left by the dead woman's boots. Paused. Shrugged. "Should be *fine.*"

Leda rolled her eyes and pushed off the wall she had been leaning against. "About time."

"I took care of the pavement outside as well." Lorelei's lips twitched in a frown, her boots appearing to float over the stairs as she descended, the mop's head sweeping across the blood on each step. "Are you going to leave your car there?" Her boot connected with the concrete floor, mop dragging along the blood-trail until she decided to throw it into a shadowed opening beneath the stairs.

"I'll come back for it later." Leda grabbed the dead woman's arm, gritting her teeth as she lifted. "Just help me get this woman down to Shade's tunnels. That bastard owes me a favour." Lorelei bounded to Leda's side, grabbing the dead woman's other arm as Leda hauled her up. "So I have a message to pass along to his hired muscle."

Chapter Fifty - Two

DONOVAN WHIPPED THE BARREL of his gun around, aiming directly at one of Lorelei's gleaming, hazel eyes. He shoved the onslaught of confusion aside as a muscle fluttered in his jaw, a scarcely perceptible warning of the anger which seared through him, of the white hot, savage fury tearing through his thundering heart. Rage spewed from his burning ocean eyes, his blistering glare enough to melt the axe which remained against Clarke's throat. His empty hand returned to Adalinda's waist, her warmth soaking through their clothes and into his skin as he applied a gentle, insistent pressure to the curve of her hip.

Reluctantly, Adalinda lowered the crowbar and stepped closer to him, her calculating gaze flicking between Lorelei and Kaleth, her bated breaths kissing the fabric of his shoulder.

Golden eyes flashed beneath dark, curling lashes.

Velvet lips hovered beneath his own.

The urge to claim them became ruinous in its' severity, an urge which seized all of him, forcing him to forget the murder, to forget the deaths, to forget himself.

The feeling of Adalinda held against him in his apartment had been enough to empty his mind. It had become overwhelming, a narcotic beginning to seep into his blood.

Donovan pressed his lips together, his grip tightening on the gun until the metal released a groan of protest.

Lorelei twitched her fingers on the axe's hilt, her eyes skimming across his gun. "Stand down or your humans don't leave here alive."

"Humans?" Clarke raised her chin, attempting to discretely lean away from the blade. Her eyes darted sidelong at Lorelei and she tightened her grip on the paperweight, still cradling the absinthe against her chest with her other hand. "What does that make *you*?"

"Something more." An amused smirk flitted over Lorelei's features, fluorescent light flashing along the razor edge of her blade. "We are blessed." She looked at Adalinda's scarf, her gaze skewering in its' intensity, whetted with accusation. "Unlike *some*."

Adalinda flinched beneath Donovan's hold, abruptly becoming impossibly still. Motionless.

A deer preparing to bolt.

Christensen scowled at Lorelei, wincing as he clutched his bruising stomach. He lifted the back of his hand to his mouth, smearing the blood still dripping over his lower lip. "What do you mean?"

Leda's cupid-bow lips sharpened in a vicious smile. "That would defeat the purpose of the game now, wouldn't it?"

Christensen swallowed, grimaced. "Are you working for Shade?"

A low chuckle bubbled from Leda's throat as she shoved the dead woman's arm aside with a gleaming, leather boot, the corpse still lying, neglected, on the floor beside her. "Shade is a maggot. *Less* than a maggot. He was *selling orphans*." Leda snarled and gestured to the steel doors lining the hall. "He bought the orphanage as a cover so he could provide *slaves* to developing countries. We freed them before you arrived and will deal with *him* later. Fortunately, his useful streak is *rapidly* coming to an end." Leda stepped forward, eliciting another flinch from Adalinda who had shifted to watch her with widening, golden eyes.

The air around Donovan began to thicken, his anger becoming a living beast as a memory of the bruised orphan darted through his mind. He brushed his hand along the curve of Adalinda's side, calming himself.

Leda smiled, deliberately looking at Adalinda's scarf.

Donovan's comforting gesture, and Leda's smile, met with a flash of panic. Adalinda shied away, tearing herself from Donovan and slamming her back against the concrete wall, crowbar raised, wide eyes skipping over the guards, over Leda and Lorelei.

Leda frowned, flicking her gaze between Adalinda and Donovan. Her brows narrowed in confusion, then rose, realisation reviving her withering smile as her focus shifted back to Adalinda's scarf. "... He doesn't know." Exhilaration dripped like saliva through Leda's clenched teeth as she spoke. "Oh, this makes it so much more fun."

Donovan's fingers loosened on his gun, his dark brows furrowing. "What's she talking about?"

Adalinda shook her head. "No." She stared at Leda, fear devouring her features. The crowbar shrieked as the metal compressed beneath her white-knuckled fists. "You couldn't possibly—"

A bark of pain tore through the hall, trailed by a flood of curses.

Donovan twisted in time to see Clarke lift her paperweight from where she had slammed it into Lorelei's hip.

"Do that again." Lorelei hissed, recovering and pressing the blade of her axe further into Clarke's throat, rupturing the flesh, drawing blood. "I *dare* you."

Clarke dropped the paperweight, muttering beneath her breath as the glass ball cracked and rolled down the last few stairs, along the concrete floor, past the toes of Adalinda's boots.

Lorelei glared at Leda, impatience lacing her angular features. "I *swear* to the Gods—"

Clarke expelled a grunt. She slipped her hand beneath the axe's haft, shoving it away with all of her strength and swinging the bottle of absinthe over her shoulder. There was a sickening crack as the rounded edge of the bottle collided with Lorelei's head, splitting the skin of her hairline, Clarke's strength not enough to render the woman unconscious.

Lorelei expelled a furious shriek. Blood dribbled down her face as Clarke darted out of her reach, leaping down the stairs to collide with Christensen.

"That is *it*." Lorelei dragged the back of her fist across her eyes, clearing away the blood. She plucked her second axe from its' sheath, brandishing the blades in her murderous grip as she stormed down the steps, leather boots stomping aggressively, hazel eyes acidic with malice. "I am going to *slice* you so fine you could be served up as *sushi!*"

Clarke swore and ducked behind Christensen, both of them moving backwards, away from the stairs and into the hall. Clarke peered over her shoulder at Donovan, her eyes wide with a desperate hysteria. "Do something."

Donovan blinked at Adalinda as she stepped away from the wall, crowbar swinging in her palm. She bared her teeth and stalked towards the stairs, past Christensen and Clarke, towards Lorelei.

Donovan surfaced from his thoughts and lunged in front Adalinda to block her path. She hissed at him to move aside as he aimed his gun at Lorelei, as his finger depressed the trigger.

The shot split the hall with the deafening strike of hammer against anvil.

Lorelei planted her boots on the floor.

The bullet exploded from the barrel, singeing the air, its' metal gleaming like a predators bared teeth.

Lorelei flicked her wrist, the corner of her mouth twitching up as the tip of the bullet collided with the vicious edge of her axe's blade.

Metal shrieked against metal, the bullet screaming as the axe carved through it.

Splitting it in two.

Lorelei twisted the axe and the halves shot past her ears, crashing into the stairs behind her head. "Oh, I'm going to *enjoy* this." She flourished her blades with the grace of a dancer. "I will take great pleasure in skinning *you* first." She pointed the tip of her axe at Clarke and slipped around a shocked Adalinda and Donovan, absently flicking her second blade through Donovan's gun.

The dark metal of the barrel peeled away, separating from the rest of the gun as if it were butter.

It hit the floor with a metallic *clang*.

Christensen continued backing away, Clarke cringing behind him as he glanced at his own gun discarded further down the hall, where Kaleth had kicked it.

"Really?" Lorelei breathed a laugh, her eyes glinting with amusement as she noticed what Christensen was doing. "I just sliced his *bullet* in half, what do you think *you'll* be able to do?"

Christensen stopped, pressing Clarke back against the concrete wall a few paces from the stairwell entrance. He swallowed audibly.

Lorelei lifted her axe.

Behind her, Adalinda raised the crowbar.

Leda stepped around Kaleth, closing the distance between herself and her twin as she shook her head. "Lorelei."

"Not *now*." Lorelei snarled, her hazel glare narrowing until it became molten, pulsing with pure, enraged fury.

"*Lorelei*." Leda seized Lorelei's arm, squeezing until Lorelei shifted to glower at her. "We were encouraged to *play* with our food." She peered at Donovan, a deliberate smirk sharpening her mouth. "Control yourself. After all, the most thrilling part of the *hunt* is the *chase*."

The warmth bled from Donovan's veins, leaving his skin cold and tingling as the ruined gun dropped from his fingers.

He remembered an axe, biting into the lowest curve of his spine.

Warm lips brushing his ear.

A smile against his skin.

"Blood's a bitch to clean up."

Lorelei set her jaw, a muscle in her neck fluttering like the wings of a bird. She cursed, stalking to Kaleth, irritably sheathing her axes and crossing her arms.

Adalinda hefted her crowbar higher as Leda drew a polished pistol from its' holster at the base of her spine, its' shimmering metal embellished with the same owl as Lorelei's axes.

Donovan remembered a gun aimed at his head, a face shadowed by loose, brunette curls.

Leda smiled and Donovan saw a cavernous room, its' ceiling embellished with iron chandeliers, the violet-eyed man lounging at the end of a long table.

"Let the hunt begin."

"You work for him. The man with the violet eyes..."

Adalinda blinked, shifting to stare incredulously at Donovan.

Leda glanced at Lorelei and her smile burst into a grin. "Took him long enough." She turned back to Donovan. "Did you think the hunt was over? Did you think you had escaped?" A grim pleasure sparked in her eyes. "Oh, no. It has barely begun. You've only had a *taste*." She raised her gun. "Now, why don't you make like prey—" The shot splintered the air, the shimmering bullet grazing the flesh of Donovan's shoulder, releasing a spray of torn flesh and crimson. Blood soaked into the fabric of his coat. "— And *run*."

Starlight

Ten Years Ago

The forest held its' breath. Watching. Waiting. Its' branches still as death, its' leaves choking the stars, thieving the pale light from a ground swallowed by gloom.

Donovan flew through the shadowed trunks, naked feet plunging into grass armed with hidden thorns, with jagged stones. His deafening heart thrashed, submerged in a frantic war against its' confines, fighting to free itself from a prison of curving bone.

The faint click of the guns' cocked hammer reverberated, the metallic sound an unbidden memory lingering in his ears.

"Let the hunt begin."

The voice throbbed through Donovan's head, a recurring taunt, inflamed by the frantic leap of his pulse, by the flash of glinting, violet eyes in the recesses of his mind.

A sharp turn flung him into the crisp water of a winding stream, its' modest current soaking the recently shredded cuffs of his trousers.

His body floated above a bed of stones, skin bleached of blood, fingers white as bone, dark hair drifting around his temples in a fluidly shifting mass.

The memory froze him, dragging him into the depths of his fear. His lungs seized. His blood shrieked as it surged through his veins, his mind abruptly trapped in that frigid lake. Drowning. Dying.

No.

Donovan ground his teeth, hauling himself from the latching limbs of terror and launched himself forward. Glistening pebbles skidded across the riverbed, irritably settling out of place in wake of his charging gait. The water would conceal his path, would provide sanctuary. He would use it, despite his fear, despite the fact that every splash hurled a vicious memory of that lake through his mind. The stream whispered, grumbled, pleaded with him to follow its' snaking course. It murmured a language of ripples, gurgling in response to the violent dash of his heels. Beads of water clung to his skin, reluctant to part with him as he fled, his breaths tearing through his lungs, his pulse hammering in his neck. The stream followed him, ignoring its' natural flow, eddying around his calves, clinging to his ankles, until he slowed, stopped, listened.

Dark brows furrowed uncertainly as Donovan peered down at the glistening surface, his lips curving in a frown.

The water ceased its' unnatural behaviour, resuming its' hushed wandering, slowing almost imperceptibly as it drifted past his shins, as if reluctant to continue its' journey.

Donovan's head snapped up, his ocean eyes searching the stretched, contorted darkness.

Shrieking hoots floated through the night's heavy mist, audible only now that his breathing had calmed, that the lashing beast trapped in his chest had quieted.

The water gurgled against the bank, lapping in the direction of the sound.

He felt a pressure in his stomach, the mild tug of a lure.

Donovan stepped forward, curiously drawn to the noise, to the howls and cries which remained at a distance, emphasised by muted thunder.

He tipped his head back, peering through a split in the naked branches above, through blanketing mist, at the faultlessly clear night sky.

The thunder did not originate from the heavens.

Donovan moved with lithe grace, slightly crouched, shifting through the night as if he were merely another shadow cast by the trees. His silence was heavy, lethal. Muscles shifted in his back with each calculated step as he abandoned the stream, as he silently swept across the forest floor.

The thundering grew louder, the hollering screams morphing into recognisable calls. Becoming haunting. Becoming human. Becoming laughter.

Donovan crept to the base of an ancient, towering oak, his palms pressing against the damp bark, his eyes gleaming in a fleeting shard of moonlight.

A clearing spread before him, its' width a deep, jade gash splitting the flesh of the forest. Figures charged across the glade, screeching silhouettes atop heaving beasts, their thundering hooves ploughing mercilessly into the soft-skinned earth. Gleaming objects swung from pale, night-bleached fists, steel swinging with fatal precision.

A razor edge winked, the tip honed to a deadly point.

Figures smashed the blades of their flashing swords, the harsh collision a blare of metal rage, as they fought for possession of a bleak shape sinking into the partially macerated grass.

The pursed lips of a bowed silhouette split into a triumphant grin, the howl of a feral creature detonating in its' throat as the steel of its' sword struck a shape partially submerged in the soil. The object skidded across the field, its' marble surface peeking through smudges of dirt.

The beasts bucked and snorted as the stone shape shot between mighty flanks and polished hooves.

It released a dull thud as it collided with the colossal trunk of the ancient oak, rolling to rest an arms length from Donovan's position.

Hooves thundered towards his place of hiding, the riders bellowing, the beasts launching at one another, smooth teeth bared, chewing and frothing at their bits.

Donovan shifted silently on the balls of his feet, stretching to the edge of the shadows to peer at the mutilated marble. His eyes narrowed, darkened to ebony by his pinching brows. He gripped the tree, bark splintering and wedging beneath his fingernails.

It was a face, a sculpted head.

Deformed, stone features screamed at him, the carving's mouth eternally gaping. Its' head tilted to reveal the jagged surface where its' neck had been brutally cleaved from its' shoulders. A single, yawning eye stared blindly through the grass, the empty space where its' twin should have been was smashed to oblivion. Great, slicing wounds marked the strikes of ruthless swords, the marble irreparably fractured, the nose shattered, gone.

A pale, ivory stallion snapped at a dark mare, yanking Donovan's attention away from the marble head. The mare lunged forward, lashing out with her rear hooves, a feral, aggravated warning. The rider of the mare lurched unsteadily in the saddle, spewing a string of curses and clinging to the pommel with his single, free hand.

Donovan retreated behind the towering oak, slowly, deliberately, excruciatingly aware of the riders closing in, their swords aimed at the severed, stone head.

He could slip around the clearing, keeping his distance from the figures, without alerting them to his presence. They were too absorbed in their game, they could not hear him, it would be difficult to track him if he chose to follow the stream. He could run, his body had yet to tire, his strength still sang through him like a vigorous current, cleaving through earth and rock, flowing with endless, terrifying patience.

The dark mare flattened her ears, her pace slowing as her rider regained his balance. Her nostrils flared, hooves stomping irritably, watching the other horses shoot past, nothing more than veins of midnight pulsing over the grass.

Donovan glanced around him, at the unfathomable forest reaching across the land, at the eternity of oozing mist and star strewn night. He could run, with no knowledge of his surroundings, of how long it would take to escape, constantly dreading the possibility that his hunters would track him, chase him with the strength and speed of the beasts beneath them. He could run and risk working his muscles to exhaustion.

Or...

Swords clashed, horses barrelling into one another as their riders fought for the marble head.

The man astride the mare dug his heels into her sides. She launched forward, neck extended, teeth bared, ears still pressed low against her skull.

Donovan uncoiled from his crouch, his decision made. He hovered at the base of the tree, naked chest expanding as he drew in a readying breath, a predator waiting to strike in the unforgiving cold of night.

Steel connected with sculpted stone, the blades edge splintering the remaining eye, sending the decapitated head soaring back across the field.

The riders wailed and howled, hurtling after it in a storm of crushing hooves and raging breaths.

The dark mare thrashed as her rider tugged the reins, her teeth snapping furiously at his knees, her mahogany eyes white-ringed and feral.

Donovan strode out from behind the oak, his hands shoved in his trouser pockets, his posture calm, nonchalant, effortlessly commanding as the mare shrieked, still fighting the rider for the bit.

Donovan flashed his teeth in a wolfish smile, his instincts welding him to the earth, watching as the mare immediately buried her ebony hooves in the dirt, skidding, rearing, flinging her rider from his saddle with a ruthless snort.

Donovan snatched the swinging reins and leaped onto the mare with ruinous grace. "Find the stream." Her ears twitched in response to his murmur of dripping honey, her taut muscles relaxing beneath his weight. She listened, requiring no further encouragement, and dashed into the forest, her feral countenance evaporating like frost beneath the morning sun.

Donovan refused to peer over his shoulder at the man sprawled on the ground, his fingers sinking into the near-frozen soil, his lips pressed in a thin line. Donovan ignored the glare he felt burning into the muscles of his back. A tangible mass of irritation and anger. A glare of depthless mud and moss. As a lone cloud drifted over the moon, bathing the clearing in a mask of darkness, and Donovan disappeared through the trees.

THE DARK MARE NICKERED her exhaustion, her smooth canter slowing, her lungs heaving beneath the confines of her saddle. Her nostrils flared, gasping for breath, her gleaming hide drenched in sweat.

Donovan dismounted, gracefully dropping to the ground and unbuckling her girth. He murmured as he worked, peeling away her saddle and the blanket beneath, slinging the sweat-soaked fabric over a low-hanging branch to air.

They had ridden the entire night, following the winding stream, pausing only to drink and catch their breath. He had pushed the mare to continue as the sun rose, as the dappled, morning light poured through the branches, shifting with their sway, and she had obeyed. She had plunged through the forest as if her life depended on it, hooves passing through the stream for long stretches, deliberately hiding their tracks before returning to the softer earth by the bank.

The mare released a snort, nudging Donovan's bare shoulder with a nose as soft as velvet. He smiled at her, placing the saddle on the branch beside the blanket and turning to sweep a tender palm over the muscled stretch of her neck. Her musky sweat slicked his skin. She huffed an appreciative breath, her dark eye glittering as she nuzzled his chest and turned her head.

Donovan's hand dropped as he stared at the white, deformed surface of her right eye.

Blind.

She was blind.

Unable to see from that single, ruined eye.

She turned her head again, blinking at him with her star-night gaze as if to question why he had removed his hand. He obliged her silent request, scratching her chin, dragging his palm down her neck, her shoulder, scratching the surface of her breast. Her eyelids drooped as Donovan lifted his other hand to remove her bridle.

Her name had been stamped in the leather.

Just above the white star marking her forehead.

"Starlight... Suits you."

The mare snorted and swished her tail, opening her mouth to release the bit, its' metal slathered with dried saliva. She immediately lowered her head to the ground and began to eat.

STARLIGHT LIFTED HER HEAD from the patch of grass she had been nibbling. Her ears twitched. She looked up.

An owl perched above her, in the branches of a tree, its' eyes of gleaming moonbeam patiently watching.

Donovan was on his knees beside the stream, cupped hands splashing the freezing water into his face and over his neck.

They had spent most of the afternoon by the river, sleeping in fits and starts, constantly aware that at any moment they might be discovered. They moved every few hours, keeping a steady pace and trusting that the river would eventually lead them to the edge of the forest. Though doubt was beginning to spread like mould in his gut.

Starlight released a warning nicker, moving towards Donovan and nudging his back with her nose, her star-night eye never leaving the waiting owl.

Donovan grunted as he pushed himself up, gaze flicking to the owl, then to the mare. "It's just an owl, Starlight. Leave it be."

She whinnied defiantly, swinging her head from side to side, then nibbling at his forearm. Her teeth gently scraped his skin.

Donovan glanced at the bridle laying beside a tree, he had replaced her saddle upon waking, leaving the bridle and allowing the mare to continue to eat.

Starlight snorted, pawing at the ground with a dark hoof.

Donovan released a sigh and strode to her side, retrieving the bridle and slinging it over his arm as she impatiently stamped her hooves. He swung into the saddle, wrapping the reins around his forearm and urging Starlight forward with a shift of his weight.

The mare began to walk, her head dipping up and down, her ears twitching irritably, though she turned obediently with the pressure of a palm on her shoulder. They had been practicing during the night and she seemed to prefer it to the bit.

She had refused to use the bridle again after that.

Starlight lifted her head, turning her blind eye to face Donovan. Her ears pricked, pointing to their right, listening to a muffled, rumbling thunder in the distance.

Hooves.

Horses.

Donovan swore, pressing his heels into Starlight's stomach, but the mare was already lunging forward and crashing into the stream. She shot through the water like a star through the sky, muscles heaving beneath her dark coat.

A howl echoed through the trees. A streak of ivory launched through the forest to their right, the stallion's rider staring at them with a bow in hand.

Donovan leaned forward, his thighs clinging to Starlight's saddle. "Into the trees. Now!" The mare veered away from the closing stallion, heading further into the forest, the trees providing them with some cover from the rider's waiting arrow.

Blood pounded in Donovan's ears. Breath heaving. Muscles heating.

The ivory streak disappeared.

Donovan glanced around, frantically searching for the stallion, the rider, the weapon.

Starlight shrieked, skidding to a halt as the stallion emerged ahead of her.

The mare's eyes gaped, her teeth bared viciously.

The rider released an arrow, its' tip pitching past Donovan's neck as Starlight twisted, leaping behind a tree.

Donovan untangled the bridle from around his forearm and held the reigns high. Watching. Waiting for the next shot.

It came through the trees as Starlight launched into a gallop, the arrow glinting wickedly as it passed through a streak of morning light.

Donovan whipped the reigns in a sweeping arc. The leather snapped against the arrow and flicked it aside.

A curse cut through the forest, sharp and lilting, as the rider nocked another arrow.

The ivory stallion raced ahead, his long legs carrying him past Starlight, circling around to cut them off as the thundering behind them grew louder. As the other horses closed in.

Donovan swung the reigns by his side, the leather whistling as it span through the air. He peered through the gaps in the looming trees for the stallion.

Ivory flashed ahead. The rider released an arrow.

The shot aimed low.

Too low.

Donovan leaned forward, attempting to block the arrows path, attempting to reach around the Starlight's neck.

The arrow's steel tip pierced her breast, carving through her flesh as if it were cream.

The mare screamed and the sound wrenched through Donovan's chest. She stumbled.

Fell.

Her body slammed into the ground, pinning his leg beneath her.

A furious, lamenting roar poured from Donovan as he hauled his leg from beneath Starlight's shuddering form. He could see the arrow, see the blood leaking from the wound. Perfectly embedded in the base of her breast. The blade piercing her strong, stubborn heart.

Donovan stared as the mare gasped, head thrashing, nostrils flaring, gaping at him with a terrified, white-ringed eye.

He lowered himself to a knee beside her, placing a hand on her cheek as silver lined his eyes.

He refused to move as Starlight went limp, her head striking the earth with a faint, destructive thud.

He refused to breathe as the light bled from her stunning, star-night eye and her final gasp rattled through her chest.

He refused to fight as the riders filled the gaps between the trees, their horses snorting, panting, shrieking.

He lay his forehead against the lifeless flesh of Starlight's cheek, closed his eyes to the dappled sunlight and murmured a prayer to the sun and skies.

The stallion's rider slid an arrow into her bow and fired.

CHAPTER FIFTY - THREE

"RUN?" ADALINDA RELEASED A baleful laugh, the sound harsh and sharp with venom. The crowbar groaned beneath the pressure of her fists. She sucked in a deep breath, shoving aside the twins' knowledge of what she was. "I've had *enough* of running." Her eyes shifted over the guards who were steadily lifting their rifles, some of them favouring bandaged shoulders. She ached to fight, to render every guard in the hall unconscious. She felt the silent rush of adrenaline, the electrified fluttering of her heart.

She adjusted her grip on the crowbar, the cool metal grazing her palm.

The force of the bullet split her skin, embedding in her flesh, snapping her collarbone.

Adalinda rolled her shoulders, loosening the taut muscles, as if the movement could dispense of the memory from the last time she had been down there.

She refused to be shot again.

Adalinda released her grip, dropping the crowbar, and listened to the metallic *clang* as it struck the ground.

She was tired of running.

Tired of hiding.

She raised her hands to her scarf, the supple fabric stroking the tips of her fingers.

A shiver of anticipation flitted across her scalp.

She could already feel the rise of excitement, feel the hall becoming perfectly quiet, the light's ordinarily invisible colours becoming vibrant and dancing across her skin. She could feel the pulse of life, of blood surging through her veins. She could feel the energy which vibrated through her, the radiant heat of her soul.

Suddenly, she could not remember why she suppressed herself, her true nature.

It was wild.

Untameable.

Exquisite.

It was sunlight, streaming through clouds.

The moon, vastly luminous in the dark.

The explosion of stars enriching the midnight sky.

It was comfort, curled on a couch before a crackling fire.

It was *her.*

Adalinda slipped her fingers beneath her scarf, her polished nails skimming the dip of her temples, the coolness of her touch seeping into her own skin.

Identical sets of hazel eyes widened, cupid-bow lips parting in protest.

Donovan's arm slipped around Adalinda's waist, the contact causing a breath to hiss through her teeth. She could feel his pulse through their layers of clothing, the fevered steel of his corded muscles hardening as he dragged her back, pressing her spine flush against his stomach. His elegant lips lowered to quietly speak, the warmth of his breath tickling the curve of her ear.

Her thoughts were lost, immediately and irrevocably, as Donovan murmured her name.

"We need to go." His voice of liquid honey spilled over her, drowning her as he pulled her backwards to the stairs.

She would do anything for that voice.

She would *die* for that voice.

Adalinda's fingers dropped from her scarf of their own accord. The vibrant, dancing rainbows of light returned to insignificant white. The sound of boots on concrete became obvious, obtrusive to her heightened senses as her anticipation fled.

The dull ache began at the nape of her neck, throbbing and extending to the backs of her eyes.

Uneven breaths rasped through the hall, the pounding in her head synchronising with the anxious, staccato taps of fingernails on glass. Clarke, tapping her bottle of absinthe, as she and Christensen backed into the stairwell, passing Adalinda and Donovan as they began to edge their way up the stairs.

Donovan gently coaxed Adalinda up the first step, his forearm bracing her waist.

The heel of her boot fumbled against the edge as she backwardly rose, her golden eyes still locked on the group lingering before her.

"Wait…" Adalinda planted her feet, attempting to remember why she was moving away.

"Adalinda." Donovan placed a hand on her shoulder, applying a whisper of pressure in order to turn her around. "We need to go."

Adalinda's gaze fell on Kaleth, his frown breaking through her confusion. "No." She struggled to break Donovan's grip, locking her fingers around his wrist, shoving her shoulders into the solid surface of his chest.

Her elbow struck his ribs, the force of the blow eliciting a frustrated grunt. "*Damn it*, Adalinda." He grabbed her arms and wrenched her around, glaring down at her with eyes of burning ocean. "Clarke and

Christensen will not heal like you if they are *shot.*"

Adalinda's attention flicked to Clarke. She and Christensen had reached the first platform of the stairwell. The medical examiner was peeking around the wall separating them from the next flight of stairs, bottle of absinthe clutched to her chest, nails still tapping it nervously.

A memory of Donovan brushed the backs of her eyes, his stunning face cold and pale. Blood coated her hands and her face. His features flickered, becoming Clarke, becoming Christensen.

Adalinda heaved an uneven breath and lowered her head in a barely perceptible nod.

She could survive no more death.

And they would not leave without her.

Donovan's fingers slid down her forearms, one hand dropping her wrist, the other lacing fingers with her own as he began his ascent, his grip on her slightly too tight. She allowed him to lead, their pace rapidly increasing until they were sprinting, launching themselves upward, multiple steps at a time.

They burst from the stairwell and into the drainage tunnel.

"My studio is the closest." Adalinda began stalking down the tunnel, towards Lorelei's bar. They could slip from the cellar and disappear with relative ease...

Donovan squeezed her fingers in a single, pulsed movement. Their linked arms pulled taut.

Adalinda stopped walking.

The Detective gestured to the stairs leading to the bathing room of the orphanage. "The car is still up there."

Adalinda set her jaw and searched the dark of the tunnel for the worn, rusted steps. "They'll be expecting us to return the way we came."

"They're behind us. The car will be faster than on foot."

Adalinda hesitated, then dropped Donovan's hand and began striding past him, dragging the torch from where she had hidden it inside her cloak. She switched it on. Light spread across the sewage-tunnel floor. Clarke and Christensen's steps echoed as they followed her, as she closed the distance between herself and the spiralling stairs, moving across the entrance of the smaller, intersecting tunnel.

Adalinda reached the stairs and leaped delicately onto them before Donovan could argue that it was not safe to go first. She ascended steadily, then hauled herself through the bathing room grate, the soft glow of the steaming pools licking across its' walls. Her scarf rustled as she shoved to her feet, listening for any disturbances in the quiet of the room as Donovan silently climbed out behind her. He reached down to assist Clark whose bottle of absinthe was still clutched to her chest. She clung to the Detective as he lifted her out, her boots sliding on the tiled floor, her fingers releasing him only to fumble with the lid of the absinthe. She gulped a mouthful, gasping and coughing when the alcohol burned her throat, her watering eyes squeezing shut.

"They're going to *hunt* us?" Christensen hoisted himself into the bathing room. He swung his legs out of the grate, struggling to conceal his trembling as he shot a glare at Donovan and Adalinda.

Clarke poured another shot of absinthe onto her tongue, the piercing in her lip glinting as she grimaced.

"Give me that." Christensen lurched off the floor and snatched the bottle from Clarke, inhaling the liquid as if it were a cure to poison.

Clarke spat abusively as he choked, seizing the absinthe with a mothers' wrath and partially twisting her shoulders to hide the alcohol. "Just because we have a group of giant mercenaries counting down from ten before they hunt us down does *not* permit you to *spill my absinthe.*" She lifted the bottle to her lips, closing her eyes and sipping delicately before replacing the lid with trembling fingers. "Besides, *I'm* the one who should be drinking because *I'm* the one with a gorgeous *psycho* who wants to *skin me alive!*"

Adalinda glanced at Clarke over the woollen cloak covering her shoulder. "We need to go." The bathing room spread before them, vast and palatial, its' silence plucking at her finely tuned nerves. "I think we just walked into the beginnings of a *very* elaborate trap." She started forward, soundless boots skimming across the tiled floor. She dodged the pools, their agitated light swirling over her billowing cloak, causing her to appear as a dream, an illusion gliding through the humid air.

Donovan retrieved the grate, the metal covering grinding as it slid into place over the tunnel entrance. There was nothing to seal it, nothing to slow the inevitable pursuit.

Adalinda slipped out of the bathing room and into the dimly lit hall, Clarke and Christensen nipping at her heels. The stench of absinthe aggravated Adalinda's headache, the throbbing behind her eyes becoming a consistent ache.

Her pace accelerated.

She hurled herself into the lobby.

Her heart galloped in her chest, pulse frantic, golden eyes searching for any sign of movement, any threat she would have to immobilise.

The room remained abandoned, heavy with predatory promise.

Her fault.

She could feel the phantom press of fear embedding in her stomach as she crossed the lobby. Hope fluttered in her chest, blooming with the intensity of a struck match as her fingers skimmed the handle of the orphanage door, closing around it, the cold metal searing into her gloved palm. She flicked her wrist and *pulled*, expecting it to be locked, expecting it to be guarded.

The door swung open and Adalinda burst into the frozen street. The stars watched from their place in the sky as she drifted over the icy pavement, frantically searching for any attackers. The biting cold cleared her head, liberating her from the confines of that stabbing ache. She expelled a calming breath, the twisting body of a cloud seeping through her lips. The road shone in the steady light of the street lamps, ice reflecting the changing colours of the traffic lights near the glowing façade of Lorelei's bar in the distance.

The rumble of a lone car broke the quiet, muted and detached.

The street remained serenely abandoned.

Voiceless.

Deserted.

Save for the dark presence of Donovan's car, its' hood gleaming in a pool of warm light.

Absently, she registered the others bursting from the orphanage. Donovan barking instructions as he marched towards his car.

Adalinda lifted her gaze to the stars, heart still slamming against her sternum, listening, attempting to calm herself.

The door of the car whispered as Donovan flung it open, swinging in front of the wheel, his boots finding the pedals and his fingers finding the key.

An owl peered at Adalinda from its' perch on a roof. It blinked down at her with moonbeam eyes, tilted its' head in mock concern.

Hide from the owls.

Adalinda glanced at Donovan as the engine sputtered. A growl of frustration spilled from his throat. He twisted the keys again, shoved his boots into the pedals, his shadowed brows knitting in concentration. A terrible grunt exploded from the car, splitting the bitter, night air with a metallic cough.

Donovan roared, thundering and feral. He hauled himself from the car, slamming the door with a sickening crash. The window shattered, the steel crunching beneath the impact. "We don't have *time* for this." Raging fire poured from him, the panic in his ocean eyes flaring as he stormed to Adalinda. "We need to leave." Donovan grabbed Adalinda's wrist, desperation trembling through his body, fear fluttering beneath his stare. She glanced at his arm, the bullet wound had healed in moments and the blood was beginning to dry on his skin.

The orphanage doors swung open.

Kaleth stepped into the street, guards filing out after him.

The scarred man raised Leda's Aegisium gun.

"*Now.*" Donovan boomed, dragging Adalinda across the road by her wrist. Christensen and Clarke were already running, disappearing down a lamplit street. Adalinda had no choice but to follow, stumbling on ice, glancing over her shoulder.

Kaleth lowered his gun and turned to the guards, barking a string of commands.

Donovan's fingers tightened on Adalinda's wrist, hauling her further down the street.

She lost sight of Kaleth just as he turned to stalk back into the orphanage.

CHAPTER FIFTY - FOUR

CLARKE STUMBLED, HER KNEES shaking, buckling, as the effects of the absinthe began to spill through. Donovan exchanged a glance with Adalinda, silently questioning, assessing her ability to keep his pace. She dipped her chin in a confirming nod and he relinquished her wrist, dropping back to where Clarke was lagging behind. He could hear the woman's breaths shuddering through her chest, erratic and ragged with panic. Donovan reached for her, neglecting to break his stride as he scooped her feather-light frame into his arms and caught up with Adalinda.

Clarke barked a protest and drove a fist into Donovan's shoulder, still defiantly clutching her absinthe. "I can run by myself! Put me down!"

"You're in no condition to run." Donovan rumbled, vaguely gesturing to the absinthe with his chin. She reeked of it, the scent of alcohol clinging to her breath.

Clarke grumble incomprehensibly, trying to pry the lid from the bottle.

"Clarke…" The edge of Adalinda's mouth dipped in a frown as she eyed the absinthe. "I think you've had enough."

"Don't tell me what to do." Clarke snapped, her words vaguely slurring. She pinned her glare on Adalinda's scarf, the smooth fabric almost appearing to shift of its' own accord. "You don't get to tell me what to do! Not when you're lying to me!"

"*Lying* to you?" The blood drained from Adalinda's face, leaving her golden eyes lightless. "I have *never* lied to *any* of you." She stared at the pavement, curling her fingers into fists. "Not *once*."

"Then you're avoiding a truth. I saw what you started to do down there. What's under your scarf?"

Donovan pressed his lips as Clarke dug her fingers into his shoulder, clinging to him as he ran, her blazing glare never leaving Adalinda.

Adalinda accelerated, her long strides flying over the road, her breaths heaving in delicate gasps. "It's none of your business if I avoid a truth."

"We're *friends*, Adalinda." Silver began to collect in Clarke's eyes, the piercing in her lip softly trembling. "Tell me the truth."

Donovan watched as Adalinda deliberately closed herself off, the muscles in her jaw clenching, her body shifting to hide her eyes, to hide whatever emotions had begun to bleed onto her face.

"I'm *protecting* you." Adalinda's anguished whisper wove among the pounding of Christensen's steps, driving an icicle through Donovan's heart. She discreetly wiped a thumb across her cheek. "Friends keep each other *safe*."

"*From what?*" Clarke seethed, her body becoming rigid in Donovan's arms. "I think we're in about as much *danger* as we can *get*!"

Adalinda drove her features to stone, her golden eyes spitting fire, the only emotion she deigned show. "You have *no* idea." The brutal, venomous ice in her voice eviscerated Clarke's anger.

Donovan felt his chest begin to ache as he watched Adalinda slam down an armoured wall, locking them out, locking herself in.

Adalinda refused to speak, refused to even look at Donovan as they ran. Her silence was agonising; it tore through him, viciously crushing him with every step she took. His instincts roared at him to comfort her, to take her hand, to say anything to distract her from her clearly destructive thoughts.

No words rose on his tongue, not even a sound floated beneath the surface.

He was choking, drowning again in that frozen river.

Clarke stared blearily, cradled in Donovan's arms, chewing the knuckle of her own finger. Her eyes were bleak and locked on Christensen as the man began to slow behind them.

Donovan shifted Clarke in his arms. When he spoke, Adalinda's name was soft on his lips, brimming with warmth to melt her despair, overflowing with ancient, intrinsic tenderness. The knot in his stomach loosened with the tension that gradually seeped from her shoulders, with the colour that returned to her features, her velvet cheeks flushing from the winter cold.

Finally, Adalinda broke her silence. She released a weary breath and when she looked at him, her golden eyes were unencumbered by her elegantly crafted shields.

Donovan's lungs seized at the raw emotion glittering within her. Her soul, scared, broken, devoid of all hope as she parted her lips and murmured with every ounce of pain and unimaginable suffering. "I am protecting you from a monster."

Clarke blinked, pulling her knuckle from her mouth, though she refused to turn or acknowledge that Adalinda had spoken.

Adalinda inhaled a shuddering breath, releasing her clenched fists, using that shield to smother her vulnerability. "I am protecting you from *myself*. I am a *monster*." The final word caught in her throat, as if her body were urgently struggling to rescind it, as if her soul clung to it with every drop of her unyielding anguish.

Donovan blanched, almost losing his hold on Clarke as she twisted in his grip. "Like *hell* you are." She spat the words with holocaustic fury, her fist bunching in Donovan's coat. "And if I hear you say that again, I will not hesitate to punch the thought right out of your skull."

"Clarke." Christensen scolded through gasping breaths. "That's not — very nice."

Adalinda slowed her steps, surveying the road before her. The street they had been following ended in the corner of a square, the isolated space extending to their right and sheltering a vast fountain, the water frozen over its' base.

"I wasn't *trying* to be *nice*." Clarke grumbled under her breath, staring at the reflective glass of her bottle as she and Donovan passed beneath the halo of a street lamp.

In the alcove of a door, a silhouette moved, faint enough in the darkness to remain unseen.

"Trouble in paradise?"

Donovan tensed, sliding to a halt. He ripped his eyes from Adalinda to focus on the recessed door of a building to their left.

A woman was leaning against the threshold.

Donovan gently set Clarke on the ground. Behind them Christensen stopped. He bent over, gasping from the run and clutching his stomach, the muscles badly bruised from Kaleth's ruthless punch.

"You look like you've been running from something." The woman shoved herself off the door. Her mouth curved in a pretty smile as she flicked a loose braid from her angular face, the length of golden beads softly sighing, quietly clinking.

Her skin shone toffee and amber as she stepped into the streetlight. *She moved like a hurricane.*

Donovan's voice held a weighted recognition, a tone of disbelief, as he narrowed his ocean eyes and cautiously stepped towards the woman. "... Asim?"

CHAPTER FIFTY - FIVE

HER GIANT OPPONENT CRASHED *to the floor before he even registered being hit.*

Asim's smile widened, her ivory teeth flashing.

"No mercy."

Adalinda whirled as another woman emerged from a shadowed alcove behind them.

Rich, chocolate lips twitched, eyes of depthless obsidian raking over Adalinda before shifting to Asim. "I believe that is what was promised when these men questioned us during our training." She tilted her head, her halo of pitch and soot curls shifting around her features as she observed Donovan with a disturbingly cunning stare. "No mercy."

Donovan clenched his teeth. He discretely moved to Adalinda, hands sliding into his pockets with feigned casualty. "Aisha." He lifted his chin in acknowledgement, shielding Adalinda with the breadth of his tense back. "... What are you doing here?"

Christensen straightened, flinching in response to Aisha's leonine grin, darting a questioning glance at Donovan as he quietly reached for Clarke.

Donovan shook his head in a barely perceptible movement, urging Christensen to remain in place as his pulse thundered through him, rumbling a string of inherent warnings and commands.

Threat.

Protect.

Fight.

Adalinda's fingers became a modest pressure on Donovan's bicep, her golden eyes glinting in the streetlight. She leaned around his forcibly relaxed form, minutely angling her head as a third woman prowled around the corner of a near-indiscernible alley.

"Why all this *waiting?*" The woman pursed her lips, her tail of champagne hair a swinging rope along her spine, violence shimmering beneath the surface of her ice-blue stare. "I get bored."

"*Patience*, Vera."

Vera sighed, looking towards the fountain in the middle of the square where a woman was leisurely seated, as if she had been there all along.

A honed smile spread over the woman's cupid-bow lips as she stretched her long legs out on the fountain's lip, her familiar eyes glinting a wicked shade of hazel. "Hunting requires patience."

Donovan ground his teeth.

The snarl that curled Vera's lip was enough to curdle the biting air. "You play too many games, *Leda*."

"Too many games?" Leda lazily dragged her gaze away from the examination of her fingernails, not deigning to move from her perch on the edge of the frozen fountain. She grinned as a voice identical to hers purred.

"I don't think there *is* such a thing."

Twin sets of hazel eyes collided as Lorelei moved from her place across the square and walked to her sister's side, their curling, brunette hair rendering them indistinguishable.

"How the hell did they get here *before* us?" Clarke hissed. Then paused, looking around. "I don't even know where we *are*."

"Oh Samantha, are you really that dense?" Lorelei's gaze slid to Clarke, lingering for a moment before she leisurely turned her head. A predator preparing to stalk her prey. "We followed you."

Clarke visibly shrank into Christensen, bleached fingers clutching her bottle of absinthe like a lifeline. "But you arrived *before* us. *How the hell does that make sense?*"

A muscle flared in Lorelei's temple, just beneath the weeping gash Clarke's bottle had left in the woman's hairline. Lorelei gestured to a car, partially hidden in another street. "We drove."

Clarke narrowed her eyes. "Where's that scar-faced bastard?"

"We left him at the orphanage. Someone had to look after those children and it sure as hell wasn't going to be me." Lorelei gritted her teeth. "Now, shut up and stop being a thorn in my ass."

"A thorn?" Clarke glanced between her absinthe and the blood clotted in Lorelei's hair. The fire returned to her jade and topaz eyes, her shoulders rolled back, her chin lifted in stubborn defiance. "Only a thorn?" The corner of her lips twitched upwards, rivalling even Leda's skewering smirk. "I thought I would at *least* be a *stake*."

The laugh which bubbled from the rooftop was strangled as Lorelei shot up a threatening glare. "Shut it, Anja."

Anja kicked her dangling legs, her calves hanging over the edge of the roof, her caramel fingers deftly twirling a pair of glistening knives. The girl's eyes of pale cerulean sparked humorously as she peered down at Lorelei, the sky a sheet of black velvet at her back, the amber streetlight reaching up to illuminate her face. "I'm not the one with a stake in my ass." She flashed a stunning grin and flicked a strand of stray, raven hair from her face with the hilt of her blade.

"Don't bait her, Anja." A shadow swayed in Donovan's peripheral vision, the foreign voice causing Anja to pout a glistening lip.

Anja swung the heel of her boot into the stone façade of the building beneath her. "But, Tzali'ka, it's just so *easy*."

Lorelei released a growl, anger stewing in her hazel eyes. She brushed her fingers over the hafts of the axes strapped to her thighs as Tzali'ka walked around the fountain, her pale scars and tribal tattoos stark against her midnight skin.

"I do not care how *easy* it is." Tzali'ka braced her arms across her chest, fingers tapping irately along her bicep. The bleached tips of her mahogany hair rustled around the shaven sides of her scalp as she shook her head, her unusual gaze of amethyst and coffee pinching at the corners like a disapproving mother. "Don't do it."

Anja simply lifted her shoulders in a noncommittal shrug.

"Who *are* you people?" Christensen's eyes fluttered incredulously between the women, his grip progressively tightening on Clarke's shoulders until she winced.

"Women who like to chat, it would seem."

"You're late." Aisha frowned, tracking the progress of a tall woman with the limbs of a willow, drifting aimlessly along the street towards Tzali'ka. Lengthy boots enveloped her calves, her ivory shirt and leather pants perfectly matching the other women's attire.

The woman stepped into the streetlight, sweeping her river of fiery, ginger hair out of her face with a sharp flick of her head. "Perhaps..." Her porcelain skin faintly crinkled around her copper eyes as she smiled, exuding acidic sweetness. "You're simply early."

"No. You're late, Iveta."

Clarke's jaw dropped and Adalinda tightened her grip on Donovan's arm, her eyes growing wide.

Iveta released an indelicate snort, waving a dismissive hand through the air. "Nevertheless, we have all arrived. I suggest calling in the guards Shade so graciously lent us."

"An army of men from his *many* illicit facilities in exchange for the removal of a body." Leda huffed a breath. "That fucking politician is both a bastard *and* a fool."

Donovan's nostrils flared at the mention of Shade as Adalinda attempted to slip around his side. He plucked a hand from his pocket and stretched out an arm to block Adalinda's path. She batted him away and strode towards Iveta, shunning the other women entirely.

"Iveta, what are you doing?"

Donovan growled a protest, taking a single step before the whetted Aegisium of an arrow whistled past his throat.

Anja grimaced innocently as Donovan shot her a glare, the bow still poised in her lap, a second arrow already nocked. She had balanced her knives so the blades pointed over the building's ledge. "I wouldn't move just yet if I were you."

"Oh, *guards*." The word became a melody as it flew from Iveta's lips, as her porcelain fingers collected her flaming river of hair and deposited it over one shoulder. "It's time to come out and play." She smirked at Adalinda.

Christensen cursed, his grip falling from Clarke's shoulders as guards flowed onto the road. More of them than had been in Shade's hidden hallways below the drainage tunnels. *Scores* of them. Giants and brutes spilled from each street, all armed with menacing rifles, the blackened steel absorbing the streetlight like a void consuming the stars.

A group of guards behind them began pushing them into the square.

Donovan ignored the arrow resting in Anja's polished bow, ignored the army of tattooed men stalking towards them, blocking every conceivable exit from the ice-laced square. He flung himself towards Adalinda, one arm securing around her waist, his ocean eyes strangling any indication of his fear, his panic, as she stared incredulously up at him. The toes of her leather boots scraped the pavement, his arm acting as a brace as he hauled her towards the closest entrance of a random building.

"Donovan." Adalinda gasped, clawing at his forearm, her glistening nails scraped at the fabric of his coat. "I can't — *breathe*." He immediately loosened his grip and she gulped a lungful of cold air, her exhaled breath the ghost of a manifesting cloud.

Donovan mumbled an apology, his attention split between the guards, the eight women and Christensen, who was herding Clarke into the square, away from Aisha and the wall of rifles at her back.

The infuriating click of a gun's cocked hammer sliced through the sounds of the guards, the laboured, frightened pants emanating from Clarke and Christensen.

Donovan froze, Adalinda still partially suspended from his arm, her swinging boots suddenly faltering in their objecting kicks.

"Ah, the sound of an armed gun." Leda sighed, gesturing with the barrel for Asim to move forward, for the guards to fully block the street. "So... *effective*."

Donovan bristled, his fear writhing through his stomach, a living beast of nausea and overwhelming panic as his gaze jerked to Adalinda.

He could not allow her to be hurt, could not allow for the return of that exposed anguish which had poured from her unshielded eyes.

I am a monster.

The echo of her words demolished him, the despair, scared, broken.

His breath caught in his throat.

She could not be hurt, not when the relief she had shown after he had woken from death shattered him so completely. Not when she raged and fought with such animated vigour. Not when she tilted her head and peered at the stars, as if they held answers, as if they might whisper to her the secrets of the universe.

The cold air seeped through Donovan's coat, through his flesh and into his bones.

Icy liquid nudged against his bloodless lips, urging him to open his mouth, pleading with him to suck in breath.

"Donovan."

Donovan blinked, once, twice, remembering the street, the guards, the dark, freezing night.

"Donovan."

His arm had dropped from Adalinda and she had turned to face him. Her palm pressed into his chest, the cool feeling of her skin seeping through his coat. Comforting. Calming.

Donovan sucked an uneven breath through his nose, exhaling through his mouth, his attention wholly on the concern hovering in Adalinda's golden eyes.

"It's alright." Her murmur came so softly, a caress meant only for him. "You're alright."

Donovan swallowed the last of his panic and turned to face Leda, his hand sliding to rest atop the curve of Adalinda's hip.

Leda deigned to move from her spot on the fountain. Donovan's gaze followed her as she skirted the square, passing Asim and joining Aisha in the mouth of the street the four of them had come through. Out of Donovan's reach. The barrel of her gun pointed at his head.

An echo of a memory.

Donovan seethed with hatred as he stepped back, angling himself between Adalinda and Leda.

The guards pressed in, moving around the women as if they were stones in a stream, rifles aimed at Christensen and Clarke, at Adalinda, as they slowly pushed the four of them back towards the fountain.

Donovan scanned the square, fear rising in him again despite the feathered touch of Adalinda's fingers on his spine. He could find no escape, nothing that did not end in his friends being shot. There was no way past the guards, all of their rifles loaded and aimed. There was no way past the women, varying weapons strapped to their figures or poised in their palms.

Christensen and Clarke mirrored Donovan's movements, slowly backing towards the fountain, the bottle of absinthe still clutched to Clarke's chest, Christensen's fists held aloft, as if preparing to fight. As if his bare skin would do anything against a barrage of bullets.

The fence of guards tightened.

Adalinda flattened her hands on Donovan's back, her fingers digging into his muscles as she nudged into the wall of the fountain. He stepped back, silently driving her to climb onto the elevated stone, staring at the sneering faces limned with grime, the darkening teeth beginning to rot.

"Donovan." Christensen edged towards him, his voice clipped, his eyes wide. "An idea would be good."

Clarke wobbled as she scrambled onto the fountain, Adalinda leaning down to assist her.

Christensen's shoulder brushed Donovan's arm, his fists still raised before his face as he muttered through clenched teeth. "*Any time now.*"

Donovan found no response, no solution hidden in the depths of his whirling mind. His pulse pounded in his ears. His thoughts bellowed at him to find an escape.

"*Donovan.*"

Donovan's surroundings became silent, drowned by the shrieking ring which reverberated in his ears, deafened by the agonising tendrils of dread gouging his flesh, filling his mind with aggressively hissing static.

He had no choice.

No alternative options.

Donovan stepped onto the fountain.

Chapter Fifty - Six

THE SEA OF TATTOOED MEN halted in a near-perfect circle, wreathing the fountain like lingering death, their grime-laden boots planted atop asphalt and pavement, their rifles aimed and armed.

A veneer of calm settled over them, reigning absolute stillness, a menacing absence of movement, crammed with raptorial anticipation.

Adalinda's gaze skittered across the sneering faces, acid scraping the base of her throat. She flexed her fingers. Her chest expanded in a cavernous breath.

Lorelei flashed her teeth in a fiendish grin, plucking an axe from her side and slowly slicing the blade through the air. The gleaming Aegisium tip halted, poised with imperturbable arrogance, aimed through the guards at the stricken heart in Clarke's heaving chest.

Lorelei's wink was the soul of derision, her hazel glare sparking bloodlust.

Adalinda watched the strands of confidence Clarke had gathered begin to split and fray. The woman's entire body trembled, a fragmented whimper tumbled from her as she fumbled with her absinthe, her cold fingers slipping on the lid.

Donovan fumed beside Adalinda, fierce and dark, a destructive force at her side. He called to a part of her which remained hidden, lost beneath the veil consuming her memories.

Leda expelled a frustrated sigh, irritably dropping the polished gun to her side. The carved Aegisium hung from her fingers. Limp. Loaded. "Honestly, I was expecting you to have remembered by now." She flicked the handle, releasing the gun so it swung precariously by the trigger guard, barrel idly hunting an innocent cloud which drifted across the star-spattered sky. "The chase is *over*. You've been *hunted* and *caught*. There's no point *hiding* anymore."

A familiar shiver prickled along Adalinda's scalp.

Her eyes flicked to Donovan.

She knew what had to be done. Knew Leda was right.

The time for hiding had come to an end.

Donovan's fingers brushed Adalinda's, electricity sparking from the point of contact, warming the blood which pulsed through her veins.

The ache behind her eyes leaked into her chest, strangling her quivering heart with cruel, vicious thorns, with biting, barbed wire.

Her fault.

The time for hiding had come to an end.

And she had to make her sacrifice.

Adalinda's fingers kissed Donovan's knuckles, a barely perceptible gesture, drowning in sorrow, in regret, as she forced herself to step away.

Monster.

The silken quality of her voice did nothing to negate the command as she began to steadily lift her hands to her scarf. "Get in the fountain."

Donovan's brows creased, his ocean eyes pinned on her fingers, on the cold, vacant air Adalinda had created between them.

Clarke paused, the lid still secured to the absinthe bottle wedged between her teeth, her nose partially scrunched in frustration as she distracted herself from the waiting rifles and Lorelei's menacing grin. "What?"

Adalinda peered sidelong at Clarke, her expression flaring challenge as she forced herself to repeat the words through clenched teeth. "Get. In. The. Fountain."

"Why?" Christensen leaned to glance around Donovan's broad shoulders, his ample lips pursed, his emerald eyes darting between Adalinda and the motionless guards.

"*Just do it!*"

Christensen flinched at the fire which flashed through Adalinda's features, savage and searing, burning with a loathing she only ever reserved for herself.

She needed them to listen, to understand what she was without truly seeing her. She needed them to fear her.

She buried the guilt which twisted her stomach, pouring her anger, and her dread, into her blazing glare.

A glare constructed of lethal nightmares.

A glare contrived of feral, molten hell.

A glare to *prove* she was a monster.

Clarke pulled the absinthe from her slackened mouth, her jade and topaz eyes gaping, her shoulders curling like a trapped animal. The whisper of a whimper trickled over her tongue as she tugged Christensen into the fountain, her soles hissing and slipping on the dense ice inside.

"Keep your heads down, focus on the toes of your boots." Adalinda did not dare let her glare falter as she turned to Donovan, not as her throat constricted in response to the shock lining his features, not as her chest caved when that shock shifted to the unmistakable frost of fear. "Do not even *think* about looking at me."

She could sense the direction of Donovan's thoughts. Wild with pain. Frantic with anger and fear.

The bodies of those murdered women slunk through Adalinda's

vision, reaping her compassion, fuelling the necessity of her choice to tear herself apart. To make them hate her before they could see the truth of what she truly was.

"You are *not* a monster." The determination in Donovan's gaze shattered Adalinda's rupturing soul. He shook his head, his rich waves of chocolate hair licking the curves of his temples. "I refuse to believe that."

Adalinda pulled her glare from him, reaching up with straining fingers to remove the transparent lenses from her eyes.

Her silence was enough to make him doubt.

She *needed* to make him doubt.

She needed him to turn around and refuse to look back.

The earth itself released a rumble, quaking beneath the groaning pavement, resonating with the intensity of Donovan's warring thoughts.

He refused to believe her capable of being a monster.

He knew *nothing* of monsters.

"No." Donovan's shoulders collapsed, proud muscles softening. The murmur which trickled from him flowed with tender conviction, with the undying belief that he could see through the hollow weapon of her assaulting anger. "You aren't a monster."

Adalinda retracted the transparent lens from her eye, watching it drop from the tip her finger, mute in its' collision with the edge of the fountain.

She should never have opened herself to them, to *him*.

Not when she knew how this had to end.

Adalinda fought the urge to look at him as she drew in a steadying breath, as she blew out an injurious growl. "Get in the fountain, Donovan."

The second lens struck the stone fountain, leaping to join its' twin as she closed her eyes, shielding against the splitting streetlight, the brightness refracting as it carved through the air. Her veins throbbed, guiding the ebb and flow of the blood which pumped through her heart. The ground vibrated beneath her boots, the sound of Donovan's movements loud, obnoxious to her heightened senses. She heard him step towards her, his soles quietly scuffing the ground.

Adalinda's eyes snapped open, the golden depths twirling and dancing in kaleidoscopic shades, alive with scintillating light, with dangerous shadow.

The world silenced as she stared at the pavement, as if it knew what would happen, as if it were smothering itself in an attempt to hide from the monster she was about to unleash.

The breath of Donovan's fingers caressed her shoulder, his touch humming through her, sentient and selfish as it dragged her back towards him, as it raised her flesh in delicate mounds, delving to heat the depths of her core.

Adalinda tore from his suspended hands with a vicious snarl. "*Stay away from me.*" She turned her back on him, crushing the whine of her heart as it painfully convulsed. "I will *not* repeat myself."

Donovan's hand hovered above her shoulder, his warmth hesitating, the seconds clinging to themselves, whispering of infinity.

Adalinda held her breath, trapping the air in her lungs, unable to move, caught in a nightmare as Donovan withdrew his hand, as his presence abandoned her.

The frozen air scraped cruel claws through Adalinda's cloak, mocking and hissing, echoing her thoughts. She waited until the hard planes of Donovan's back shifted into her peripheral vision, until her chest became hollow, a dead bird's empty cage.

Adalinda straightened her shoulders, smothered her anguish.

She hooked her fingers beneath the velvet length of her scarf.

And dragged it from her skull.

MONSTER

Ten Years Ago

LIGHT BLED THROUGH THE *gaping door before her, illuminating the burnt-orange fabric of her torn and tattered dress. Its' shredded skirt revealed the length of her thigh. The strap of one shoulder hung, as if defeated, its' ruined length dangling below the pale flesh of her breast, the nipple beaded against the cold, stale air.*

The figure was no more than a shard of silence, drifting to a halt inside the threshold of the room. It raised the lantern, watching as the light lapped at the cold, stone floor, flickering irritably as if disgusted by the layers of wet and filth.

"You wish to know why you're here?" The figure's voice sent shivers over her scalp, the language a sweet combination of syllables, rich and elegantly flourishing. "They are scared of you." The figure gestured sharply to the open door, to those who remained hidden beyond its' patiently waiting maw.

Her chains sang broken melodies as she shifted, her bare feet grazing the rough ground, the same language rasping fluently through her dry and aching throat. "... And you are not?"

"No, I am not." The figure lifted the lantern, allowing warm light to caress the smoothly sculpted curves of its' hooded face. A man's face. His lantern-lit gaze sparking an unnatural shade of violet. "I happen to be of the opinion that you should be released."

"Released?" She quirked a brow suspiciously, rolling her shoulders to soothe the ache of her arms still suspended above her head. The iron shackles pinched and peeled at her skin as a drop of water resonated through the chamber, devouring a fleeting moment of ruminating quiet. "At what cost?"

The man shrugged and prowled closer. "At no cost."

"You would have me believe that you are doing this out of the kindness of your own heart?"

The man slowed to a graceful stop, his perfect mouth splitting to produce a bone-white smile. "Well, now that I think about it... There is one thing."

"And what might that be?" She stepped forward, lengthening her spine to peer up at the man with the violet eyes, her features suffused with challenge.

His grin widened, ivory teeth reflecting the lantern's fluttering warmth.

Her stomach dropped.

"Ask me why you're here."

She hesitated, taking a breath to unwind the tension knotting her throat. When she spoke, the words were slow, reluctant, as if she was uncertain she truly wanted to know the answer. "... Why am I here?"

"Because, my dear." The man pivoted on his heel, lantern swinging, reflecting in the vertical surfaces of the walls. "You are a monster."

The words were a ruthless slap across the face, snapping the sanity back into her. She glanced at the echo of him, only now noticing the mirrors which lined the cell as he prowled to the door, his free hand reaching for a panel, for a light switch.

"I'll be back soon with a meal and a plan." The man shot a wicked grin over his shoulder, his violet stare pleased with the disquieted expression spilling onto her face. "I'll let you become reacquainted with yourself."

"What are you—"

The violet-eyed man flicked the switch, abruptly flooding the chamber with blinding, white light, and dragged the door shut behind him.

A hiss burst from her throat. She flinched, clenching her eyes shut and listening to the deafening thud of the door as it was locked, the metallic sound resonating through the room.

A string of flaying curses shot from her lips as she waited for her pupils to contract, waited until she could endure the vividly refracting light, the dancing rainbows skittering across the room.

Her brows twitched, a crease forming between them as her mind replayed the man's words.

Because, my dear. You are a monster.

"I'm not a monster." She curled her fingers into stubborn fists. "I'm not—" Her scalp sent a shiver down her spine and she paused, blinking at the blood collecting in pools of crimson on the floor, leaking through the cracks and edging towards her toes. "... Am I?" She lifted her eyes to the mirrored surface of the door.

A woman stared back, her skin smothered in dust, her pale arms decorated with veins of dribbling blood, running down her wrists and dripping from the bends in her elbows. The air abandoned her lungs as she met her own gaze, her irises shimmering and shifting like the flames of a raging fire. She swallowed, and the arid surface of her throat screamed for water, as she forced herself to raise her eyes to the area she had compulsively kept hidden beneath her burnt-orange scarf. Feeling the incessant prickle of her scalp. Finding the cause.

Monster.

She lost her balance.

Her limbs disintegrated beneath her, the leather brace callously ploughing into her ribs.

THE MIRROR

And she retched translucent bile onto the floor.

Part Three

A Battle Of Gods

Chapter Fifty - Seven

ADALINDA'S IVORY SCARF whispered its' relief, dropping from her fingers and gathering in a supple, woollen pile beside her boots. Its' edge rustled against the layer of dense ice coating the fountain's water, the frozen surface groaning as the earth beneath it softly quaked, as if gradually stirring in its' slumber.

The biting cold drove into Adalinda's exposed scalp like a whetted blade through porous flesh. Her skin quivered, a blend of shock and delight shivering down her neck and shoulders.

"Don't look at her!"

Adalinda smiled, listening to the panic in Leda's voice as she shouted at the guards.

"Keep your Gods-damned eyes DOWN!"

Life poured through Adalinda's veins, its' energy tingling with anticipation, dancing in response to the refracting light which kissed the ice-laced pavement. She raised her eyes from the ground, lazily dragging them along the bodies of the guards before her, relishing in the knowledge that they could not bring themselves to move, could not force themselves to run.

Not from her.

Never from *her*.

With her paralysing, golden eyes and her mercilessly prickling scalp. Her skull.

Consumed by a writhing halo of scaled death.

A streamline shadow caressed Adalinda's jaw, the smooth body nudging affectionately. Its' scales of cream and chestnut rustled, its' forked tongue flicked, scenting and savouring its' freedom despite the harrowing winter cold. Adalinda tilted her head to brush her cheek against its' side. She lifted her fingers to gently stroke the underside of its' inflated hood. Her purr of approval vibrated in her throat as the body rose to tangle with the rest, to hiss with the seething, gleaming snakes sprouting like coiled vines from her scalp. Cobras. Their bodies brushing her shoulders and curling around her neck, their jaws yawning to reveal the glinting barbs of dripping fangs, their narrowed eyes perfect, venomous replicas of her own.

The ruthless smile spread across Adalinda's face, churning in the fathomless depths of her paralysing gaze. Heat flooded her core, wild and exquisite, grazing fevered fingers down the length of her stomach and seeping over the curves of her thighs.

With each thud of her heart, her pupils stretched, slicing her irises like a chasm splitting the earth.

Her stare impaled the guards, flicking between them like a harlot in the street. She watched the fear spew from them in corporeal waves, smelled the scent of rancid sweat as it began to coat their clothes. They gaped, unable to act on Leda's orders, too incapacitated by their shock which crept steadily through the frozen air and into Adalinda's skin. She could feel it wriggling through her mind like maggots through rancid meat. As she basked in their narcotic panic.

Bathed in their breathless screams.

Enjoyed the wicked angles of their pinched faces as they fought the paralysis spreading through their limbs, locking their lungs until they could no longer draw breath. Until they gaped and gurgled and gulped. Their impotence both delicious and nauseating in its' pleasure.

Leda swore, glancing at Aisha, then Asim.

The other women were already moving, seemingly unaffected as they wove through the paralysed men.

Iveta snarled in disgust as her shoulder brushed a guard, the blood crystallising in his veins, the crisp sapphire threads straining against his bleaching skin and stretching over his contorted face. Crimson spat across his eyes, the capillaries violently bursting to deliver a crawling flourish of ever expanding blood.

The effects spread through the guards as Adalinda sliced them with her ferocious stare, each impossibly tense, their red-rimmed eyes locked on the undulating mass which wreathed her head.

Their dread itched in the depths of Adalinda's cells like a crust of drying gore.

Vulgar and putrid.

Immoral and callous.

Stunning and *glorious*.

Adalinda realised she was starving.

She wanted *more*.

A whisper of regret flitted through her.

She doused it.

The euphoria would linger after the slaughter, shielding her with the tenuously iridescent film of an arsine bubble. Toxic. Like a floating, bloated corpse. The knowledge patiently waiting in the bowels of her mind.

Every addiction requires withdrawal.

Adalinda began to drift around the edge of the fountain, circling it. Silent and gracefully stalking.

Pale tendrils, like feathering frost, bloomed across the toes of the guards' boots and the tips of their fingers, steadily climbing in intricate swirls. It swept over their skin, their clothing, sliding into their mouths and crawling over their bloodshot eyes. The pale threads petrified with a satisfied hiss, the crystalline veins darkening to sapphire as the guards flesh slowly, agonisingly, solidified. Stone consumed their muscles and ingested their bones until they stood atop the pavement, utterly motionless.

Perfect. Shrieking. Sculptures.

Of murderous marble.

The exquisite brutality of it left Adalinda trembling, her gaze smouldering, slitted pupils dilated, silken lips deliciously loose. Electricity skittered beneath her skin. Her cobras relaxed, lowering themselves to drift over her shoulders, their tongues leisurely flicking across her neck.

Indolent.

Sated.

The guards' lingering fear melted inside her, settling into a millpond calm as something murmured in the back of her mind. A voice of warmed honey. Another of vicious steel.

Adalinda wafted to a halt in the place she had dropped her scarf. Her boot crushed one of her discarded lenses as a flash of movement caught her attention, hauling her away from the dark veil smothering her memories, the mental barricade beginning to crumble.

A man was crouched behind one of the petrified guards, his broad shoulders taut, his face turned away. Another lunged between a pair of stone legs, careful to keep his eyes on the ground.

A few of her snakes hissed, lethargically rising to peer at the figures, at the remaining guards who were wise enough to hide, avoiding the curse of her monstrous gaze.

Adalinda's brows furrowed as the earth released a tremble, waking beneath the pavement and unleashing a terrible, rumbling shudder.

She stumbled, eyes growing wide.

The earth split.

Part of the street collapsed, devoured by a tremendous, Godlike force.

A guard screamed as he fell into the darkness of the rift, trailed by a stream of stone guards, their bodies rolling, crashing, shattering.

The ledge of the fountain tore apart mere inches from Adalinda's feet, shattering the dense surface of ice, shards of rock tumbling into a deep gash in the ground.

And Adalinda's memories erupted.

They incinerated the dark veil which had been their prison, visions lancing behind her eyes in a barrage of ruinous thunder.

Memories of who she was.

Memories of warriors and blood.

Memories of glittering, ocean eyes and an excruciatingly devastating smile.

Adalinda steeled herself.

She did not hear Clarke's frantic squawk, nor the yelp which burst from Christensen, as their boots broke through the ice and they plunged into the escaping water of the fountain.

She did not see the silhouette circling above, its' broad wings gliding through the dark night sky, its' penetrating, moonbeam eyes fixed on her.

She was too focused on the hushed breaths of Donovan's quiet steps, on the wave of utter adoration that consumed and submerged her snakes.

Adalinda's eyelids fluttered closed and she watched through the eyes of her cobras, drinking in Donovan's scent of woodsmoke and pouring rain, revelling in the ruthless set of his broad shoulders, the pulse crashing in his elegant neck, the cold, hard fury blazing in his ocean glare.

She watched his mouth tear open.

Watched his lips peal back as he bared his teeth.

A deafening roar shredded his throat. And the world exploded.

Chapter Fifty - Eight

Donovan's memories detonated, mauling the dark veil which had been their prison, visions skewering the backs of his eyes.

Memories of who he was.

Memories of warriors and blood.

Memories of gleaming, golden eyes and an excruciatingly devastating smile.

Rage tore through him with severing talons. Cold, numbing fire surged through his veins. His ocean glare burned with the livid ferocity of a woken volcano, spewing its' unrelenting wrath as a figure crept through the shadows beneath the petrified guards.

Donovan could feel them, those of the guards wise enough to remain hidden. He could sense the water in their bodies, the vibration of their movements through the moisture in the air.

A guard launched at Adalinda, his eyes clenched shut, his gun aimed at her chest.

Donovan's mouth tore open, his lips pealed back as he bared his teeth.

A deafening roar erupted from his throat and the world exploded.

The cleave in the earth began to give way, forcing Adalinda to move, her steps luxuriously feline as her eyes snapped open and she twirled aside.

Donovan planted his boots and fired a soundless command, forgotten power flooding through him as the stars snuffed out, annihilated by a mass of bruised, savage clouds.

Thunder split the heavens, a vicious strike bereft of lightning.

Sentient water burst from the tunnels beneath the pavement, shooting in great, destructive waves. It wrenched the surviving guards from their places of hiding and slammed them into buildings, their mortal skulls cracking, shattering with the force.

A manic, delighted laugh burst from Leda as Lorelei reached her and grabbed her arm, hauling her away from the water which poured from a drain by her feet. The women scattered, slashing at the liquid with their various weapons, the frigid tentacles churning and seizing, dancing across the pavement and through the frosted air.

The surviving guards thrashed, muscles cording in their necks, struggling against the coursing liquid which pinned them to the walls. Water surged around their bodies, shoving down their throats, flooding into their nostrils and ears. Skin and clothing peeled and split against the rough, stone buildings, smearing the surfaces with bright pools of crimson, clouding the water with curling bursts of blood.

The bodies of the guards convulsed, their lungs filling with the rose-flushed liquid.

And they drowned.

Gurgling. Choking.

The life bleeding from their wide, panic-stricken eyes until they glazed over, stared blankly, drained and devoid of soul.

Donovan released his hold on the water and the dead guards fell, the sounds of snapping bones and slapping flesh a melody against the pavement as he turned to stare at *her*.

She stood atop the fountain's ledge, beautiful lips curved in a vivid smile, adoration gleaming in her stunning, golden eyes.

He felt the breath rush from his lungs.

His heart skipped a beat in his chest.

He stepped across the tear he had sliced in the earth, ocean eyes focused entirely on her, their surroundings forgotten, the women and their weapons meaningless.

Her cobras writhed, their tongues flicking out to scent him as he stopped beneath where she stood, his simmering gaze locked with her own.

And when he spoke, her true name was syrup and venom dripping from his lips.

"*Medusa...*"

Chapter Fifty - Nine

His ocean gaze consumed her, the ache in his eyes, the relief on his face, seizing her heart and setting it alight. He stood like a God beneath her, powerful and beautiful, intense with desire, the scent of him, of woodsmoke and rain, banishing the lingering stench of blood.

A radiant smile lit Medusa's features, pure adoration pouring through her as she lowered herself into his outstretched arms. Forgetting, for a moment, all of the broken bodies and petrified remains, the gruesome garden of screaming marble. Because all she saw was him. All she *felt* was *him*. The heat of him enveloped her like the warmth of a fire on a frozen winter night. His arms stole around her, his fingers spreading over her curves, one hand supporting her back, the other cupping the arch of her thigh. His beautiful mouth curled towards his gleaming, depthless eyes, his smile mirroring her own, each desperate emotion fighting for dominance after being trapped, compressing, in the recesses of his mind. "Hello, darling."

That was all it took, two simple words, which set fire to Medusa as if a match had been struck and thrown, spinning, into a tank of gasoline. She quaked in his arms, her lungs shuddering relief as, slowly, ever so carefully, she lowered her mouth to his, dangerously aware of his body pinned to her own, hoping against hope that he would not again be stolen, that she would at least be gifted with a lingering moment, an *eternal* moment, only ever fastened to a kiss.

Medusa's moan fluttered into his mouth, her breath merging with his, her body filled with want, her core clenching desire, her heart growing and growing until it filled her chest and wanted *out*.

One of his hands reached up to massage the nape of her neck, his arms contracting, his muscles flexing, hard against her back, firm against her stomach. She shivered, and the shiver became a tremble when his tongue flicked over the silken flesh of her lower lip, a deprived groan resounding in his chest as he deepened the kiss. The taste of him flared each memory Medusa had forgotten, stoking the fire in her veins, inducing a surge of heat which flared through her stomach, undulating below her navel like the building of a wave, molten hot and infinitely ravenous. Because to have been deprived of him was to have been deprived of her heart, her vitality. And with him in her arms, their lips moulding, their tongues tasting, the vibrant effervescence of life came crashing down and she realised exactly how bland her world had been before...

... Before.

Medusa tangled her fingers in his velvet hair, breathless and shattering in his arms. Her snakes shivered over her scalp, some winding their bodies around his wrist, others whisking their tongues over his skin, peppering him with besotted kisses. He relaxed his grip, lowering her to the ground. Liquid heat swelled as her stomach slid against his own, the splintered ice parting quietly beneath the press of her boots. His devastating lips brushed across her cheek, pressing a feathered kiss behind her ear, trailing down her neck, teeth scraping, tongue stroking, leaving her breathless and evaporating as her snakes wriggled with delight, enchanted by his every touch. Medusa gasped as he gently bit the curve of her shoulder, nuzzling aside the collar of her cloak...

And she remembered where she was.

A night-dark street filled with stone corpses and dead men, their bodies near glowing beneath the amber flood of lamplight.

While she kissed her love.

And forgot herself in him.

Her fault.

Monster.

The heat in her evaporated, doused with ice-cold horror.

She had done this.

She had *murdered* those men, near a hundred of them, with barely a thought.

With barely a *glance.*

Medusa hissed as her love pulled her closer, his hands roaming the plane of her back, his tongue tasting the salt of her skin. "S-stop."

His hand slid over the arch of her hip, a roguish smile playing across his lips. Until he sank his teeth into the soft flesh of her shoulder and caught her as her knees buckled.

"*Poseidon!*" Medusa pulled back, breath heaving in her chest, blood pounding through her like a midnight storm. She glared as he straightened to his full height, his arms still curled around her waist. "Now is *not* the time."

Poseidon simply smiled, his mouth curving like a satisfied cat as Clarke choked behind them.

Monster.

Medusa ripped herself away, ducking her head behind her lover's shoulder. "Damned gods and their appetites." She snatched for her scarf, trembling as she tied the length around her head. Her snakes hissed aggressively, refusing to be confined. She growled at them, pleaded with them, urging them to calm and reassuring them that she would remove the scarf later. Once it was safe.

Poseidon lifted Medusa's chin with gentle fingers and heat shot through her as he leaned in, his breath drifting over the skin of her neck as he murmured softly in her ear. "You know *nothing* of my appetite."

Shivers coursed down the length of Medusa's spine. Her snakes writhed erratically, envious beneath the prison of her scarf. She leaned forward, nipping at the lobe of his ear with gently grazing teeth and smirking as he released a shuddering breath. She kept her voice low, rich as velvet, smooth as silk. "Oh, I know a *few* things." Medusa stepped back, drawing her lips away and dragging the tip of her finger over the powerful curve of his collar. She gazed up at him through her lashes, quietly admiring his smouldering eyes, savouring the warmth which burned in her chest.

Poseidon widened his predatory smile, the twisted corner of his mouth sharp with starving promise as he parted his lips to speak.

And the bottle of absinthe dropped from Clarke's slack fingers. Shattering the quiet and smashing across the ground at a gaping Christensen's feet.

Medusa ducked, hiding behind Poseidon as he span.

Clarke was opening and closing her mouth, no words escaping as she stared at the stone guards, at the sea of dead and paralysed men.

Medusa's scalp began to prickle.

Monster.

The light guttered in her eyes.

Her fault.

Two women had been killed because of her.

One-hundred guards murdered. Slaughtered.

By *her*.

Medusa glanced at the sky, at the bruised bodies of Poseidon's clouds, the storm's thunder momentarily quieted. Her eyes narrowed at a silhouette circling above. An owl, examining her with moonbeam eyes, its' broad wings gliding through the air, its' feathers rustling irritably.

"We need to go."

Poseidon turned back to Medusa, a question in his eyes.

"We need to *go*."

He looked up and saw the owl.

A growl vibrated in his chest.

He turned to Christensen and Clarke.

"No." Medusa shook her head, closing her eyes against the regret as Poseidon frowned at her. She could see herself in the darkness of her eyelids, see the slitted pupils of her golden stare, the thrashing snakes framing her face. "We can't take them."

"Medusa, we can't just leave them…"

"If we take them, they'll *die*." Medusa opened her eyes, let him see the pain, the fear. She pointed to the broken lenses at her feet, the only shields she had against her lethal gaze. Even if she hid her snakes beneath a scarf, her stare would kill, a glance would paralyse. "If I look at them I could *kill* them! I am *dangerous*. I'm *still a monster*, Poseidon. We can't—"

"Do you know, that might be the most intelligent sentence I've ever heard escape your slanderous mouth?"

Medusa recoiled, responding instinctively to the familiar, steel resentment in that sonorous voice.

Poseidon stepped onto the fountain's ledge at her side, his arm sliding around her waist.

A woman had materialised on the roof beside Anja. She held out an arm, waiting patiently for the drifting owl to swoop down and perch just above her wrist.

The creature narrowed its' eyes of pale moonbeam, its' feathers rustling aggressively.

"Medusa." The woman's silver eyes glinted like sharpened blades. Her hair spilled in dark, auburn curls over the assured set of her shoulders, a coat of caramel and ivory fur draping over her lithe figure. "I was expecting you to have provided more *chaos*. I was at *least* anticipating a *challenge*." She gestured in a sweeping movement to the stone guards, the soaked, bleeding men Poseidon had killed, the fissure severing the pavement. "*This* is *hardly* worth the visit."

Christensen groaned as he rubbed his temples, trapped in a cloud of confusion, of disbelief, with Clarke still opening and closing her mouth at his side. He peered up at the woman standing regally atop the roof. His brows furrowed as he squinted into the dark. "... *Wise?*"

The woman cocked a brow, dragging her glare from Medusa to blink at Christensen. "... Not quite." She rotated her shoulders, tilting her head in an avian movement as she returned her attention to Medusa. "I believe your lovely companions are at somewhat of a disadvantage, not knowing who we are."

Medusa snarled at the silver-eyed woman, at the woman who was not quite Wise, at the woman who was a *deceiver*. Her nose crinkled and she opened her mouth, a few choice words poised on her lips.

"Ah—" The Deceiver held up a hand, ignoring the growl which thundered in Poseidon's chest. "As *immensely* as I would enjoy a conflict, I have other business to attend to." She gestured to the army of stone guards, their rifles forever aimed at the fountain, their faces forever paralysed in their haunting, silent screams. "This was a message and I need to ensure that it is received." She pivoted on her heel, the winter breeze teasing the fur of her opulent coat as she disappeared from the ledge.

Anja retrieved her bow and knives, pushing herself up and glancing at Poseidon with an apologetic grimace before trotting after Wise.

When Medusa looked back around the square, the other women had disappeared without a trace.

Chapter Sixty

MEDUSA LAUNCHED HERSELF from the fountain, fire blazing through her veins, anger flaring as she glared at the empty roof stained with the Deceiver's presence.

And Iveta.

Iveta.

Iveta had manipulated her, just as thoroughly as the Deceiver.

Medusa shoved the stone guards aside as if they were nothing more than hollow shells, ignoring their contorted features infinitely screaming agony, cursing herself for not seeing Iveta's alliance sooner.

She would find the woman later.

Leaden thunder crashed in the heavens as the stone guards struck the pavement, shattering like porcelain beneath Medusa's unnatural strength. The porous rock of their skin and muscle smashed to shards and dust, leaving stark bones of solid granite to bathe in the warm embrace of the street's surrounding light.

Blood crawled down the walls in a series of butchered trails, like fingers reaching for the pavement, spattered with bone and smeared with gore. The drowned guards lay crumpled, drenched, their broken remains composing a sonnet of Godly massacre.

Medusa shoved the last of the guards from her path, stalking in the direction the Deceiver had disappeared. Her anger howled as her nails sank into the palms of her fists, her countless lost memories accumulating in an unbearable flood.

Three thousand years she had been trapped in her curse.

Three thousand years of being taunted, then killed, over and over, her memories drained like blood from a butchered swine.

Killed and placed like a pawn on a board.

Used.

Discarded.

Again.

And again.

The trembling began like a poisonous plague, creeping through Medusa's hands, squirming through her straining muscles. She would not lose this time. She would not watch the light seep from Poseidon's eyes. She would not hear his breath hitch, his heart stop.

Not again.

Never again.

She would tear this world apart if only to stop the endless torture, if only to find a shredded fragment, the shallowest gasp, of peace.

"*Medusa.*" Poseidon had followed her. He grabbed her arm, hauling her around to face his chest, heaving with the fierce breaths of a wrathful God. "What are you doing? You'll get yourself killed."

Medusa snarled, baring her teeth. She glared at Poseidon, anger leaking from her in a churning, boiling torrent. "Then *help* me." She ripped her arm from his grip, stepping away from him as heat flared in her core, as her anger flickered in response. "Either help me or leave. I'll not be prey to her demented games any longer."

Poseidon shook his head, the tempestuous waves of his dark hair rustling against his temples. "This is not the way to stop her and you know it."

"No." Medusa gritted her teeth. "I will not cower. Not to her and *not* to you." She swallowed the tightness constricting her throat, pouring acid into her glare as she met his gaze. "Don't ask me to wait, I will not watch you die again."

"And I'll not watch *you* die again." Poseidon stepped forward, looming over her like a shadow. "You've no weapons to kill her, Medusa."

"Then I will *find* some."

"There are *none here*." A low growl resonated deep in his chest. "You know what she is. *Who* she is."

Medusa lengthened her neck, exposing her throat and jutting her chin with iron resolve. "I know what *you* are, who *you* are, and if you can be killed then *so can she*."

"She has the resources—"

"To kill you? Then I'll find *them*. I'll *take them*. I'll steal the Aegisium." Medusa clenched her jaw, listening to the stubborn groan of her teeth. "Will you help me or not?"

Poseidon's pulse flitted in his neck as he stared down at Medusa, rigid fists near splitting his knuckles, boots stubbornly planted on the iced-over pavement.

His eyes smouldered like dark coals, brimming with adamant determination.

"No."

He did not give her a reason.

Medusa pursed her lips as her heart seized painfully in her chest. She released a frustrated sigh, her breath a ribbon of shimmering mist dissipating in the night. "*Fine*." She pivoted on her heel, straightening her back, raising her chin, shoving the ache of his refusal into the depthless abyss of her rage. "So be it."

Poseidon remained where he stood, watching her stalk around the corner of a building, her simmering gaze stubbornly scanning the rooftops for movement. He stood and savoured the cold, the winter sting on his cheeks, with his features deeply shadowed beneath a pool of amber streetlight.

Finally, he released a repressed breath, came to a decision and began to walk, tucking his hands into the pockets of his coat.

Christensen and Clarke still stood in the fountain, the black depths of the crevice slashing the ground beside their feet. Their eyes yawned wide. Their mouths hung agape.

Poseidon did not look back.

He drifted out of the streetlight, passing the corner Medusa had taken, the street now muted and empty of life. And as he strode into the jaws of the night he plucked his phone from his coat, the screen as bright and blinding as the midday sun.

He frowned at the phone. Dialled a number. Lifted it to his ear.

It rang twice before it was answered.

HOLLOW

TEN YEARS AGO

THE ARROW PIERCED HIS HEART.

Donovan jerked awake with a tormented cry. Thunder detonated above, the furious explosion quaking the ground. He hauled himself up. Muscles taut. Lungs seizing.

The mattress beneath him was soaked in sweat. The covers tangled and twisted. One pillow lay crumpled against the harsh, stone wall.

His eyes flew to the night darkened window. Silhouetted rain pounded against the glass, the drops near deafening as they beat against the tiled roof. The scent of storms crept through the room, stalking the shadows which stretched across the floorboards and carpet. The fabric was clean of dust. Absent the blood from the wound that had sliced Donovan's chest.

He felt as if that had been long ago.

Another lifetime.

Donovan suppressed his exhaustion as he slid from the bed, rubbing a hand across his newly bearded face. His fingers brushed one of its' elaborate, mahogany supports. He remembered clinging to the carved post, fighting to keep his legs beneath him as his consciousness threatened to disintegrate. He remembered the pain in his chest, the sickening feeling of blood pouring from the wound, his head light from blood-loss, his breath a wet gurgle as the crimson liquid leaked into his lungs.

He remembered the pain.

Days of pain.

Weeks.

Of running.

Of fighting.

And hiding.

Each time waking back in this room, with the memory of a knife through his neck, or an axe in his back, or a sword through his chest…

… Or an arrow through his heart.

That had been the worst.

Watching Starlight die.

He knew it could not have been imagined.

And yet, as he walked through the darkened room, thunder rumbling in the bruised-black sky, he could not eradicate his doubt.

The wounds he had suffered were mortal.

He should have died in that frozen lake.

He should have died that first day on the carpet, and again in that forest.

He should have died.

Donovan opened the window. A fist of rain blasted through the room, launched by the wind as it howled inside. The bed's velvet curtains whipped and lashed. The carpet drowned as water spread across the floor.

Donovan leaned over the window ledge, his hips pressing against the broken stone. It had been so long since he had struck it, shattered its' surface and sent it crumbling to the floor.

Donovan blinked against the rain. The water drenched his hair and beard, pelting his exposed skin. Stinging. Clinging.

Calling.

He shook his head, water flying from the ends of his hair, streaming down his nose, dripping from his lashes. The calling stopped. And it left him hollow. It left him lost. With a profound sense of absence and a void in his heart, as there was in his amnesic mind.

Donovan stared at the harrowing drop, at the lanterns faintly flickering along the paved walkway far below, almost completely obscured by the storm.

His heart fluttered.

He felt the cavity between its' beats.

Absent.

Hollow.

Lightning crashed, streaking across the sky in a furious flare like the veins of a luminescent beast.

For a moment Donovan's eyes lit, a vivid flash of blue streaking through the fibres of his irises, the colour swimming, rippling, dying with the light.

And still he felt it.

Hollow.

Thunder struck. The tower vibrating beneath its' force.

Donovan recoiled from the window, the soles of his feet splashing across the patterned carpet. He slammed the windows shut. Glass shuddering with his force. Frames rattling with the wind. He stepped back, retreating, inexplicable fear roiling in his gut, until the flesh beneath his knees collided with the bed and he stopped. Water falling in streams down his skin. Saturating the waistband of his trousers. Creeping lower.

The fear became worse.

It merged with the hollow. The terrible, echoing hollow.

The feeling was like a parasite, crawling beneath his skin. Multiplying and eclipsing. Expanding like a horizon.

Hollow.

Hollow.

It beat and thrashed. It absorbed and consumed.

Hollow.

Hollow.

Hollow.

Hollow.

He felt it in his soul, in his heart, in his mind.

It chanted with the rain.

Hollow. Hollow. Hollow.

His hands flew to his ears, fingers tangling hair, water pouring down his face.

Hollow. Hollow. Hollow.

A roar exploded from him in an agonised wave.

Thunder struck the air, its' vibrations shaking the earth.

The rain stopped.

His pulse slowed.

The hollowness fled.

Donovan gasped, arms dropping to his sides, knees quietly quaking.

He stared at the window, then the pool of water on the carpet, its' surface reflecting the dull light of the cloud-choked sky.

The thunder ceased.

Donovan dragged a palm across his soaking face. His fingers vaguely trembled as he drove them through his hair. His nails scraped his scalp, water collecting between his knuckles and spilling over the back of his hand as he released a strangled sob.

His mind felt fragile, frail as fractured glass.

Donovan closed his eyes and an unsteady breath filled his lungs.

He saw himself die, over and over.

No.

No.

He had not been dead.

He could not have died.

If he had then what did that make him?

Donovan opened his eyes and glanced at the stairwell entrance.

He needed to leave.

He needed to escape.

Fear danced in his throat, tugging at his veins and playing with his pulse.

His heart stumbled.

Death. There was so much death...

No.

Donovan shook his head, strangling his fear.

He would not be afraid.

And he would not wake here again.

His feet were silent as stone as he padded towards the door.

Chapter Sixty - One

The Deceiver

The Deceiver drifted through the building like mist in a field. Slipping past the doorman. Watching as a silhouetted figure locked its' forearm across his throat.

His breath hitched.

His eyes rolled back.

The silhouette detached from the doorman and followed the Deceiver a few steps behind, creeping in the shadows of her wake, anticipation dripping from every breath.

The Deceiver hummed to herself as she walked, the song an ancient melody, sweet and cloying, thrumming with morbid accusation as a memory of Medusa darted through her skull. She frowned, stepping into an elevator, still humming as it rose, the silhouette hovering at her back.

A talon stretched from the bed of her nail, curling around the tip of her finger in a beautifully injurious arc.

The elevator chimed and the doors slid open.

The Deceiver stepped into the penthouse, sweeping through the hall and smoothly sliding her talon into the door's lock. It swung open on perfectly oiled hinges, hushed as leaves in a breeze. Barely a whisper. Nary a warning.

Moonbeams poured through the penthouse's towering windows, bathing the opulent lounge in a transient sheen of night. The Deceiver strode across the room, her silver eyes flashing like a dancing warrior's blade.

She found the bedroom and idly leaned a shoulder against the frame of the door.

Blankets sighed as the figure they concealed shifted in his sleep. His breath peaceful. His features serene. So confident in his safety. So certain that his fragile lungs would keep drawing life from the air brushing his lips. His midnight hair trailed across his forehead, the rumpled, tangled strands streaked with washed-out grey.

The sheets around him were creased in the aftermath of pleasure.

The girl must have been dismissed. Like a trinket. Used and discarded.

The stench of sweat still hung in the air, plaguing the room with its' stale odour. It lingered beneath the curl of smoke seeping from a smouldering cigar and the sickening tang of sugared mint drops on the nightstand, beside the ash tray.

The Deceiver smiled.

She delighted in this place.

This moment.

Poised between what was and what would be.

The power of knowing, when others were so oblivious, living like worms rotting in the shadows.

Her talon carved a pattern in the plastered wall, gentle as a lover's kiss, her shoulder still leaning lazily against the threshold of the bedroom.

Oh, how she delighted in this moment.

She breathed a contented sigh and slipped into the room, the moonlight licking her skin, her shadow prowling across his bed.

The Deceiver's trailing silhouette lingered by the door as she lowered herself onto the man's covers, the fabric sighing blissfully beneath her thighs. She grazed her talon across the tenuous flesh beneath his chin.

And his bitter, obsidian eyes flew open.

The Deceiver released a shushing hiss, cupping a hand over the man's mouth. Her smile sparked in the depths of her gaze as she felt his uneven breaths heating her palm. "Hush, now. We wouldn't want to wake the neighbours, my dear Shade."

Shade shuddered beneath the Deceiver's grip, struggling to scramble away, his fingers frantically clawing at the covers.

The Deceiver merely shifted, dragging the smooth side of her talon down his cheek. Her smile bloomed as he froze, as she repositioned the point beneath his chin. "Do you know why I'm here?"

Shade swallowed, his throat bobbing precariously against the tip of her talon, and shook his head.

"I don't appreciate men taking advantage of my warriors." The Deceiver leaned forward, pressing her talon into Shade's skin, watching as he winced and a bubble of blood broke the surface. "*Especially* when she is under orders *not to harm.*" She tightened her grip on his mouth. "... And I *hate* slavery." Shade began to spit a muffled string of curses, the spray of saliva drenching the Deceiver's palm. She glanced at the doorway and jerked her head, gesturing for the silhouette to enter.

A superior smirk crooked the corners of cupid-bow lips.

Hazel eyes narrowed, eagerly simmering.

Leda sauntered to the foot of the bed, her knuckles popping as she squeezed each fist, her fingers flexing in fluid movements.

"I suggest you begin with the removal of his tongue." The Deceiver lifted her glistening hand from Shade's mouth, disgust limning her features as she wiped his spit on the sheets.

A sleep-rusted bellow burst from Shade, ice freezing his furious glare. "*Bitch—*"

Leda leaped onto the bed and slammed her boot into his ribs, silencing him.

The Deceiver smiled at the wet sound of fracturing bone, at the raking coughs of Shade vomiting onto his pillows. "Your guards are dead. Those orphans you were selling as *slaves* have been freed." She stood, elegant as the spread of an owl's wings, her flashing gaze pinning Shade as he swore through his violent retching. "I expect you won't lay another unwanted hand on a woman..." She plucked a bronze knife from the inside of her coat, admiring the owl carved into its' ivory hilt. "Not now, nor in the afterlife." The Deceiver held the blade in the palm of her fist, feeling the razor edges press into her flesh as if it were no more than a blunt plaything. She offered the hilt to Leda. "Take your time, my warrior, we wouldn't want him to die without suitably repenting."

Leda's lips split in a lupine grin as she took the whetted knife, the owl carved into its' hilt cruelly gleaming. A hyena's cackle clawed from her throat, the sound roiling elatedly. "It'll be my pleasure."

The Deceiver tilted her head in a smooth motion, indicating Leda could begin, as she strode to the door.

Shade heaved one final time and hauled his sleeve across his mouth. He released a seething snarl. "*Whore.* I'll make you—"

Leda's fingers snapped out and his words were cut off by a gurgling shriek. The shriek of claws shredding glass. The shriek of a feral creature. As Leda slid the pale knife into Shade's gaping mouth and sliced the muscle of his tongue.

Clean through.

She threw the lump of wet flesh onto the floor, smirking as blood spewed from Shade's gaping mouth. "Call me a whore again, you *Godless* shit."

Shade choked, gasping, shuddering, crimson spilling over his chin in a torrent, blood staining the dark fabric of his sheets. The metallic scent of it fused with the residual reek of sweat, with the persistent smoke of the smouldering cigar and the sickly sweet tang of mint-drops.

Shade's skin blanched to a deathly pallor.

His fingers clawed at his bloodied face.

The Deceiver paused at the threshold of the room, her talon effortlessly retracting into her finger. "Leda dear, there's a half finished cigar on the nightstand..."

Leda shoved her boot into Shade's stomach and flicked the knife in her palm, holding him down while he convulsed. "So?"

"Fire and flesh." The Deceiver glanced over her shoulder, malice flashing across her features like a streaking summer storm. "Be creative." She turned and resolutely left, Shade's screams abruptly cut short as Leda tore through his sheets and shoved the fabric into his mouth.

Chapter Sixty - Two

Theodore

A CURSE SPILLED THROUGH the night as Theodore distracted himself with the heating on the dashboard of his car. He glanced through the windscreen, the glass clouding with fog, his mud and moss gaze scanning the street.

The pavement glittered beneath the blinding flood of his headlights, the frozen ground littered with starless shadow.

A figure paused as it moved into the street. Silent as the night. Furious as a storm in the gloom.

She peered at his car with glowing, golden eyes.

Theodore sucked a calming breath through his nose, gradually releasing the air from his mouth and twisting the radio's volume controls. A melody poured from the speakers, drowning the reality of his trembling hands. He began to mouth the lyrics. Then began to sing. His fingers struck up a beat on the wheel, the pristine leather smooth beneath his touch. He wriggled further into the heated seat, his eyes slowly drifting shut, his voice imperceptibly hitching. He could feel the heart cringe in his chest as he waited for the woman to approach, as he had been instructed, though his instincts screamed at him to run.

Theodore tensed, fear driving through his veins.

Running was not an option. It never had been and it never would be.

Not from them.

Theodore dragged his hand over the steering wheel of his new car.

A gift...

... Basically.

Who left a car like this on the side of the road? It was just *asking* to be stolen.

Especially when his own now had a broken window.

It was too damned cold not to have a window.

The corner of Theodore's mouth twitched up, remembering the excitement he had felt at seeing the silver lightning which burst like shimmering veins over the car's ruby-red doors. He had picked the lock, felt the leather seats heating beneath him, and had fallen in love. He had driven for hours through the night-dark streets, listening to the roar of the engine and the screech of the breaks, until he had arrived here.

Sitting.

Waiting.

For the woman with a predator's gaze.

Theodore flinched as the door was flung open.

A hand grabbed his collar, hauling him from his seat and slamming him into the wall of a building across the pavement.

"Hey! *Ow!*" Theodore swore as the woman shoved again, crashing the crown of his head against the stone. He groaned and blinked, attempting to banish the spots swirling across his vision. "I didn't *do* anything!"

"Oh really?" A laugh swept beneath the still blaring music, devoid of humour, entirely too familiar. "You call *killing* me 'not doing anything'?"

Theodore grimaced at Medusa's fuming features, his fingers curling around her forearm as she pinned him to the wall. "You remembered..."

"*Oh*, I remember."

"You can't possibly *still* be mad about—"

"About you *stealing* into my home? About you *slicing* my *throat* in my *sleep*?" Medusa snarled, teeth gleaming as she dragged Theodore towards the bonnet of his car.

"No!" Theodore grabbed her wrist, yanking at her unwavering grip on his collar, his heels scraping across the pavement. "No, Medusa! *Not the car!*"

"It has been almost three thousand years since you killed me, slaughtered me, like a *God-damned coward!*" Medusa threw Theodore into the bonnet, the ruby metal denting beneath the force. "I will *never* forgive you such a *violation!*"

The breath burst from Theodore's lungs, a fit of coughs raking through his chest as she lifted a pale fist and leaned forward.

"No! Not the face!" Theodore flung his arms up, shielding his face from the ferocity leaking in wrathful hisses through Medusa's teeth. He swore under his breath, knowing this was what he had been waiting for. He was simply a distraction in a cruel, ruthless game. Though her anger was far worse than he had expected. He took a deep breath. "I thought you'd be less angry after you..."

Medusa tensed, her whole body becoming rigid as she narrowed her paralysing eyes, as the blood drained from the knuckles of her raised fist, the skin becoming white. "After I *what*?"

"After you and Poseidon..." Theodore raised his dark brows suggestively, peering through the gap between his shielding forearms. "You know..."

Medusa's anger momentarily flickered. Her velvet lips pursed. Her threatening fist faltered.

Theodore stared at her, his arms dropping slightly. "You haven't—"

Medusa growled, the fire returning to her tenfold. She reached for the mirror protruding from the car door, her fingers hovering above it like brutal claws. "Say another word and the mirror gets it."

Theodore cringed, trying to hold the words in.

He couldn't do it.

"— Made *sweet, sweet love?*"

The screech of tearing metal pierced him as Medusa ripped the mirror from the car and hurled it across the street. Her glare burned into his flesh. Her teeth flashed in the streetlight.

Theodore howled his grief, staring at the gaping hole in his beautiful, stolen car. "Why would you *do* that? *That was so unnecessary!*"

"If you *ever* insinuate that you know *anything* about my relationship with Poseidon again, I will not hesitate to crush your damned car until it is nothing more than a useless pile of gleaming *tin*."

Theodore blinked at her. "But—"

"Shut your mouth, Perseus, or *so help me...*"

He lifted a frantic finger to his lips, shushing her with a vicious hiss. "Quiet! You'll blow my cover!"

Medusa's hand dropped from his collar. She blinked at him incredulously. "... Curse the gods." Hatred fluttered beneath her graceful features as she stepped aside. "I loath you."

Perseus shoved himself off the car, grief straining in his chest at the sight of the dented metal, at the thought of his true name on her lips.

He supposed he had *kind of* asked for it...

Perseus frowned. "I *like* being Theodore and I'm *tired* of being *her* errand boy." Silver eyes flashed through his mind as he caught a glimpse of his reflection in the windscreen, the alluring features, the disarming, inviting mouth. "Do I *look* like an errand boy to you? I should be courting mortals and using my significant assets for something *pleasurable! I have needs!*"

Medusa tilted her head back and glared at the sky, exasperated. The pulse throbbed in her throat as her fingers curled, then flexed, and she released a mocking sigh. "Alas, I am *Perseus* and I've been making an endless stream of stupid decisions since the day I was born." She turned to him and raised a brow at the gaping car door, gesturing to the meticulously painted lightning which stretched across the ruby paint in striking silver. "Son of Zeus, the mighty yet absent Father! Oh, how I *suffer!*"

"You would be *particularly* adept at role play." Perseus twisted his lips in an appreciative smirk, the heat in his veins banishing the thread of fear in his stomach as he stepped forward, peering down at Medusa. She truly was a staggering sight, wrath burning beneath her elegant features, sharp and stunning, soft and alluring. He felt her breath, the heated cloud of it kissing his skin. "Under the right tutelage you might even rival myself."

"And I suppose you'd be the one to teach me?" Medusa glared at him darkly, nary a glint of mirth in her gaze. "Don't flirt with me, Perseus. I'm poisonous."

Perseus lowered his head, cautious of the near imperceptible writhing beneath the veil of her scarf. "And you might kill me in my sleep?"

A dark chuckle climbed Medusa's supple throat. "No. I would watch the light seep from your eyes knowing that you had put up a fight and that it *wasn't enough.*"

Perseus swallowed the discomfort crawling through him, refusing to back away from the promise in her eyes as the heat in his veins turned to ice. "Why am I still standing?"

"I want her Aegisium weapons." Medusa clenched her teeth, a muscle in her jaw fluttering irately. "And I have a feeling you know where to find them, since you've been so *conveniently* positioned in my way. I'm assuming she instructed you to keep me busy."

Perseus lifted his shoulders in an impassive shrug as he straightened to his full height. "What if I don't feel inclined to help?"

Medusa's mouth curled in a brutal smile. "Then we find out just how much of that mortal blood runs in your Demigod veins."

'Tell me, Perseus, if a demigod is killed, do they return? Or do they die a mortal death?'

Perseus flinched at the memory. The gleaming, silver eyes flicking through his mind. The cruel, glorious smile pinning him like prey. Her amused laugh echoed, chilling his trembling bones and leaving him weak with unbearable terror.

'Shall we see just how immortal you are?'

Perseus crossed his arms, fear twitching through his features.

Finally, he released a shuddering breath. "Alright, but I'm driving."

FEAR

TEN YEARS AGO

THE RANCID SCENT OF BURNING bile assaulted her senses, mutilating her throat, torturing her nose. Blood congealed on her arms in glutted rivers, the scent of iron mixing with vomit, the wounds in her wrists mercilessly throbbing as she hunched over the cold, stone floor. Her golden eyes glittered. Vision blurring. Salted tears forming cleansed streams down her sweat and dust-ridden cheeks.

She froze as scales scraped metal. As writhing bodies shot prickles over her scalp.

A snake slithered around the manacle imprisoning her neck.

Her nostrils flared, eyes yawning wide as another lowered its' elongated body, hovering in front of her face. Its' forked tongue tickled her skin, tasting her tears as it shifted, as it swayed.

She clung to her chains. Held herself steady. Using the cold, gnarled metal as a makeshift anchor.

Her entire body convulsed, struggling to smother a shuddering sob. She could feel them all as they squirmed around her skull. She could feel their bodies writhing across her shoulders, tangling in a twisted mass atop her head. She could see through their eyes. She could taste through their mouths.

She could lose herself in the eternal susurrus of their whispering scales.

A gleaming string of bile dribbled from her lower lip. Nausea mauled the lining of her stomach. Insufferably aching. Incessantly cramping.

She swallowed thickly, straightened, spat the remaining bile into the puddle on the floor and watched the murky vomit ooze towards her naked feet.

She shuddered.

Enough.

It was enough.

She glared at the cobra draped in front of her face. She could taste the residual tears and dirt still lingering on its' tongue.

She ground her teeth as it leaned forward. As it tipped its' head. As it gently nuzzled her cheek.

Golden eyes locked with slitted pupils as the cobra snapped forward, a curved trail of shadowed sand abandoned in its' wake.

"Calm yourself." Her scalp prickled in anticipation as she mimicked the movements of the snake, leaning forward to meet it. "I won't hurt you."

The fear evaporated, the memory of her first moments in that desert sinking over her, calming her.

The snakes would not hurt her.

Her snakes would not hurt her.

She focused on their movements, on those reaching for her chains, irritation flowing through them as they examined the steel, as they reached towards the leather brace confining her ribs.

The cobra which had nuzzled her cheek began to rise, reaching for the confines trapping her wrist.

The iron taste of blood and metal blossomed on her tongue as the snake tasted her shackle, the morbid bloom spreading until it filled her mouth, almost erasing the acidic bile clinging to her throat.

The cobra hissed.

Struck.

She grimaced in pain as its' fangs collided with the manacle, as every snake atop her head flinched.

Froze.

She heard humming. A hollow rhythm beyond the bleak, metal door.

A mass of serpentine heads twisted, tongues flicking out to taste the air.

The scraping thud of unbolted locks echoed through the cell, resonating off the mirrors panelling the walls, glass softly trembling in their frames. The door swung open. The light beyond was choked by the flood of white still illuminating her stale, barren cell.

The violet-eyed man stepped in. Elegant as an owl. Hair rustling. Coat whispering. A burnt-orange scarf draped around his neck.

His body was recurrent in the mirrors. Reflections upon reflections upon reflections.

An army of violet-eyed men.

He held a tray of food and water, balancing it on one hand, and lifted a ring of gleaming keys with the other. "I trust you've had enough time to reacquaint with yourself." The man shot her an amused smile, gracefully crouching to set the tray on the floor.

She did not respond.

Could not respond.

Her throat was sandpaper. Dry as ice.

Confusion trickled from her snakes as they tasted the decaying air. Their bodies reached for the violet-eyed man, their eyes unblinking, their breath a ceaseless hiss.

Her cobras paused, then violently recoiled, thrashing in recognition.

A flood of impossible fury burned through her veins.

Her fingers tightened on her blood-coated chains.

Her breath shuddered.

Her shoulders trembled.

The violet-eyed man straightened, holding the keys towards her as if she could take them. He swung them on their ring, tilting his head and listening to their tuneless chant as he stepped over her pool of vomit, looked her in the eyes. And when he spoke, his voice was polished steel, smoothest silk and savage tempest.

"How would you like to rid yourself of those chains?"

CHAPTER SIXTY - THREE

POSEIDON WATCHED THE GLOWING windows of Shade's penthouse from across the night-shadowed street. He leaned against a frost-slicked wall, boots planted on the icy pavement, hand laid flat and facing the moon as water gently rippled in his palm. His gaze was dark as death, stare locked on the orphan-slaver's building.

Orphan. Slaver.

Poseidon released a menacing growl. The water in his palm began to mould and take shape. The smooth surface expanded, the ripples rose in circular ridges, furrowing to form a skin of shimmering, watery scales.

A coiled cobra.

Water flowed through the body as if streaming through a crystal tube, pockets of air capturing light, sparking, disappearing, as the fluid began to tremble, then shake.

It lift its' head.

Its' body trickled sentience, the water gaining life and breath and sight.

His life. *His* breath. *His* sight.

The water-cobra spread over Poseidon's palm, curling its' tail around his wrist. Its' black-water eyes snapped to Shade's window. In the light of day it would not have seemed real, with the sunlight pouring through its' transparent scales, but the day reveals all and the night hides terrors. And in the dark the liquid glinted, appearing born instead of made.

Though to him it was nothing.

A mere drop in a vast, endless sea.

Poseidon's returned power was a storm in his veins, coursing through his muscles, thunderous beneath his skin. For the first time in ten years Poseidon felt awake. Alive.

He felt like a *God.*

Poseidon slid one hand into the pocket of his coat, his beautiful mouth curving in a devastatingly lethal smile. Darker than the black beneath the earth. Darker than the absence between the stars.

Poseidon's smile was like a knife. Hellfire glinting in his eyes.

He angled his head and began to *listen.*

Muffled howls leaked from the penthouse, leaching through the curtained windows like the souls of men just dead. The howls were of despair. Of agony and prayer.

The splintering sanity of a tortured man.

Shade.

Poseidon had tracked the Deceiver through the streets, had followed her until she entered Shade's building and now he waited, filled with eternal, confident patience.

Another strangled shriek floated to him through the cold, barely audible over the subtle breeze.

He doubted a human would hear.

He would have preferred to be the one performing the torture, as one performs a ballet or a harmony or an act. If that had been the case he would have let the orphan-slaver scream, he would have watched Shade beg and choke and writhe, he would have forced

Shade to stare at his own blood as it spilled like tears from his wounds.

But Poseidon was not performing the torture. So he settled in to listen and enjoy the piquing fervour of Shade's screams.

Until they shifted and his mind produced a scream far worse, far more terrible, than those streaming from above. A three-thousand year old memory. A scream that had torn a wound in the very air he breathed. And turned it to poison in his lungs.

It was the scream of a girl who had become a monster.

Poseidon exhaled, long and slow. He shoved the remembered scream aside.

He had had enough of this game. This *punishment*.

Three thousand years was enough.

So Poseidon stood alone in the night-dark street, the cold body of his liquid-cobra coiled around his arm, licking the air with a tongue that could not taste. He focused on its' scales, smooth and hard as sculpted glass. And there he waited.

And waited.

Finally, a figure emerged from Shade's building, ethereal in her grace, one hand stroking the fur of her coat, the gleaming-silver moon of no comparison to her eyes. She slipped through the door and let it swing closed. Then stopped to examine his presence, her gaze lingering on the cobra.

Its' head flattened against his palm, its' body tensed around his wrist.

"I have to say I was initially surprised that you left her like you did... Although, you always have managed to provide more of a challenge."

Poseidon's fingers curled in fists. The cobra stopped like rusted clockwork, slid from his arm and fell, splashing across the pavement in a puddle beside his boots. He released a mirthless, steaming chuckle. "I simply decided I had tired of playing your *unending* games."

"Fancy that." The Deceiver combed her fingers through her silken, auburn hair, the waves whispering as they tumbled over her shoulder. "It only took you three thousand years."

Poseidon shoved himself off the building, striding to stop before the woman with her silver eyes. He peered down at her, feeling his power kick and thrash. A power that was not unending and had not been for a very long time. Since his Aegisium armour had been stolen, and a weapon along with it. Melted down and reduced to nothing more than *knives* and *bullets*.

Poseidon loosened his fingers and relaxed the strain in his shoulders, still standing over the Deceiver with the quiet certainty of a God. "I have a proposition for you."

The Deceiver watched him for a moment, searching his eyes. She stepped closer. "... And what proposition is that?"

Poseidon smiled, corrupt and stunning, and told her what she wanted to hear.

Chapter Sixty - Four

Leda

LEDA SAT ON THE CORNER OF Shade's bed, legs crossed atop the covers, bloody hands sinking into the sheets by her side. Her eyelids were soft and drooping, serene as a reaper in the presence of death. The Deceiver's bronze and ivory knife rested by her feet, soaked in blood from hilt to tip, the carved owl patiently watching beneath a handprint of still-wet crimson.

Blood drenched the mattress beneath Shade's mutilated corpse, the metallic scent creeping through the room, as rich and intoxicating as an aged and vintaged wine. Crimson plastered his hair to his face, the strands matted from his thrashing and soaked with his sweat. It coated his lashes, his lips, his teeth, leaking into eyes staring sightlessly at the ceiling, dribbling from the lump of his swollen, severed tongue.

Leda took a deep breath, savouring the perfect silence, smirking at the sour stench of urine and the soiled remains of his torn and crumpled sheets.

In the end, he had drowned in his own blood, suffocating as she poured it down his gurgling throat, unable to breathe through the crimson gore choking the bruising mess of his shattered nose.

He had howled. He had flailed. He had convulsed. And he had died.

And now she sat, listening to the drip of blood onto the floor. Eyelids aflutter. Warm as a babe.

Content and idly dreaming.

The Deceiver shifted, dragging the smooth side of her talon down Shade's cheek.

The woman was ferocious and beautiful as a recently sharpened blade. And just as lethal.

She was mercy. She was power. She was the dark before the dawn.

She was the earth and the moon and the stars shining bright.

She was everything.

And she was *perfect*.

A sigh danced across Leda's tongue, her mouth curving in an appreciative smile. Her heart floated, weightless in her chest.

"Picturing how Her Intelligence will smile when she hears of the damage you've done?"

Her Intelligence.

The name had been given to the silver-eyed woman by her warriors. Though it was never used in her presence. It was merely an avoidance of using her false name.

Wise. For the moment.

Leda leisurely tilted her head. She rested her cheek against her own shoulder and lifted a hand, lazily sweeping her blood-stained fingers through the air. She kept her eyes on Shade's weeping corpse as her twin stepped into the waking light of dawn, her figure no more than a silhouette against the glass.

Lorelei groaned in disgust, the toe of her boot nudging an oozing lump of flesh on the floor. "*Please* tell me that's *not* the bastard's tongue."

Leda shifted slightly, her hooded, hazel eyes drifting to Shade's tongue, the flesh coated in drying spit and blood. "He was deserving."

"I don't doubt it." Lorelei scanned Shade's naked body, his abdomen barely shielded by a blood-bathed sheet. She raised a brow at the wounds decorating his stomach, stabbing and slashing through organ to bone.

Bleached skin peeled back from the muscle of his chest, the right pectoral brutally exposed.

Circular burns puckered in sickening welts, dusted with ash and spattered in blood.

"... Cigarette burns?"

Leda gestured vaguely towards the dwindling cigar in the ashtray on Shade's nightstand, a thread of smoke still wafting from its' tip. "Cigar."

Lorelei narrowed her eyes. Nodded.

Leda lifted her gaze from the awkward angles of Shade's arms, his shattered ribs and snapped fingers, bloody teeth both fractured and missing, fragments of bone peaking through skin. "... I assume you're here because '*Her Intelligence*' sent you."

"Can't I ever simply be here because I care for my sister?"

A laugh split Leda's mouth, her smile gleaming like the moon, as she carefully wrapped her fingers around the hilt of the blood-stained knife and lifted it off the sheets. "You're here because you care for your sister *too much*. You followed me when I *specifically* told you not to and now you're in this as deeply as I am."

Lorelei lifted her shoulders in a casual shrug, dismissing Leda's comment as if the broken man laying slaughtered on the mattress were nothing more than a child's lost toy. "I've grown into the role."

Leda stretched her legs, boots leaving crimson smears on the clean section of sheet beneath her. "It only took eleven years."

"I don't regret it." Lorelei pressed her lips together, meeting Leda's identical gaze, ignoring the freckles of crimson strewn across her sister's face, the blood soaking her shirt and pants. "I wouldn't take it back. I followed and I will keep following you to the ends of the earth."

"Perhaps it's time *I* followed *you.*" Leda's smile softened as she swung her boots to the floor and rose from the bed, knife swinging inattentively by her side. "What, exactly, did Her Intelligence want?"

"She was approached by Poseidon."

Leda paused, the blood on her boots soaking into the carpet. "What did he do?"

Lorelei combed her fingers through her hair, frowning slightly as they caught in a tangle of tresses, matted with her own blood. "Nothing... He *spoke* to her."

"What did he *say*?"

Lorelei shook her head, her curtain of brunette hair sighing. "I don't know. I arrived when they finished. I was asked to disable the building's cameras, erase the security footage and retrieve you."

"What did you do with the guard in the entrance?"

"I made sure he was still unconscious and locked him in a supply closet."

"Bound and gagged?" Leda stepped forward, moving towards Shade's bedroom door and leaving a fading trail of bloody bootprints in her wake.

Lorelei stared, one eyebrow climbing in an unimpressed arc. "... Seriously?"

Leda tucked her knife into her coat, disregarding the ruined fabric partially painted crimson. "Were we instructed to go anywhere *specific* after having dealt with Shade?"

Lorelei raised her fingers to her temple, to the bruise blooming around the sliced and grazed skin. She could still taste the blood where it had spilled down her face and entered her mouth. Her skin and hair were caked with it. Lorelei let her hand fall to her side, glancing at her leg. Clarke's glass paperweight had left a sickening bruise beneath her trousers. She had checked. She was still limping slightly from the blow. "We were instructed to go on a hunt."

"I was hoping you'd say that." Leda wiped her bloodied hands on her shirt and plucked her coat from its' place on the couch. She slid her arms through the clean sleeves before turning to Lorelei and grinning. "Let's hope they were intelligent enough to make this difficult."

"I highly doubt it." Lorelei smiled and lead her sister out of Shade's penthouse, not bothering to look back at the man's corpse.

A Girl With Cerulean Eyes

Ten Years Ago

Donovan crept through the halls, no more than a wraith against the shadows waiting between the windows. The clouds outside were softly crying, he could hear the drops tapping against the glass. Beads of water still dripped from his hair, trickling down the planes of his naked back as he peered into a familiar room. The dining hall. The ceiling's tremendous beams now floated in darkness, the iron chandeliers cold, their candles doused. The carved, stone fireplace held embers almost dead, nothing like the beast of roaring flames he remembered from that first night. The embers barely illuminated the table in the centre of the room, its' polished surface empty, its' cushioned chairs bereft.

The violet-eyed man was nowhere to be seen.

"Let the hunt begin."

Donovan silenced the man's voice as it began to ring in his head.

He left the room as it was.

Soundless.

Deserted.

And continued down the hall.

THE WAXED FLOORBOARDS FELT *warm beneath Donovan's bare feet as he skirted the edges of a ballroom. Muted colours bathed the floor, the dull light outside casting echoes of stained-glass across the haunting room. The windows were palatial, towering mosaics of abstract glass which speared towards the roof. Chandeliers hung above, from arched wooden beams, their crystals twinkling like blood and starlight, quietly reflecting the shadows and the painted windows light.*

A figure stood reverently beneath it all, dark cloak falling around subtle curves to gather at her boots in a pool of absorbing black. Donovan could hear her tranquil breaths, her soft murmurs of devoted prayer. She touched fingers to her forehead, then her temples, and lowered her arms, head gracefully bowed, dark curls spilling from her upraised hood.

Donovan watched from the darkness as she turned, straightened her shoulders and strode towards the door. Her steps reverberated through the silent ballroom, cloak fluttering behind her in a darkened stream of night.

Donovan trailed her through shadows, creeping forward with lethal grace. He followed as she disappeared into a stairwell, the stone steps coiling in a steep ascent. He paused as she slipped into a dimly lit hall, rain pattering against the windows and sliding down the glass, causing shadows of the droplets to streak across the floor.

The woman stopped before a room near lost to darkness between the windows, its' presence exposed only by a thread of amber light spilling beneath the door. Donovan hovered in the darkness of the stairwell as the woman tentatively opened it, cautiously scanning the empty hall before moving inside.

She did not notice as Donovan strode to the door and slipped in after her, nothing but a dark figure looming at her back. Quiet as the stars. Calm as a mountain in a floating mass of clouds.

He reached for a vase on a table beside the door.

And slammed the ceramic container into the woman's head.

The vase shattered.

The woman dropped.

She lay on the carpeted floorboards. Unmoving.

Donovan stepped over her unconscious form, careful not to tread on the sprawled fabric of her cloak or the ceramic shards of the vase. He scanned the room, an office, its' walls decorated with painted maps, its' floor spotted with antique terrestrial globes and wooden filing-cabinets. One of which had been left open.

Donovan crossed the room and began rifling through the open drawer, scanning document after document.

Wyatt Shade.

...

Diana Laurenti.

...

Donovan frowned, shoving the drawer closed and reaching to open the next.

A quiet gasp stopped him.

He turned, bathed in shadow, without a shirt, hair a tangled mess, the rough strands of a beard dominating his face. To find a girl, no more than six, staring at the woman still unconscious on the floor.

Wide eyes of palest cerulean lifted to stare at Donovan, the child's delicate, caramel fingers clutching a file tightly to her chest. Her throat bobbed as she chewed her lip, then tip-toed around the unconscious woman's head, stepping over a strand of her curling, brunette hair.

The girl paused, looking up at Donovan as if he were a wild beast.

He lowered himself to a knee, allowing a reassuring smile to tug at his mouth.

She glanced at the file in her hands, then held it out to him.

He accepted it with a flutter of anticipation. "What's this?"

"Shhh." The girl slapped a hand over his bearded mouth, lifted a finger to her lips.

Donovan grunted, brows narrowing.

The girl slowly pulled her hand away but kept her finger on her lips, glaring at him pointedly.

Donovan nodded, watching as the girl dropped her hands to her sides and pointed at the file.

"Open."

"… I thought we were being quiet—"

"Sssshhhh." The girl hissed. She tapped her finger against the file. "Open."

Donovan frowned, the creases between his brows deepening. He opened the file. And found a photograph of himself staring out.

Detective Areus Donovan.

Donovan blinked, glancing at the girl. She gestured for him to continue.

He read the files, lowering himself to the floor as he shuffled through the details of his past. He was a detective… who had gone missing during a murder case. Presumed dead. Last seen by Chief Akilah Wise almost three months ago… There was a photograph of her, auburn waves strangled in a knot atop her head, silver eyes bright as the new moon.

She looked familiar.

As if he knew her.

The file dropped from Donovan's hand, pages spilling onto the floor.

The woman who had saved him, dragged him from that frozen lake, she had known his name. How had she known his name? How had she known where to find him?

And the violet-eyed man.

He had known, too…

Donovan gritted his teeth, panic rising in his throat.

The rain striking the windows of the hall became deafening.

He felt the void between the beats of his heart.

Hollow.

Hollow.

Hollow.

Donovan dragged his fingers across his beard, through his matted hair. Hollow. Hollow. Hollow.

A soft hand settled on the curve of his shoulder.

Donovan looked up, feeling his panic falter.

The girl stood at his side, frowning deeply, her gaze filled with concern.

"I need to find her." Donovan scraped the papers back into the file, grabbing the photograph of Akilah Wise, along with a page detailing the address of his own apartment. He folded them, then shoved them into the pocket of his trousers. "I need to escape."

The girl let her hand drop from Donovan's shoulder. She glanced at the woman still unconscious on the floor.

She was beginning to stir.

"Quiet." The girl lifted her finger again to her lips and began to walk, moving towards the hall. She paused by the door and looked back, pale eyes determined. "Follow me."

Donovan glanced at the file in his hand, then at the pouring rain outside. The papers would soak if he exposed them outside. He placed the file in the cabinet and closed the drawer, assuming that was what the girl had come in here to do, then followed her into the hall. She grabbed his finger, her small hand closing around it, and dragged him through the night-dark castle, past empty rooms and closed doors, paintings and stairwells, ballrooms and dining rooms, until they came to a kitchen with a discreet, unadorned door on the other side of the room. An exit.

The girl dragged Donovan into the kitchen, then stopped. "Wait here." She released his finger and raced back out before he could stop her.

Donovan looked at the exit, listened to the rain steadily falling outside. The door rattled in the wind. The windows shuddered in their frames.

Donovan felt the fear creep up on him.

Felt the space between heartbeats—

The girl stepped up to his side, taking his finger and smiling innocently at him. "Done." She was clothed head to toe in an oversized raincoat.

Complete with hat and boots. Both far too large for her tiny head and feet.

Donovan frowned at her.

How long had he been standing there?

"What?" The girl shrugged and dragged him to the exit. "I didn't want to get wet." She pulled the door open and a burst of saturating rain howled inside. Her hat blew off, disappearing into the dimly lit kitchen. "Damnation." She cursed under her breath, then pursed her lips, eyes going wide. She glanced at Donovan. "... Don't tell anyone I said that."

Donovan chuckled.

The girl narrowed her eyes. "Shush." She stomped out into the rain, ducking her head against the onslaught of water which drenched her ebony hair.

Donovan closed the door behind them. "Why are you here?"

The girl shook her head, stubbornly clinging to Donovan's finger as she led him around the stables. He could hear the storm-nervous horses inside, snorting, nickering. Could see an afterimage of the arrow as it pierce Starlight's breast—

Donovan stopped. Rain pelted his naked back, streamed from his hair and beard.

The girl tugged on his finger.

"Why are you helping me?"

She glared at him, water dripping from her lashes and onto her cheeks. "Because every time you come back, you're bleeding." She yanked on his finger, stomping through a puddle and continuing through the rain. "I don't want to watch you bleed anymore."

A knife through his neck.

An axe in his back.

A sword through his chest.

An arrow through his heart.

Blood.

Darkness.

Death...

Donovan rumbled a growl, the thunder echoing his anger, his frustration.

He had not been dead.

He had not been dead.

The girl released his finger. They stood before another set of stables, this one quiet, absent the equine noise. She trudged to the stable doors and knocked, rapping her knuckles rhythmically against the wood.

She pressed her ear against the door.

Waited.

Donovan grumbled and glanced around. They had gotten here too easily. There had been no guards to stop them. No weapons. No fight.

"... What are you doing?"

The girl scrunched her little nose in concentration. "Listening."

"It's empty." He could sense it, somehow, through the rain.

She didn't respond, simply kept her ear against the door. After a moment she pulled away and nodded. "It's empty."

Donovan grunted, striding forward and shoving the wooden door open. He marched inside, the girl following in his heels.

"Will this help?"

Donovan felt his mouth fall slack. The stable had been modified, the pens removed. It still smelled of horses and straw and dirt. But also leather.

And automobiles.

Motorbikes, cars, snowmobiles, modified dune-buggies. All covered in heavy grey cloths layered with dust.

Untouched.

The girl tugged on Donovan's trousers, looking up at him with wide, serious eyes. "Will it help?"

Donovan knelt beside her, throat growing tight and tears pricking his eyes. "Yes." His voice was crumpled paper as he gently grasped her shoulders, grinning beneath his beard. "Yes, it will help."

"You won't bleed anymore?"

Donovan shook his head, pulling the girl into a quick, dripping hug. "Thank you." He whispered, letting her go and pushing to his feet. "Are you going to be alright?"

The girl shrugged, stomping back to the door in her oversized rain-boots. "Don't get caught."

Donovan watched her leave, her tiny, hunched form disappearing into the rain.

He turned and strode further into the stables, grabbing a tarp and tearing it from a matt-black dirt bike.

A leather jacket lay over its' seat, helmet atop it.

Donovan frowned, pulling them on even as his heart gave an anxious stutter. He jogged to the rack of keys hanging beside the door, scanned them, grabbed a set and jogged back to the bike.

He swung his leg over the seat and kicked up the stand, shoved the key into the ignition and twisted. Flicking the kill switch. Jabbing the start button.

The engine roared to life, muting the rumble of thunder and the constant, pelting rain.

The wheels spewed dust as Donovan shot over the stable floor and through the still open door, speeding out into the night, to the wet, mud-slicked forest. The rain soaked through his clothes, reaching for the photograph of Chief Akilah Wise and the paper with his address.

He kept going.

Screaming through the forest.

Dodging trees.

Jumping streams.

Surging through the mud.

An owl watched him go, its' moonbeam eyes glowing silver.

And back in the castle, the violet-eyed man smiled.

Chapter Sixty - Five

MIST BILLOWED THROUGH THE air in an endless breath, curling over the cobblestones and swallowing the streets in a curtain of blurring white.

Adalinda rested her gloved fingers on the roof of Perseus' car. She stood motionless beside the gaping door. Nothing more than a shape in the mist.

She knew this place, though she could not see it, knew the buildings and their walls, knew the broken windows, the wilted vines, their hidden façades lurking beyond the mist. She knew the gentle curve of the road, the feel of the cobblestones beneath her boots. She was calmed by its' desolation. Content in its' solitude.

She felt her studio silently calling from its' place along the street.

Another life.

Another lie.

Medusa slammed the car door, veins of painted lightning flashing across its' steel. Her golden eyes glinted pleasure as Perseus released a yelp.

"Why don't you just stab me in the heart? It would hurt less."

"And end your prolonged suffering?" A cold smile tugged at Medusa's lips, her gaze sliding to Perseus, to the tortured grimace twisting his features as he carefully slid from the car. He flinched as she stepped forward and tapped a finger on the bonnet. "I think not."

"How did you come to be so cruel?"

Medusa searched the mists, the smile falling from her face. "... You know the answer to that."

Perseus paused, watching the vast, white mass before them eerily shift, the mist curling through the night air as if stirred by a non-existent breeze. "You're sure you want to do this?"

Medusa raised a hand, fingertips lightly brushing the edge of her scarf. "I don't have much of a choice. She can use those weapons to kill Poseidon." Medusa lowered her arm, cloak rustling against her sleeve, heart twisting as Poseidon's refusal to help echoed in her mind. "... I can't let that happen again..."

Perseus exhaled a reluctant sigh, his breath disrupting the curling mist as he moved forward, his form becoming a faded, grey shadow. "Come on. It's this way."

Medusa followed, her snakes quiet beneath her scarf, their muscles tensed, waiting. She knew her actions would likely end her life, knew she would wake again with no memories, her mind a dark void, her past an opaque shadow.

Scattered.

Suffocated.

Lost.

Medusa's fingers formed fists, the creaking leather of her gloves hidden beneath her rippling cloak.

She was willing to make that sacrifice.

She would not watch Poseidon die.

Not again.

"... Doesn't look like anyone's home..."

Medusa froze mid-stride, her eyes widening. Perseus stood before a window with his face pressed against the glass, his hands shading his brow so he could see inside.

Medusa grabbed his jacket and hauled him away from the building with a muted hiss. "*What are you doing?*"

Perseus stumbled to a stop and straightened, peeling her fingers off his shoulder, delicately brushing away the creases she had left in his sleeve. "I've had a long week. I thought I'd take a nap."

Medusa pursed her lips, stewing.

"I'm searching for signs of life." Perseus pointed to the door beside the window, its' surface pressed into the stone as if retreating from the mist. "What? Do you think I'm just going to waltz in the front door with a blindfold and a lollipop?"

Medusa crossed her arms and narrowed her eyes. "I wouldn't be surprised."

Perseus stared at her, blinking, the corners of his mouth tugging into a frown. "Ye of little faith." He rolled his shoulders as if in preparation, then pivoted and marched to the door. "I'm only going to do *one* of those things."

Medusa watched blankly as the Demigod slammed his boot into the door.

As the wood fractured.

Slightly.

Perseus barked a curse, clutching his foot and hopping atop the frozen cobblestones. "How does Poseidon *do* that?"

Medusa smirked and loosed her fists. She strode forward, calmly grasped the doorknob and stared directly at Perseus as she ripped the lock from the door, splinters spraying across the pavement.

Perseus dropped his foot. "Oh, of course *you're* able to do it."

Medusa gently nudged the door open and stepped aside, gesturing for Perseus to enter. "I believe waltzing was mentioned."

Perseus exhaled an indignant huff. "I loathe you."

"Believe me, the feeling is mutual. Now, waltz."

Medusa waited as Perseus stalked inside, hands shoved into pockets, grumbling under his breath. She waited in the cold as damp mist kissed her cheeks, the night air icing her blood. She waited. Shivering. Until she was certain Perseus was alone. The only sound the echo of his boots.

Medusa glanced over her shoulder.

The mist twisted, shifted, as if recoiling from the open door.

She closed her eyes, a sigh escaping as she felt Poseidon's absence lingering in the air beside her.

Where are you?

Medusa smothered her flutter of concern as Perseus called out, "There's no one here."

She opened her eyes and stepped through the door.

To find herself standing in a dark, cavernous hall.

The building had been eviscerated.

Disembowelled.

Gutted.

Its' interior had been entirely removed to exhibit a floor of exquisite marble. Leaves and vines decorated the stone, spreading from the edges of a sunken, circular platform, its' edge surrounded by shallow steps and positioned in the centre of the hall. Enormous, stone columns divided walls of lavish balconies, their edges draped in silk, their carpets stretched beneath alluring divans and tables bursting with exotic fruit. The stone pillars shot towards the ceiling, their tops transforming into curving arches which effortlessly supported the expansive roof, its' surface painted swirling scarlet, almost like the flames of hell.

"... This was her entertainment for the ten years it took you to regain your memories." Perseus stared at the single, looming mirror enveloping the farthest wall, its' reflection of the hall framed in sculpted bronze. Shards of streetlight poured through the building's many windows, muted by the dense mist and pooling on the floor. Perseus' voice echoed, spreading and dancing across the stone, as he spoke. "Whenever she grew bored of tormenting you, or Poseidon, she would come here. Although she enjoyed the first stages, watching you attempt to survive in the desert, prompting Poseidon to provide varying degrees of sport."

Medusa frowned at Perseus' reflection, confused. His gaze of mud and moss became momentarily empathic, brimming with intelligence. She felt a faint trepidation lingering in her blood as she watched him, his posture impossibly calm, like the sea before a storm.

As if he were simply contented to wait.

"I came for the weapons, Perseus. Where is the Aegisium?"

Perseus shrugged in resignation, hands still tucked in his pockets. "Relax, I told you the place was empty didn't I?"

Medusa glanced at the balconies, at their tables bearing untouched fruit. She kept her voice low, no more than a murmur. "You'll forgive me my mistrust."

Perseus strolled towards the mirror, moving to one of the two shadowed passages hidden behind the final columns at each side of the hall.

"If I find myself ambushed, Perseus, I'm going to kill you. And I promise, it will not be pleasant."

Perseus stiffened almost imperceptibly before clearing his throat and clicking his tongue. "Honestly, anyone would think I deserved this devout hatred. I'm just a man trying to find a form of self-preservation that doesn't end in him being skewered on a stake."

"A stake isn't *nearly* creative enough."

"Now you're just being mean."

"I was unaware that I had ever stopped."

Perseus shushed her. "You'll wake the neighbours." He moved through the entrance of the passage, squinting into the dim space, steps resounding through the room. He drew a hand from his pocket and placed it on the wall, feeling his way through the dark.

Medusa trailed him into the shadows, her eyes slowly adjusting to the shift in light. "I thought you said no one was home."

"I was being poetic."

"You were being an ass."

"I loathe you."

"Yes, that has been established." Medusa bit her lip to stop the corners from curving in a smile. "I thought you wanted me to be quiet."

"I did." Perseus removed his hand from the wall, dusting it on his trousers as he continued to walk. "Your poisonous quips are hurting my ears."

The breath of a laugh escaped Medusa's mouth.

Perseus stopped, cocking his head in her direction. "Was that a laugh or a cough?"

Medusa shrugged, her cloak silently grazing the wall as she caught up with Perseus. She could feel his eyes on her, his gaze sending shudders over her scalp.

"The weapons are through there." Perseus gestured to a waiting entrance, its' threshold vacant, bereft of a door. The room beyond flickered a candlelit amber. "It's basically a museum. Most of the weapons are so ancient they're useless. If I'm going to be honest, which I usually am, it's a little ostentatious."

"That's a brave statement, considering our circumstances." Medusa paused, keeping her voice low, keeping her murmur soft as clouds. "If you're heard, you might end up skewered on that stake you mentioned."

Perseus glanced along the passage as he stopped, his form consumed by shadow beside the light of the glowing entrance. He held out an arm, barring Medusa's path. "... I don't expect you to listen to me, Medusa, but were I you, I would run."

Medusa's snakes shifted in warning.

She ignored them and stepped forward, feeling Perseus' arm press against her stomach as she peered into the room.

And her heart dropped to her stomach like a stone through a lake.

CHAPTER SIXTY - SIX

IVETA

THE SLEEK LENGTH OF A KATANA balanced delicately in the woman's grasp, as naturally and as subtly as a branch in a tree. The blade she held as if an extension of her self, amorously admiring her reflected beauty in its' steel. She smiled and saw the curve of her lips, lifted her chin and watched the light dance across the fiery river of her hair, blinked and glimpsed the dip of pale lashes fluttering over the gleaming surface of her sultry, copper eyes. And her skin. Her skin seemed...

Pale.

Iveta frowned, dragging her eyes from her reflection to search her surroundings.

Glass cabinets greeted her with the reflection of a wraith, her faded features interrupted by slashes of colour, by ancient weapons rusted-blue, by knives and daggers, guns and bullets, polished yet incompetent, too small to be used as a mirror.

And she hated using her phone. The screen was hardly adequate.

Iveta released a despondent sigh, glancing once at her reflection in the katana once more before slipping it into the leather sheath in her lap. She rose from her place lounging on a cushioned bench and swept to the back of the room. Towards a lustrous, bronze shield poised between a pair of double-bladed halberds, spearheads protruding from their tips of their wooden hafts, their metal rusted blue with age.

Iveta drifted to a halt before the wall-mounted shield, admiring her skin which gleamed bronze in its' surface.

The lips of her reflection curled in an enamouring smile.

For she had never seen such grace and poise.

And surely neither had Narcissus.

Chapter Sixty - Seven

MEDUSA PUSHED PERSEUS' ARM away, slipping around him and into the room.

Iveta stood before a bronze shield, fingers daintily combing her hair as she angled her chin, admiring the slender arch of her creamy neck. "Do you know how long I've been waiting?"

Medusa paused, gaze flicking to the silk-wrapped hilt of Iveta's sheathed katana as the woman turned, a dark glint sparking in her copper eyes. A dark glint which had called a hundred men to their deaths. As if their lives meant nothing. As if their families meant nothing.

Medusa strangled the memory of the guards, their bodies devoured by stone.

Slaughtered by nothing more than her murderous stare.

Monster.

Medusa swallowed thickly, aware of the faint ache creeping through her flesh, aware of the waking throb whispering in the back of her skull.

She craved to do it again. To watch the blood crystallise in their veins, their skin harden to stone, their bones to granite.

Every addiction requires withdrawal.

She had not been counting the minutes.

A mistake.

A fault in judgement.

Soon it would begin to hurt...

"*Medusa.*"

Steel flashed.

Medusa span, barely avoiding Iveta's katana as it sang past her throat.

"Were you even *listening*?" Iveta snapped, blade reflecting cabinets of weapons, feet sliding in an elegant sweep as she straightened from her attack and sheathed her katana. "*Pay attention to me.*"

Medusa stumbled back. Breath hitching. Heart thumping. "You're insane," she breathed.

"I have been waiting for nearly an *hour*! Do you understand how *long* that is? It feels like an *eternity* for a social creature like me! What on *earth* did Perseus have to say that was so *damned interesting*? He may be attractive but he has the brain capacity of a *newt.*"

Perseus sucked in a wounded gasped. "A newt?" He slapped a hand over his heart as he stepped into the room. "A *newt*? You know what, Iveta? I've just decided that I don't *like* you very much. You, my dear, are what some might call a *heinous bitch.*"

Iveta rolled her eyes, lashes indelicately fluttering. "Perseus, if you don't shut your lovely mouth you may well find my katana emerging from the back of your skull. Now stand over there, look pretty, and stay the hell out of this."

Perseus brushed his gaze across the sheathed katana. Shot Medusa a rueful grimace. "... Self-preservation." He shrugged and ducked out of the room.

"Perseus." Medusa cursed, watching the hem of his coat disappear down the passage. "*Perseus.* Get back here. PERSEUS! If you leave me I swear to the stars I will find a stake and I will *show* you *exactly* what it feels like to be a *kebab!*"

Iveta clicked her tongue against the roof of her mouth, rolling a palm over the pommel of her katana. "Well, doesn't that sound gruesome."

Medusa flashed her teeth, glare glinting her rage. "I'll deal with *you* in a second."

A sunshine laugh tinkled in Iveta's throat, melodic as birdsong, fresh as squeezed citrus.

Then the smile abruptly fell from her face. "No. I don't think so."

Steel sang as Iveta pulled her katana from its' sheath, the blade flashing her reflected beauty.

The woman lunged, her weapon spearing for Medusa's heart.

Medusa recoiled. Twisting and spinning around the blade in a death-defying dance. Cloak billowing. Boots buoyant. Floating like a leaf gently kissed by the wind.

She reached the wall.

And her fingers closed around the elongated, wooden haft of a double-bladed halberd.

Medusa tore the weapon from the wall, its' supporting hooks ripping from the plaster in a white-dusted spray. She swung the axehead, teeth bared and gleaming as Iveta leaped away. Stumbled. She caught herself on a glass cabinet filled with ancient knives, barely escaping the halberd's spearhead as its' tip grazed her collar. As the axe slammed through a separate cabinet.

Split the wall behind.

Stuck.

Glass exploded. A vicious snow of glittering shrapnel icing the floor.

Perseus peeked into the room.

Winced.

Retreated.

Iveta lifted a hand to the base of her throat, her fingers coming away slicked crimson with blood.

Her copper eyes widened.

A scream of feral fury tore from the woman's throat and she lunged at Medusa, her katana slicing the air. "*That's going to leave a scar!*"

Medusa dropped, swinging beneath the haft of the halberd, its' blade still lodged in the wall.

It held her weight as the katana sliced over her head.

Beneath her scarf, her snakes tensed. And Medusa pivoted, wrenching the halberd from the wall, watching as its' hooked edge snapped, the rusted tip remaining embedded in the layer of stone below the plaster.

The metal beneath the broken tip glinted, near glowing in the room's candlelight. Impossibly sharp and appearing to ripple. Molten bronze and silver swirling like mist beneath glass.

Medusa stared at the shimmering metal, the corner of her lip curving in a delighted smile. "Clever." She glanced at Iveta, assessing the woman's graceful crouch. The katana remained poised in the woman's porcelain hands, her ginger hair draped in a fiery cascade over one shoulder. "She hid the Aegisium in a rusted-bronze shell."

Iveta altered her grip on the katana's hilt. "She's always clever. Always one step ahead." Her skirt pooled on the floor as she shifted her weight. "It doesn't matter whether the blade is of Aegisium. It doesn't matter that a God bled himself over a forge to create armour and weapons of Godsblood and bronze." Iveta released a rose-petal laugh. "A weapon is a weapon. An axe is an axe. An inanimate object. The skill is with the fighter."

"I would agree with you." Medusa quirked a brow. "If a regular weapon could pierce a God's skin."

"Aegisium will only pierce a God's skin if you *hit* him." Iveta smirked, gesturing to Medusa's halberd. "And if it's made of *his own* Godsblood. *Poseidon's*, specifically."

Medusa narrowed her eyes. "Why do you think I came here?"

"To steal the weapons that were forged of Poseidon's melted-down armour. After all, we can't kill a God without his Aegisium." Iveta tilted her head, her cruel gaze locked on Medusa's. "You're a monster playing heroine, Medusa. You wish to save a God before he falls." Another laugh, this of spring and flowers, of storms and hail, of whispering, smoking sanity. "He's already fallen."

Medusa glanced towards the passage entrance, revolving the halberd in her palms.

Dread began to rot her stomach.

"For all you know he may be dead. She may have *slaughtered* him."

Acetic fear rose in Medusa's throat. She tightened her grip on the wooden haft.

"Hung him from his Godly neck. Skin sliced. Blood leaking."

Ocean eyes stared sightless at the ceiling.

Blood stained her skin. Her hands. Her face.

"No." Medusa shook her head as a darkness crept into her vision like whispering tendrils of smoke, swallowing the memory whole.

Every addiction requires withdrawal.

"Perseus—"

Perseus' disembodied voice echoed through the passage outside. *"Self-preservation."*

Silver eyes glinted cruelty.

Monster.

The halberd's wooden haft groaned beneath Medusa's fists. The blood drained from her face. "No." Cold ripped through her muscles. "Not yet."

Iveta blew a draping lock of hair out of her eye. "You can't fight a withdrawal, Medusa. You know that better than anyone."

Medusa gritted her teeth, the ache in her skull spiking, fading. "Why are you doing this? Why are you with *her*?" *The Deceiver.*

"I am with *her* because she showed me strength in a time of weakness." Iveta shrugged. "I'm doing *this* for the fun of it." She stepped forward, katana slicing for Medusa's hand, aiming to slash the gripping muscle. To force Medusa to drop her weapon.

Medusa pressed her lips.

She swung the halberd at Iveta's katana, knocking the blade from the woman's grip. She flipped the haft. Jammed the blunt end into Iveta's exposed stomach.

Iveta flew backwards. Crashing through a cabinet. Body shattering glass. Shelves splitting in half. Weapons falling around her like ancient, rusted rain. Tearing and grazing her porcelain skin.

The katana screeched to a stop, blade near buried in a pile of shattered glass strewn beneath the bronze shield, from the cabinet Adalinda had shattered earlier.

Iveta slumped to the floor, raised a hand to the back of her head and found her hair matted with blood. Scrapes and scratches marred her skin. Crimson dribbled down her grated forearms.

Medusa stormed forward, coming to a halt by Iveta's feet. "Which of the weapons are Aegisium?"

Iveta clenched her teeth, refusing to reply as Medusa lowered the gleaming point of the halberd's spearhead, holding it barely an inch from the woman's eye.

"Answer the question."

Iveta flinched. "I don't know."

"Then I suggest you sit quietly while Perseus and I check them. You even *mention* Poseidon again and I will nail you to the wall. Do you understand?"

The muscles in Iveta's throat flexed as she swallowed. She glanced at her katana.

It was too far to reach.

The woman chewed her lip, her eyes flicking to Medusa's halberd.

She dipped her chin in a shallow, grudging nod.

"Good." Medusa pressed the rusted spearhead into the flesh of Iveta's brow. "I'll not kill you if you move." She trailed the point down the woman's cheek in a suggestive kiss, terrible memories flashing behind her golden eyes. "But you'll wish I did."

Again, Iveta nodded, the movement quivering like a windblown leaf.

Medusa lifted the halberd and the woman released a shuddering breath, dropping her face into her palms.

"Perseus." Medusa turned to the door. "Why don't you come in here?"

"... Because I don't have a death wish."

Medusa scanned the room, staring at the rusted weapons. Swords. Knives. Bullets. She would have to snap the tips of each blade, removing the ancient bronze, searching for any Aegisium that might be hidden beneath. She knew not all would be of Godsblood and bronze.

A memory of silver eyes sliced through Medusa's skull.

The Deceiver was too intelligent for that.

"It'll take less time if you assist me."

Boots shuffled on stone in the passage. Perseus cleared his throat. "I don't care."

Medusa closed her eyes and inhaled a calming breath, aware of Iveta now sobbing on the floor. The woman had spread herself over the tiles, surrounded by a spray of smashed glass. Her arms were bent beneath her downturned face, fiery hair spilling over bleeding forearms and weapons that had fallen from the ruined cabinet. Her floor-length skirt was bunched around her knees.

She had always been melodramatic. But she was never stupid. She would stay where she was and she wouldn't fight.

That was all Medusa needed.

Slowly, Medusa released her breath, aiming her voice at Perseus. "What if I asked nicely?"

Perseus slunk to the entrance and peered into the room. He watched as Medusa cracked open an eye. "I'm listening."

"... I won't kill you if you help me sort through the weapons and find out which are Aegisium."

Perseus furrowed his brow, mouth curving in an evaluative frown. "Well... that wasn't a *blatant* threat." He waited a moment, assessing the room, the shattered cabinets, the weapons scattered across the floor.

Finally, he released a suffering sigh.

"*Fine*. But you're doing the heavy lifting and if I strain something, you're carrying me."

ADALINDA VEIL

TEN YEARS AGO

"HOW WOULD YOU LIKE TO RID yourself of those chains?"

She was impaled on his violet gaze. Unable to move. Unable to look away. Anger that was not hers thrummed beneath her skin. Her snakes hissed. Long and low.

The violet-eyed man leaned forward and narrowed his eyes. "Quiet."

The hissing stopped.

The anger cooled.

She felt the man's breath on her cheek as he reached up, the keys in his hand dully winking.

The collar released her neck and clattered to the floor.

Again, the man reached up, unlocking her bloody shackles.

One arm dropped, then the other. The empty chains swung calmly from the ceiling as her knees collapsed beneath her weight. Her ribs drove into the leather brace around her chest and the breath burst from her lungs.

The violet-eyed man tutted as he crouched, keys kissing locks, manacles falling from her ankles. "How are you to walk out that door if you can't even stand on your feet?"

She coughed. Gasped. Wet remnants of bile burning in her throat. "I'll — manage."

The man smiled to himself, remaining in his leonine crouch and peering at her through those unnaturally gleaming eyes, as if he enjoyed her filth and blood soaked visage. "Perhaps some food will help." He flicked the keys. Pushed himself up. "Water as well. Though I'm afraid a shower will have to wait, you'll just have to deal with the smell."

She cleared her throat, viscous phlegm spitting onto her dust-dry tongue. "Where are we?"

"Underground."

"... In a prison?"

The violet-eyed man hummed confirmation, plucking a knife from beneath the draping fabric of his coat. The metal glinted, near glowed, seeming to ripple like molten bronze and silver in the blinding white light.

She flinched. Felt her snakes tense.

"Hold still. Untying all of these straps is a waste of time." The man strode around her until he stood at her back. His boots still silent. A faint smile still curling his lips. "I assume they used the brace so a prize such as yourself would remain in one piece. Styx forbid your weight on those shackles should sever any tendons."

"Styx..." The word was familiar. Her brows creased slightly, a frown shadowing her features.

She glanced at her weeping wrists, the torn, blistered flesh, the dried blood climbing her forearms in morbid streams. The wounds almost appeared to diminish before her eyes.

She kept her concerns to herself.

"This may sting a little."

A curse, bright and flaming, spat through her clenched teeth as the man swiped his knife up the back of the brace, the tip carving a shallow gash in her back.

She collapsed, knees crashing to the floor, one hand slipping in the pool of her vomit as blood began streaming from the wound.

The violet-eyed man eyed her back, his hand catching the brace as it swung from its' suspended chain. The corner of his mouth twitched as he shrugged. "It's shallow. It'll heal."

"Bastard."

"Quite possibly..." He walked around her, frowning at her hand, still planted in the greasy vomit. He tucked the knife back into his belt and tossed her a handkerchief which had been hidden in his sleeve. "Clean yourself up, dear. We have a lot to do before you leave."

She glared at him. "Like what?"

"Firstly, eat and drink. Secondly, give you a false identity. And finally, remove you from the country. The first of which is simple, the last of which is easier said than done."

"Doesn't anyone know you're here?"

The violet-eyed man smiled, flashing his pearly teeth. "The guards have been dealt with. Not that anyone would check on you considering your... unique abilities."

Her frown deepened and her snakes shifted uncomfortably. "What are you talking about?"

"You don't remember?" The man's smile became a grin. The grin of a shark. All whetted points and serrated edges. "Dear, you turn people to stone. Just one look and—" He snapped his fingers. "Blood crystallises in their veins. Skin frightened to porous rock. Bones petrified to granite..."

"Who are you?"

"My dear, the question is not 'who am I' but 'who are you' and if you can't remember that, we're going to have a problem because I did not come here to give a history lesson."

She was silent for a moment, plucking the handkerchief from the floor and wiping at the vomit between her fingers. "M..." She could see fragments in the corners of her mind, trapped but not entirely hidden by the dark, rippling void, like the hole a bullet tears through flesh, leaving an empty space, rapidly filling with blood. "Medusa." The name snapped into place, a single memory floating in absence. A triumphant gasp slipped through her parched lips. "My name is Medusa."

"Good, we're getting somewhere." The violet-eyed man reached into his pocket, retrieving a compact, leather satchel. "I had a passport made for you, along with various questionably-legal documents. Your name is now Adalinda Veil and you're a sculpture artist..." At this he paused, smirked. "Mildly symbolic, don't you think?"

"If the sight of me turns people to stone, why do you seem to be immune?"

Again, the man reached into his pocket, producing a vial of shimmering, golden fluid. "A very special active vaccine. The last of its' kind, in fact. The science is rather complex. I believe it's a mixture of your blood and the venom from your cobra. This is injected into the vessel and integrated into their DNA sequence via the nuclei. Basically, it forms a mutation allowing the cells to be petrification-resistant."

Medusa finished cleaning her fingers and discarded the handkerchief on the floor. She could feel the cold seeping into her flesh, the blood retreating from her toes. "Apparently it's effective."

"Apparently." The man dropped the vial back into his pocket and placed the leather satchel on the tray of food. "Perhaps you should eat before we continue our conversation, you sound like you swallowed a barrowful of nails."

Medusa scowled, pressing her palms into a dry section of floor and shoving herself to her feet. She stumbled slightly, aware of the stale air licking her single, naked breast. Beading her nipples.

The man gestured to a plate of bread, seemingly oblivious of her exposed skin. "I suggest you eat slowly for fear of emptying your stomach again."

Medusa carefully lowered herself back onto the floor, knees softly aching, torn wrists itching. She seized the pitcher of water and brought it to her fractured lips. The cool liquid dribbled over her tongue, rinsing down the acidic burn of bile, calming the partially forgotten throb of her dehydrated throat. She set the water down, ignoring her body's thirst for more, and began to pick at the slices of bread.

The violet-eyed man leaned against a mirrored wall, waiting as Medusa carefully ate.

Her stomach cramped irritably, threatening to regurgitate every mouthful.

She stopped. Shook her head.

The tray of food shrieked as she pushed it across the floor.

"I can't..."

The violet-eyed man shrugged. He pulled the burnt-orange scarf from his neck and walked over, handing it to her. "Put this on." He opened his coat, retrieving a small case. Contact lenses. "And these, they're specially made so you don't paralyse anyone. The scarf won't be enough on its' own, your gaze will still be lethal, if exposed long enough."

Medusa nodded, deftly tying the scarf around her head. She rinsed her hands with water before sliding the lenses into her eyes, then glancing at her uncovered breast. "I don't suppose you have a change of clothes...?"

"No." The man crouched beside the tray of food, lifting the water jug and removing a cloth which had been catching its' condensation. He shook it out, opened its' mouth to form a bag. "We are going to need to cover your face, though."

Medusa shied back as the violet-eyed man shoved the bag over her head.

"I'll take it off as soon as we get there."

"Bastard." She snarled, trying to pull away, stone floor scraping her knees.

The man sighed and lifted the bag until he could look her in the eyes. "Do you want to stay here? Because if you do, keep struggling."

Medusa scrunched her nose at him. "Why did you give me the contact lenses and the scarf if you were just going to cover my face with a bag?"

"Because your face is recognisable and we don't want to be followed. Any more questions?"

Medusa pursed her lips and shook her head.

"Good." The man smiled. "Now, keep your mouth shut and follow as directed." He lowered the bag over her head, hauled her to her feet and dragged her out the door.

MEDUSA WAS ON A BOAT.

She could feel the gentle sway of the deck beneath her bare feet. Hear the lap of water against the hull.

The violet-eyed man had helped her into the back of a van, instructed her to keep the bag over her head, and left her. They had driven for what felt like hours. Hours sitting in the dark van.

Sweating.

She had taken the bag off, despite his warning, occasionally using it to dry her face.

She had pulled it back on when they had stopped.

And now she stood on a boat.

Bag over her head.

Breeze kissing her exposed breast.

She could hear men and women murmuring.

Along with a shrill, lilting voice.

"Why on earth does the poor thing have a bag over her head?"

Medusa flinched.

Her scalp began to prickle.

"And someone find her a dress that doesn't look like it was stolen from a homeless person." The woman paused, foot tapping on the deck. "... Now. Right now."

People began scrambling across the deck as a set of cool fingers hooked beneath the bag, lifting it over Medusa's head.

Medusa squinted, raising a hand against the bright, afternoon sun.

A woman was standing before her, dressed in flowing floral and cream, fiery hair tucked into an enormous, dip-brim hat. "So you're my new sculptor." The woman smiled. "How lovely. I'm Iveta, gallery curator and owner. Lover of arts." She held out an introductory hand, then paused. "I suppose we should get you a bath first, shouldn't we..."

Medusa looked down at her naked breast. She fumbled with the torn strap of her dress, lifting it to cover herself as a woman stalked across the deck, a deep-blue slip bundled in her arms, her hair embellished with beautiful, golden beads.

Iveta turned to the woman. "Take the dress to the bathing-room. Miss Veil requires a shower."

The woman's burning umber eyes pinched irritably. She flicked a strand of beads from her face and grumbled as she stalked back the way she had come.

Iveta smiled, clapping her hands together. "Wonderful! We head off in five." She gestured for Medusa to follow the woman with the dress. "I'll meet you for dinner. We'll be a few days on this yacht, then we'll take a short flight inland and you can see your new home."

Medusa's frown twitched. She reached for the scarf around her head, aware of the snakes shifting impatiently beneath it, then followed the woman with the dress belowdeck.

She spent an hour in the bathroom sitting by the door, staring at the wall and fighting her tears.

Too easy.

It seemed too easy.

But she steeled herself and bathed, then met Iveta for dinner and forced herself to accept that she had been freed. Because to consider that it had been too easy would be to drive herself insane, thinking about why the violet-eyed man had helped her, why he had given her to Iveta, why Iveta had almost no questions about her past and simply accepted Medusa without a second look.

So Medusa forced herself to become Adalinda Veil. She forced herself to sleep and talk and eat, despite the fact that she woke each night screaming and each day the memories of the desert haunted the dark behind her eyes. She became Adalinda Veil. And then she became a sculptor. Hiding her failed works in a vault above her studio, banishing the broken pieces with ruined features and uneven proportions to the airless, metal tomb. With each spoiled sculpture she learned, surprised to find that her instincts would guide her if she took the time to listen, if she took a breath instead of a frustrated scream, if she let the beating of her heart measure the space between her strikes. She learned. In far less time than she should have. She became the woman she was pretending to be. The role she needed to constantly play. And on occasion, for a moment, for a breath, she would forget who she was. She would forget what was hiding beneath her scarf and she would overlook the fact that she was, and forever would be, nothing more than a monster.

Chapter Sixty - Eight

Medusa marched through the shadowed passage, Aegisium halberd gripped in one hand, lips held firm and golden eyes sparking.

They had broken every blade. Scraped a length of rusted bronze from every single weapon. And *none* of them had been Aegisium.

None save the double-bladed halberd, its' rust now partially stripped, the Godsblood and bronze seeming to twist and curl as the exposed metal reflected the dull passageway light.

Medusa had searched the upper levels, finding nothing but mould and dust.

She had searched the second passage, veering off from the main room with its' mirror and its' balconies.

More mould.

More dust.

A gleaming lounge and kitchen hidden among deserted rooms.

Still no weapons.

Still no Aegisium.

So she would improvise. Hoping against hope that Poseidon's heart was still beating. That his memories had not again been stolen, as they had been before...

Medusa gritted her teeth, banishing her memories of Poseidon's deaths. Blood and knives. Torture and pain.

Over.

And over.

In three thousand years she had not been able to save him once.

Not once.

The knowledge ate at her insides like acid on steel. Burning and tearing and feasting.

Not once.

Monster.

And where was he now?

Dead.

Dying.

No.

Medusa's polished nails severed crescents in the halberd's haft.

He wasn't dead. If he were, she would have felt it.

She hefted the weapon with both hands, holding it across her body at a pitching angle as she stalked from the passage like a storm ready to strike. She knew who would be waiting for her, outside in the cobblestone street, with a smile carving her face and a wicked glint in her silver eyes. The Deceiver would be waiting. And she would be death. Swift as sparks, or the flare of a match, or the shock of a wrathful detonation.

Medusa felt a fist tie her stomach in knots.

She needed Poseidon's Aegisium to end this. As long as the Deceiver possessed the weapons, she and Poseidon did not stand a chance. Medusa's only choice was to give the Deceiver what she wanted.

A challenge. And a fight.

With the hope the woman would let slip a clue that would lead Medusa to the hidden Aegisium.

Medusa rolled her shoulders and shifted the weight of the halberd in her arms.

Foolish as it was, she would fight. In order to save Poseidon.

That was all she had wanted. Every second, of every day, for three millennia.

Despite her frequently wandering memories.

Despite his absence.

Despite her pain.

He was her oxygen, her life, her love.

And she *would* save him.

Not matter what.

Medusa stormed towards the building's entrance, her boots silent on the vast, marble floor. She strode past the sunken, circular platform, its' empty steps sending a chill to her bones. Past the pillars and balconies, their silks still draped beside tables of untouched fruit.

Perseus trailed slowly behind her, hands in his pockets, fidgeting with something he had stolen when she wasn't looking, something that clinked faintly each time he moved his fingers. He was quietly murmuring to himself about self-preservation and a face too pretty to be murdered.

Monster.

Medusa's countenance darkened as she swept out the still open door and into the brightening dawn, her caramel cloak kissing the cobblestones, the double-bladed halberd braced in her arms. Sunlight poured through the mist-shrouded street, concealing her surroundings in an eerie sheet of white. But all she could see was murder.

Women with smiles sliced in their throats.

Men devoured by stone and drowned in the street.

Death and torment and betrayal.

Her fault.

And yet, it wasn't.

Not entirely...

Medusa drifted to a halt, listening to the silence of a seemingly abandoned street.

She knew the Deceiver was close. Knew the woman would be waiting for the perfect time to strike. So, Medusa would draw her out. Make a scene. Show her defiance.

She opened her mouth to shout, the anger of three millennia like fire and oil beneath her skin, the Deceiver's true name gaining weight as it gathered on her lips—

"I wouldn't scream, if I were you."

The voice was ice and steel.

And the Deceiver's name withered on Medusa's tongue, disintegrating like petals in vinegar.

An innate sense of fear began to slide around her rage.

Her snakes tensed beneath her scarf.

She tipped the double-bladed halberd, aiming its' spearhead into the blanketing white.

All it took was the woman's voice.

A single sentence and Medusa's confidence dissolved.

Her head began to ache with the pain of withdrawal as the Deceiver emerged from the mist, smooth as death from darkness.

Perseus edged over the threshold of the abandoned building, saw the woman, winced.

An amused smirk lit the Deceiver's features as her shimmering eyes locked on the Demigod. "I assume you appreciated my gift, Perseus. I chose not to give you the keys. I know how much you enjoy a good *distraction.*"

Perseus muttered a curse under his breath, his mud and moss eyes flicking in the direction of his car. "I was hoping that was an act of fate."

The Deceiver released the melodic hum of a laugh as she stopped before the tip of Medusa's halberd. "Technically, it was." Her lips curled in a disastrous smile as she reached out a hand, pushing Medusa's weapon aside with the ease of wings displacing air. As if Medusa's strength were non-existent. As if her teeth were not gritted, her muscles not straining.

The Deceiver took a step forward and rested her fingers on Medusa's cheek, tenderly caressing the cold-flushed skin. "I see you found the Aegisium."

Medusa lifted her chin, nostrils softly flaring. "Not all of it, unfortunately."

"'Unfortunately'..." The Deceiver smiled, the soft curve of her lips incapable of masking her predacious cunning. "That implies my actions in separating the weapons were not deliberate."

Medusa tightened her grip on the halberd, feeling dawn's winter chill begin to seep through her clothes, the damp of the mist only making it worse.

"You know as well as I, Medusa, that nothing I do is *anything* if not deliberate."

Medusa fought the weight of the other woman's stare as her hands began to tremble, as the ache of withdrawal gradually climbed to a throb. "Where is the Aegisium?"

The Deceiver's smile did not falter as she trailed her fingertips down Medusa's neck. "The weapons are hidden where you will not find them. And they are guarded enough that you could not reach them, even if you did."

Medusa clenched her teeth, exhaling a breath as she raised a wall against her countless, teeming memories. Life and death and failure. An unwavering will to survive. "You underestimate me."

"No." The Deceiver hooked her fingers beneath the collar of Medusa's cloak, pulled until Medusa could feel the woman's breath on her skin. "I do not."

A shiver rolled over Medusa's flesh, skin growing cold, heart beginning to stutter.

Her knees began to quake.

Her strength threatened to lapse.

The blood drained from her face as she realised what was happening.

Every addiction requires withdrawal.

... She had run out of time...

The Deceiver tilted her head, watching a sheen of cold sweat collect on Medusa's brow. "How many mortals did you kill, dear one? Near a hundred? Perhaps more?" The sigh of a breeze blew an auburn curl into the woman's face. "And how long does it take for the effects of withdrawal to set in...?"

Medusa shuddered, feeling sick. The snakes beneath her scarf began to shift, the prickle of their movements enveloping her in a cloud of need. The need to remove her scarf. The need to end a life.

A smile spread across the Deceiver's face, wild and utterly haunting. "You were not counting."

A mistake.

A fault in judgement.

The light in Medusa's golden eyes flickered.

A voice in her head screamed at her to *run.*

"It will make the withdrawal worse, to stand out here in the mist. After all, cold-blooded creatures don't fare well in winter... Perhaps we should warm you up."

The Deceiver curled her fingers further around Medusa's collar.

Lifted.

And *threw* her across the street.

For an eye-blink, Medusa was blind and weightless.

She slammed into a wall, the halberd slipping from her fingers, her head snapping against stone. Pain flared in her skull as her snakes were crushed beneath her scarf and black spots spat across her vision.

She collapsed to the pavement.

Coughing.

Gasping.

"I must admit, I wasn't sure Shade would provide enough of a distraction. He was, after all, simply *convenient*... Possibly a little *too* convenient..."

Medusa's eyes darted in the direction of the Deceiver's voice, then landed on the shadow of the fallen halberd resting a few feet from her head. The mist was pulling away from it, as if the sheet of white had chosen to retract just enough for her to see.

A groan escaped Medusa's throat.

She shoved herself to her feet and stumbled towards the halberd. Head throbbing. Breath hitching.

The Deceiver materialised out of the mist at Medusa's back, observing as Medusa crouched, as she hefted the mass of the Aegisium weapon.

"... Though, he proved sufficient in the end."

Medusa span. Eyes wide. Teeth bared.

She swung the halberd with everything she had.

And the Deceiver caught it in a single hand. The wooden haft striking her palm. Its' edge, sharp as the moon's taunting smile, a bare breath from slicing the woman's temple.

The Deceiver lifted an auburn brow, gazing at the bronze and silver ripple of the halberd's beautiful blade. "Shade was an appropriate sacrifice, I think. I would have enjoyed torturing him myself... Alas, I left that privilege to another." She tore the halberd from Medusa's hands and seized the nape of Medusa's scarf. Her fingers squeezed, snakes hissing beneath her grip, as the Deceiver tossed the halberd into the mist.

A smile glittered in her silver eyes as she dragged Medusa across the cobblestones.

Medusa thrashed, hands clawing, boots kicking as she scraped across the uneven ground.

As the deafening roar of an engine split the quiet of the street.

Perseus.

Leaving.

A dark chuckle collected in the Deceiver's throat. "You're being abandoned." She hauled Medusa off the cobblestones, smiling into golden eyes. "You are *alone*."

Fear began to crawl over Medusa's bones, consuming her fragile calm.

She strangled a cry as the Deceiver cast her aside, as she ploughed into the ground.

The breath burst from her lungs.

She heard the crack of bones in her side.

"And where is Poseidon?"

Medusa gasped, a soft moan rolling over her tongue.

Pain flared in her ribs. White-hot and burning.

"*Where is your God?*"

Medusa planted her hands beneath her, forcing herself to stand.

She clenched her teeth.

Smothered her fear.

Searched the mist for movement.

"Your God is gone, Medusa. He *left* you."

Medusa lunged away from the voice, teeth sinking into the flesh of her cheek. She was silent. Even as the blistering pain lanced through her side. She stifled her shuddering breaths as she stumbled, as her ribs nauseously shifted.

"I sent Leda and Lorelei to hunt your friends... What are you fighting for? Why do you still resist?"

The shadow of a fist drove into Medusa's fractured ribs.

She screamed as bones shattered.

"You have nothing to fight for. Are you really that stubborn?" The Deceiver grabbed Medusa's shoulders. Twisted. Drove a knee into Medusa's stomach.

Medusa heaved, vomit painting the cobblestones in a sickening sheen.

The Deceiver stepped around Medusa's hunched form, delightedly watching the string of bile leak from Medusa's mouth, just like it had in that cell, in that prison. The woman lowered herself until her lips brushed Medusa's ear, her voice a chilling whisper, her breath merging with the air. "Honestly, I think you're just a fool."

The Deceiver stepped back.

And was consumed by mist.

Medusa clutched her stomach with trembling hands. A broken moaning dragged itself over her tongue. Tears glittered in her golden eyes.

Her vision blurred.

She could feel her broken ribs, the bones sickeningly loose in her chest, pressing into her lungs as a sob tore through her.

"What did you think was going to happen when Perseus brought you here?"

Medusa flinched as she heard metal scraping across stone. Not from the direction the Deceiver had thrown the halberd, but from another direction entirely.

"Did you think you would find those weapons? Did you truly believe the building would be conveniently *deserted*? ... No..."

Medusa forced herself to straighten, pain bleeding her vision black and choking the effects of her withdrawal.

"You are a *monster*, Medusa... And deep down you know that you are deserving of this. *That* is why you came. *That* is why you're here."

A shape swung from the mist. A spear. Its' wooden shaft driving into Medusa's chest. She felt the crack of her sternum, felt the blow in the marrow of her bones as it launched her back across the street.

"Because how could *anyone* love a creature like you?"

Medusa struck the earth, cloak tearing from her neck as she skidded across the cobblestones, sliding to a halt atop the ice and stone. Blood leaked from beneath her tattered clothing. Her grazed skin wept, staining the pale fabric a blossoming crimson. She stared up at the swirling mist, her vision fading in and out, her heart crumbling beneath the truth of the words. A question she had asked herself repeatedly for as long as she could remember.

"*Because how could anyone love a creature like you?*"

Her snakes slithered, their movements faint, tangled tight beneath her scarf. The winter air crept into their scaled bodies, slowly freezing their blood.

... *Monster.*

Medusa felt her fear dissolve, her pain and anger doused.

She felt cold.

Empty.

Useless without Poseidon.

A tear trickled from the corner of her eye, leaking down her temple and falling onto her scarf.

She watched a glittering flake of snow as it drifted through the mist, landing delicately beside her head.

"This is your fault, you know."

Medusa stared, the snow multiplying above her, scattered, dancing.

She rolled onto her side, numb to the pain of her broken ribs, numb to the cold seeping into her bones. Her fingertips were bloodless beneath the fur-lining of her gloves. Her head felt light and her thoughts were beginning to slow.

She had been mindless to think she could fight the Deceiver.

Especially without the help of her God.

But she would stand.

She would *always* stand.

Monster.

Medusa's arms trembled as she slowly pushed herself up, focusing on the layer of vomit still coating her tongue. She watched the flurrying snow as it wandered and settled on the ground.

The mist began to clear.

Monster.

Medusa raised her head.

The Deceiver stood with her spear in the middle of the street, fur coat sighing, dark hair a silken river. A frown darkened the woman's features as a figure leaped from a rooftop, his muscles gracefully shifting beneath the rippling fabric of a charcoal coat.

He landed silently, like a shadow on the road.

And his voice of dripping honey tore a whimper from Medusa's throat. "She's had enough."

Medusa struggled to keep her arms from collapsing as the pain returned in a brutal flood. Slicing through her lungs. Splintering her heart. She'd thought him gone. Perhaps tortured. "No…"

"She's had enough." Poseidon gestured to Medusa with a dismissive hand. "She's broken. She cannot fight."

The breath caught in Medusa's chest as bile rose in her throat. "Not him. You can't have him…"

The Deceiver glanced at Poseidon, lips pressed in an irate line.

Medusa shoved herself to her feet, broken ribs digging into her lungs, teeth clenched until they groaned. And then she screamed. All of her pain and anger. All of her broken bones and bruised and aching limbs. All of her love for a God she could never fully reach. "YOU CAN'T. HAVE. HIM!"

"My dear, I don't think that's entirely your choice." The Deceiver flicked her hand. Morning sunlight glinted from the blade of her spear, the Aegisium halberd laying, discarded, across the street. The woman lowered her chin in a nod to Poseidon.

And water began to slither in streams from the grates.

Medusa stepped back, disbelieving. She lifted her gaze from the water to stare at Poseidon, her lips parted in confusion. Terror gripped her as she began to retreat, any remaining heat leaching from her blood, leaving her cold, leaving her shivering. "… Poseidon?"

The water spread across the cobblestones in a rippling pool, trickling forward and surrounding her boots.

Medusa's trembling hands began to visibly shake.

She stumbled to a stop.

The water circled her, trapping her on a patch of frozen ground.

Snow melted on its' surface as the liquid crept towards her.

The cold soaked into Medusa's bones. Her thoughts became lethargic as the ice slowed her blood. She shook her head. Focused on the pain. Focused on the screaming stab of her broken ribs, flaring with every inhaled breath. "Poseidon…"

"Medusa."

Her name on his lips was a sword through her heart.

"I'm tired, Medusa. Haven't you had enough?"

Her snakes had stopped moving beneath the confines of her scarf, their bodies were cold, her temples throbbed. She looked at Poseidon, searching the impossible depths of his devastating gaze. She looked at him and the last of her strength vanished, evaporating in the wake of his defeated resignation.

Tears filled her eyes, spilling over her cheeks.

Her fault.

Monster.

The Deceiver strode forward, her spear in hand. "This is exactly what I was trying to avoid. This is why you became a monster. Don't you see? Men make us *weak*. They speak beautiful lies that make you feel warmth, passion. And then they break you. And *still* you refuse to listen. You refuse to stop *loving*. I want you to remember this the next time you think me a villain. I was trying to teach you. I was trying to *shield* you from this *pain*." The Deceiver stepped through Poseidon's pool of water, the liquid parting for her boots. She wiped the tears from Medusa's cheeks, removing them before they could freeze on her skin, and pressed the tip of her spear to the space beneath Medusa's sternum. "Betrayal can destroy even the strongest of us."

The Deceiver drove the spear through Medusa's stomach.

The steel tip severed flesh. The wooden shaft scraped past bone.

And emerged from Medusa's back coated in a layer of warm, dripping crimson.

Medusa choked, curling her fingers around the Deceiver's wrists, her snakes twisted and seizing. Her eyes locked on Poseidon and she found his features bleak. Defeated.

Hollow.

The Deceiver pulled Medusa further onto the spear. The wood slid through Medusa's stomach as the woman pressed Medusa to her chest, squeezing in a sympathetic embrace. "Do you understand now?"

Medusa released a shuddering breath, vaguely aware of the falling snow, her eyelids delicately fluttering. She could feel herself slipping. The pain dragging her down.

Her voice was almost lost as she whispered. "... *Never*..."

Chapter Sixty - Nine

THE PAIN WAS RUSTED KNIVES, on salted nails, on frozen fire and burning ice. Impossible as the star-stained sky. Ever expanding. Never ending. The pain was an entity. A seething mass of darkness and death with a smile that could slit wrists, strangle throats, mangle skin. And a gaping black hole where empathy should have been.

There was no trough to pain's brutality.

Only peaks.

Upon peaks.

Upon peaks.

Upon a whisper.

"Wake up."

An inaudible groan spilled from Medusa's lips.

"*Wake up.*"

Pain ploughed across Medusa's cheek, blossoming behind her eyes, rattling between her teeth. Her face snapped to the side, neck twisting beneath the force of the slap.

Her golden eyes fluttered. Dull. Glazed.

A bloom of crimson spread across her bloodless, stinging cheek.

Medusa lifted her head, squeezing her lids shut as it lolled back, as vertigo gave her a brutal shove.

Again, she groaned, pain coaxing bile into her throat.

She was pale as death. Half-conscious.

And impaled on the brutal spike of a gleaming, bronze hook. Hanging from the ceiling. The toes of her boots barely scraping the floor of a dark, cavernous hall. Its' walls entirely removed to expose decorated marble and a sunken, circular platform, its' edge surrounded by shallow steps and positioned in the centre of the hall.

Where Medusa slumped.

With the hook protruding from the hollow beneath her ribs, the metal scraping her sternum, slicked with blood and flakes of bone.

Medusa stared absently at the ceiling painted scarlet, gazing up a length of chain attached to a clasp in the roof. Her throat caught as she attempted to swallow. She was blinded by pain as soon as she moved. As soon as she leaned forward...

She clutched at the metal, trying to breathe, trying to support her own weight as it threatened to crush her sternum. Her fingers slipped on the blood. Crimson beneath her nails. Crimson staining her fingers. Her palms. Her wrists.

A scream of frustration tore from Medusa's lungs, desperate to stop at least a sliver of the pain.

Tears formed pools in the lids of her eyes. Blurring her vision. Salting her cheeks.

Finally, her fingers caught on the hook and lifted the pressure from her chest. Her relieved sob wrenched her torn muscles. Her spine scraped against the side of the hook.

Another scream.

Another groan.

Hands squeezing.

Arms trembling.

She could see figures through her tears, lounging on the lavish balconies between the stone columns. Eating from tables piled with exotic fruit. Drinking. Smiling.

"H-*help*."

The Deceiver walked slowly around the lowest step of the sunken platform, twirling a small blurred object in her fingers. The woman circled Medusa like an owl circling prey. "My dear, help abandoned you long ago."

"P-Poseidon."

The woman's silver eyes glinted. "Poseidon abandoned you too. I sent him after Perseus."

Medusa's hand slipped.

Caught.

She captured her scream between clenched teeth.

"I have your mortals, too. Poor, sweet creatures. Opened their mouths for gags like starving babes for the teat."

Medusa heard a muffled string of what sounded like flaming curses. Her eyes flicked to a mound of bloodied clothing near the entrance of the building. Light poured from the windows above, dust motes dancing in the sun and drifting towards Clarke and Christensen who lay bound and gagged on the floor. Blindfolds over their eyes, cloth stuffed in their mouths, hands tied behind their backs and ankles tied to their wrists.

And Clarke was thrashing. Cursing through the gag. Platinum and lavender hair tangled and matted and damp with sweat.

Identical women stood above them, one with axes strapped to her thighs, the other with polished, Aegisium guns.

Lorelei drove her boot into Clarke's exposed stomach.

Christensen bellowed as Clarke grunted. As she fell quiet.

The Deceiver continued to circle. Still calm. Smiling now. "And I have you. *Swinging* from the ceiling." She paused as she tilted her head. "No... That's not quite right, is it?" She reached out and shoved

Medusa's fractured ribs.

Medusa's scream drowned out the groan of swinging chains.

The Deceiver blew out a contented sigh. "*Much* better."

Medusa gritted her teeth against the torture, her grip tightening on the swinging hook, her lapsing stare focused on Christensen and Clarke. "Let them go. Th-they did *nothing*."

The Deceiver's smile sharpened. "Didn't they?" She turned towards Leda. Gestured with one hand. "Untie them, then. Remove the blindfolds first."

Leda's lips split in a lupine grin. She dropped to a crouch beside Christensen and reached for his blindfold.

Medusa's scalp began to prickle. The shiver of snakes crept down her neck, stretched over her shoulders. Hoods inflated. Mouths hissing.

A cobra slid beneath her chin.

And Medusa went impossibly still.

Her scarf was gone.

Her lenses were broken.

The realisation woke the hunger within her, its' dark tendrils spreading across her vision.

Starving.

Craving.

"NO!" Medusa screamed as Leda's finger slipped beneath Christensen's blindfold. "NO! No! *Leave them alone!*"

Leda began to drag the cloth up the bridge of Christensen's nose. She met Medusa's eyes, curling her lips in an indolent smile.

"No! *Please!*" Medusa turned to the Deceiver, muscles tearing over the calmly-swinging hook, golden eyes wide and pleading. "P-please. *Don't* h-hurt them. *Please.*"

The smile faded from the Deceiver's face. She flicked a hand towards Leda and nodded her head.

Leda obediently replaced the blindfold.

A sigh shuddered from Medusa as her head drooped forward, pain howling and throbbing and shrieking through her limbs. She could feel disappointment lurking beneath her relief, barely more than a grain of sand in a desert.

Every addiction requires withdrawal.

The symptoms were lost beneath the pain, but the *want* still lingered.

And it would get worse.

So much worse.

Medusa took a shallow breath, forcing herself to speak through the agony skewering her stomach. "Why the h-hook? N-not really your s-style is it?"

The Deceiver paused, then stepped down into the centre of the sunken platform, still twirling that small object in her fingers.

... A remote.

She pressed a button on its' surface and a course, scraping sound crackled over hidden speakers.

"I'm in hell."

Medusa lifted her head, recognising the ghost of her own recorded voice as the hook swung to a languid halt.

"I died in the desert and this *is hell?"*

Delusional laughter poured through the hall.

"What? No fire? No tempests? No demons?!"

Medusa's words spat from the speakers in a tangle of languages. Harsh and dry. Louder now. Encouraged by splintered sanity.

"Where is the river of boiling blood and fire? The lake of frozen ice with its' drowning spirits? I find myself disappointed by your lack of creativity!"

The frenzied racket of shaking chains hissed over the speakers.

"Why don't you try something new? Drown someone in their own blood. Or try a meat hook speared through the stomach. Now wouldn't that be brutal? Join the adults, you bastard! Why don't you try some damned barbed wire?!"

The Deceiver lifted the remote. Stopped the recording. "*Someone* has been doing some reading. Nine circles of hell, weren't there? *Inspired.* I thought for once I would take your advice. Drowning in your own blood. A meat-hook. Barbed wire. The three of them together would have been a *little* overkill, if I'm being honest. So I settled for one. Which, I'm inclined to say, has proven *delightfully* effective."

Medusa coughed, grimaced as metal wrenched flesh and black stars spread across her vision. "You should l-listen to me m-more often."

"Perhaps I should." The Deceiver tucked a warm finger beneath Medusa's ashen chin, leaning forward to inspect the darkening bruise on the cheek she had slapped. "I rather enjoyed our time in that cell. Watching you vomit every time a snake touched your skin. You were so dehydrated after being in that desert, I thought you might die on me again." Her eyes of swimming silver flashed like burning stars, then shifted to an unnatural shade of violet. "Alas, you did not."

Medusa snarled. "The v-violet-eyed man." Her arms began to violently shudder, her own blood slowly growing viscid beneath her grip. "Th-that was *you.*"

The Deceiver blinked and her eyes were silver. "Ah, the pieces are finally falling together."

Medusa adjusted her grip, her crimson fingers sickeningly sticky, pain flaring as the metal hook slid through her stomach, scraping bones and tearing muscle. "... Y-you killed those women."

The Deceiver frowned, the corners of her perfect lips crinkling. "They were unfortunate casualties."

"W-why?"

"Why does the sun shine? Why does the moon disappear during the day?"

"Why did you k-kill them?"

"... They became liabilities, as your darling mortals have become. Leena got too close to Perseus so I killed her and placed some convincing evidence in her apartment, suggesting she had been besotted with your work." The Deceiver smiled, dropping the remote into a pocket of her luxurious fur coat. "It's in the details, really. You have to make it believable. Anna, on the other hand, made something she didn't understand and began asking too many questions." The Deceiver retrieved a vial of shimmering, golden liquid from another pocket. "I asked her to recreate this for me. The active vaccine seems to become less effective after a few years, so my warriors require a steady dose to keep them immune." The Deceiver placed the vial back in her pocket. "Anna was successful... Unfortunately, she was also *curious*."

"Why not t-take their m-memories?"

"A waste of good resources. You know I can't just snap my fingers and wipe their minds."

"What did you do to Poseidon?"

"Absolutely nothing." The Deceiver smiled pleasantly. "He came to me of his own accord."

Medusa's gaze grew vacant as pain clawed through her stomach. She could feel the cold metal, like a disease waiting to kill, draining her life as her body struggled to heal.

A mortal would have died from her wounds almost immediately.

Instead, she was tortured by them.

She did not know which was worse.

Vaguely, she heard the building's door open, felt a breath of iced air on her bruising cheek. Flakes of snow wafted into the room in a swirling burst of chilling white.

Medusa forced herself to look up.

Just as Poseidon strode inside, the double-bladed halberd gripped in one hand, dragging Perseus with the other tangled in the back of his coat.

Poseidon tossed Perseus forward.

Kicked the door shut.

His voice was enough to stop Medusa's heart.

"The golden boy. As requested."

The Deceiver frowned, turning to Poseidon's snow-dusted form. "You took longer than I had anticipated."

Poseidon stared at the Deceiver, his ocean eyes cold, flat. "I was on foot. He was driving a car."

The Deceiver flicked her gaze to Perseus who stood beside Poseidon, fuming.

"I don't know what it is with you people but for the love of all things decent *stop threatening to kill me!* A man can only handle so much! Just because I'm a Demigod does *not* mean you can *use* me whenever you *like!*"

Clarke, who had begun to squirm again, suddenly went very still.

The Deceiver quirked a brow. "... Are you finished?"

Perseus ground his teeth, nostrils flaring. "Not even close."

"Then you can join the mortals on the floor." The Deceiver gestured to Poseidon, turning back to Medusa as Poseidon grabbed Perseus by the arm and shoved him towards Christensen and Clarke.

Poseidon released a low growl. "Sit."

Perseus opened his mouth, then glanced at the Aegisium halberd still clenched in Poseidon's palm. He shut his mouth. Sat. Crossed his arms over his chest and muttered profanely under his breath.

The Deceiver tapped a finger on her lip, ignoring Perseus as her silver stare crushed Medusa's snakes. A crease wove between the woman's brow and she reached towards the cobras. "The cobra is a fairly miraculous creature, don't you think?" The Deceiver gently trailed her knuckles along a set of gleaming scales, her touch soft as winter down, subtle as the brush of lashes caressing skin.

Medusa shuddered as her grip shifted on the hook, the metal tugging through her stomach.

The Deceiver leaned forward, seized a lethargic cobra. Medusa's snakes slowly recoiled, the trapped cobra struggling weakly in the

Deceiver's grip. It hissed and writhed as the woman squeezed its' neck.

The creature's panic shot through Medusa like a raging arrow. Her nostrils began to flare. Her heart pulsed in her ears.

"Cobra venom is a vicious neurotoxin. It destroys nerves and tissue, causing paralysis, even death." The Deceiver turned the cobra in her hand. It opened its' mouth and spat a furious hiss. "If this venom enters your blood stream, your body will fight and you will be caught between paralysis and death. Conscious yet unable to move. Awake and in ceaseless pain." The woman glanced at the tattoo on the inside of Medusa's wrist. "I'm sure you remember by now."

Medusa narrowed her eyes, dragging her thoughts from the depths of her pain to glare at the Deceiver. She remembered being strapped to a chair, unable to move as the woman tapped the tattoo into her wrist.

"The venom did not dry with the tattoo's ink when it was first administered. Your body absorbed it all." The Deceiver frowned and dropped the cobra. "That was mildly disappointing, I must say."

The snake fell to Medusa's shoulder, its' body curling around her neck.

"I'll draw it out this time, make sure it lasts longer." The Deceiver beckoned to a woman partially hidden in the shadows beneath a balcony, her fiery river of hair a knotted tangle, partially stained with blood.

Iveta smiled sweetly as she swept from the dark, her scraped hands gripping a velvet-lined box, her chin dipping reverently as she proffered its' contents to the Deceiver. The bronze knife rested inside, its' blade smoothly arced, its' carved ivory handle nestled in a cradle of smoothest velvet. A crystal glass of poisoned-sunshine glistened at its' side.

Cobra venom.

The Deceiver removed the knife from the box, twisted its' curving blade in her hand and dipped the point into the crystal glass.

"Now…" The Deceiver curled her lips in a wicked-sharp smile as she lifted the blade from the pool of venom and aimed it at Medusa. "Shall we begin?"

CHAPTER SEVENTY

POSEIDON FELT HIS MUSCLES TIGHTEN. His eyes were caught on Medusa. Skewered on a hook. Hanging from the ceiling. Blood dribbled from her stomach, leaking through her clothes and staining her hands. A pool of crimson was beginning to spread beneath her feet.

Medusa looked at him and he saw her pain, saw her strength. The defiant tilt of her chin. The determination blazing like a star beneath her stare, burning in darkness that would have smothered all other light.

His heart stopped.

The sting of barbed-wire filled his chest.

He had known she would be hurt.

He had known she would be tortured.

He had thought he could survive it.

Venom dripped from the arched knife in the Deceiver's hand, its' glinting point lowering to Medusa's breast.

And Medusa's strength faltered, like a candle in a breeze. Almost imperceptibly. Her bloody grip tightened on the hook. Her arms shook. Her skin bleached to a colourless white. She pursed her lips to hide their tremble.

He had thought he could survive her torture.

He had been wrong.

Poseidon lunged across the hall with a feral, night-dark roar. His fingers sank into the Deceiver's hair, yanking her thick, auburn tresses and dragging her across the marble floor. Away from Medusa.

The Deceiver twisted in Poseidon's grip. She tossed the knife aside as she broke his hold and lowered herself into a fighting crouch. The blade sang sharply as it struck the marble floor, skittering to a stop in the shadowed alcove beneath a balcony. "I was wondering how long it would take you to break."

Poseidon growled. Stalked forward. Tossing the double-bladed halberd to the side. He knew in this moment he was not going to need it. "This is not what we agreed."

The Deceiver chuckled, low and arctic. "Yes, it is."

She lunged.

And they collided.

Smashing and striking like a howling, hailing storm.

Thunder in the heavens.

Earth shaking beneath.

She moved like a warrior and he like a beast. All muscle and anger and growling, savage fury. Neither one leaving a mark on the other. Though their fists were as fast and as heavy as lead.

Poseidon grabbed the Deceiver by the neck and threw her with a thundering, inhuman bellow, picturing how she had thrown Medusa through the street. The Deceiver crashed through the building's foremost wall, shattering stone and tumbling rubble. She slid over the cobblestones, her neck bowed forward, her tangled hair streaming. And struck the door of the building across the street.

Poseidon stood before the wall's gaping hole. Shoulders heaving.

Breath snarling. Lips peeled back from clamped and groaning teeth.

Perseus leaned to stare out the hole in the wall as Clarke and Christensen shouted around their gags.

Poseidon stepped forward, moving to continue his fight, but Medusa released a frustrated growl and he turned back. Fire licked through his veins as he crossed the room, seizing the double-bladed halberd and glaring at the women on the balconies, daring them to challenge him, daring them to fight.

No one moved.

And no one spoke.

They simply watched as Poseidon strode to Medusa, as he swung the Aegisium axehead, cleaving the barbed tip from the hook with effortless grace.

Medusa gritted her teeth as Poseidon set the halberd against the steps and lifted her from the hook. Slowly. Gently. She strangled a scream as the metal scraped through her stomach, as it slid free. Poseidon cradled Medusa in his arms, watching her as the blood-soaked hook swung empty on creaking chains.

They stood for a moment, the monster and the God, lingering in the centre of the hall. Medusa panted softly as she clutched her wounded stomach. Her legs dangled over his arms. A bead of sweat trickling down her bruised and swollen cheek. Her clothes were torn, her wounds from the street barely beginning to heal. Snakes huddled around her bowed head, gently nudging her cheek, carefully flicking their tongues over her bruises and her scrapes. She lifted her golden eyes to meet his and lowered her chin in an appreciative nod. Her smile was weak, insubstantial. "For a moment there I thought you were actually going to let her do it."

Poseidon stared at her for the space of a breath, watching the light return to her striking gaze, watching her translucent smile become opaque, then a solid quiver. "... I was..." He set Medusa on her feet, aware of her fractured ribs and open wounds, observing the hand she kept clutched to her stomach. "I made a deal with her. I told her that I would stand aside if she let you live, if she let you keep your memories, but I walked in that door and saw you *hanging* there—" Poseidon glanced over his shoulder at the hook, bloodied and broken, at the pool of Medusa's blood spreading across the floor. "I couldn't leave you like that. Even if she was going to release you when she was finished, you would have been too damaged to properly escape."

Medusa lifted her hand from her stomach, examining the torn flesh painted crimson, before replacing it and increasing the pressure. "Ever the gentleman." She winced as she took a step forward and Poseidon nearly gathered her back into his arms. She stopped him with a shake of her head, remaining stubborn in her strength, though he knew she was grateful for his arm as he wrapped it around her bleeding back and helped her climb the steps, using his boot to flick the discarded halberd into his hand as he went. "Next time you decide to make a deal involving my torture, perhaps discuss it with me beforehand."

Poseidon chuckled, pressing a kiss to the snakes atop Medusa's head. "I'll keep that in mind."

They walked towards Christensen and Clarke, still bound and gagged on the floor. Poseidon glared at the twins as Leda and Lorelei grudgingly retreated, their hazel eyes narrowed, their fingers brushing their weapons. He did not look away from them as he spoke to Perseus. "Take Clarke and Christensen to the car. Remove the gags. Keep the blindfolds."

Perseus stood from his position cross-legged on the floor, eyes darting to the ruined wall.

He crouched beside Clarke and removed her gag.

Clarke spat onto the marble, wriggling as Perseus moved to untie her wrists. "*Mother of Death*, that gag tasted like *dirt* and *worms*. Can someone please explain to me *what is going on*? Did that bitch *seriously* just call us *mortals*?"

"You *are* mortals." Perseus grunted as Clarke's wrist slipped from the rope and she elbowed him in the abdomen.

Clarke growled under her breath, wiped the spit from her mouth with her sleeve. "I don't know who you are, Mister, but you can go right outside and suck some cobblestones because I don't like your *tone.*"

Perseus paused, looked at Medusa whose features were pale and tense. "I've seen this one before... In the gallery." He leaned down, inspecting Clarke's blindfolded face. "What was her name?"

"Clarke." The medical examiner spat.

"Clarke. Cute." Perseus nodded to Christensen who was struggling to spit out his gag. "Not as cute as him... But still cute."

Clarke stilled, a blush creeping up her neck as the ropes fell from her ankles and she pushed herself up. "I see what you're doing, trying to distract me with your compliments, but *I* am not cute, I am a *fearsome warrior queen!* And there's no way in *hell* I'm going to forget my situation because some boy with a pretty voice and soft skin starts sweet-talking me. I just got kidnapped and beaten. I want to know what is going on. I want to know who this strange man is. And I want a cup of blessed tea... Wait..." Clarke stopped moving. "... I know that voice." She reached for the fabric over her eyes. "Is that *Theodore?* God damn it, I can't see a bleeding thing through this blindfold."

"*Don't—*" Medusa's cry turned to a scream as she reached out, stiffening in Poseidon's grip and gasping through the pain of her tearing wound.

Clarke leaped into the air. Swearing. "*What?* What is it?"

Perseus threw Christensen's gag aside, stepping over the detective to untie his wrists. "Have you not read the stories of the *dreaded* Medusa?"

Medusa shot Perseus a flat glare as Christensen dragged his hands from the ropes, flexing his fingers to stimulate the blood-flow.

"Clarke, she turns people to stone by *looking* at them. What do you *think* is going to happen if you take that blindfold off? Did you not see *the hundred dead guards*? You know, the one's she *just killed*?"

Poseidon felt Medusa flinch against his side.

Clarke dropped her hand from her blindfold. "... But it didn't affect Donovan... And Theodore, who is dishing out the compliments, doesn't seem like *he's* made of granite."

"Complicated." Perseus muttered as he dragged the rope from Christensen's ankles. He threw it aside and vaulted to his feet, eyes again darting to the building's ruined wall. "Don't have time. Need to run." He hauled Christensen up, grabbing the man by the shoulder, his other arm snaking around Clarke's waist. "Now. Right now. My life is at stake. Don't want to die."

Clarke frowned, staggering as Perseus pulled her through the hole in the wall, over the stone and rubble aftermath of a God's wrath and a thrown Deceiver. "What are you *talking* about? Can someone just *explain* to me what is going on? *How is Adalinda now Medusa?* I thought Medusa was a *myth!* And people don't just *come back from the dead!* They *stay* there! Wherever 'there' is..." Clarke stumbled, trying to find Poseidon. "Where is 'there' by the way? Did you see anything when you were dead, Donovan?"

"No." Poseidon gave no more explanation as he followed Perseus, his arm carefully bracing Medusa, his fingers still gripping the Aegisium halberd. Medusa moaned as they moved into the cold street, snow delicately dancing from a solid grey sky. Her snakes burrowed into the warmth of her neck.

Poseidon glanced at the door he had flung the Deceiver into.

It was hanging open.

"Perseus."

Perseus stopped, turned to Poseidon.

"Take Medusa."

"What?" Perseus blanched, the colour draining from his face. "No.

No way."

Poseidon's mouth curved towards his chin. He scrunched his brow as he guided Medusa towards Perseus.

Perseus shook his head. "No. That was *not* the plan."

The impossible ocean gleam of Poseidon's eyes darkened with his impatience. "It is now."

Medusa arched her neck, peering up at Poseidon. "What plan?"

Perseus stepped back. "We agreed to run."

"No. *You* agreed to run." Poseidon growled.

"Not with her! She'll kill me!"

Medusa ground her teeth, pressing her fingers harder against her wound. "*What* plan?"

Poseidon turned to Medusa, bowing his head over her own and gently pulling her close. He could feel the pulse thumping in her chest, see the concern creasing her brow, the moisture of cooling sweat glistening on her skin.

He pressed his lips to hers, the kiss as sweet as fresh plucked fruit, as bitter as zested lemon and salted tears. He ached, not being able to touch her, to savour her as she deserved to be savoured. To worship her like a sated craving. With dancing lips and tasting tongues and hands and skin and heat and sweat. He ached as he pressed his lips to hers, their mouths melting together as if they were congruous, a harmony of skin and spirit, each seeking refuge in the comfort of the other. The kiss was soft as feathers and filled with longing. The longing of three thousand years, wanting to be together and never quite having the chance. Torn from each other at the very last moment, the cruel and brutal end to a beautiful, heart-breaking tale.

The kiss was broken practically the moment it was given.

A promise.

And an apology.

Poseidon's words were a whisper, breathed onto Medusa's lips. "I'm going to finish this and give you a chance to escape." He pulled away from her before he could change his mind, saw her eyes widen, saw her mouth open to form a protest. He saw an echo of Medusa in that night darkened street, the deaths of a hundred men still fresh on the pavement, their stone forms left, abandoned, around a shattered and leaking fountain.

"Will you help me or not?"

Poseidon's pulse fluttered in his neck as he stared down at Medusa, rigid fists near splitting his knuckles, boots stubbornly planted on the frozen pavement.

His eyes smouldered like dark coals, brimming with adamant determination.

"No."

Poseidon had watched her walk away, her back ramrod straight, her chin raised in defiance, anger streaming from her like heat from scalding sand.

He had watched her walk away.

He had pulled his phone from his pocket.

And as he strode into the cold, dark night, he had called Perseus.

"... I need a favour."

Poseidon shook the memory free of his mind, focusing on the open door of the building across the street.

Still no sound.

Still no movement.

"No. Poseidon. No. *Goddamnit.* We agreed that I would bring Medusa here while you tried to convince 'Wise' that you were on her side." Perseus took a step forward, stomping his boot on the cobblestones. "That's all. That's *it. You* were to take it from there. This is *not my fight.*"

Poseidon paused, fingers drumming the haft of the halberd as he turned to scan the building for movement. "Then you should have fled a long time ago."

Perseus shook his head, fingers curling into fists as his mud and moss eyes flared. "No."

Medusa was staring at the ground, her snakes reaching down her neck, their heads lost in the collar of her shirt, seeking warmth. She was quiet. Listening. Processing. Cornered like prey and attempting to think of an escape. "I won't let you die again…" It was a murmur, nothing more, appearing as if to no one but herself. She knew better than to argue against Poseidon's decisions, to argue with a God was to intrinsically lose, though she knew he could hear her, as well as if she spoke into his ear, and it was not in her nature to stand aside, to let him save her. It never had been and it never would be.

Poseidon straightened his shoulders, gripping both hands on the Aegisium halberd as Medusa turned to Perseus, still pressing her hands against the gaping wound in her stomach, blood still rushing from the wound in her back.

"Get Clarke and Christensen in the car. Take them somewhere safe."

"No." Clarke crossed her arms, black blindfold like a dark shadow across her squinting eyes. "Christensen and I aren't *being taken* anywhere. I know I'm a *little* insane but I want to get off the crazy-train. Right fucking now."

Poseidon felt Medusa's eyes flick over his back, like the kiss of a moth among falling snow.

She planted her feet. "I'm staying."

Poseidon's heart gave a butterfly flutter, the air's moisture collecting around him as if it were a glistening shield, disrupting the billowing flakes of snow. His skin heated. His fingers began to tingle, the sensation creeping up his arms, through his chest, up his neck.

He did not need to tell the water what to do.

Medusa sucked in a gasp. Poseidon could almost feel her outrage as she glared at the water which had begun to climb her boot, its' rushing current tethering her to the ground so she was unable to move. Unable to fight.

Medusa hissed a violent curse in a language long forgotten, lashing

Poseidon with a murderous glare as he walked further into the cobblestone street.

Buildings rose above him like cliffs from a ravine, dead and withering vines obstinately clinging to sand-stone façades, iron railings curling before dusty, fractured windows. Snow settled on the surfaces to create a soft, white shroud.

His boots did not crunch, though they left prints in the gathering snow.

His breath clouded at his lips.

The Aegisium halberd gleamed in the morning light. Bronze and silver Godsblood shimmering like shifting mist.

Bronze and *his* Godsblood.

Poseidon lifted a hand to the curving point of the halberds' blade. He pressed a finger into the tip, felt the sharp sting of splitting flesh, watched a bead of silver and crimson dribble from the wound, as if starlight had fallen from the heavens, fusing with molten fire.

Divinity tangled with humanity.

The darkness had hidden it when he had been shot in the basement.

The wound in his finger healed in an instant and he rubbed the remnants of Godsblood away with the pad of his thumb.

"Don't do this." Medusa fought to pull her boot from the water, palm still shoved against her blood-soaked stomach. He could hear the pain in her voice. "We can *run*. I'm not leaving you to stay and fight alone."

Poseidon paused, closing his eyes. He felt her words bury themselves deep inside his chest.

She was right.

They *could* run.

But that would not change their fate. They would simply be running in circles. Always with the same end result.

Her.

The Deceiver. With her glinting silver eyes and her wickedly cunning smile.

Always hunting.

Always taunting.

Always one step ahead.

The door the Deceiver had disappeared through began to creak open on broken hinges. Loud and leisurely. Leaving a cavity of fear like the waiting silence of an empty forest.

After a twig has been snapped.

Poseidon adjusted his grip on the halberd, snow dusting his dark waves, brushing past his lashes, collecting on the broad shoulders of his draping, charcoal coat.

The door groaned and the Deceiver prowled through, a profane smile carving her face. The spark in her silver eyes sang of thorns and thistles and blood, so much blood. And in her lax, swaying hands the woman who was not Wise, the woman who was a lie, a cunning manipulation, a brutal, murderous *deceiver*, carelessly wielded the terrible, beautiful might of Poseidon's Aegisium trident.

Long since stolen.

Assumed forever lost.

Poseidon felt his disbelief melt into betrayal, a more profound betrayal than it *ever* had the right to be. The trident whispered to him, called to him, just like the rain when he had forgotten himself, when he had opened the tower window and felt the downpour soaking his face, felt it stinging, clinging, calling. Making him feel empty.

Hollow.

And that was all it took for the absence to return. The vacant pit buried in his soul. The void between the beats of his rapidly pulsing heart.

His Aegisium trident and with it, the one thing that had not yet returned, the one severed slice of his power that had been lost to him for almost three millennia.

For even Gods had their limits.

Poseidon stared at his trident. Felt the hollow transcend to a ruinous, deprived *hunger*.

Even Gods had their limits...

An idea his trident was about to eradicate.

As soon as he held it in his hand.

CHAPTER SEVENTY - ONE

MEDUSA STARED AT THE AEGISIUM trident, forged of Poseidon's Godsblood and bronze. She had believed it destroyed, melted with Poseidon's armour to create an arsenal of Aegisium death.

A terrible, knowing dread rose like a beast from the depths of Medusa's soul. She began attacking the water which trapped her leg, clawing at the liquid, tearing at her boots. The gaping wound in her stomach *screamed*. Blood consumed the fingers she kept clutched to the ruptured flesh, droplets of crimson streaming down her wrists. Her vision blurred. Pain, there was *so much pain*. She could feel her strength waning, sucked from her limbs with the blood pouring from her wounds.

She glanced over her shoulder at Christensen and Clarke.

Felt a ravenous, starving hunger.

A simple fix.

If only she could remove their blindfolds...

Monster.

Medusa recoiled, disgust shoving the thought aside. The ache of withdrawal had worsened beneath the hurt, becoming a constant, leaden thrum, a ringing in her ears, a tremor in her hands. Her breaths were shallow and deafening. The morning light was *blinding*. Cold sweat slicked her brow.

In her mind she watched Clarke and Christensen turn to stone.

Monster.

Medusa shook her head.

The street snapped back into place.

She focused on Poseidon and the water caging her boot. Every movement was agony. Broken bones and tearing wounds. She held in her screams. Clenched her teeth and forced them down. Her ribs shifted like fingers, digging into her lungs. Her breaths were becoming wet. Desperate.

The Deceiver lifted the trident and pointed the bladed-prongs at Poseidon. The prongs rose in smooth, lethal arcs, carved with beautiful, ancient text, the haft embellished with shards of pearl and shell and bone. "Give me a challenge and I may return your trident." She smiled. "It's calling to you. Can't you hear it?"

Poseidon rolled his shoulders, flicking the halberd in his grasp.

The Deceiver hummed a laugh. "I thought you could."

Medusa pressed her lips, lifting her leg and trying to slide her foot from her boot. The water climbed over her knee, consumed her thigh. Medusa released a frustrated, wordless shout. She glared at her love. "*Poseidon.*"

Poseidon's head twitched towards her voice.

"Poseidon, please. Let me go, I can *help* you."

The Deceiver twisted Poseidon's trident, a smile lighting her face. "Don't do this alone."

Poseidon angled the halberd, holding it diagonally across his body. He did not move. He knew better than to strike first.

Medusa pressed her open hand further into her wounded stomach, blood coating her fingers in a sticky crimson glove. "Poseidon..."

Poseidon ground his teeth, adjusted his grip on the halberd. "No, Medusa."

Medusa's vision blurred.

She blinked tears of pain from her eyes.

She could do nothing as the Deceiver launched herself at Poseidon.

CHAPTER SEVENTY - TWO

THE DECEIVER RELEASED A warrior's scream. She ran at Poseidon, her boots silent as a grave, the fur hem of her coat churning up the falling snow. She thrust the trident towards Poseidon and he twisted around her attack, mist cloaking his body, clouds darkening in the sky.

The earth began to tremble.

Poseidon followed the momentum of his twist, swinging the halberd towards the Deceiver's spine. She smiled. Span. Blocked the attack with the trident, shoved the halberd away and thrust forward.

Poseidon launched himself backwards.

The trident's edge scraped his side, drawing blood.

Perseus cursed under his breath as he hauled Clarke and Christensen into the car, slammed the door and edged back towards Medusa.

The Deceiver threw the trident to her opposite hand, admiring the gleam of Godsblood on its' edge. "How disappointing. You've grown *weak*, Poseidon."

Poseidon bared his teeth. He launched into an attack, closing the distance, feinting left, swinging the edge of the halberd towards the Deceiver's stomach.

The Deceiver leaped back, the halberd's blade carving through her coat and barely missing her skin. She hit the cobblestones in a crouch with one hand on the ground, her boots gliding backwards over the snow and the ice. She slid to a stop and straightened. Span Poseidon's trident in an elegant, sweeping arc. "... You ruined my coat."

Poseidon gritted his teeth. Thunder rumbled through the bruising clouds as he stormed forward, snow falling in swirling gusts, the ground shuddering beneath his feet. Beats of heated power resounded through his bones, surging with his blood, aching beneath his skin. It wanted to escape. *Needed* to escape. He breathed out, releasing a whisper of power.

The cobblestones beneath his feet began to crack.

The Deceiver smirked, tucking the trident's haft beneath her arm, bladed-prongs aimed at the ground.

Poseidon attacked.

And the Deceiver began to dance.

Ducking. Weaving. Spinning. Avoiding each and every assault. She didn't lift the trident. Didn't fight him back. She just smiled. Dropped. Rolled. Shoved herself up and kept herself moving.

Poseidon roared a frustrated bellow. Power blazed through his veins, the deafening beat of it smothering his thoughts. He charged, slamming his shoulder into the Deceiver's stomach and tackling her to the ground.

She hit with a sickening crack.

The cobblestones fractured.

Crumbled.

Collapsed.

The Deceiver fell and Poseidon followed, devoured by a shower of dirt and shattered stone. They dropped through the air, weapons gripped in weightless fists, teeth bared, growls echoing.

And slammed into the streaming water at the base of a drainage tunnel.

Medusa's shout reverberated off the walls.

Poseidon shoved the Deceiver's head beneath the numbing water.

Felt his breath catch in his throat.

The fear crept up on him...

Poseidon's grip faltered.

The Deceiver tucked her knees and *shoved*, throwing Poseidon off. She rolled to the side and rose, wiping the water from her face, scraping her soaked hair back. Still holding his trident. Still smiling.

She fell into a crouch. "That all you've got?"

Poseidon ground his teeth, stretched his neck. He banished the fear of drowning in that frozen lake and stood, water streaming around his boots, the sound near deafening as it rushed through the tunnel.

The water was his.

It was *his*.

As was the thunder and the quaking of the earth.

Poseidon pointed the halberd at the Deceiver and smiled right back.

He was no *prey* to be *hunted*.

He was a *God*.

And this woman had been playing with him for *far* too long.

The water beneath the Deceiver began to rise, climbing her shins, soaking her legs.

Holding her down.

The tunnel above her began to crumble, broken brick and cobblestones falling with dirt and snow.

And the Deceiver began to laugh.

Laugh.

She looked up at the crumbling ceiling, eyes glittering, teeth gleaming. A section of the street collapsed, crashing to the ground and spraying her with snow-coated rubble. The Deceiver lowered her chin and leaned aside as a plummeting slab of cobblestones exploded to her left. "A trap." She grinned, her teeth a white streak among the shadows and falling debris, looking at Poseidon with pure, undiluted delight. "How *strategic* of you."

Poseidon kept the smile on his face, dark and sinister. "I thought it might provide a challenge."

"Certainly, it does." The Deceiver tilted her head as another slab of stone broke away from the street, right above her head. "But I fear you've yet to remember who I am." She ripped her legs from the water, dashing forward as the mass of stone struck the ground at her back, a wall of water spraying after her. She slammed the trident into the floor and *flung* herself into the air, spinning and landing beside Poseidon.

Poseidon pivoted, swinging the halberd.

The Deceiver caught the blow between the trident's bladed-prongs and *twisted*, snapping the halberd's wooden haft.

Poseidon grunted and stepped back, losing his grip on the broken weapon.

It fell to the water at his feet.

The Deceiver clucked her tongue. "Should've seen that coming."

She drove the trident towards Poseidon's chest. He caught it, the bladed-prongs slicing into his palms.

And his power *detonated* inside him.

He felt the water in the air, beneath the earth and in the clouds. He felt the snow and the rain and the mist, the oceans and rivers, streams and frosts. He felt it all. Everywhere. Vast and infinitely fathomless.

Poseidon's ocean eyes began to glow.

And, for a moment, he hesitated.

The Deceiver tore Poseidon's trident from his grip. She glanced up at the ruined ceiling of the tunnel, then jumped. Through it. Disappearing over the crumbling edge and leaving Poseidon feeling hollow.

Lost.

His power stolen.

Again.

Poseidon leaned forward, bracing his bleeding hands on his thighs. Water gushed around his boots, vaguely slowing as it passed. Whispering. Calling.

His heart fluttered.

He felt the cavity between its' beats.

Absent.

Hollow.

Hollow.

Hollow.

Hollow.

Thunder broke the heavens.

The falling snowflakes shuddered.

A roar erupted from Poseidon in a furious, agonised wave. Water collected beneath his feet and *lifted*, forming a wave, shoving him towards the street above. He rose through the ruined ground, deaf to Medusa's struggling, ignoring the Deceiver's warriors, their backs now pressed against the walls of the building, watching him with curious eyes.

The snapped halberd floated to the surface, the water lifting the Aegisium blade until Poseidon could catch its' splintered haft in his hand.

Behind him, Perseus reached for Medusa.

She spat a curse and he backed away.

As Poseidon stepped onto the cobblestones.

Breaths heaving.

Eyes still dimly glowing.

He called the mist, obscuring the street.

He called the snow, the frozen flakes condensing in a beautiful, flurrying mass.

He spread the water across the ground and searched for the subtle shift of air, a breeze disrupted by limbs and clothing. He could sense movement through the moisture, the shape of his trident in the mist. He did not need to use his eyes to see. He felt the Deceiver as she flew at him, her shadow streaming through the mist.

He lifted the halberd. Swung the broken haft.

The blade slammed into the Deceiver's side and she was thrown back across the street.

Poseidon dispersed the mist.

Stepped forward.

And found the Deceiver lying on the ground, still clutching his trident.

She shoved herself upright, rolled her shoulders, cracked her neck and smiled. "That was a decent blow." She pressed a hand to her side and her palm came away clean. There was no wound from Poseidon's Aegisium halberd. No bruises or broken bones. No blood pouring from broken skin.

Medusa growled a warning.

Poseidon shifted to find Leda, her Aegisium gun held to the back of his head.

The Deceiver had *allowed* him to hit her. As a distraction from Leda's approach.

Poseidon snarled.

The Deceiver stalked towards him, his trident swinging calmly in her grip.

"N-no." Medusa grimaced, nostrils flaring, blood pouring from her wound. She had let go of it and was struggling against his water, both hands wrenching at her leg. Despite knowing it was useless. Despite being on the other side of the cavernous cleft he had torn in the street. "No! *Poseidon!*"

Poseidon reached to grab Leda's arm.

The woman stepped out of his reach, shifted the barrel and aimed at Medusa.

Poseidon froze.

Leda smirked. "Make me shoot her. I dare you."

Medusa shook her head, pressing her lips together and yanking at her leg. Still fighting. Always fighting. On the other side of the chasm, separated from the warriors and the Deceiver.

... She had a chance to escape...

Poseidon set his jaw, turning to face the Deceiver as she approached.

He released the mist and snow.

The water fell from Medusa's boot.

His love stepped forward.

And the Deceiver struck, plunging the bladed-prongs of Poseidon's trident into his stomach, his heart, his throat.

Poseidon choked, glancing sidelong at Medusa.

His love screamed at him as Perseus grabbed her, struggling to hold her back from the chasm's crumbling edge.

The Deceiver lowered herself to one knee as Poseidon collapsed, caught on the trident and choking on his own blood. He could feel the warm liquid filling his throat as the Deceiver leaned forward to whisper in his ear, smiling to herself and humming contently under her breath. "I think, perhaps, you forget, Poseidon." A talon stretched from her finger and she gently stroked its' curve down the length of Poseidon's bleeding neck. "Or you simply have yet to remember..." She breathed against his ear, her touch near banished beneath the shuddering of his body, her words near silenced by the excruciating pain. "... You are not the only God." She gritted her teeth and shoved, plunging the trident in to its' haft.

Poseidon's vision went black. He felt the Deceiver's grim smile as the Aegisium sliced through him, severing his muscles, shattering his spine, tearing out his back.

Warm blood bubbled in his mouth.

His eyes rolled back.

And the darkness of death consumed him.

Chapter Seventy - Three

MEDUSA STILLED IN PERSEUS' HOLD. She watched the light bleed from Poseidon's eyes. Felt her desperation and fury sputter. Then go out. A void unfurled in her mind, consuming her panic and sorrow, swallowing the tears which had threatened to pour down her cheeks, and the ever-present effects of her withdrawal.

Her ragged breaths calmed.

The frantic beat of her heart began to slow.

Touch and colour and sound disappeared. Leaving the street bleak. White snow falling on grey cobblestones and melting in the swelling streams of Poseidon's blood.

She had seen him die. Countless times.

And, for the first time, she found herself numb.

Not enraged.

Not nauseous.

Not disbelieving.

Simply tired.

Drained.

Unable to feel self-pity or blame as she lifted her gaze from Poseidon's impaled form, blood and bone fragments protruding from his back, and looked at the Deceiver.

Medusa raised her chin, shrugged Perseus' hand from her shoulder. "Get in the car."

Perseus hesitated.

"Get in the car and start the engine, Perseus. It's time to leave."

"... But—"

"He's dead. I can't help him if I don't leave with my memories in tact."

Perseus opened his mouth. Closed it. Scrambled to the car and threw himself inside.

The engine woke with a turbulent roar.

Medusa shot a glare at Leda as the woman lowered her Aegisium gun, she could feel the eyes of the warriors watching her from the sidelines, waiting for her to scream and fight as she had so many times before.

She would not make those same mistakes again.

Medusa took a deep breath of winter air, turned her back on Poseidon's lifeless corpse, and walked away.

No one tried to stop her.

The Deceiver planted a boot on Poseidon's shoulder and pushed, yanking the trident from his lifeless body and flipping it. Crimson sprayed from its' blades and dribbled down its' haft to soak the Deceiver's gloved fingers. She leaned against the trident, bloodied prongs aimed at the sombre, snow-filled sky, and turned to flash Leda a sly, knowing smile. Then she bent and grabbed Poseidon's coat, dragging him back across the cobblestones as Medusa slid into the passenger seat beside Perseus.

Perseus stretched an arm around the back of Medusa's seat, craning to look over his shoulder. He accelerated. Wheels skidding, then catching and launching them backwards out of the once-deserted street.

Medusa's eyes slid closed, Poseidon's corpse a haunting visage behind the darkness of her lids. She heard the curses of Clarke and Christensen sprawled across the back seat, felt the jolt of the car as Perseus hit the breaks, shifted gears and accelerated.

The snakes coiled around her neck did not move.

The numbness did not retreat.

She left Poseidon. *Abandoned* him.

... And found herself wondering if she had made the wrong decision...

Epilogue

River

"There are five rivers that lead to the underworld…"

River frowned as she perched on her cushioned chair, her bruised skin still dappled with purple and yellow and a sickening olive-green. She was staring at a man through an open door across the room, he had been tied to a chair with his head bowed forward and his dark-chocolate waves obscuring his shadowed face.

… He looked familiar…

River didn't think he was breathing. Not with the amount of blood morbidly painting his chest and throat.

"… Are you listening, River?"

River blinked, turning to the woman crouched in front of her, her silver eyes brighter than the moon in a midnight sky.

River nodded. Of course she was listening.

"Good." The silver-eyed woman gracefully stood, hair rippling over her shoulders as she adjusted her fur coat. Part of it looked torn, as if it had been sliced by a blade. "This will be important." She glanced towards the open door, smiling contently at the man who wasn't breathing. "There are five rivers that lead to the underworld, two of which are *particularly* useful, the others... less so. The first is the river Lethe, of oblivion. If ingested, its' water steals memories." She paused, smoothing the fur lining her collar. "The second is the river Styx, of hatred." The woman smiled as the man who wasn't breathing began to stir.

He took a breath.

"Can you guess what its' water might do?"

River frowned, the movement making her bruises ache. "It would make you hate...?"

"Exactly! Clever girl." The silver-eyed woman leaned forward and fondly poked River on the nose. "Now run along, I think Tzali'ka might be looking for you. Why don't you ask her if she has any cookies?"

River grinned. She leaped off the cushioned chair and ran across the room, skidding out the door as she went to find Tzali'ka.

Behind her the silver-eyed woman walked to a set of drawers and removed two vials of clear liquid.

She slipped into the room with the man who was now breathing.

And calmly locked the door.

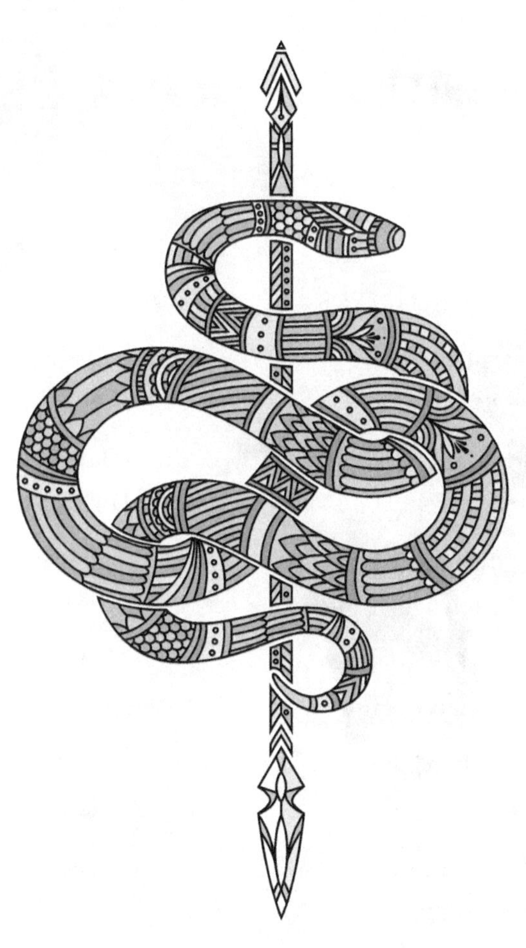

Pronunciation Guide

<table>
<tr><td>

Main Characters

Areus Donovan:
Aar - ee - us | Don - o - van

Adalinda Veil:
Ada - lin - dah | V - ay - l

Samantha Clarke:
Fearsome - warrior - queen

Christensen:
Kri - sten - sen

Akilah Wise:
Aa - kee - lah | Wi - ze

Diana Laurenti:
Die - an - ah | Law - ren - tee

Wyatt Shade:
Ba - st - ar - d

River:
Un - bro - ken

</td><td>

Covert Warriors

Leda:
Lee - dah

Lorelei:
Lor - e - lie

Tzali'ka:
Tsa - lee - ka

Anja:
An - yah

Aisha:
Ai - ee - shah

Asim:
Ah - sim

Vera:
Vee - rah

Iveta:
Ee - vet - ah

</td></tr>
</table>

AUTHOR'S NOTE

In the words of Samantha Clarke: "*. . . Well, shit.*"

. . . That was a rollercoaster. . .

I hope I managed to make you cry. Or laugh. Or feel *something* - whether it be anger, or excitement, or irritation. Honestly, I hope you want to throw the book across the room and scream in my face, because that would mean I created a story worth writing, that would mean the tears and the frustration I went through to bring this into the world were all worth it. And, hell, isn't that was reading's about? Smiling and chuckling to yourself on one page and crying into a pillow on the next?
I guess the best thing to say about *The Mirror* is that it required a *lot* of unending belief. There were countless times while writing it that I wanted to quit, just put the damned story down and forget it. But in the end I decided to work through my negativite thoughts

because I wanted to see if I could finish something. I wanted to believe in myself. And I think that somewhere along the way, I did just that. I made something real. I wrote a *five-hundred page* book, I designed it *in it's entirety* and I proved to myself that I am capable, I am creative and, no matter what, I will perservere.

No.

Matter.

What.

I learned to believe.

And I hope that wherever you go next, you'll learn to believe in yourself too. Because, let's be honest, if you survived reading this book you can pretty much survive anything.

So, be strong.

Never give in.

And always, *always* believe.

ELLEN A. HUNT

www.ellenahunt.com
Instagram: @ellen_a_hunt
Facebook: /missellenahunt

Post and hashtag *#themirrornovel* if this story made you cry... or throw the book at the wall. It will undoubtedly make the author smile, but *don't* share any *damned spoilers*.

Acknowledgements

Thank you to the people who helped and supported me through the writing of this book.

To my wonderful Mother, thank you for reading and editing *The Mirror* without complaint, even though almost every time you pointed something out that could be improved upon, it escalated to an argument.

To my amazing friends Mikaela and Rainer, who never once doubted me and who have faithfully read every chapter of this book - sometimes twice, as they were rewritten.

To my siblings, who got frustrated with me for never being sociable and disappearing into my room almost every night to write, yet they still read and critiqued anything I gave them.

To my Father, who is always supportive and full of love, and who probably won't read this because it doesn't have a happy ending.

And to anyone else who has helped me along this journey.

I will be forever grateful.